Little Bit Crazy

CHRISTY MARCHAND

Little Bit Crazy

Chapter 1

Maggie Parrish sighed, closed her book and tugged the brim of her floppy hat lower on her forehead. Sleep had been impossible her first night in the little beach house and a morning nap near the water was her first order of business. She was worn out, not just from yesterday's long drive, wailing along to bad-ass-girl music – salute to P!nk, Kelly and Gaga – but also from tossing and turning alone in an unfamiliar bed, unable to stop dwelling over impossible why's and what if's.

Ugh. She was a mess.

Sliding down farther on her chaise lounge, she willed herself to concentrate on the rhythmic sound of the surf washing onto the shore. The weather was ideal and the narrow stretch of beach was peaceful. Maybe too peaceful? Maybe Orange Beach would have been a better choice. There, the sound of the surf vied with music, jet skis, and boats towing parasailers. Here there were no distractions from her glum thoughts. Of course, when the reservation was made months back, she hadn't known she'd end up here alone and in need of distraction. One upside to being alone, though, was that she didn't have to put on an act to keep her friends and family from worrying about her.

Down the beach a few hundred yards away, children spilled

energetically from another house, followed by a trickle of adults carrying beach gear. They were the only others on the beach, but it was early. A little closer, a lone man leaned against the railing of a deck that stretched along the front of an impossibly enormous beach house; all sharp angles, neutral color, and the obligatory wall of glass windows. Was he here alone, too? She doubted it. Any minute now a woman would join him, maybe even a couple of kids. A happy little family, ready for sun and sand castles. Squashing a sharp yearning, Maggie closed her eyes and concentrated on the sound of the surf. Just because her life was upended right now didn't mean she wouldn't have happier beach days someday in the future.

She dozed lightly, peripherally aware of the sun and breeze and the distant sound of children's voices. After what seemed like only seconds, she sat up with a snap, knocking the hat off her head and the book from her lap in the process. A faint cry nudged her awake and something felt wrong, really wrong. She put a hand to her chest and blinked in confusion, trying to gather her fuzzy thoughts and pinpoint what had startled her. She squinted against the glare of the morning sun and scanned the shore.

A child, no more than two or three years old, had apparently wandered away unnoticed from the group down the beach. She had been knocked down by a forceful, churning wave and was struggling in the undertow. Maggie saw a glimpse of a little hand, a flash of a bright red swimming suit, and frothy water. For a horrible moment everything but that flash of red fell away and all she could feel was the loud thudding of her heart. The stretch of sand between her chair and the child looked infinite and her body felt heavy and unwieldy as she tried to rise from her chair, but she willed her legs to move and at last she was up, bolting towards the water.

Garrett Long crossed the wide-planked deck of the beach house, towel draped around his neck, second mug of coffee in his hand. He and his sorry excuses for golf buddies should have teed off hours ago. The big lugs were sleeping like well-fed babies and he didn't have the heart to wake them up. Having a lazy start to the day felt good. Besides, they had the whole week to play golf. He was glad they had nagged him into making the trip.

Reaching the railing, his attention was caught by the sight of a woman leaping off of a beach chair and sprinting toward the water like the hounds of hell were nipping at her heels. He squinted to make out where she was heading and watched as she flew into the water, her arms outstretched. She plunged below the breaking waves and was out of sight for a moment, and then rose with something in her arms.

A child. She had a child in her arms.

The incongruity of the scene playing out before him in contrast to the beautiful, sunny morning made him freeze for a split second. The mug slipped from his hand, coffee splashing, and then he was on his way, too, eyes fixed on his target. He couldn't get any traction in the soft sand and it seemed to take hours to cross the distance separating them.

The woman was stumbling out of the breaking surf with the limp child in her arms when he finally reached them. "I've got her," she panted, her face pale, her wet hair plastered across her face.

Thank God she was fast. What could he do? He knew nothing about CPR. His gaze ricocheted around but there were no lifeguards and he didn't even have his phone on him to call 911. His whole body clenched at the realization that he was useless. All he had was a towel, which he threw down onto the sand at the woman's feet.

She sank down to lay the little girl on top of it and he dropped to his knees beside her. "What can I do?" he managed. Unhearing, she proficiently rolled the child onto her back and tilted her head back. Garrett waited, fists clenched, as the woman cycled between chest compressions and mouth-to-mouth breaths.

She knew what she was doing. The relief he felt was profound.

"Marisa!" A dark-haired girl came charging down the beach, shrieking, her eyes wild with fear. "Marisa!"

Garrett rose and managed to catch her and hold her back so that the woman could continue her efforts on the child uninterrupted. "Let her work. She's got this." The girl clutched at him and began praying as other members of her group came running behind her, voices clamoring. Garrett motioned them back with his free arm. They surrounded the woman and child more closely than he liked, and hovered, holding one another, crying and speaking anxiously in Spanish.

The child coughed and choked, opened her eyes and began to cry. The group let out a collective breath and the furor increased. The woman rocked back on her heels and dragged a sandy hand across her brow. Their eyes met, hers huge with relief, and Garrett felt a rush of understanding. He nodded at her and bent to scoop the child from the towel, handing her to her sobbing mother, and then helped the woman to her feet.

"Good job," he said, patting her on the back, and then felt sheepish. 'Good job' was adequate for a successful pass reception or well-timed tackle, but was embarrassingly lame for someone who just saved a life.

The family members were loud with relief and excitement, crowding the woman as they pressed effusive thanks on her in a language she didn't understand. Garrett edged away, eager to escape before he was recognized. He didn't need photos online announcing to everyone where he was or what he was doing, and even at the beach people had their phones at their fingertips, ready to take photos whether they asked permission or not. He needed to get away, back to the beach house.

When he reached the fringe, he threw one last glance over his shoulder and stopped abruptly. The woman's face had gone from pale to white and she swayed slightly in the center of the group. She was about to go down, damn it, and nobody else could see it.

Ignoring the voice in his head that warned him against bringing attention to himself, he began nudging his way back into the overexcited group. Couldn't they see they were crowding the woman too tightly? That she needed air? "Excuse me, sorry, let me through." The group finally realized that the woman wasn't well. He reached her and slid a supportive arm around her waist just as her knees buckled. Catching her easily, he pulled her up against his side. "Too much excitement," he said to everyone and nobody as he used his free arm to try to push their way back out again.

Smiles of relief turned to frowns of concern as they separated to let him pass with her tucked under his arm, and a fresh volley of rapid, unintelligible conversation followed him as he waved them and their concern away dismissively. Towing the woman along, Garrett sent a glance towards the chair where she had been sitting. He could just take her there and set her down. He didn't need to get involved. She'd be fine.

He was only a couple of steps away from her chair when he made the mistake of looking down at the same instant she looked up. She looked shattered. She was trying hard not to cry but a tear slipped down her cheek.

Well, crap.

She'd saved a little girl's life, with zero help from him. The one chair suggested she was all alone. It would be pretty insensitive to just drop her off and walk away. He could keep an eye on her for a minute, make sure she was okay. It was the least he could do.

He changed direction and headed for the beach house.

Okay, this morning was off the rails big time.

Maggie gave up trying to walk beside the man and just bumped along, squashed against his side by a muscular arm, her bare feet only occasionally skimming the sand.

When she started feeling light-headed in the middle of all the people, their eyes connected and, the next thing she knew, he was cutting his way through the crowd toward her like a disgruntled arrow. He was so tall she had to twist her head to try to catch his expression but it was hard to read. Was he frowning? It occurred to her that he wasn't steering her toward her chair. Did he have bad intentions? It didn't seem likely. A bad person wouldn't have come to help, would they? Should she be worried? Should she be worried that she wasn't worried? It felt good to have someone to lean on for a minute.

But he wasn't hers to lean on. He was a complete stranger. "You can let go of me now. I'm okay." She swiped at her face, embarrassed by her tears.

"In a minute." He continued to make his way up the path leading to the modern beach house. "You were about to face plant. Let's make sure you're steady first."

"Can I try to walk?"

"I don't know. Can you?" He stopped and eased his grip slightly, allowing her to try to stand on her own. Her legs felt noodly but they worked. She looked over her shoulder to see the little girl's family and the child safe in her mother's arms, and relief surged through her. Another glance up at the man's face showed he was watching the group, too, and then his gaze dipped to hers.

"You did good," he murmured, and her breath hitched a little.

"Hey, Garrett, what's going on?" Another man, tall with dark hair and ripply muscles, ambled toward them on the path. "Looks like there was some excitement down there."

Garrett? Maggie looked up at him again. There was something vaguely familiar about him but she couldn't think what it was. Was he one of those personal injury lawyers with a million billboards along the interstate? A news anchor or something? Maybe it would come to her if she sat down for a minute but figuring him out wasn't a priority. She wanted to dry off. Get warm. Process what had just happened. Offer up a prayer of thanks for CPR classes and the little girl's well-being.

The man jerked his head towards the people still clustered by the edge of the water. "A kid got away from her family and our neighbor here saved the day. Get her stuff, would you? That's her chair over there."

The dark-haired man threw astonished looks at Maggie and the crowd of people still congregated at the edge of the shore. "Sure thing, man."

Apparently still unconvinced that Maggie could move along under her own steam, the man put one firm hand beneath her elbow and the other at the small of her back. He steered her up the wide steps of the beach house, across the deck and toward the wide sliding doors to the interior. Maggie balked. He stopped, tilting his head questioningly.

"I can't go inside. I'm too wet." She waved weakly down to her legs. She felt small and slight and very cold, wearing nothing but her ancient one-piece suit and what seemed like half the sand from the beach crusted onto her knees and feet. She would make a mess in his designer living room.

He gave a noise that sounded part amused and part annoyed and propelled her inside despite her protests. Here was a man who didn't have to clean up after himself, Maggie thought wryly. He turned her in the direction of a deep leather sofa and gave her a nudge. "Why don't you sit and I'll get something for you to drink."

It wasn't really a question, though, was it? Apparently he was also a man who was used to bossing people around. Wearily she sat, wincing at the water dripping from her body onto the sofa. Something hot to drink would be nice but a towel would be better.

"What would you like?" he asked her from the vast kitchen area, opening the refrigerator and looking inside. "Water? Green tea? Coffee?"

"I think I've had enough water, thanks." The lighthearted tone she'd aimed for came out sounding a little on the feeble side. "Coffee sounds wonderful. A towel, maybe, too, if it's not too much trouble?"

Jerking to a stop, he looked at her with a pained expression. Without a word he strode out of sight, beyond the kitchen and then returned with a large towel in each hand. "Sorry. Wasn't thinking."

Maggie felt her eyes prickle again when he handed them to her and she felt him looking at her but she didn't trust herself to speak. What was wrong with her? There was no reason to blubber over towels, especially in front of a stranger. She might be feeling a little exposed and out of her element but she was no crybaby. Inhaling a deep breath, she managed to twist one towel around her body and use the other to swipe at her hair.

He stood there a moment longer, frowning, and then returned to the kitchen. "Coffee's coming right up."

"Thanks." She tried to distract herself by looking around the vast room. It was at least ten times bigger than her modest rental. It had a high-vaulted ceiling and was decorated in cool grays and pale, beachy blues. She sat on one of two gray leather sofas angled toward a dramatic fireplace and a wide flat-screen television. There were expensive looking accents and even a couple of big sculptures in the corners of the living area. All very la-de-dah.

No sign of a wife or children, though. Maybe the second guy who was getting her stuff was this guy's boyfriend? She shot a glance toward the kitchen where the man waited, one hip leaning against the counter, for the coffee to drip.

She hoped he wasn't gay. Not that it mattered to her one way or the other.

The kitchen boasted gleaming white cabinetry and a giant marble topped island and, wait, was that a giant silver octopus light fixture over the island? Yes, it was. Indeed it was. Maggie stared at it in amazement. Ultra la-de-dah.

She felt the need to break the silence and say something. Anything. "I don't understand what happened."

"You saved a little girl's life, that's what happened," the man replied matter-of-factly.

Maggie tore her gaze from the octopus light fixture. "I mean afterwards. Getting dizzy like that."

After the coffee stopped dripping, he stirred a lot of sugar and cream into the mug. "Seems perfectly natural to feel overwhelmed after something like that, especially when you've got so many people closing in on you." He crossed the room in a loose, long-legged stride and handed her the mug.

She accepted it with a grateful nod, wrapping her cold hands around its warmth. Despite his efforts, she had the feeling he'd rather her not be there. He didn't have a lot to say and he seemed to have a hard time looking at her. Or maybe he was just shy. No matter what it was, it wasn't any of her business, and as soon as she downed this coffee she was out of here.

He eased down on the ottoman in front of her, his gaze impassive. "You seemed to know what you were doing. Are you a doctor?"

Maggie shook her head. "No, I teach kindergarten." She tried not to think about that infinitesimal moment of complete nothingness when she couldn't remember even the first thing she had learned from her CPR class. Thank God the fear had passed and the training kicked in.

"Kindergarten teacher, huh?"

"Yep." Maggie sipped at the sweet, hot coffee and eyed him over the rim of the mug. Instead of dwelling on her initial panic and what still felt like a heart-stopping close call at failure, she made an effort to concentrate on her host. He might not be the chattiest guy in the world, but damn. Just – damn. He didn't really need to talk, now, did he? He could just stand and rotate slowly and she'd write a thank-you note.

Silky dark brown hair, close cropped on the sides and longer on top, sapphire-blue eyes with dark lashes longer than hers on her very best make-up day, a scarred chin, and chiseled cheekbones. Muscular, ropy arms stretching the sleeves of a plain blue t-shirt and unremarkable athletic shorts. His legs, though, now those were remarkable. Muscular and tanned, and too long for the low ottoman. His knees, one of them scarred like his chin, were in danger of bumping into hers.

That creeping familiarity was still there, but she still couldn't place him. Maggie dropped her gaze and stared at his bare, sandy feet. It was safe to look at feet.

Damn it, even his feet were handsome. As well shaped as the rest of him. Maggie squeezed her eyes closed.

"Are you fading again?"

"No." She kept her head down. It felt dangerous to look at him, like looking straight at a solar eclipse.

He lifted her chin with a finger.

Aaaaannd now he was touching her.

Her adrenaline started pumping like crazy and her face felt hot. From one finger.

His expression was searching. "I'm not convinced." His pulled his hand back.

Aaaaannd now he wasn't anymore.

"It's just that I only took the CPR class a little while ago. I didn't expect to have to use it so soon and I couldn't think straight when I first got her out of the water." Maggie shivered and drank a sip of coffee. That tiny little girl, in her scarlet swimming suit, with her precious face, so still and pale. The fear that she hadn't gotten there fast enough, that she wouldn't be able to save her. "I almost choked," she whispered, rotating the mug in her hands.

"But you didn't. You saved her life. How about tossing me a blanket or sweatshirt or something?"

Maggie blinked. Who was he talking to? She flushed when she spied two enormous men, dressed in shorts and golf shirts, frozen on the sleek metal staircase. Their faces were still and sympathetic and she realized they had heard every word.

"Got it," one of them said before disappearing up the stairs. He returned a moment later, treading lightly despise his bulk, with a maroon sweatshirt in his huge hand. "Here you go, brand new and all yours."

Maggie managed a smile and took it from him. "Thank you." Clumsily she pulled it over her head. Oh, that was nice. Dry and heavy and warm. After folding the damp towels, she held out an arm and managed a light laugh at the length of sleeve that dangled far past her hand. "And look, a perfect fit." Her comment broke the cautious mood and the men chuckled.

"Hey, here we go. I got your stuff." The man who had been dispatched to retrieve her things loped into the room from the deck, her beach bag and hat dangling from one hand. "But your hat's squashed." He held it up apologetically.

Whoa-kay. This man was almost as handsome as the one sitting inches from her with longish black hair, dark brown eyes and a profile that was a cross between an Italian statue and Elvis Presley. Who were these men? Male strippers? And what terrible thing had she done in a previous life to deserve being dropped into their midst like waterlogged roadkill?

Blinking back into the moment, she waved dismissively at the hat. "No great loss."

The Elvis doppelganger deposited her bag and hat at her feet and then moved lithely to pluck a baseball cap from the top of the kitchen island. "But you need a hat at the beach. How about this one?" He presented it to her with the air of a knight presenting a gift to his lady.

Smiling at him, Maggie took it and turned it in her hands. "Renegades," she read aloud, fingering the monogrammed lettering. She tugged the sweatshirt away from her chest, which was easy to do, to read the wording on front. "Denver Renegades." She tilted her head up to offer a smile to each of them. "Y'all must be really big fans. I'm a Saints fan, myself. Are y'all from Denver?"

They all began to chuckle.

What? What had she said that was funny? Maggie sent a questioning glance at the man still sitting inches from her. He had the barest trace of a smile.

"Yes, we are." He rose from the ottoman and moved to sit farther away. Crossing an ankle at his knee and stretching a sinewy arm along the back of the sofa, he avoided meeting Maggie's perplexed look and waited instead for the others to compose themselves.

Suddenly all the details fell together and clicked in Maggie's mind. That's why he looked so familiar. She had seen him on television, wearing a helmet, shoulder pads and snug spandex. His face, his size, the size and bulk of his friends, the monogramming on the cap and lettering on the sweatshirt. For the second time that morning, Maggie felt as though the blood was draining straight out of her body.

Sweet baby Jesus.

She was sitting, like a piece of chicken coated with sand instead of flour, swallowed up inside a 3X sweatshirt, beside Garrett Long, a multi-million-dollar quarterback. The man owned two Super Bowl rings and the hearts of countless women across the country. Maggie gaped wordlessly at him for what felt like forever and then, feeling woozy all over again, leaned forward to carefully set her mug on the floor and drop her face into her hands.

The chuckles drew to an abrupt halt and Maggie felt her end of the sofa shift as Garrett slid closer.

"You all right?" She felt a light hand on her back.

She nodded without lifting her head. "I'm so embarrassed." Her response was muffled in her hands. "I know who you are now. You must think I'm an idiot."

"Not at all," he replied.

"It's just that you're not where I expect you to be." She lifted her face to look at him. Wait, that didn't sound right so she tried again. "I mean, you expect to see football players at football games, not at the beach."

That elicited broad grins from Garrett's teammates while he just looked at her with the barest hint of a smile.

"Not that you can't come to the beach," she plowed on

desperately. "Of course you can come to the beach. You can go anyplace you like. I mean, look at you. Who's going to stop you? It's just that – It's just that –" Maggie groaned and dropped her face back into her hands.

Kill me now.

Great bursts of laughter erupted from Garrett's teammates. But not from the stoic quarterback. Maggie peeked through her fingers and saw he was still studying her with faint amusement, like she was a curious science experiment gone awry.

Painfully aware of how silly she sounded, rambling about where professional athletes were allowed to go, Maggie struggled to get up from the deep sofa. It took two tries, the first attempt a pathetic, unsuccessful lurch that landed her right back where she started, but on the second try she made it to her feet. "Uh, thanks for everything. I've got to go now."

Rising beside her, Garrett waved meaningfully at his friends and they obligingly composed themselves "Why don't you sit back down and finish your coffee first? And we should've introduced ourselves. I'm Garrett Long and these are my teammates, Dominic Moretti, Wayne Spence, and Demario Murray."

The three men nodded at her, friendly smiles on their faces.

"And you are?" Garrett inclined his head in question.

"Margaret Parrish," she replied obediently, anxiously shifting her weight from foot to foot. "Or Maggie. My friends call me Maggie." Oh, heavens, they didn't care what her friends called her. "Thanks, but I've really got to go." She tried to push the long sleeves up so she could grab her bag and ruined hat but the sleeves insisted on sliding back down.

Sleeves one, Maggie zero.

"It was nice to meet you. Thanks for everything." Was that the third or fourth time she'd said thanks for everything? They probably got the idea. She looked across the room. She had a long way to go to get to the sliding doors and she felt like she should say something else, but what? "Go Renegades!" she concluded, lifting her arm like a demented cheerleader.

Another burst of laughter from Garrett's teammates and a look-fast-or-you'll-miss-it grin from him.

Oh my God, had she really cheered for them? Like Spartan cheerleader Cheri Oteri on Saturday Night Live? Why yes, yes she had. Cringing hard, Maggie managed to fight past her sleeves to grab her things and then speed-walk toward the open sliding doors.

"Wait, you forgot your hat." Dominic, aka Italian Elvis, a huge grin on his ridiculously good-looking face, picked the baseball cap up from the floor where it had landed when she stood. "Come on, I'll walk you back to your place." He gave her a wink that she felt in her knees.

Garrett slanted an unreadable look towards him and took the cap. "I've got her."

No, no, no. She wanted out of there, with no interference. "Oh, you don't have to. I'm fine. Steady as a rock. The coffee helped. Honestly."

"I insist." He took the bag from her and dropped the baseball cap inside before turning to his teammates. "You guys want to go ahead? I'll meet you at the club later."

It looked like Mr. Inscrutable was going to walk her back whether she wanted him to or not. It was a short walk, thankfully, and in minutes she'd be alone again. Where, no doubt, she'd relive every embarrassing bit of babble for the rest of her natural life.

He followed her down the stairs and to the path to the beach. She glanced sideways at him at the same moment he glanced at her, and she quickly averted her eyes. Awkward. What did you talk about with a millionaire quarterback? She hated to think about what a sight she must be, with her wet hair plastered to her head and the giant sweatshirt flapping below her hands and past her knees.

He seemed comfortable with the silence. That was just as well because she was keeping her stupid mouth clamped shut, and in just a few moments they were at the path to her rental. She slowed to a halt. "Well, here we are," she said lamely, looking up at him. Man, he was tall. "Thanks again for everything."

Was that the fifth time?

His mouth quirked. She guessed that was his go-to smile for crazy people. "Sure thing." He handed her the straw bag. "Well, it was nice to meet you, Maggie Parrish. Hope the rest of your vacation is a little less exciting."

"You, too," she said, before leaving him on the path. Once inside the door, she leaned against it, her head tipped back.

Gah, what a morning.

Go Maggie.

Chapter 2

Garrett watched her slip inside the door, comically swallowed up in Dwayne's sweatshirt, before making his way back to the beach house. A kindergarten teacher, of all things. Apparently kindergarten teachers were made of stern stuff these days as that had been some heroic rescue. He recalled her racing towards the surf like a flash, long legs flying, and her subdued confession that she had almost fumbled. He hadn't seen it that way. He hadn't noticed her falter for even a split second when she carried the little girl out of the water and proceeded to save her life. She'd risen to the challenge while he'd just stood there, no help at all.

That wouldn't happen again; he was going to sign up for a CPR course before the season started.

And afterwards, yeah, she'd looked decimated. She'd made no mention of having anybody waiting for her so he was glad he had ignored his initial impulse to just leave her on her own. He knew from experience that it could be hard to settle down after an intense adrenaline rush. He could've done a better job looking after her, though. He should've gotten her a towel without her having to ask.

After mixing and drinking a smoothie, he checked the clock and saw that he had enough time for a short run before meeting the guys at the golf course. He tugged on running shoes, did a few stretches, and glanced up and down the beach. There were considerably more people out now. Hopefully he wouldn't be recognized or approached.

Maggie was already back on the beach, he saw, sitting in her chair under an umbrella, her new Renegades cap on her head and a book in her hand. That was good; she was clearly fine now. He set off along the edge of the beach and she glanced up as he passed in front of her. He lifted a hand in an understated wave as he ran past. Dipping her chin in acknowledgement, she gave him a nod and then immediately dropped her head to her book again.

Huh. He didn't know whether to be pleased or not. He hated attention and he was glad she hadn't turned out to be the distraught, clingy type, but this was zero attention. He realized he was being unreasonable when he ought to be grateful. He was there to hang out with his guys and play some golf, not hit on a cute kindergarten teacher, even one with big brown eyes and an amusing propensity to ramble.

About a mile down the beach, his phone buzzed. His assistant's photo filled the screen. He tapped the screen for Facetime. "Hey, Claire."

"Well, there you are." Claire Marshall looked concerned. "Just a heads up that you've made the news."

"What are you talking about?" He wiped away the sweat trickling down his face with his free arm. Glancing around, he saw a group of people setting up chairs and umbrellas a few yards away. He turned his back to them and hunkered down, trying to look inconspicuous.

She turned the phone so he could see the screen of her desktop computer. There was an enlarged Instagram post with a photo of him hauling a wet and limp Maggie out of the crowd on the beach with the text "QB Garrett Long at Torrance Bay Beach! Rescued little girl! Who's the woman?"

Damn. That hadn't taken long. "I didn't rescue anyone."

"No? What happened? I've already gotten calls. What do you want me to say?"

"Same as always. No comment."

"Okay, no comment. Can you at least tell me what happened?"

Claire had been his assistant for the past few years but they went way farther back, to when he was a kid. She was used to his brusque manner but he knew it frustrated her sometimes. "Yeah, of course. The kid wandered off from her family and got into trouble. The girl saved her. I really didn't have anything to do with it."

"Then why are you carrying her away?"

"She was about to pass out and nobody else noticed." Garrett gave a sideways glance to the group of people and saw that they were eyeing him curiously.

"Are they both okay? The kid and the girl?"

"Yep. Everybody's fine."

"Well, that's a relief."

"Yep." He chanced another glance and winced when he saw recognition blooming on their faces. Any second now and they'd be headed in his direction.

"You know the press is going to show up, right?"

"Yep." Rising, he pulled the brim of his cap lower and started walking.

"So you'll be back in Denver sooner than expected?"

"Probably. Is that it?" He picked up speed and started jogging. He'd like to get away but if somebody called his name, he'd have no option but to respond. Be friendly, shake hands, sign autographs, pose for pictures, talk football.

Please don't call my name.

He heard Claire sigh. She'd been relieved that he had decided to come with the guys on their annual golf trip to Florida. She and his sister acted like he was becoming a recluse but that wasn't the case. He just liked laying low and minding his own business during the off season.

"Just text me when you'll be home."

"Will do." He disconnected, shoved the phone in his back pocket and blew his breath out in disappointment. The guys were going to have to find another fourth for golf because the Instagram tag would have his location out there for anyone to see. No more anonymity this week. No hope of just chilling on the beach. It was only a matter of time before the media showed up and he'd be trapped. It wasn't just the media, either. Fans could be worse, especially the women. He'd had way more than his share of obsessed stalker types who were hung up on his status or his looks. It was the unfortunate reality of being a professional athlete. He loved the game, appreciated the fans, and understood his responsibilities, but damn, he wished he could have some privacy, at least during the off season. But no, one Instagram post and he was done.

Ahead he saw Maggie again, still reading her book. He glanced around, up and down the beach that was becoming congested with couples, kids, families, and then there she was, all alone, and he couldn't help wondering why. Alone or not, he'd have to let her know that her photo was online and that sobered him up real quick. She needed to be warned about the inevitable invasion into her privacy, and the sooner, the better. From their brief interaction, he felt reasonably confident she wouldn't freak out about it but you never knew. The last thing he wanted was drama.

He slowed to a walk a few yards away. "Hey again. Feeling better?"

She didn't respond and he frowned. When he got a little closer, he saw she was wearing earbuds. He moved a little closer, casting a shadow, and she glanced up. Removing her earbuds, she set her tablet down. "Sorry, did you say something?"

She certainly hadn't been waiting for him to go past her again, that was clear. "Just asked if you were feeling better."

She nodded. "Yes, thanks."

He nodded back and then felt awkward when she didn't elaborate. It occurred to him that he was accustomed to women tripping over themselves to talk to him but Maggie, no longer flustered as she'd been earlier, seemed content to wait for him to speak.

Damned if he could think of an easy segue into his unhappy news.

"You look hot. Want some water?"

He watched as she blinked, a blush coloring her cheeks. Her reaction to her own innocent comment was obvious and kind of cute. Lifting the hem of his shirt up, he swiped at his face to hide his smile. "That'd be great."

Her eyes dropped to his abs and her blush deepened before she leaned over to unzip the top of a small cooler. Pulling a bottle from the ice, she untwisted the cap and handed it up to him.

"Thanks." Her action amused him even more. It reminded him of his sister, who tended to forget he was a grown man. "And for opening it."

She made a face. "Sorry, it's a reflex. I can't tell you how many bottles I open and juice boxes I stab in a week."

He gestured to the footrest of her chair. "Mind if I sit?"

She looked surprised but nodded her permission and pulled her legs up to give him room.

He dropped to sit on the low foot of the chair. She had great legs, he noticed, long and slim, but that conservative, navy blue one piece swimsuit of hers sure wasn't doing her any favors. In fact, the best thing he could say about it was that it looked comfortable. Well, she was a kindergarten teacher, not a spindly runway model, and in any case, he wasn't there to try to take it off of her. Drinking another long pull of water, he couldn't help wondering why she was hiding her curves.

None of his business.

"Got some news that might affect your beach time. Somebody took our picture earlier and it's already online."

She looked confused. "Someone took our picture?"

"Yeah. And posted it on Instagram." She had nice eyes, too, and some little freckles. Very girl-next-door-ish.

"That was fast. Is that normal? For you, I mean?" She seemed mildly interested but not concerned. He knew that would change.

"Try Googling my name and see what comes up." He grimaced, hating how self-important that sounded.

She dug through her beach tote, pulled her phone out of a plastic bag and tapped it on. "Just your name?"

"Yep."

She tapped the phone, waited for results and then blinked. "'QB Garrett Long at Torrance Bay Beach! Rescued little girl! Who's the woman?'" she read aloud, and then looked at him with open-mouthed horror. "Oh my God, I look like something dead that washed ashore from a shipwreck!"

Her reaction to the photo made him bite back a smile. "Surely not that bad?"

"Pretty bad." She enlarged the photo on the screen with her thumb and index finger. "It looks like you're trying to drag an albino octopus or something," she continued, squinting at the screen.

An albino octopus? He had to hide another smile.

"Well, the headline isn't so bad. The picture's awful, for sure, but it's not like they printed my name." She turned the phone sideways and tried enlarging it again. "It's obviously you, but who would really know or care that it's me?"

He took it and examined the photo. "You're right, your face isn't clear." He handed it back. "But the bad news is that it's just a matter of time before the press shows up and starts snooping. They're going to want a story."

She frowned.

Now she was getting it.

"A story about us?"

"Yep."

"But there is no story about us," she said matter-of-factly.

He wished it were that simple. "It won't matter."

She sat up straighter and scanned the beach, as if she could spot a reporter or photographer among the beachgoers. Apparently nobody looked suspicious because she turned back to him. He decided not to explain to her about long range zoom lenses.

"I'm sorry," he found himself adding. She hadn't asked for this.

She shrugged, her expression untroubled. "Why? It's not your fault. I'm grateful to you for grabbing me before I passed out. The headline could've been 'Kindergarten Teacher Accidentally Trampled by Happy Family.'"

He found himself smiling again at her sense of humor. "That wouldn't have been good, either."

"Look, don't worry about it," she said lightly. "It'll be fine."

She was naively optimistic if she didn't believe reporters would hassle her.

"Honestly," she continued, looking at the photo on her phone again. "I'm only upset that I look so awful in the picture. I wouldn't mind at all if I looked wonderful. At any rate, don't worry about it. It's far from the worst thing to happen to me lately."

He tilted an eyebrow in question.

She scrunched her face as if she regretted making the last remark, then drew in a deep breath. "This week was supposed to be my bachelorette party but my fiancée dumped me and I couldn't get my deposit back for the rental. Turns out you can't get a refund for being dumped." Her shoulders stiffening, she looked away from him.

Damn. Garrett could see that, despite her breezy explanation, she was struggling to maintain her equanimity. "Well, that really blows," he finally said.

"On a blowing scale of one to ten, it blows ten thousand," she agreed ruefully. "And last night, my best friend called to tell me she can't make it after all so I'm thinking of just throwing in the towel and heading right back home tomorrow. The beach isn't much fun alone." Sighing, she gazed off at the water and then blinked and looked embarrassed. "Oh, wow, sorry, didn't mean to sound all whiney. I hate whiners, don't you? This," she waved her hands to encompass the area around her chair. "This is now a whine-free zone."

He wasn't sure what to say to that, or to half of what she'd said, but he felt the need to try to cheer her up. "Pretty sure that doesn't count as whining," he replied.

She shot him a grateful smile. "Kind of a shame about the photo, though. There are worse things than being linked with – wait for it –" She tapped another quick search into her phone, then, giving him a cheeky grin, showed him the photo that popped up. "'The NFL's hottest quarterback.'"

He closed his eyes and rubbed his forehead. That damned article and that stupid shirtless photo. What he did for a living and what he looked like was not the sum total of his existence but, more often than not, it was all people saw. All they wanted to see. He would never understand why total strangers cared about him beyond his ability to lead an offense, and it was ridiculous to be admired for a random accident of genetics.

Especially when those same genetics might someday rise up in less than agreeable ways.

"Turn that off." He aimed for a light tone but wasn't sure he achieved it. He freaking hated the internet sometimes.

She laughed and did as asked, dropping the phone back into her bag. "You know you're pretty. You should just own it. In fact, I can't think of anything I'd love more than for my stupid ex to see a photo of you dragging me off someplace. Is it awful that I want him to be jealous?"

Her artless honesty eased his frustration. He thought about the Instagram photo and the imminent media invasion and had an idea. Maybe a terrible idea, but she seemed harmless. Not the crazy drama type. The media was coming, no doubt about it, and he had the ability to put a different spin on the inevitable story. But did he want to?

"Oh, well." She dipped her head to adjust the brim of her new cap, and then looked back up at him. "I don't think your paparazzi will be an issue if I get out of here first thing tomorrow morning."

He considered her silently, still mentally debating whether or not to go out on a limb. She hadn't asked for an autograph or a photo, and there was none of that giggling or posing, or worse, clamping onto him like he was community property. All things considered, her actions that morning, her indifference to his fame, her humor, and that disgrace of a swimsuit told him everything he really needed to know about her.

"Would you really like your ex to see a photo of the two of us?" he asked abruptly.

He couldn't believe he was going to do this, but there was something about her that appealed to him. He figured she deserved a break.

"Because if you do, I might be able to help you out with that. Want me to be your rebound?"

Chapter 3

Wait, what? Maggie gaped at him. What did he mean? Had she even heard him correctly? Despite her flippancy about her broken engagement, the truth was she was still feeling pretty wrecked and was in no state to even think about another relationship.

And why would he ask such a thing? He was Garrett Long, for heaven's sake. The NFL's hottest quarterback wouldn't go around offering himself out as a rebound.

She realized he was still waiting for her reply. "I'm not sure what you mean," she finally managed. "I mean, you're gorgeous and I'm sure most women would jump at the chance to let you rebound the freaking hell out of them but I'm kind of off men at the moment."

Garrett's mouth quirked into a half smile. "Well, thanks for that, I think. I'm not suggesting a real relationship. I was thinking that if you really want a photo, we could make that happen. There's going to be press whether we like it or not. Why not decide what we want the story to be, instead of them?" He finished off the last bit of water and squashed the bottle. She held out her hand and he blinked and then gave it to her.

Of course he wasn't suggesting a real relationship. She stowed the empty bottle back into the cooler. "So what's your plan? I'm all ears."

He squinted thoughtfully toward the water, seemed to sigh, and then looked back at her. "How about this – let's go out for dinner, let them take some photos, make your ex think twice, and everybody's happy. Except your ex, hopefully." He frowned a little, like he was suddenly having second thoughts. "If you want to," he added. "Your call."

Maggie stared at him. Did he say go *out* for dinner? She'd Googled him after he'd walked her back to her place, and the running theme in everything she'd read was his determination to keep a low profile. No, not just low. Invisible. He was like the Howard Hughes of the NFL. Why then, would he offer to make an exception for her? They were strangers. She finally found her voice. "Dinner out, like out-out?'

His lips tilted a bit. "Yes, out-out."

Huh. "Okay, as evil plans go, it's super enticing. But wouldn't going out to dinner be in direct conflict with your – policy? You know, to stay out of the news?"

Propping his elbows on his knees, he clasped his hands together and squinted off toward the water for a moment, then turned back to her. "Yeah, it is. But it's for a good cause, right?"

Wow, he was really offering to do this for her. He wasn't just eye candy; he had a heart. "Aw, you're nice." She punched him playfully on his bicep, and then opened her eyes wide when she realized what she'd done. "Uh, sorry." Smacking him on the arm? His throwing arm? His zillion-million-dollar-contract throwing arm?

He rubbed his arm and acted like he was checking for a bruise.

Look at that. He did have a sense of humor.

His mouth quirked into that half smile again, and damned if it didn't feel like a lava lamp was rippling in her stomach. "Annywaay," she said, drawing the word out. "That's a really kind offer." There was no reason for him to go out of his way for her but here he was, offering to do a nice thing way outside his own comfort zone for a relative stranger. "Wait, do you somehow know my ex? Mason Robillard? Is that why you're helping me?"

He bit back another smile. "No, I don't know him. So what do you say? Do you want to have dinner tonight? Pick you up at seven?"

Maggie thought about Mason seeing a photo of her holding onto hunky Garrett Long's big muscular arm, all smiles and happiness. It was a no brainer. But wasn't Garrett dating someone? She had scrolled through a ton of photographs of him with various ridiculously beautiful women. From what she'd gathered, his most recent conquest was an actress in one of her favorite Netflix dramas.

"I know it would be a pretend date, but won't your girlfriend mind?"

"Girlfriend?" he asked, brow furrowed.

"Aren't you dating Vanessa Kaplan?"

He looked at her for a long, cool moment. "If I was seeing someone, I wouldn't suggest dinner. That's not who I am."

Oh. Damn. Open mouth, insert flip-flop.

"Of course you're not. I'm so sorry."

Garrett sighed, his expression inscrutable. "Forget it. So, do we have a date?"

Should she be a little excited that he was single? No, she shouldn't. It was nothing to her. His invitation was just a weird good deed. A weird good deed by a gorgeous single quarterback.

No. Just stop it.

She nodded. "If you're game, I am, too. How can you be sure we'll get our picture taken?"

"Trust me," he replied wryly. "There's no escape."

Well, then. It appeared as though she was going on a date with Garrett Long. A kind of pretend date, but a date nonetheless. This was going to go down in the history books as one of the most unexpected days of her life and it wasn't even over yet. "Well, in that case, you'll have to excuse me." She rose from the chair, touching his shoulder briefly for balance. "Apparently I'm having dinner tonight with the NFL's hottest quarterback –" She paused, grinning when he huffed. "And I have a lot of primping to do." She dropped her book in her bag and picked up her cooler.

Rising, he glanced at his watch. "You do know it's not even noon yet, right?"

"A lot of primping," she repeated firmly. She was pleased when she saw the trace of another smile. He was a bit of a puzzle, with his measured remarks and his guarded glances. It might be fun to see how many of those reluctant smiles she could get out of him before the night was over.

She could do with some fun for a change.

After a shower and a short nap, Maggie felt almost cheerful. She hadn't felt truly cheerful in a while. She was generally pretty upbeat but since the break-up she'd been stuck on an emotional Tilt-a-Whirl with no safety bar, lurching between miserable and murder-y.

She was still agog over the fact she was going on a date with a man whose face and body sold everything from sports drinks and watches to menswear and luxury cars. It didn't matter that it was a fake date. In fact, thank God it was a fake date. All she hoped for was a really good photograph where she looked a lot less water-logged Amy Farrah Fowler and a whole lot more sexy Penny, and that Garrett looked like – well, just exactly how he looked.

Now the big question: What was she going to wear? She hadn't packed anything special; just shorts and jeans and t-shirts, and that wouldn't do at all. Maybe there was time to dash into St. Augustine and look for something? If things worked out, and Mason did happen to stumble across the photo online, she wanted his eyes to pop and his jaw to drop. She wanted him to wonder if perhaps he had made a terrible mistake and to beg her to forgive him.

Despite the voice in her head telling her not to do it, she picked up her phone and began scrolling through her photos. She really ought to just delete them all. Looking at all of the pictures of Mason's handsome face was painful. These photos were of the old Mason, the guy who had swept her off her feet with over the top romantic gestures and sweet promises. Back when she was his dream girl, his soul mate, and he couldn't wait until they were married and had a big family of their own.

But then he went to work at a boutique investment company and the Mason she fell in love with turned into someone she didn't recognize; someone who preferred hoity toity luxury suites instead of tailgate parties and golf weekends with his jerk of a boss over picnics with her. And then the day came when he told her he didn't want to marry her after all.

He told her he would always love her as a very dear friend. Blah blah blah.

They both deserved passion and excitement. Blah blah blah.

One day she'd thank him because she'd find true love and realize it was all for the best.

Blah blah blah, in bold and all caps.

What he was really saying was that all of the things he'd once loved about her were now boring and basic and he was tired of her. And it hadn't taken him long at all to find a new love. Her phone had been blowing up with friends furious on her behalf that he was already dating a girl from his company. A willowy, exotic girl who had the whole smoky eye make-up thing down cold. The polar opposite of basic and boring.

Maggie swiped an angry tear away. She definitely didn't want him back but she did want him to see that she wasn't wasting away, nursing a broken heart. She started deleting photos quickly, before she could change her mind and then she asked Siri to identify one or two boutiques where she might find something befitting a date with a demi-god. Grabbing her keys, she stomped out of the beach house.

It was on.

In less than an hour she was pushing open the door of a chic little shop in St. Augustine where a mega-tanned sales assistant with perfect eyebrows wasted no time approaching her. Normally Maggie liked to fend off over-eager clerks but today was the exception. Today she needed all the help she could get.

"I need a revenge dress. You know, the kind of dress that will make my ex cry? Got anything like that?"

The young sales assistant looked thrilled. "Oh, I know exactly what you want," she said excitedly, leading Maggie to a rack of brightly colored shirts. "We just got these in."

Maggie touched one of the garments. It was the most marvelous silky fabric but she shook her head. "No, I want a dress. It has to be a dress." Mason had always admired her legs so she wanted them to be on maximum display.

"But these are dresses." The assistant pulled one out and held it against her body to show Maggie. "See?"

Maggie squinted at it doubtfully. "Are you sure?" She took it and held it up against her own frame. Yikes. There was short and then there was this little scrap of a dress. But if she wanted to show off her legs, this would definitely do the trick.

The girl rifled through the rack, pulling out several of the so-called dresses. "Here, take these and try them on. I think you'll like them."

Well, why not? Lifting her chin, she followed the clerk to the dressing room.

Maggie the basic kindergarten teacher might not wear a teeny tiny dress like this but Maggie the kick-ass-revenge-goddess definitely would.

Chapter 4

She had made a mistake. A terrible, terrible mistake. Biting her lip, Maggie looked at her reflection in the bathroom mirror and broke into a cold sweat. What had she been thinking? The dress, if that's what you wanted to call it, the one looked so amazing and flattering at the trendy (aka expensive) little boutique, now felt like a porn star's negligee, and the strappy sandals the sales clerk had assured her were perfect felt like twisted ankles waiting to happen. Was it too late to change into her jeans?

She heard a knock on the front door.

Yep, too late. Gritting her teeth, she walked carefully toward the front door, picking up the purse she'd also bought in her delirious fit of spending. Here went nothing. Taking a deep breath, she opened the door.

Garrett Long stood waiting in all his chiseled glory, an unreadable look on his face that morphed into a distinctly startled expression as he took in her appearance.

"I know, I know." Maggie winced at his reaction. "It's terrible. It's all wrong. This is not me. I don't know what I was thinking." She took in his appearance as well, charcoal slacks and a black and gray hounds tooth button-down that just screamed custom tailoring. Shirts didn't ordinarily fit like a second skin, did they? His shoulders looked a mile wide; his sleeves were pushed up, showing off muscular forearms and a Tag Heuer watch. The neck was open at his tanned throat. Mercy. He looked like a million dollars. Which he had, she thought disjointedly. Multiple millions. She was so far out of her league with him it wasn't funny, even if it was a fake date.

"You look gorgeous," she said accusingly. "What are we going to do? I can't go out like this. I look terrible."

He swallowed and blinked. "Maggie?"

She tilted her head in confusion. What was wrong with him? "Garrett?"

He stood back a step and looked at her again, up and down and back up again, slowly.

Maggie felt hot suddenly. All over. She looked down at her dress, what there was of it, and then back up at him. "Say something. It is terrible, isn't it? I told the sales clerk I wanted a kiss-my-ass dress but I think I went too far. I can change, really."

He gave her a smile, a real smile, one that made her knees feel a little wobbly.

Or maybe it was the shoes. She was definitely wobbly in the shoes

"It's the opposite of terrible. You look –" He shook his head slowly. "You look very nice."

He sounded like he meant it. Maggie relaxed. "Oh, thank God. I was about to have a meltdown." She stepped out of the doorway and pulled the door closed behind her. "I was thinking about going back to murder the sales clerk."

She heard him chuckle and felt his hand at her elbow, leading her across the porch to a car on the driveway. He opened the door of the passenger side and she carefully slid into the seat.

Uh, yikes. Note to self: try sitting in a dress before buying it. In a sitting position it was almost up to the top of her thighs. She tugged on the hem a little desperately as Garrett circled the hood.

Yeah, so far she was nailing this date thing. Yay Maggie.

He opened his door and slid into the driver's seat, his gaze sliding to her legs, then quickly back up at the steering wheel. Looking slightly bemused, he started the engine, backed the car down the drive and pulled out onto the highway.

It was very quiet in the car for several miles. Garrett seemed to be engrossed in his own thoughts so Maggie didn't know if she ought to instigate a conversation or not. She was a little afraid of what might come out of her mouth. And if she did make an attempt, what should she talk about? She didn't know enough about him to know if they had anything in common beyond landing on the same stretch of beach, and she sure wasn't going to rely on anything she'd read online.

Should she ask him about football? Did he get tired of that? She didn't know a lot about the Denver Renegades. She did know a good bit about the Saints but she didn't think talking about a rival was polite. Maybe she should steer clear of football entirely.

Maybe she'd just be quiet. Probably the best option.

She eyed him surreptitiously. It was ridiculous for a man to have such a perfect profile. Honestly, he looked more like a movie star than a football player. Those lips, wow. Just wow.

"So you went into town today?" He gave her a quick side-eye.

"Yes." Maggie was so relieved to have a topic. "I spent a month's salary on this get-up. I'm brand new down to my undies."

Oh sweet baby Jesus.

His flash of a grin came and went so quickly she wasn't really sure it had happened.

Enough of this. She was the boss of her own mouth. "Sorry, too much information. Where are we going, anyway?"

"A place my assistant chose. It's supposed to be nice."

"Your assistant?" Did he not know how to pick a restaurant himself? "Is that a normal thing for her to do?"

He nodded. "She does the research and reaches out to the

place so they know we're coming. That way we have more control and they get some publicity."

"Hmm. So no such thing as spontaneity, then."

He glanced over questioningly.

"I mean, like, 'oh, that burger place looks good, let's try it.'"

"Sure, but it can turn into a real spectacle. And speaking of spectacles, here we are." He pulled the car up to a valet station outside a stately brick building.

Maggie glanced through the windshield and caught her breath. A mass of people, some holding expensive looking cameras and others wearing variations of Renegade team clothing and holding up smart phones, were waiting behind a thick cord running from the valet podium by the street to the door of the building. She could see them jostling for elbow room, and the noise level was rising. She felt a prickle of unease.

Garrett took the keys from the ignition. "Wait for me to come around for you, pivot so you can step out on both feet, then just hold onto me and smile."

"Wait, pivot, step out, hold on, smile." She gave him a firm nod. "Okay. I've got this." She watched him step up out of his seat and circle around the front of a car, seemingly oblivious to the furor a few feet away. Weird to get such specific direction on how to get out of the car but he clearly had more experience with this kind of thing than she did. She'd do whatever worked to avoid flashing her lady bits. Taking a breath, she eyed the excited group again and her worry grew. This was starting to feel like a very bad idea. Was it like this for him all the time? Ugh, she felt sorry for him. And he was doing this for her. A photo to make Mason jealous. A photo her parents would also see. And the other teachers, and her principal, and her student's parents. And her pastor! In this tiny excuse of a dress! Why was she just now realizing this? Maggie considered the console between the seats. Could she climb over it and just drive off? Forget the whole thing? It wouldn't be a very nice thing to do to Garrett, but –

He opened her door, interrupting her panicky thoughts, and

held out his hand. When she hesitated, he gave her an encouraging little smile. Okay, she could do this. He wouldn't let her stumble. Her eyes fixed on him; Maggie swallowed, did the pivot thing and stepped out of the car. The noise level rose like a dull roar in her ears but Garrett tucked her hand in the bend of his arm, gave her a slight squeeze, and led her back around to the entrance. She kept her fingers wrapped around his hard forearm as he handed his keys to the wide-eyed valet. When he turned them toward the group, the din subsided somewhat but the sound of cameras clicking revved up.

"Hi guys," he said calmly. "Nice to see you all. Hope everybody's having a good night."

And the flashes – mercy. They were enough to trigger a seizure. Maggie shifted a little closer to Garrett. He dipped his head towards hers. "Evil plan a success," he breathed in her ear.

She blinked up at him and was surprised when he gave her a little wink. A wink! She smirked at his unexpected humor in the face of the jostling furor.

"Who's your date?" one of the photographers called, and then others started shouting questions, vying for his attention

Yikes. Maggie drew in a deep breath and straightened her back. Their intensity was overwhelming. What were so many Denver fans doing in Florida? Was this normal? She heard more than one woman shouting "I love you, Garrett!" Seriously? What were they thinking? She sure hoped nobody flung a pair of panties or a bra in their direction. She was not down for that kind of behavior.

Garrett held his hand up again. "This is my friend, Maggie Parrish." He squeezed her hand again. Maggie remembered what he had said so she tried to smile. Normally, like a human, not like a frightened capuchin monkey.

"And she's not used to all of this so we're going to go on in and have a nice meal now. Thanks for coming out." Ignoring the next wave of shouted questions, Garrett led Maggie to the front door of the restaurant where an ecstatic maître d' waited.

"Mr. Long!" he exclaimed, clasping his hands together. "We're so honored to have you and your lovely guest dine with us this evening!"

While the man gushed, Maggie glanced around the elegant interior of the restaurant where the other patrons, seated at white linen covered tables, eyed them just as avidly as the crowd outdoors. She straightened her shoulders and drew in a deep breath.

Pretend they're kindergarteners. It's the first day of school and they're more afraid of you than you are of them.

"And Miss Parrish," the man said, startling Maggie with his use of her name. "Please let us know if there is anything at all we can do to make your evening memorable in every way."

"Thank you so much," she managed. He didn't have to do a thing to make the evening memorable. It was already memorable. And astonishing. And frankly terrifying – all without anyone's help.

The man finally ran out of steam and, waving off the other staff, personally led them through the dining room to a small anteroom with three private, high-walled booths.

"That one." Garrett gestured toward the farthest booth, and Maggie sank gratefully onto the plush banquette. Just a tug or two to make sure her dress hadn't crawled up to her waist and she was set.

The man garbled a few more moments before finally withdrawing and wide-eyed wait-staff poured water for them with noticeable side glances. Maggie glanced at Garrett, who took the attention in reserved stride.

Once he scuttled away, Maggie turned sideways to look straight at him.

"All of that – the media and the people, just because you're eating out – that was – that was –"

"Ridiculous, right?" He shook his head ruefully and toyed with the heavy silverware.

"I feel so sorry for you. What a kerfuffle."

His eyebrow quirked. "A what?"

"Kerfuffle. You know, a commotion."

"Kerfuffle." His lips tilted into a smile. "I call it a shit show."

Maggie grinned. "I use kindergarten language."

"Well, the kerfuffle was necessary to guarantee the success of your evil plan."

Thinking of Mason made Maggie frown. It probably wasn't healthy to hope he'd see the photo and suddenly realize he'd made a terrible mistake. Stop thinking about him. Right this minute. She drew in a breath and glanced at Garrett to find him studying her with an unreadable expression.

"Chin up." His voice was soft. "That's not the look we're going for."

He was right. Now wasn't the time to think about Mason. In fact, never would be a good time to think about Mason. "You're absolutely right." She drew in a deep breath and gave him a big smile. "After all, I'm on a date with Garrett Long tonight, the NFL's hottest –"

"Yeah, yeah," he interrupted her, gifting her with one of his wry half-smiles. "Enough of that."

"No, seriously." He didn't seem very used to being teased, which made it even more fun. She wondered if she could get him to laugh again. It was hard work but definitely worth the effort. "You're a big deal and I'm doing this all wrong. I should be gazing at you with lusty adoration like those women outside." She fluttered her eyes at him in demonstration.

He shook his head. "Lusty adoration, huh?"

"Hey, I read romance novels. I know the lingo."

He was trying not to smile. It just made Maggie want to try harder. "You do realize you were only seconds away from being pelted with panties, don't you? I bet you have a collection, don't you? A drawer full of random panties at home?"

He dropped his chin and rubbed his forehead. "No, Maggie, I don't."

"It's okay," she smirked, patting his arm. "I won't tell anyone."

Their waiter appeared, a bit calmer than his predecessors. Maggie suspected that Garrett was relieved to have the topic of panties interrupted. They were presented with menus and a wine booklet, and the waiter recited the specials before disappearing again.

"Would you like some wine?" Garrett opened the booklet to study the options.

Maggie drank a sip of water. "No, thanks. I only drink wine with my girlfriends in very secure locations."

He raised one eyebrow in question.

"One glass and I can't stop talking; two and I get really handsy; three and you'll have to haul me out of here draped over your shoulder."

He closed the book. "Handsy?"

Ah, there it was, that smile sneaking out. Maggie nodded. "I'm a hugger– most Southern girls are – and wine, well, it tends to make me super affectionate. You'll be amazed to know that sometimes total strangers don't appreciate a good hug."

"You don't say. Give me an example."

She pursed her lips thoughtfully. "I guess the most embarrassing example was this one time in the French Quarter when I got a warning from a police officer for hugging his horse. Excessively hugging his horse, apparently."

Garrett choked a little on a sip of water.

"The horse didn't mind," she added, giving him a helpful little thump on the back. "Just the officer."

His grin was spectacular. Mercy. Maggie felt the liquid, loopy thing again, all the way to her toes.

"You're making me really want to order wine, just to see what kind of trouble you get into."

"Not tonight, superstar. No wine for me, not in this dress and with your friends with cameras outside."

"Good point." She could see he was actually trying to tamp down the smile but wasn't having much success.

"I am hungry, though." Maggie scanned the offerings on the

menu. "I wonder what's good here. Seafood's always a good choice on the coast but I think I'm in the mood for some beefcake. Oh, I'm sorry, I meant beef steak."

He tried to glare at her but she could tell he wasn't far off from laughing again. "I'm so sorry," she lied, grinning at him. "It's just that it's hard not to tease you. I mean, look at you. You're so pretty."

He laughed out loud. "You really enjoy giving me a hard time, don't you?"

Yay! She finally got him to laugh again. "Come on, I bet you wouldn't like it if I fawned all over you. I bet that gets old."

He nodded. "It does. I hate it. Like the guy who met us at the door with all his yapping and flapping. I'd like to just walk in someplace and sit wherever I want, with people acting normal around me."

He was so earnest. Maggie put her menu down and gave him her full attention. "Is it like this for you all the time?"

"Just when I go out in public," he answered wryly.

Yikes. "How do you cope so well with it?"

He lifted his shoulder in a half shrug. "Sometimes I don't."

Maggie remembered an article she'd read about him going after a reporter who asked some nosey questions about his family. It had turned into quite a scuffle. "It must take a lot to get to the point of wanting to punch someone," she mused aloud.

Wincing, he rubbed his forehead.

"Just the wrong question asked the wrong way on the wrong day," he said finally. "I understand I represent my team and the franchise, and I'm fine with that, but personal stuff should be off-limits. The public doesn't have the right to know about my private life."

Maggie touched his arm in sympathy. "I'm sorry. I'm ashamed to be part of the problem."

"What are you talking about?" His expression was puzzled but wary.

"You know, Googling you today. Reading articles and making assumptions. It's exactly what feeds the monster and makes your life difficult."

He squinted at her. "Have you always suffered from an over-active sense of responsibility?"

She shrugged. "No, but I sure don't want to treat anyone like an inanimate object instead of a person with feelings."

Garrett propped an elbow on the table, rested his chin on his hand and studied her face for a long moment. A little flustered by his scrutiny, Maggie looked down and fiddled with her cloth napkin until the awkward pause was interrupted by the returning waiter.

"Have we made a decision?" The waiter blinked, realizing he had interrupted a moment. "Or should I come back?" he asked.

"No." Garrett turned his attention to the man. "I'll have the special, and she'll have –" he looked at Maggie.

"Me, too," she said, relieved to no longer be on the receiving end of that disconcerting gaze. For a second there, she'd felt a trickle of something alarming, like he was doing a fingerless Vulcan mind-meld on her and could read all her thoughts.

The waiter looked confused. "Which one?"

"Sorry?" Garrett asked.

"Which special?" the waiter asked.

Maggie hoped Garrett had paid attention earlier when the waiter had spouted off all the specials, because she certainly hadn't. She busied herself with a sip of water and looked off into the distance.

"You first, Maggie," Garrett said, a little smile playing around the corners of his mouth.

Maggie wondered if he suspected she hadn't been paying attention. "No, you first," she said, a little desperately.

His smile quirked again. "The fish one," he told the waiter.

"The fish one, yes! Perfect!" she echoed.

"Very good," the waiter declared, looking very proud of both of them.

As soon as he was out of earshot, Garrett looked at her, another quick smile flashing on his face. "I didn't have the heart to ask him to recite all the specials again. You were no help at all."

"What if there hadn't been a fish one?"

"There's always a fish one," he replied. "What about you? 'The fish one, yes, perfect!'"

Oh, look, now he was teasing, too. Maggie was delighted. Just as soon as the teasing began, it ended; his expression stilling as if he realized he was relaxing and didn't want to. "So are you still planning to leave tomorrow?" He shook his napkin into his lap.

He was definitely a puzzle. "Yes. I might as well get back to Baton Rouge. I want to find a new place to live."

Garrett blinked. "Baton Rouge? I've got a good friend there; Ty Hurst. He's an old teammate."

Maggie looked at him in surprise. "I know him. Well, not him so much, but I know his wife, Eleanor. Their son, Nicholas, was in my class last year."

"That's a crazy coincidence."

"It sure is," Maggie agreed. "Nicholas is absolutely adorable, and Eleanor was my class parent. She made my life so much easier. I hope I get all their kids."

He shook his head. "What do they have, three now? I can't keep up."

Maggie smiled. "There's Nicholas and the twins, Lauren and Nicole, and Eleanor told me at the end of the year that she's expecting number four."

His eyes widened. "It's got to be a zoo at their place."

"Sounds wonderful to me," she admitted. "I'm an only child. I want a big family. Huge, even. How many is the right number for you?"

He hesitated for a moment. "Actually I don't see myself ever getting married, much less having kids."

Huh. That sounded sad and lonely. "Ever?"

He shrugged. She could tell he was uncomfortable with the direction their conversation had taken. "Just not my thing," he said shortly.

Uh oh. She could practically see his walls going back up.

Abort! Change the subject!

"What about you? Heading back to Denver?"

"I haven't decided. I can still play golf without a lot of fuss but hanging out on the beach will be impossible." He drank a sip of water. "New place to live, huh?"

Maggie nodded. There was no way she could continue living in the house she had happily shared with Mason, even though she loved it. She would find a new place and then survive the summer that should have been filled with the wedding and the honeymoon and the new life she and Mason were starting together.

"Maggie?"

She snapped back from her musings. "Sorry," she said quickly.

"He did a number on you, didn't he?" His voice was quiet. Sympathetic.

"It was sudden," she said helplessly. "Out of the blue, really. One minute I had this clear vision of my life and then everything changed overnight." She looked at Garrett earnestly. "But things don't really change overnight, do they? Or people? How did I miss the signs?"

He looked away, lips pressed together. "People are good at hiding things," he said finally. To her surprise, he reached for her hand. "Look, I've only known you, what, a couple of hours? I can see you're great. Don't waste time mourning for a guy who can't see it." He squeezed her hand and let it go. "I just hope things work out for you the way you want."

How did she want things to work out? She didn't think she wanted Mason back but she did want a little bit of her pride back. She dashed away the one tear that had escaped. "You're really nice."

"I'm really not," he replied firmly. "You just caught me on a good day."

"I don't believe you." She was firm, too. "Look at the trouble you've gone through tonight."

"No trouble. We both had to eat, right? And you're a lot prettier than my teammates." He closed his mouth as if he regretted the last statement.

She was startled and cautiously flattered by his remark and wasn't sure how to respond. He probably didn't mean anything by it. It was probably the kind of thing he automatically said to women. No biggie. "I bet I eat less, too, right?"

He seemed relieved by her response. "That's for sure."

"So tell me," she began. "What do you do during the off season, besides playing golf with your teammates?"

He shrugged. "Nothing exciting. Work out, read, eat things I shouldn't. This week is kind of an annual thing, but otherwise, I spend most of the off-season at my house near Grand Lake. The season's pretty grueling so it's good to just relax."

"I love having the summer off, too. Not that teaching kindergarten can be compared to playing professional football," she added quickly.

"I don't know. Sounds pretty exhausting to me. Why'd you pick kindergarten?"

"Kindergarten is such a huge year." Maggie leaned forward. "It's the foundation for more than just a child's academic future, it's where they begin learning and practicing skills they're going to use the rest of their lives. It's like being an ambassador to aliens from another planet and teaching them how to understand our culture." She broke off, suddenly a little embarrassed.

He tilted his head and waited.

"You know, like 'No, Brock, we do not lick water fountains. That might be acceptable on your planet, but here on earth we prefer to drink the water coming out of the fountain.'"

He chuckled. "It sounds like you love what you do."

Maggie nodded. "I do, but don't get me wrong; there are days when I'd like to run for cover. You might have one child start off in a bad mood, and before you know it, everyone's crying."

"I think I'll stick with football."

"What, you've never had to deal with all your teammates crying at one time?"

"Well, there was that one time when we lost the NFC championship," he said, straight-faced. "That was pretty intense. Bunch of babies."

Maggie laughed and he smiled at her.

"Uh, excuse me."

Maggie looked over to see a pretty girl in a short black dress standing by the edge of their booth, her eyes trained on Garrett. Maggie looked at him, curious to see how he would react. She was struck by how quickly he had reverted to what she already recognized as his default guarded expression.

The young woman didn't seem to notice his reticence. She batted her eyes and edged closer toward him. "I'm so sorry to bother you, Garrett. I'm a huge fan and I was wondering if I could please get a picture with you?" Not waiting for his response, she handed her phone to Maggie, moved to perch beside Garrett, and put her hand on his arm.

Oh-kay. Maggie looked down at the phone to ensure it was in camera mode but Garrett took it from her and passed it back to the woman.

"Sorry." He didn't look sorry at all, with his face shut down and his tone flat. "We're on a date and we're back here to have some privacy."

The phone back in her hand, the woman blinked in surprise. "Oh, of course, I'm sorry." She shot a sour glance at Maggie and then reached quickly to drop a folded piece of paper by Garrett's water glass. "Have a nice night."

Maggie watched her sway out of sight and then turned to Garrett, open mouthed. "Wow."

"Sorry about that." He shook his head slightly, looking openly irritated.

"Is that her phone number?" She nodded toward the bit of paper.

"I don't know." He picked it up and crumpled it into a tiny ball.

Maggie held out her hand and he handed it to her reluctantly. She smoothed it open to find a name and number, and then looked at Garrett, shaking her head in amazement. "Wow. Just wow. Imagine how mad I'd be if this were a real date. Her name is Amber. Sure you don't want to keep her number?"

He grimaced. "I'm sure."

"She was awfully pretty. Just think. You might be able to add to your panty collection."

He narrowed his eyes at her and Maggie winked at him. "Gotcha."

Chapter 5

Back at her rental, Garrett pulled the car into the drive, killed the engine and then stepped out to circle around to Maggie's door. She didn't wait for him; she opened it herself.

He gave her a chiding look. "That's my job."

Making a face at him, she dug in her bag for the key to the door. "You're taking this date thing way too seriously. You can relax now."

He shoved his hands into the front pockets of his pants. "It was a nice evening."

Maggie could swear he sounded a little bit surprised. "It was." She walked to the door, aware he was following her. Unlocking it, she hesitated. What was she supposed to do now? Did he expect a kiss? Surely not. They'd already established this was a pretend date. Did he expect to come inside? Did she want to invite him inside? What would she do with him if she did and he said yes? Invite him to play Yahtzee? She felt a little curl in her lady bits as other, super inappropriate ideas sprang to mind.

Like ripping that fitted shirt right off of him, buttons be damned, and biting those biceps.

No.

She was not the kind of girl who entertained those kinds of

ideas. She wasn't interested in a real rebound fling and anyway, this was Garrett Long.

Who was absolutely the most delicious looking man she'd ever seen in her life.

Maybe she could be that kind of girl for one night?

No.

They'd had a good time and all, but he was way too – just too everything. And she was still way too raw from her break-up. She couldn't think of anything more ridiculous than him wanting to do anything other than say good night and make a swift exit.

But he wasn't leaving. He was still standing there. All six-plus feet of him, all muscle-y and gorgeous, with a contemplative look on his movie-star face.

She fidgeted with her bag. "Did you want to come in?"

What had just come out of her mouth? "Or do you want to leave? I'm sure you want to leave. Don't you? Because it's really late."

He glanced at his watch. "It's not ten yet. Is that late?"

Maggie bit her lip. Ten o'clock wasn't late, not really. At least not for a twenty-nine-year-old woman. Maybe Mason was right. Maybe she was boring.

"I've got an idea," he began, interrupting her thoughts of self-loathing. "How about a walk? It's a nice night and it's too dark for anyone to bother us. And it might be my only chance. I'd go by myself but that's pretty lame."

She hesitated.

"If you want to." He suddenly looked uncomfortable. "No pressure."

Would she rather stay in her rental and play Solitaire on her phone or go for a walk with arguably the handsomest and most surprisingly kind man she'd ever met in her life? Was she completely hopeless?

No, she was not. She was certainly mature enough to go for a walk on the beach. Because that's all it was, a little walk. Maybe she'd even be able to pry another smile or two out of him.

"That sounds nice," she said finally. "But I can't take these horrible heels another second. Do you mind waiting until I change into something less Real Housewives of Florida?"

He looked pleased that she had agreed. "Great, I'll do the same, and meet you by the water in –" He glanced at his watch. "Twenty minutes?"

"Deal. Twenty minutes." She opened the door and slipped inside, then popped her head back out. "Last one there's a rotten egg."

Garrett returned to his car, glad he had managed to extend the evening a little longer. It was funny; while he and the guys were playing golf, he'd seriously reconsidered his out-of-character invitation. The only reason he hadn't backed out was because he didn't have Maggie's phone number and he wasn't enough of a jerk to ghost her. Then he figured he'd just get it over with as quickly as possible and go on his way. It hadn't occurred to him that he might have a good time.

He had really had a good time.

It wasn't like he wanted to get Maggie into bed. She wasn't his type at all. He preferred women who wanted what he wanted; something casual without any expectations. Maggie had hopes and expectations written all over her. But he still liked being around her. There was no knowing what she was going to say next. Hell, he didn't think she even knew what she was going to say next.

Anyway, it was just one evening. Tomorrow she'd be on her way back to her life in Baton Rouge and he'd soon be on his own way back to Denver. Two ships passing and all that.

And then he only had a month or so left to suffer through and it would be time to get back to work. He was ready for it, too. More than ready. Long hours at the facility, six days a week. The relentless challenge and thrill of the game. It was what he lived for. The game and his role gave him purpose and he was a little lost without it during the off season.

Back in his room at the rental, he stripped off his dress clothes. He was glad his buddies were still out because he didn't want to have to explain his evening. They were always on him about loosening up, Dom especially. He didn't want them to get the wrong idea. Maggie was a nice girl but it wasn't going to lead to anything. It wouldn't lead to anything precisely because she was a nice girl.

He thought back to when she opened her door earlier and he got his first look at her in that slip of a dress.

Whoa.

That dress. Her 'kiss-my-ass' dress. He smiled. The silky stuff it was made of had skimmed her body in all the right places, and her legs had looked a mile long. He shook his head in appreciative recollection. It had really taken him by surprise. And her face when she opened the door? Hilarious. It hadn't been a calculated bid for attention; she was really panicked. In his opinion the sales assistant deserved a bonus.

Her hair was a nice surprise, too. A warm brown that reminded him of caramel; falling in tousled waves, brushing the thin straps that crossed to the low back of her dress. Not that overdone bleached blonde or other colors not found in nature. It was the kind of hair that invited a touch, to see if it felt as soft as it looked.

He'd actually felt a little uneasy in the car at first because the change from kindergarten teacher to bombshell had been so startling.

Her appeal wasn't just based on her appearance, he mused, searching through his bag for a pair of shorts. He'd dated plenty of women who were stunning. Maggie seemed different. She wasn't shallow or vain; she was straightforward and natural and she was funny as hell. But most surprising of all was her unexpected empathy regarding his absurd celebrity status. He didn't often voice his frustration because he knew that, in other people's opinions, he had very little to complain about. Any sign of impatience or irritation on his part, no matter how justified, made him look like a first-class asshole. Maggie, however, seemed to see the bullshit for what it was. That was unusual and refreshing.

Tugging on a pair of shorts and a shirt, he heard his phone chime. He picked it up from the bed and saw his sister's face on the screen. He usually enjoyed catching up with Emily but he wanted to get back to Maggie. He tapped the answer key and headed into the bathroom. "Hey, Em. What's up?"

"Garrett! I have a huge favor to ask," she began.

He grabbed a towel and tossed it over his shoulder. "Huge, huh? Can I just say no right now?"

"No, you can't. I really need your help. Is there any possible way you could watch Lilah for us for a couple of days?"

Garrett halted, shocked into speechlessness. He couldn't imagine watching his niece for an hour, much less a couple of days. He'd never even been alone in a room with her.

"Dan's got a work thing in Savannah and I'm going with him. I was thinking maybe it would be a good opportunity for Lilah to get to know her Uncle Garrett a little better."

Lilah was five years old, and as cute as she was, she might as well be from another planet. He couldn't believe Emily would even consider such an idea. "You're kidding, right?" He headed down the stairs.

She dashed his hopes. "No, of course I'm not kidding."

Garrett frowned. "You do realize I'm the worst possible choice for a babysitter, don't you?"

"You're the perfect choice. You're my brother and I trust you more than anyone."

"You're really desperate, aren't you?"

"I'm so desperate!" she laughed. "But I really do trust you,

Garrett. I know you'd take great care of her. And who knows, maybe you'll even enjoy it a little bit."

He sighed. His sister rarely asked anything of him. She was the steadfast fixture in his life, the only person who understood the emotional scars he carried from his childhood because she was scarred along with him. He stopped on the stairs, drumming his fingers on the baluster. It was a terrible idea. Really, really bad.

But he couldn't say no.

"I'll hate every second," he finally said, moving down the stairs again.

"Is that a yes?" Emily sounded ecstatic.

"When do you leave?"

"Tuesday. I'll be back Saturday."

"Go ahead and make your plans. I'm in Florida right now but I'll get home in time."

She squealed. Wincing, he held the phone away from his ear. "Oh, Garrett, you're the best brother! I can't thank you enough! I'm so –"

"I'm regretting it already." He was only half kidding. "Look, I've got to go right now, but I'll get back to you tomorrow."

"Wait," she said quickly. "I wanted to tell you one more thing."

She hesitated. Garrett got a familiar, unwelcome feeling. "What?"

"She called me again."

Yep, he knew it. He could always tell when she wanted to talk about their mother. "And?"

"She sounded really good. I think she's made a lot of progress at the new place."

Garrett stopped on his trek across the room, waiting for it.

"She wanted to know if we would come see her."

Easy. "No."

"Would you at least think about it? We could go together."

"No."

Emily sighed. "Just think about it and we'll talk about it later, okay?"

His sister was nothing if not an optimist. "It's always going to be 'no', Em. Look, I've really got to go now."

"All right," she said. "Love you."

"Love you, too," he said, disconnecting. Glancing at his watch, he realized he was taking too long. Maggie might think he changed his mind and wasn't going to show.

Maggie hurried to change and slip outside to the beach but once she reached the edge of the water where waves were gently lapping at the sand, she started having second thoughts. She ought to be packing her things and preparing for an early morning and another nine-hour drive. Ugh. And then home to her empty house, with nothing to do when she got there but mope. She didn't even look forward to seeing her parents or her friends because they were all worried about how she was handling the break up. She was tired of talking about it. Talking about it didn't change anything.

She crouched down to the wet sand and drew an "M & M" with one finger and then watched the surf wash it away. Just like that, three years gone.

"What are you doing down there?"

Garrett's low voice startled her. She lost her balance in the shifting sand and tipped over sideways, losing a flip flop in the process. She looked up to find he had changed into a pair of shorts and a t-shirt as well, was barefoot, and had a towel slung over one wide shoulder. It was a relief to see him in casual clothes again. Not that he looked any less handsome, just more approachable. Plus she liked his legs. A lot. Powerful thighs, defined calves, even his knees were pretty. Who had pretty knees? And all of those parts dusted with just the right amount of hair. Sitting on the sand gave her a great view. Garrett's legs put Mason's legs to shame, like comparing redwood trees to pine needles.

"Maggie?"

She blinked and looked up. He had a half-smile on his face that made her suspect he was aware she'd been gawking, and then she remembered he had asked a question. "Just doodling." Was her face red? It felt red.

"Is falling over part of doodling?"

She gave him a mock-glare from her low vantage point. "I fell over because you startled me, sneaking up so sneaky-like."

He offered her his hand. "I didn't sneak up sneaky-like."

He had big hands. She'd noticed that at dinner. That was a thing with quarterbacks, right? She allowed him to tug her to her feet and then glanced down ruefully at the sand all over her hip and leg.

He was looking at her legs, too. "Here, use this." He handed her the towel.

"What took you so long, anyway?" She slid her foot back into her runaway flip-flop, swiped at her backside hurriedly and handed the towel back to him.

"Well, somebody had to be the rotten egg." He squinted at her shirt. "'Teaching is important but summer vacation is importanter'?"

She looked down at her shirt and smirked. "I've got lots of teacher t-shirts. What can I say? It's my jam."

He dropped his gaze and then put a hand on her shoulder to turn her slightly. "Missed some." He crouched to brush sand from her leg. He must be on a mission to dust off every single microscopic grain of sand, with his big warm hand. Her stomach did the inverted roller coaster lava lamp thing again.

Oh-kay.

So…

He was taking a long time.

Finally he rose, tossed the towel back over his shoulder, and she let go of the breath she didn't realize she was holding. "Thanks," she managed.

"Want to walk to the pier?" He gestured down the beach towards the long concrete pier extending into the water.

"Sure."

They set off companionably. Now she was glad that she'd agreed to the walk. The beach was serene at night, almost devoid of other people, and the salty scent of the breeze was cool and refreshing.

"Nice, huh?" Garrett nodded toward the sky as they moved along the ribbon of dark sand closest to the water.

Maggie paused to give the sight her full attention. The moon was almost full and it seemed larger than normal, hanging low over the water in a deep blue and purple sky. It reflected onto the ocean's low waves, creating the effect of several silvery moons reaching for the shore. "Gorgeous." She hugged herself, rubbing her upper arms. "Kind of science fiction-y."

"Science fiction-y?"

"You know, like the huge moon of Endor."

He cocked his head in question.

She sighed. "Star Wars? Return of the Jedi?" She acted out brandishing a light saber and made the whooshing noise. "You know, the one with Ewoks?"

He started laughing and mimicked her 'whoosh.'

Oh my God, she loved his laugh. "Don't tell me you're not a fan of Star Wars?" She slanted a smile at him. "Wait, I know. You're all about Captain America. I get that about you."

"Star Wars and Captain America are okay. He gave her a considering glance. "I'm more about Harry Potter, myself."

She stopped in her tracks and gaped at him. "Shut up!"

"Okay." He continued walking, straight faced.

She hurried to catch up and smacked him in the arm. "I love Harry Potter!"

"Ouch." He rubbed his arm. "What is it with you and your

need to hit me?"

Laughing, Maggie bumped him with her shoulder, too, earning a bonus amused side-eye. "I would never have taken you for a Potterhead in a million years."

He looked offended. "Why not? What kid doesn't want to find out they're a wizard?"

"And go to school at Hogwarts," Maggie added.

"And play Quidditch on a flying broomstick," he said.

"And do spells with a magic wand."

"And sneak around under an invisibility cloak."

"And drive an enchanted car."

"And fight dragons."

He hadn't missed a beat, and Maggie burst out laughing again. "Okay, here's the most important question of all, for the win. Which Dumbledore is best?"

He made a scoffing sound. "Original Dumbledore. No contest."

Maggie did a little dance. "Right? The second Dumbledore was the worst!"

They grinned at one another, and Maggie felt her heart thump, hard. He was full of surprises. Underneath that gorgeous poker face, the big old gazillionaire quarterback ambling along the beach beside her was as much a Harry Potter nerd as she was. Mind officially boggled. "This was a good idea." She rubbed her arms again as they walked along. "I wouldn't have done this on my own."

"I'm glad you came." He drew the towel off of his shoulder. "You should've brought a jacket."

Maggie hadn't realized she was chilled until he draped the towel over her shoulders. "Thanks." She clutched the ends together. "Were your friends back?"

"No, they'll probably be out for a while yet. All night, if Dom has anything to do with it."

"Dom was the one with black hair?"

He gave her a sideways glance. "Yeah."

"He's pretty."

He gave her another glance, an unreadable one.

"Not as pretty as you, of course," she teased.

He rolled his eyes. "Shut up."

She smirked at him. "Would you have gone out with them, if you hadn't taken pity on me?"

"For dinner but not afterwards. You saw what it was like at the restaurant so you can imagine what it's like at a club."

She imagined it would be a hundred times worse. At least at the restaurant, the other patrons continued on with their meal and they were able to dine in peace. Well, with the exception of Amber, of course. In a club, packed with people in various stages of tipsiness, he'd need a bodyguard or two because there would be Ambers coming at him from every direction. Maggie tightened the towel around her body. "So you would have stayed in alone?"

"More than likely. Why? Are you feeling sorry for me again?" He gave her a wry glance.

"Your life is different than I would have imagined."

He shoved his hands into his pockets. "What did you imagine?"

She thought about it. "Having the freedom to do what you want, when you want?"

"Well, you know better than that now. What else?"

"Cliché superstar stuff. Lots of traveling, parties, extravagant lifestyle, multiple homes, a Jay Leno garage full of fast cars, lots of –" She broke off abruptly. Best not to say 'lots of women.'

He lifted an eyebrow. "Lots of –?"

"Friends?"

He gave her a look that told her he knew what she stopped short of saying.

"Of course now I know you don't exactly get to do what you want, when you want; not without being hassled anyway."

He didn't reply. They continued walking, and the silence

stretched between them.

Ugh, she had accidentally dialed him right back into his quiet mode.

Finally he spoke. "I'm not the partying type anymore. I like traveling under the right circumstances; I have one car and one truck, a house in Denver and a place in the mountains. I don't have many friends outside of football. That's it. I'm pretty boring, actually."

Whew, she was relieved he was talking again. "You're the opposite of boring." She shoulder-checked him again. To her delight, he bumped her back, but he was so much bigger that she stumbled a little. His arm shot out and caught her, steadying her. "Whoa, big guy." She flashed a grin up at him. He was looking down, his blue eyes fixed on her, and her breath caught in her throat.

He cleared his throat. "What about you?"

Maggie had to think furiously to remember the question. "I have a huge desire to travel but not, unfortunately, the finances; my social life revolves around children's birthday parties and Mexican food with my best friends; I live in an old house with terrible plumbing, and you saw Lucille out front."

He lifted his eyebrow. "Lucille?"

"My car."

He blinked. "'Lucille'?"

"She's red."

Still nothing.

She held her hands out, palms up, and made a 'duh' face at him. "You know, like Lucille Ball. Red. Red hair. What, you don't have names for your vehicles? That's sad."

The look he gave her looked like a cross between amusement and concern for her mental health. "And the friends? That you have Mexican food with?"

Maggie smiled. "Sharon, Alicia and Toby. They'll be speechless if a picture does turn up online, and believe me, that'll be a first. Sharon and I teach together. She's married to Mark and they have an adorable little boy. Alicia and I shared an apartment when we were in college and I've known Toby since first grade."

"One of those was supposed to meet you here, right?"

She was surprised he remembered. "Yes, Sharon. Well, everyone was, originally, but –" She shrugged. "You know." No reason to bring up the doomed bachelorette celebration again.

"Yeah," he said quietly.

They walked silently for a few moments.

"So, what time are you leaving tomorrow?"

She hated to think about that long drive. "As early as I can. Seven maybe?"

"I'll be leaving earlier than planned, too. Got a call from my sister and she needs me to babysit."

Maggie thought she misheard him. "She needs you to what?"

"Babysit," he repeated, nodding at her doubtful expression. "I know. She's pretty desperate, apparently."

It was the last thing she could imagine him rushing home to do. "How old is her child?"

"Five." He grimaced. "I don't know anything about five-year-olds." He slowed down and eyed her intently. "But you do. You have any advice?"

"Well," Maggie said thoughtfully, "the main thing to remember is to keep him well fed and try to wear him out."

"She's a girl," Garrett's tone was apprehensive. "Does the same advice apply?"

Maggie couldn't help laughing. "Yes, girls aren't a different species. Keep her busy and you'll be fine."

"Busy doing what?"

He was looking at her like she was the font of all wisdom. Seriously? Had he never been around children before? Or been a child himself?

"Games, puzzles, finger paint, coloring books; that kind of stuff. And you can always fall back on television. Appropriate television, of course," she added quickly. "No Nightmare on Elm

Street or anything like that. You could even get the Disney channel."

He nodded. "I don't have anything for her at my house. Where do I get the right kind of stuff?"

Maggie felt a tinge of worry. Did his sister realize he was completely unprepared? "Do you want me to make a list of stuff? You could order online and have it delivered in plenty of time."

He nodded thoughtfully. "Yes, that would be great."

"We'll sit down at the pier and go phone shopping. You'll be all set. She'll think you're the best uncle in the world."

"I'll settle for just keeping her alive." From his tone, Maggie didn't think he was joking. When they reached the pier, they found a bench and he handed her his phone. Choosing an assortment of books and toys took her longer than she expected because it was a little hard to concentrate with him sitting beside her, long legs outstretched, hands clasped behind his head. "There." She gave him back his phone and pointed to the shopping cart. "You won't need all of that but it gives you a lot to choose from."

"Great." He glanced down and hit 'place your order'.

"Orrrr –" she dragged the word out, shaking her head in wonder, "You can just order all of it."

He shrugged. "Money well spent. Say, how would you feel about giving me your telephone number? Just in case of an emergency."

Maggie was taken aback by his request. "Sure, if it makes you feel better." She took his phone again and added her name and number to his contacts page. "There you go. But you'll be fine."

"You're the only kindergarten teacher I know. You're the pro here, not me." He pressed 'call' on his phone and she watched as he listened until her voice mail began and then pressed 'end'. "There, now you've got my number, too." He rose and stuffed his phone in his back pocket.

Huh. She had Garrett Long's telephone number. She'd have to think about that staggering bit of information later, when she could freak out about it properly. She stood up and they began the walk back. "Don't you have any friends with children that you can call? Some of your teammates have kids, don't they?"

"Yes, but I'd rather not expose my deficiencies to any of them. I'd never hear the end of it."

"What about your assistant, the one who picked the restaurant?"

"She's on vacation. Believe me, she didn't hesitate to remind me of that when I texted her about finding a restaurant."

They talked the rest of the way back about his niece. It was nice, how concerned he was about making her visit a success. When they reached the path to her rental, they both drew to a halt.

So this was it. Maggie knew she'd never see him again and it felt weirdly sad to say goodbye. Meeting him was completely bizarre; spending the evening with him took bizarre up a whole other level. She sure hoped there was going to be a photo online, because if there wasn't, nobody would ever believe she'd been on a date with him. Maybe she should ask for a selfie with him? Ugh, no.

She drew in a deep breath and looked up at him. "Well, Garrett Long, it's been quite a day, hasn't it?" She pulled the towel off her shoulders and handed it to him.

Tossing it back over his shoulder, he smiled down at her. "Indeed it has, Margaret Parrish."

Maggie didn't know what to say next and it seemed he didn't, either.

"I enjoyed meeting you," she finally said. "Thanks for rescuing me this morning and arranging the whole revenge-photo dinner thing."

"My pleasure," he said, rocking on his heels. "I hope it works out for you."

They stood there another awkward moment. "And good luck with your niece."

"Thanks."

He still didn't move.

Invite him in, invite him in, invite him in, her lady bits chanted. She mentally hissed at them to shut the frick up.

"And I hope you make it to the Super Bowl again," she added awkwardly.

He flashed that quick grin at her again. "Me, too."

"Sooooo….." She drew in a long, long breath. *What the hell.* She could dredge up enough courage to kiss him on the cheek. Of course she could. Just a friendly thank-you-and-goodbye kiss. That was the ticket. Just to be able to tell Sharon and Alicia and Toby that her lips had touched his skin.

But just as she raised up on her toes and lifted her face, he dipped down, and the kiss that should have landed quickly and casually on his cheek ended up squarely on his mouth.

On his perfect, sultry, almost too-pretty-for-a-man mouth.

"Oh my God!" Scrambling backwards, Maggie clapped a hand over her own mouth. "I so did not mean to do that!"

The corners of his lips were twitching. "It's okay, Maggie."

She could tell he was trying his best not to grin. Her face felt so hot. She must look like a tomato.

"Seriously, it's okay. I don't feel violated. Not real bad, anyway."

Oh, God, she might cry from the horror. "I was going to kiss you on the cheek, you know, just a little bye-bye kind of friend kiss, but you moved, and I wasn't quick enough, and honestly, it was an accident." Gah, she was doing it again; rambling, stammering, and explaining too much.

"Do you want to try again?" He tapped his cheek, radiating amusement.

Gah! "No, but thank you." Death would be so welcome. Flight seemed easier. "So, good night then!" she chirped weakly, turning on her heel. Just get to the door. Eyes on the door. Carefully, carefully. Do not make things worse by doing a face plant. Just get inside. Just a few more steps. Almost there.

"Hey, Maggie."

She reached the door, grabbed the knob, and threw one last, red-faced look over her shoulder.

Garrett was standing in the same spot, that giant Endor moon over his shoulder. The grin on his face was spectacular. "Go Renegades!" He lifted his arm in a cheer motion.

He was teasing her and, despite her scorching embarrassment, she loved it. "Go Renegades," she agreed, before slipping inside the door and closing it behind her.

And lightly touched her lips. Her lips that had touched his lips.

What a day.

Chapter 6

Maggie woke at 6:30 a.m. to the sound of knocking on both the front and back door of the beach house. She stumbled out of bed, headed for the front door, and was reaching to open it when she heard several voices on the other side. Suddenly wide awake and apprehensive, she sidled up to the window beside the door and tilted one of the slats of the wooden blinds to peek outside.

There were men on her porch, armed with cameras, having conversations with one another as casually as if they were at a sporting event.

Yikes. Garrett had warned her, but she hadn't really thought anyone would show up on her doorstep after one dinner. She wasn't famous on her own like the women he normally dated. How did they even know where she was staying?

She dropped the slat carefully. There was no way she was going to face them, wearing pajamas and sporting crazy bed head. She guessed the best option was to get ready to leave as planned, make as dignified an exit as possible, and hopefully reach the safety of her car without incident. Once inside, she would simply drive off and not look back.

Hurrying back to her bedroom, she tugged her jeans and a top on and began tossing the last of her things in her duffle bag. The knocking continued. It was a creepy feeling knowing there were strangers out there, lying in wait.

Inspiration struck and she carried her bag to the front door, then went to the back door and opened it a tiny bit. The group on the back steps snapped to attention, pointed cameras her way and began calling questions.

"How long have you and Garrett Long been dating?"

"How did you meet?"

"Is he inside with you now?"

She imitated Garrett's calm, raised hand and to her surprise, they quietened down. "If you'll be patient and wait here, I'll be back out in just a minute." Closing the door, she locked it quietly and then tiptoed to the front door. A stealthy peek through the window showed the men on the front steps hustling around the back.

Adrenaline rushing, Maggie slung her purse over her shoulder, readied her car keys, picked up her bag, and took a deep breath before opening the front door quietly. Sprinting to her car, she opened the door, pushed her bag in and over the console to the passenger seat, and slid inside.

Success! Starting her engine, she backed out and stepped on the gas just as the group of reporters came careening back around to the front of the beach house, cameras aloft. They didn't look happy at all.

Suckers.

She hadn't been on the road for very long when she remembered she'd put her cell phone on silent mode before making her dash to the car. She pulled over at the first opportunity and glanced at the recent call page.

Lord have mercy. There were over a dozen missed calls and texts. Was the hoped-for revenge photograph already online?

She did a Google search and then gave a little gasp. There it was; a clear head to toe shot of her and Garrett outside the restaurant last night, with the caption "Garrett Long's new romance?" Him, all swoony in his dark outfit and her in her colorful dress. Maggie drew in a breath, not sure if she was horrified at the length of leg she was showing or delighted with the overall image. She certainly looked delighted *in* the photograph.

Smiling like the cat who got the canary, the cream, the laser dot, and the feather on a string all at once.

And Garrett's expression – hmm. The man was so ridiculously good looking. The way he was smiling down at her was downright unsettling. She knew the exact moment the photo had been snapped; that surprising instant when he leaned down to whisper 'evil plan a success' right by her ear. She remembered him tucking her hand into the bend of his arm, but she didn't remember him placing his other hand on top of it.

It looked like a photograph of two people who were on a real date. It may have begun as a make-believe date, but by the end of the night, it felt like more. She hadn't expected to enjoy talking with him so much. Hadn't expected his empathy or quiet humor. Hadn't expected the attraction she felt to keep escalating, the desire to touch him to eclipse her immature plan to provoke Mason.

No, the pretend date hadn't felt all that make-believe by the end of the night.

Garrett eased down the staircase, awake before his friends again, and dropped a pod in the coffee maker. He gazed out of the windows and saw people already congregated about midway between the house and the water. *Awesome.* The sun was barely up and it was already a damned circus outside. The gate at the front of the beach property was locked. That hadn't prevented eager fans and determined reporters from finding a way around the neighboring properties to congregate on the beach-side of the house. There wouldn't be any run on the beach today. He couldn't even go sit outside on the deck. He may as well fly back to Denver.

He hoped Maggie had managed to get away without being hassled. It was crazy to think that he had only met her yesterday morning and now here he was, worried about her well-being. He thought about texting her, but hesitated. He'd enjoyed going out with her but they both knew it was a one-time thing, just a little innocent exercise to provoke her ex.

Thinking about it prompted him to pick up his phone and type a search into Google. There it was, the photo she wanted. He hoped she was happy with it. Ignoring the headline and text in favor of enlarging the photograph, he shook his head slightly, still a little staggered by Maggie's transformation. He didn't think he'd ever forget her hilarious anxiety when she first opened the door. Her silky little dress was far from the standard kindergarten teacher uniform.

Which begged the question, what did kindergarten teachers wear these days?

He sat down on the sofa with his coffee and, on a whim, typed in a new search: Maggie Parrish kindergarten teacher Baton Rouge Louisiana.

Well, look at that. Kindergarten teachers had pages nowadays. He tapped the link and smiled at a photo of Maggie and a group of children, all wearing wide grins and paper crowns on their heads. She was wearing a red dress and her hands were resting on the shoulders of the children standing nearest to her. He could see an engagement ring on her left hand.

Her ex was a stupid bastard.

He clicked the link to "About Miss Parrish" and found another photo, one of those traditional school photos with a generic blue background. In it Maggie's head was tilted slightly, her hair was shorter, just brushing her shoulders, and she was smiling like she was dreaming up mischief.

It was the same look she had when she'd encouraged him to call the girl who'd interrupted their dinner. Garrett snorted, remembering how annoyed he was when the girl handed Maggie her phone without so much as a glance. And Maggie had taken it, remaining pleasant even while being disrespected.

She was something else. Too nice for her own good.

He returned his attention to his phone to read the paragraph beneath her photo.

> My name is Maggie Parrish. This is my fifth year teaching kindergarten at Broadmoor Elementary. I am a Baton Rouge native. I graduated from the University of Louisiana – Lafayette with a Bachelor's degree in Early Childhood Education with a focus in Gifted Development and graduated from Louisiana State University with a Masters of Education.
>
> I absolutely love teaching. I teach because there is an excitement and joy that is unexplainable in seeing young children making new discoveries daily.
>
> I like Baum's doberge cake, Harry Potter, dogs, and the New Orleans Saints.
>
> I don't like centipedes, mushrooms, or scary movies.
>
> In my free time, I like to read, garden, and spend time with family and friends.

No big surprises there. He knew her enthusiasm for teaching was real because she'd practically glowed when she talked about it at dinner. The kids in her class were lucky. He bet she was one of those teachers that kids never forgot. He could still remember his own elementary school teachers; he especially remembered the looks on their faces when he and Em showed up in clothes that were dirty or too small or lacking lunch money or supplies. He vividly remembered which ones were kind and which ones weren't, and there was no doubt in his mind that Maggie was one of the kind ones.

He looked at her photo again. It was a good picture. Before he could think of a reason not to, he saved it.

Putting his phone aside, he drank some of his coffee. The walk after dinner had been a good idea. He had enjoyed their easy talk and her delight over his Harry Potter confession. He'd liked watching her while she sat beside him with his phone in her hand, picking out things for him to buy for Lilah. She'd been so earnest; biting her lip, like choosing some toys was the most important thing in the world at that moment. And then she'd coached him about things like snacks and nap time. Thanks to her, he felt a lot more optimistic about looking after Lilah.

He'd opened up more than he'd meant to during their walk that was for sure. He was so used to clamping down on even the slightest scrap of personal information. But something about Maggie made it easy for him to relax, to answer questions and feel okay about asking some of his own without worrying that she was going to read too much into it. He liked how she bumped him when she was amused, how she laughed when he bumped her back and almost tipped her sideways. For a minute he'd wanted to drop his arm around her shoulder and tuck her under his arm. Not in a romantic way, more of a – of a platonic, playful way. Like he would with Emily.

Right?

Maybe?

He frowned.

Maybe not.

If he was going to be honest, when she'd kissed him on the mouth by accident, he'd wanted that kiss. Maybe not such a quick one, either. Definitely not a quick one. But she'd been horrified.

Like, clapped-a-hand-over-her-mouth horrified. On the one hand, he was relieved she hadn't been playing him but, on the other, her distress had been disappointing. He couldn't recall a woman ever being anything but eager to kiss him. Eager for whatever he wanted.

Yeah, he was an ass, but truth was truth.

So basically, he liked Maggie because she was real and she saw him as a person, not a body or a paycheck. But he wasn't what she wanted. Pretty ironic, if you thought about it.

But for the best. Definitely for the best. Maggie was a nice girl, too nice for him.

Despite the success, despite the fame, despite anything good, he was just like his father. How many times had he been told that? He was just like his father, and he wasn't dumping that shit on anyone.

He picked up his phone again, returned to the photo he'd saved, and deleted it.

"Lilah, you remember Uncle Garrett, don't you?"

Garrett smiled at Lilah. She really was cute in her little pink dress with her blonde hair tied up in an enormous pink bow. "Lilah, you've sure gotten big since the last time I saw you."

She frowned at him.

"I've got some toys and things for you," he added hopefully.

She frowned at him again. Apparently she was not easily bribed.

"Do you remember Uncle Garrett's dogs?" Emily asked Lilah.

"Dude and Buddy can't wait to see you again," he said encouragingly.

Unimpressed, Lilah hid her face in Emily's shoulder.

"She's tired from the drive," Emily said apologetically, stroking

Lilah's back. "And I hate to rush off but I've got to get to the airport."

Garrett hated to see her rush off, too. Probably even more than Lilah.

Emily stooped down to put Lilah on her feet. "Lilah, mama's going to go now but I'll be back in just a few days."

Lilah clutched at her mother's legs. "No, mama," she whimpered.

"Yes, Lilah," Emily said firmly. "You're going to have such a good time with Uncle Garrett. He's a lot of fun."

Lilah looked up at Garrett and started crying. She wasn't buying into that line, not even a little bit. "No, mama, not gonna stay, gonna come with you." She wrapped her arms even more tightly around Emily's legs, her sobs increasing.

"This is so unlike her," Emily told him as she tried to gently pry her child off.

Garrett was beginning to feel a little panicked. So much emotion coming from such a small package and he was going to be left alone with her? For days?

"She's not a picky eater, but I'd avoid too much sugar. I've packed clothes for every kind of weather," Emily said. "And you have all the information and telephone numbers of where we'll be, right?"

Garrett nodded mutely, watching his sister wrestle with Lilah's locked arms. So far Lilah was winning the battle to stay connected.

"Mom called again." Emily looked at him hesitantly as she continued to try prying Lilah loose. "She's doing really well."

"Em, don't."

Emily ignored him. "She's taken up painting."

"Why do you keep telling me all this stuff when you know I don't care?"

She frowned at him. "If you really didn't care, you wouldn't have helped me find the best place for her or insisted on paying for it."

"Claire helped you and I just don't want you trying to pay for it," he said shortly. "Don't you need to get on the road?"

Emily sighed. "We'll talk about it when I get back."

He gave her a warning glance.

Emily lowered her voice. "Whatever. Look, you're just going to have to take her. She's not going to let go on her own."

"Physically rip her away from you?" he murmured back. "That's not going to go well."

"Just do it," Emily said in a whisper, straightening. "And I'm going to run for it."

Garrett looked at his sister with horror.

"Do it," she hissed.

"Come see me, kiddo," he said weakly, putting his hands around her small frame and pulling her inexorably off Emily's legs. "Tell mama bye."

He felt her body stiffen in his arms, and her sobs kicked up to howls.

"No, no, no, no, no!" she wailed, one small arm swatting at Garrett, the other reaching for Emily. Oh no, that was the wrong thing to say.

This was a nightmare. He felt as traumatized as Lilah. "Em, I don't think this is going to –"

"Mama loves you!" Emily called as she threw him one last apologetic glance and disappeared through the front door.

"– work," he finished weakly, looking at the closed door and trying to keep his hold on the squirming and bawling she-demon in his arms.

"No, no, no, no, no!" Her shrieks were ear-piercing and she started beating at his face with both hands. For something so small, she was lethal. If he didn't get her calmed down, he was going to end up with a black eye or bloody nose. He stooped to put her feet on the floor, and as soon as he let go, she shot like a bullet to the door, still screaming.

"No, Lilah!" He sprinted after her. Luckily she couldn't

manage the handle and he was able to get between her and the door, but then it turned out to be not lucky after all because she took the opportunity to head butt him in the groin before running, still wailing, through the house toward the French doors to the patio.

"Ahhh," Garrett slumped against the doorframe, clutching his traumatized body parts. He could hear her shrieking and yanking at the doors. Thank God the back doors were locked.

He limped toward the den by the kitchen and collapsed onto the sofa, watching Lilah yank with all her might on the door handles, screaming at the top of her lungs. She wasn't heartbroken anymore, she was as mad as a little pink hornet.

He had to handle this. He was not going to be defeated by a five-year old in the first two minutes of her stay. He was going to wait this temper tantrum out and then lay down some ground rules. If he could lead an offense to victory in the fourth quarter when they were twenty points down, he could do this.

But five more minutes of ceaseless shrieking felt like thirty. Defeated, he limped out of the great room to find his phone.

Since returning home, Maggie had been busy fielding calls and texts from friends and family who were agog at the discovery she'd gone out on a date with Garrett Long. A couple of local reporters had contacted her as well, and she'd shut them down as quickly as she could. It was surprising that one chance encounter with a celebrity could affect her own life, so far away from Florida or Colorado, and she was ready for the furor to die down.

And now, Mason, the person for whom all the revenge effort had been made, was standing on her threshold, wearing a tentative smile along with a suit she'd picked out for him. She hadn't seen him since the day he backed out of their engagement and her life.

She really didn't want to see him now.

She glanced down. Nope, still not wearing socks. Idiot.

"Hi, Maggie." He smiled at her as if he hadn't ripped her heart out and tap danced on it. "Can I come in?"

Maggie-before-fake-date would have slammed the door in his face but Maggie-now was in a slightly better place and a little curious to know why he was there so she held the door open and watched him walk in. He sat down on the end of the sofa they had picked out together and amped up the wattage on his smile. She noticed, from where she stood, that his hair was thinning a little bit on top. The discovery made her happy.

"How've you been?" He beamed at her.

Seriously? "Oh, you know. Canceling venues, begging for refunds, putting my wedding dress up on eBay." She crossed her arms over her chest. "Stuff like that."

He had the grace to look disconcerted. "You know I'm sorry about all that."

'About all that'. Gah. "How's your new girlfriend?"

He looked even more embarrassed. "Uh, fine."

"Why are you here, Mason?" she asked bluntly.

He flushed slightly. "I've got a favor to ask."

A favor? Was he for real?

"I saw the photo of you and Garrett Long," he began.

So Garrett's kind gesture hadn't been in vain. She wished she could feel more delight about it. Now she just felt embarrassed that she'd wanted to get a dig in at a man who was too stupid to wear socks with his suit.

His practiced smile wasn't having the desired effect and he started to look a little uncomfortable. "Perry saw it, too. He was really impressed. He wanted me to ask if maybe you could ask him to participate in our company golf tournament in August."

Maggie gaped at him, unable to put words together. Perry was Mason's boss, and she had never liked him. He had always acted as though teaching was a dreary career and would openly shut her out of conversations as though she couldn't possibly have anything of value to say. But now he was impressed because she'd gone on a date with a football player? It was astonishing that Mason thought she'd want to help him.

Mason really was stupid, she realized.

Going bald and stupid. She'd had a lucky escape. She could see that now.

"It would be a real coup for me if he agreed," Mason added.

She found her tongue. "You want me to ask Garrett Long if he'll make an appearance at your company tournament?"

Mason had the grace to look embarrassed. "I didn't think you'd mind."

Not mind? Maggie could not fathom his reasoning. In what universe would she ever consider pimping Garrett out for her clueless ex fiancée? She glared at him in outrage. "I wouldn't ask that of him in a million years, and you've got some –" she shook her head "–some incredible nerve showing up here to ask such a thing."

"Come on, Maggie," he cajoled. "Why are you so mad at me? You've moved on, too. You looked pretty happy to me in that photo. I mean, Garrett Long!"

Here was the flip side of the revenge photo. Instead of being jealous, Mason thought she had moved on. He thought they could be buddies. She narrowed her eyes at him. "It was one date, Mason. It's not serious, like he and I are in a relationship or *engaged* or anything."

Mason's mouth bobbled open but nothing came out.

Yeah, that's right. "And you can tell Perry for me that he can kiss my sweet teacher's –"

Her phone rang in her purse. She dug for it, ready to put this conversation behind her. She gaped at the name on the screen.

Garrett Long.

Mason caught her reaction and stood up to look as well. "Not in a relationship, huh?" he said indignantly.

Maggie pointed to the door. "You need to leave right now."

Moving a few feet away, she pressed the answer button. "Hello?"

"Hey, Maggie, it's Garrett. Garrett Long. Got a minute? I could use your help."

Maggie could hear what sounded like shrieking in the background.

"Ask him." Mason was at her elbow. "Just ask him."

Maggie jerked away from him. Why was he still here? "Go away!"

"Go away?" Garrett asked. "Okay, sorry, I –"

"Not you," she said quickly. "Someone else. What's the matter?"

"Can you hear that?"

Maggie heard the wailing a little better, as if Garrett were holding his phone closer to the source. "Is that your niece?"

"Yes, and she hasn't stopped screaming since my sister left. I don't know what to do. What do I do?"

Mason waved his hand near her face to get her attention. Scowling at him, Maggie moved to the front door, opened it, and waved her own hand in a 'get out' motion. "How long has she been at it?"

"I don't know, fifteen minutes? Four hours?"

Turning her back on the door, Maggie bit back a laugh. "She's having quite the tantrum, isn't she?"

"You have no idea. She smacked me around a little, too. I'm going to have bruises."

Maggie laughed out loud. "Here's the plan. Did you get snacks like I suggested?"

"Yes. Cookies, popsicles –"

She interrupted him. "Popsicles are perfect. Make a huge production of getting the popsicles out of your freezer without really looking at her and I'll bet she does a one-eighty."

"Without looking at her?"

"No direct eye contact. None. Think of her as a wild animal."

She heard him chuckle. "Okay, I'll try it. Thanks a lot."

"Good luck!" She tapped the phone off and pushed it into her jeans pocket.

"Why didn't you ask?" Mason appeared at her elbow again.

Good Lord, did he not understand the concept of leaving? "I'm never going to ask," she shot back. "Go away, Mason. Go far, far away and don't ever bother me again." Putting her hand on his back, she propelled him through the open door and then grabbed the knob to close it.

Mason stuck his shoe into the doorway to stop her, a hurt expression on his face. "This isn't like you, Maggie."

"It's like me now." She nudged his foot away and then closed and locked the door.

Chapter 7

Garrett felt a little more optimistic after he hung up the phone. Just hearing Maggie's voice and picturing her smile gave him confidence. *Think of Lilah as a wild animal. No eye contact.* He could do that. Rising, he limped toward the kitchen and opened the freezer.

"Look at this," he said loudly. "Popsicles!" He made a lot of noise removing the box from the freezer, watching Lilah from the corner of his eye. She stopped shrieking and was directing a narrowed look over her shoulder in his direction, her hand still on the door handle. "Mm, looks like we've got red and purple and blue."

Lilah let go of the handle and turned toward him. Tear stains streaked down her face and he could see her little chin still quivering a little bit.

"I wonder what flavor Lilah likes," he continued loudly. "I bet she doesn't like blue."

She took a tiny step in his direction.

"I like blue. I think I'll have a blue popsicle. Mmm."

He heard her whisper something, and he slanted a cautious look in her direction "What was that? Does somebody else like blue popsicles?"

She took another tentative step in his direction. "I like blue popsies," she whispered a little louder.

"You do?" he asked in mock surprise. "Would you like a blue popsie?"

She gave a tiny nod.

He took a popsicle out of the box and held it up. "Do you want me to open it for you?"

Another tiny nod. Garrett felt elated. Thanks to Maggie, he had this. He had the key to Lilah's heart right there in his freezer.

"Alrighty then." He walked around the island and hunkered down a few feet away from her. He began unwrapping the popsicle. She began taking little steps in his direction. "You can sit right here at the island and have a blue popsie."

"Sit in there." Lilah nodded towards the den.

"No, sit here," he repeated, nodding toward the island. This was it. This was the defining moment. Who was the alpha? Him or Lilah? He held his breath.

She eyed him a minute, then nodded.

Resisting the impulse to pump his fist in the air, he handed her the popsicle. He rose and lifted her to the bar stool before she could react. She settled there, intent on her treat, and gave him a hint of a smile.

"Do you like pizza?" he asked.

"I like pizza," she agreed, her lips and tongue turning popsicle blue. "I like cheeses but not the gween stuff."

Pizza without the green stuff, check. Everything was going to be just fine.

Maggie looked around the table at her three closest friends, sitting on the edges of their seats at their favorite Mexican restaurant. They'd been texting her nonstop since the morning the photo had appeared online. This was the first time they'd all been free to get together. After Mason's annoying visit and Garrett's surprising phone call, she was more than ready for a jumbo margarita and girl time.

"Aren't you glad now I couldn't join you?" Maggie's friend, Sharon, jabbed her in the ribs. "You might never have met him otherwise!"

"Ow." Maggie jabbed her back. "I wouldn't say that but I am glad I was on the beach that morning."

"So what was he like?"

Trick question. Morning-Garrett had been aloof, Restaurant-Garrett had been pleasant, and Beach-Walk-Garrett was delightful. And all of them were gorgeous. "He was nice. I doubt I'd have seen him after the first time except that picture showed up online and he stopped to warn me that the media would probably turn up."

"That doesn't explain how you ended up going out on a date with him." Toby leaned forward. "Come on, get to the good stuff."

Maggie laughed. "Calm down. It wasn't really a date. I told him I wished I looked better in the picture so Mason would see it and that's when he suggested going out. He knew there would be cameras and he was helping me get a better picture."

"A revenge photo," Sharon mused.

"Exactly!" Maggie smiled at her best friend.

Toby shook her head. "Sorry, Maggie. I'm not buying it." She reached for her phone again, and this time she pulled up the photo taken outside the restaurant. "If it looks like a date and smells like a date, and Garrett Long is looking at you like he's looking at you in this photo, that's a date, my friend."

Her three friends nodded knowingly at one another.

"It certainly fooled me," Sharon said.

"It was supposed to look like a real date," Maggie insisted. "That was the whole point."

"You shouldn't waste one second thinking about Mason," Alicia interjected. "You're so much better off without him."

"Hear, hear." Sharon lifted her margarita.

"That's not even up for debate," Toby agreed. "But back to Garrett Long. Did you have revenge sex, too?"

Maggie choked on a mouthful of margarita. "No!" she sputtered. "We took a walk on the beach, and I helped him order toys for his niece. Then we said goodbye."

"A walk on the beach?" Sharon asked.

"At night? Was the moon out?" Alicia added, winking at Toby.

They were determined to make more of the interaction than was warranted. Maggie was just as determined to set them straight. "Yes, it was night time, and yes, the moon was out, but all we talked about was his niece and I made him a shopping list on Amazon."

"So no chemistry at all? Not even a smidgen of hanky panky?" Sharon looked disappointed.

Maggie hesitated. Did giant flapping butterflies in her stomach count? Or that mortifying missed-kiss?

"Oh, ho ho!" Toby cackled. "I knew there was more to the story."

Maggie pressed her hands to her cheeks. "Not really. When I was saying goodbye, I thought I'd be brave and kiss him on the cheek, you know, like you do with friends, but somehow I –" She knew she was blushing and she hated it. "Kissed him on the mouth for about a tenth of a second."

All three of her friends inhaled sharply, like all the oxygen in the room had disappeared.

"What did he do?" Alicia demanded.

"Kind of laughed," she mumbled. Gah, she wished she hadn't told them.

"I'd take that tenth of a second," Toby said, looking at Maggie with admiration.

"And you haven't heard from him since?" Sharon asked.

Maggie hesitated again.

"You have!" Alicia crowed. "You have!"

Sharon made a 'gimme' motion with her hands.

Maggie sighed. "He's babysitting his niece. She was having a tantrum, and he called for advice. We talked for two minutes. That's all."

Her three friends eyed her suspiciously.

"I promise. I mean, come on," she added, "He's Garrett Long. He's a superstar gazillionaire athlete who dates models and movie stars, and I'm – well, I'm me."

"You are amazing," Sharon said indignantly. "He'd be lucky to have you."

"So lucky," Alicia nodded.

"Damn right he would be," Toby concluded.

"But do you want to know what I think?" Toby considered Maggie over the rim of her margarita glass.

Maggie wasn't ever really sure she wanted to know what Toby thought.

"I don't think you've heard the last from your superstar gazillionaire athlete, Maggie. And I want to borrow that dress."

After Lilah finished her popsicle and he'd managed to clean most of the sticky mess off of her, Garrett turned on the television and started a Disney film. With Lilah settled on the sofa to watch, he'd taken the opportunity to take a hurried shower.

He turned the corner back into the kitchen and came to an abrupt, horrified stop.

The film apparently forgotten, Lilah was sitting on the floor with Dude on one side and Buddy on the other, several opened bottles of finger paint scattered around her. There was paint on her dress, her face and in her hair, there were puddles of paint on the floor and somehow there was even paint on the refrigerator. The two dogs, delighted to be part of the fun, were smeared from snoot to tail with thick globs of the stuff.

I was only gone five minutes, he thought wildly. *Five minutes.*

Lilah caught sight of him and beamed at him. "Come paint, Uncle Garrett." She gestured toward Dude. "Doo's a lion and Buddy's a tiger."

"Is that so?" he said, rubbing his forehead.

"Mmm hmm." She poured some orange paint directly into her hand, and on the floor, and smearing it on Buddy's chest. "They likes it."

Maggie had just stepped into the shower when her phone started ringing. A phone call at midnight was never good so she slipped and skidded her way into the bedroom, only to have it stop ringing as soon as she reached it. Naturally. Towel clutched around her dripping body, she listened to the voice message.

"'Hey Maggie, it's Garrett Long again. I've got some problems here. Can you call me back as soon as you get this? It doesn't matter how late it is. Just call, okay?'"

She played it a second time, puzzling over the tone of his voice. She couldn't quite identify it. Panic? Desperation? Shaking her head, she tapped the call button.

He answered on the first ring. "Maggie, hey, thanks for calling back."

It was definitely desperation. "Hi, Garrett. Is everything okay?"

"Well, if by okay you mean there's finger paint on every surface in my house and Lilah's been throwing up pizza and blue popsicles all evening like something out of a horror film, then yes, everything's okay."

She tried hard not to laugh. "Oh, Garrett."

"Man, it is so bad. Look, this is going to sound crazy but is there any way possible, any way at all, you could possibly fly to Denver and help me here?"

Wait, what?

"I know it's asking a lot, but honest to God, I'm in over my head and you're the first person I thought of."

"You want me to fly to Denver?"

"Yes. I'll take care of the arrangements; all you have to do is show up at the airport."

The idea of seeing him again made her tingle all over but was he inviting her because he wanted to see her again, too, or did he just see her as a potential babysitter? She squashed the notion that he wanted to see-her-see-her. She was no Netflix actress. He needed babysitting help. And she'd put the finger paint in his shopping cart and suggested popsicles so it was kind of her fault.

But it wasn't like he was just across town. Was it normal for him to fly people across the country to help him out? Maggie shook her head in confusion. "Garrett, I know you've got other options. You must have friends with wives and children who could help you out and there are private babysitting agencies you can –"

"No," he interrupted her. "Please. I want somebody here at the house around the clock. I want to look after her but I need help. I trust you, Maggie."

Maggie was at a loss for words. "We spent maybe four hours together," she reminded him. Four really nice hours, minus the embarrassing stuff, but still. Not exactly a firm foundation for asking someone to fly across the country to babysit.

There was silence on the other end for a moment. "Four hours was plenty of time for me to see what kind of person you are," he said finally.

Aww. That was nice, even if it was a little nuts.

"And I want you to know, it's all above board. I think of you as a friend. Strictly friends."

She didn't want to think too hard about why that stung a bit. "Of course," she said in a cheerier tone than she felt. "Strictly friends."

"And I'll pay you, you know. Anything you want. And you said yourself you've got time on your hands," he added. "Looking for a new place can wait a few days, can't it?"

It was a crazy idea. She didn't do crazy things.

But she could, if she wanted to.

She glanced at the bed she used to share with Mason and frowned. Everywhere she went she was reminded of him and the canceled wedding. School didn't start again for weeks. That was a lot of time to fill. And she'd never been to Colorado. She could rent a car and see the mountains. That could be fun. She could sight-see until it was time to set up her classroom. Going to Colorado was sounding better and better.

"Okay," she heard herself say.

"Okay?" he repeated. "Yes!"

Maggie drew in a big breath. Yes, she'd do it. She'd throw caution to the wind and fly across the country to help a completely competent man, one who could afford a team of professional nannies, look after one tiny little girl. Why not? It was time for her to stop being so tame and predictable.

"Baton Rouge doesn't have any direct flights but there's one out of New Orleans at eight a.m. that will have you here a little after ten. Is that possible for you?"

He had already looked at flights? "Eight a.m. tomorrow morning? As in, eight hours from right now?" She was a little worse for wear from too many margaritas and an eight a.m. flight would mean getting up at the crack of dawn to get to the New Orleans airport on time.

"Well, there's one that leaves at six a.m. and arrives a little after eight –"

"No," Maggie said quickly. "There's nothing a little later, like ten or eleven?"

"Well, yeah. Is eight too early?"

He sounded so dismayed. Maggie sighed. "No, eight is fine."

"That's great. I'll text you all the information," he said, relief evident in his tone. "Just be at the airport and I'll take it from there."

"You know this is insane, don't you?" she asked him. "What if your instincts are all wrong and I turn out to be a psychopath?"

"If you're a psychopath who can help me manage a five-year old, I'll take my chances."

Garrett pulled his truck into the passenger pick-up corridor at the Denver airport. As he edged along behind other vehicles, he looked for Maggie in the throng of travelers waiting for rides. He glanced over the seat and was glad to see Lilah was content for the moment, buckled into her car seat, clutching a Barbie doll in each little hand.

He spied Maggie standing alone near the curb ahead, texting on her phone and biting her bottom lip in concentration.

Man, she looked good. He edged his truck into an open spot just ahead of her. She was dressed simply, wearing skinny jeans, a red t-shirt with Ragin' Cajuns emblazoned on the front, and red Converse Chucks. She had a leather bag hoisted over one shoulder and a pink camouflage duffle bag at her feet. He liked the fact that she was wearing her Renegades cap again, with her hair pulled into a bouncy pony tail threaded through the back.

He reminded himself that she was here to help with Lilah, nothing more. Having a woman stay with him was way outside his comfort zone. Even when he was seeing someone, he preferred going to their place, keeping his home private. Of course this wasn't a hook-up, and desperate times called for desperate measures. The only reason he even felt halfway okay with her being here was because he knew she was still hung up on her dumbass ex. His plan was to be friendly but keep her at an arm's length.

It was only for a couple of days.

Piece of cake.

He slipped on his sunglasses in an attempt to go unnoticed, put the truck into park and jumped out. "Maggie!" He lifted a hand. When she turned to look, she flashed her big smile and waved back.

He jogged over quickly to grab her duffle bag. "Hey." His gaze swept over her face as he automatically moved to hug her.

Wait, no. He wasn't a hugger. He found himself frozen in a half-reaching stance.

"Hey yourself." She took the extra step toward him to give him a quick, amiable squeeze with one arm, her eyes glancing everywhere but at his face.

He was relieved by her casual welcome. Looked like they were on the same page. "Thanks for coming. How was your flight?" He took her bag, opened the passenger door for her and closed it once she was seated. Circling around, he put her bag in the back seat beside Lilah and then got back into the truck behind the wheel.

"It was fine, thanks." Maggie hopped into the passenger seat and twisted to look over her seat. "Hi, there, Lilah." Garrett watched her from the corner of his eye as she directed her big smile at Lilah. "I'm Maggie. I like your dolls."

Garrett glanced over the seat to gauge Lilah's response. She held her dolls up for Maggie's inspection. "Bobbies," she announced happily.

"Yes, I see. I like Barbies, too. Maybe we can play with them together."

Lilah beamed at her. "We can play school with them?"

"Yes, indeed. That's right up my alley." Maggie straightened and shot a swift glance at Garrett. "This is the angel that had you tearing your hair out?"

"You wouldn't have called her an angel last night when her head was revolving and spewing pizza and blue popsicle in every direction."

Maggie huffed in amusement. "I'm glad she's fine now. How long will your sister be away?"

"She'll be back on Saturday."

Maggie looked confused. "Three days from now?"

He felt a little embarrassed. "I know, it isn't very long, but trust me, I can't take another night like last night on my own. The tantrum was bad enough, but when she started throwing up, I completely lost it. I didn't know whether to call 911 or rush her to the hospital or what." He gave her a sideways glance. "And talk about gross. I threw all the sheets and stuff away."

Maggie laughed. "You did sound traumatized." Looking out of the window, she spied the sweeping range of mountains in the distance. "Wow, wow, wow. Look at that. They're massive. I didn't realize. Pictures don't do them justice, do they?"

He gave her a sideways glance. Was it his imagination or was she looking everywhere but at him? "You've never been to Colorado before?"

"No. They're really something, aren't they?" She was leaning forward, gazing through the window. "Do you ski? I always wanted to learn how to ski. It looks like so much fun. And snowmobiling looks like fun, too. But not cross-country skiing. That looks hard. Obviously we don't get much snow in Baton Rouge. People absolutely lose their minds when we get even a dusting."

He liked how she rambled sometimes. "My contract doesn't allow me to go skiing, unfortunately."

"Really? That's a shame." She looked so disappointed on his behalf. Maybe, after Emily came back, he could take her up to his place on Grand Lake. Again, strictly as friends. It would suck for her to come all this way and not experience the mountains up close.

"Hey, I was thinking," she said, interrupting his thoughts. "Maybe we can stop by a grocery store on our way to your place? You know, pick up some things I can fix that Lilah will like?"

"I don't expect you to cook. I can cook or we can order in."

She looked surprised. "You cook?"

"Yeah, during the off season. I'm pretty good in the kitchen."

"Really."

Her skeptical expression amused him. "Yep. Your only job is to help me keep Lilah happy. And keep her from leveling my house. And we need to discuss your compensation."

"My what?"

"Compensation," he repeated. "I'm paying you for your time here."

"Don't be stupid," she huffed. "You bought my ticket. Which reminds me, why on earth did you book a first class ticket? Anyway, I'm glad to help out. I don't want you to pay me."

"Did you just call me stupid?" It was the first time he'd ever been scolded for buying a woman a first-class ticket. Being called stupid certainly wasn't the norm, either. Emily and his assistant, Claire, never minced words with him but Maggie was the first woman in a long time that didn't fall all over themselves trying to flatter him. He liked it.

She grinned. "No, I warned you not to be stupid. That's different."

He was going to pay her for her time. He'd wait and bring it up again later. This was strictly a business arrangement. "Hey, did your ex see the photograph from the restaurant?" he asked.

Turning toward him, she finally looked right at him, her expression indignant. "Yes! And you would not believe what he did!"

"What?"

"He showed up at my place to ask if I would get you to come to his company's golf tournament!"

Her irritation was palpable. "Well, I do love to play golf," he said with a straight face. "Have him send me the details."

Maggie's mouth dropped open in astonishment.

Hah, he got her. "Just kidding. What did you tell him?"

She made a face at him. "That wasn't funny. I told him to go away and never bother me again."

"Your expression just now was funny," he argued. "Did he go away?"

"Yes, after telling me I wasn't acting like myself." She looked very satisfied.

Garrett was glad to see she had her confidence back. When she'd crumpled at the restaurant in St. Augustine, he'd wanted to track the bastard down. Just like he would if someone hurt Emily. "We're almost there." He nodded ahead at the turn into his neighborhood. "How do you feel about dogs?"

Maggie's face lit up. "I love dogs! Do you have one?"

"Two. Rescued pit bulls." He waited to see her response. Pit bulls had a bad reputation. Even some of his teammates had been nervous about his boys until they met them and discovered they were just huge goofballs.

"Pitties! I follow several pit bulls on Instagram. I can't wait to meet them. What are their names?"

Of course she'd be unbiased. He should have known. "Dude and Buddy."

"Cute names. I grew up with dogs. I wanted one so badly but Mason wasn't a dog person." He turned onto his street. "Wow, Garrett, this is your neighborhood?"

He nodded. "Been here a couple of years." Most of the homes in his neighborhood were set far off the street, out of sight behind gates and long, curving driveways. His was no exception. He'd had a penthouse downtown when he first came to Denver, but it was too easy for people to lie in wait. He wasn't about the night life anymore. And here, he had a yard for the dogs.

He turned into the driveway. The arched metal gates swung open. He eased down the driveway to the house. He glanced at Maggie, whose brown eyes grew big as she saw the house come into view.

Chapter 8

Maggie took in the mammoth proportions of Garrett's home. It looked like a castle, complete with wood banding, arched windows, and even a tower with a conical roof. Like something you'd see next to a fjord in the Swiss Alps, not near downtown Denver.

"Are you kidding me?" she murmured. "All that's missing is a moat."

Garrett came around the front of the truck with her bag. "I had the moat filled in," he said with his usual straight face as he passed her to lead the way to the front door. "Can you unbuckle Lilah?"

Snickering, Maggie opened the back passenger door and freed Lilah from her car seat. She held her arms out to be lifted and Maggie propped her on her hip before reaching in and retrieving the dolls. Lilah accepted the dolls, stuck them under her small arm, and squirmed to be set down. Maggie obediently placed her on her feet and followed her up the wide stone steps to the door.

"Gotta go potty," Lilah announced, hopping from one foot to the other.

When Garrett opened the door, Lilah ran across the wide foyer to the back of the house, apparently familiar with the route to the nearest bathroom.

Maggie looked around, taking in the wide curving stairway that led upstairs from the foyer to a railed loft area, to a formal dining room on the left and a library-ish looking room on the right. Light flooded in from floor-to-ceiling windows in each room. The furnishings were elegant and there was a glossy grand piano in the room on the right.

"Do you play the piano?"

"No." He placed her duffle bag on the floor beside the staircase. "It came with the house."

"Houses here come with grand pianos?"

"This one did."

"Of course it did." She ran her hand appreciatively along the curved banister. "Why wouldn't it?" She was rewarded with another quirk of a smile.

"There are five guest bedrooms upstairs." He nodded upwards. "You can use any one of them you like, or there's a guest house on the other side of the garage if you'd rather have a little more privacy."

"Where's Lilah sleeping?"

"I took a twin bed mattress from one of the rooms upstairs and put it on the floor in my room. I was worried about her waking up in the middle of the night and being scared."

"Good thinking. Does the twin bedroom have two beds?"

"Yes."

"Well, let's drag it back upstairs and I'll stay in that room with her."

He frowned. "There's no reason for you to share a room or sleep in a twin bed when I've got all these other rooms."

"Garrett, I couldn't care less. Lilah's the priority here. I'm sure I'll be very comfortable." She waved an arm to take in their surroundings. "How could I not be?"

"If you're sure." His expression was doubtful.

"I am."

He shrugged. "Okay. There's another set of stairs by the kitchen. You can get upstairs that way. Downstairs too."

"What's downstairs?"

"Game room, safe room, media room, and a wine cellar."

"Wine cellar?"

"Yeah. It's empty, though. I'm not much on wine."

Of course. An empty wine cellar to go with the grand piano that nobody used.

"Come on." He led the way through the foyer area, through a vast great room with twin chesterfield sofas and more floor-to-ceiling windows flanking a stone fireplace. He gestured toward a wide hallway leading away from the right side of the room. "Office, my room, home gym, sauna and steam room are all that way."

Sauna? Steam room? Seriously? Dumbfounded, Maggie followed him through a wide arched opening on the left which led to another space that held a dream of a kitchen, an informal dining area and smaller living area with a fireplace and a flat-screen television over the mantel. A vast wall of windows and French doors stretched from the kitchen area to the den area.

She would not want to have to clean all these windows.

"My assistant's office, the laundry room, and the garage are all that way." He gestured carelessly toward yet another hallway off the den.

"The assistant who's on vacation?"

"Yeah, Claire. And this is where I mainly hang out." He waved a hand to take in the den area adjacent to the kitchen.

Maggie looked around. It was too large to qualify as cozy but it was definitely the homiest of the rooms she'd seen so far. There was an oversized leather sofa with a chaise on one end, bookended by two stone topped tables, a massive upholstered coffee table and a deep chair with an ottoman. Clearly a man's room. Two dog beds were in front of the hearth and the biggest flat-screen television Maggie had ever seen was mounted above the mantel. She moved toward the wall of glass to take a look outside. Of course there was a giant pool with a rock waterfall, an elevated hot tub, and a covered outdoor kitchen with a fireplace. Beyond the patio area was a deep yard, almost a field.

She peered out the window. "Where are your dogs?"

He glanced outside. "Probably irritating squirrels. They'll be scratching at the doors any minute."

Lilah reappeared, still clutching her Barbie dolls.

"Did you wash your hands?" Garrett asked her, eyebrow tilted. Lilah eyed him and Maggie bit back a smile. She knew that look too well. Lilah was wondering whether or not to fib.

"Let's wash them again, together," she said, saving Lilah from replying. "I need to wash mine, too. Will you show me where the bathroom is?"

Lilah nodded. "Uncle Garrett has lots and lots of bafrooms," she announced, pronouncing Garrett 'Gawet'. "This one's best 'cause it's close to in here where I plays the most." Maggie followed her to a half bath off the kitchen and they washed their hands together, Lilah chattering the whole time about all the bathrooms in the house. She really was adorable. Despite her meltdown the previous night, she had clearly settled in with her uncle.

"Your Uncle Garrett bought you some toys and things, didn't he?"

Lilah lit up. "Uh huh, you wanna see?" She took Maggie's hand and led her back to the den.

Garrett opened one of the French doors and gave a whistle. "Here they come."

"Doo and Buddy!" Lilah squealed.

Maggie watched as two large pit bulls, both white and tan, gamboled into the room and bounded around Garrett, tails wagging so hard that their rear ends swayed madly from side to side.

"Okay, guys. Okay, calm down." Bending to rest on one knee, Garrett tried to pat them as they vied for his attention. "Somebody here for you to meet. Okay, jeez." One of them licked him across the mouth. "Chill, Dude." He wiped his face with his arm. "Have some dignity."

Maggie laughed at their antics and at Garrett's unsuccessful efforts to calm them.

"Look out." The dogs spied her and immediately abandoned him and careened toward her, tails still flailing. Maggie sank onto the floor and let them sniff her open hands before patting their huge velvety heads. They waggled around her as they had done with Garrett, sniffing her up and down before flopping down and showing her their stomachs, paws in the air. She obliged by scratching their tummies and laughed at their ecstatic expressions.

"My ferocious guard dogs," Garrett said dryly, rising. "And if you notice, Dude here has still got traces of yellow paint because Lilah decided he's a lion, and Buddy's more multi-colored because he's a tiger."

"But I isn't allowed to paint them anymore." Lilah joined her on the floor. "'Cause dogs don't supposed to be painted."

"That's right." Garrett ruffled Lilah's hair. "Paint is for outside, right? On paper, not on Dude and Buddy?"

"Right," she agreed, scratching Buddy's ears.

"Want to go show Maggie upstairs?"

Lilah nodded. "There's bedrooms and more bafrooms," she told Maggie. "So many of them."

"Would you like to share a room with me? We can have a girls' room together."

Lilah beamed at her. "A big girls room?"

"And after Maggie's settled, do you want to go swimming?"

"Yes, yes, yes!" she cried. "I gots my swimsuit and my floaty shirt!" She tugged on Maggie's hand. "Come on! I need help!"

"Runs in the family," Garrett quipped, flashing a wink at Maggie.

Gah. That wink got her every time.

When they came downstairs again, Garrett smiled at the sight; Lilah, wearing a tiny ruffled polka dotted swimsuit and Minnie Mouse flip flops, and Maggie in an oversized t-shirt that read 'Do not make me use my teacher voice'.

"Are you joining us?" she asked, a hair band between her teeth, pulling her hair up into a ponytail. Garrett tried not to notice that her t-shirt hiked up with her motion, exposing the long length of her tanned legs.

"Come swimmin', Uncle Garrett!" Lilah chimed, pulling on his hand.

He looked down at her. "But I don't know how to swim," he told her solemnly.

Lilah put her hands on her narrow little ruffled hips and eyed him suspiciously. "You has a pool, Uncle Garrett! You has to know how to swim!"

He and Maggie exchanged amused glances. "You got me. I'll come out in a little while, okay?"

"Okay!" She grabbed Maggie's hand. "Come on, Maggie!"

He watched as Maggie allowed Lilah to tug her out of the door and toward the pool. Dude and Buddy careened into view and launched themselves at the pair. After an extended bout of petting, Maggie slathered sunscreen on Lilah's face and thin little arms and legs, and wrestled the flotation shirt over her swimsuit. Then Lilah smeared sunscreen on Maggie's face, and Maggie's scrunched up face made Lilah giggle.

Their interaction made him smile. Flying Maggie to Denver had been a stroke of genius. He turned to the refrigerator to get a bottle of water, uncapped it and turned back to the window. He could tell Maggie was encouraging Lilah to jump into the water, but Lilah hung back, apparently a little anxious now that the big moment was at hand.

Garrett watched as Maggie shimmied her shirt up and over her head and tossed it onto one of the chaise lounge chairs.

Whoa.

The water went down the wrong way and he coughed. Maggie wasn't wearing the grandmotherly swimsuit he remembered from the beach; she was wearing a miniscule red bikini. Still coughing, he watched her dive smoothly into the pool and then surface gracefully. Placing one hand on the edge of the pool, she showed Lilah how to pinch her nose and then held her arms out in invitation. Lilah didn't hesitate; she pinched her nose and jumped in, and when she bobbled back up, he didn't know which of the pair looked more delighted. Maggie hoisted Lilah to the edge of the pool, and then, with her palms planted on the edge, effortlessly lifted herself out as well. Water sluiced down her body, down the valley between her breasts and down the length of her long, shapely legs. She lifted her arms and tightened her ponytail, innocently arching her back in the process.

Garrett felt the blood rush south to his groin. He slid his hand into his jeans and adjusted himself, uncomfortable mentally as well as physically because this was all wrong. She was here to help look after Lilah. That was all. She was off-limits, not just because of the friends-only agreement but because Maggie was the kind of girl who deserved a happily-ever-after. He wasn't a happily-ever-after. He never would be.

He heaved a deep breath and headed for the privacy of his bathroom. After he took care of his personal problem, he'd find other things to do while they enjoyed the pool, and get back into the game when everyone was dry and fully clothed again.

"Garrett?" Maggie crossed the great room toward the hallway leading to the other side of the house. He hadn't shown her this area. She didn't think it was off limits, but she was still a little reluctant to go any farther without an invitation. Damp from the pool, the cool temperature inside the house made her shiver despite her dry shirt.

"In here." His voice came from the first room on the left.

She hesitantly walked to the doorway and peeked around the corner. It was his office, another oversized room with a wide desk centered in front of a wall of windows looking out on the pool area. Cases jammed with books lined one wall and a large television was mounted on the opposite wall. Two tufted chairs faced the desk where Garrett was sprawled back in the leather desk chair, a sheaf of papers in his hand, a pair of narrow reading glasses low on his nose. He looked at her over the top of the glasses. "Hey, everything okay?"

Just when she thought he couldn't be any sexier, he had to go and put on a pair of glasses. Maggie felt a tingle all the way down to her toes, and then scoffed at herself. He was a man wearing glasses. Glasses suggested that his eyesight was weak, didn't they? There was nothing sexy about weak eyes.

He tugged them off and tilted an eyebrow in question.

That eyebrow. Another freaking tingle. She tried looking over his shoulder instead of directly at his face. "Do you mind if I make some lunch for Lilah?"

He looked startled, and rose, dropping the papers and his glasses on the desk top. "Oh, damn, what time is it?"

"Almost two. I'm fine, but Lilah needs to eat."

He rounded the desk swiftly "I'm sorry, I lost track of time. I meant to throw something together a while ago." He passed by her in the door but she held back, realizing that the shades on the windows, which were opaque from the exterior, were crystal clear from the inside looking out. Had he been able to see her cavorting around the pool like a demented camp counselor? Maggie edged toward his chair and peered outside. Even from a sitting position behind his desk, he had an unobstructed view to the entire pool area. Horrified, she turned and slowly followed him to the kitchen. Packing the skimpy bikini she'd bought for her honeymoon had seemed like a great idea back home, but now she wasn't so sure.

In the kitchen, Lilah was perched on a bar stool. "I want a peanut butter sanwich," she stated firmly. "Peanut butter with no bones, and with grape jellies, not apple."

"No bones?" Puzzled, Garrett looked at Maggie.

Maggie gave him a weak smile. "I think she means creamy, not crunchy."

He smiled. "Oh. That makes sense, I guess." Opening the refrigerator door, he leaned to look inside. "I know I've got peanut butter; let's just hope I've got grape jelly." After shuffling things around, he withdrew a jar with a look of victory.

"Let me help," Maggie said, tightening the towel around her body. "Where's your bread?"

"No, sit." He ducked into the pantry and then reappeared with bread and a Costco sized container of peanut butter.

"We is so hungry, Uncle Garrett," Lilah chastised him, a frown wrinkling her little forehead.

"I bet you are. Uncle Garrett messed up. Sit," he told Maggie again. "I've got this."

"If you don't mind, I think I'll run up and change. And this little chickadee can change after lunch, okay?" She gave Lilah's braid a gentle tug. Lilah nodded, her attention fixed on her uncle who was slathering peanut butter onto slices of bread.

Maggie hurried upstairs and into the bathroom. Dropping the towel and peeling off her long t-shirt, she eyed herself critically in the bathroom mirror. The bikini looked okay as long as she was standing still but she certainly wasn't slim and toned like the women she'd seen with Garrett in photos online and, unfortunately, there had been no standing still while she had been entertaining Lilah. There had been a lot of silly jumping. She really, really hoped he hadn't been looking out of the window when she had been doing the silly jumping.

When Maggie returned downstairs in dry clothes, Lilah was eating a sandwich and Garrett was leaning against the kitchen counter, finishing off a rice cake smeared with peanut butter. "I made you a sandwich," he added, licking smudges of peanut butter from his fingers. "Is that okay?"

His careless act hit Maggie like a brick. Maybe she was naïve or just plain stupid but when he'd asked her to come help him out, it hadn't occurred to her that reading glasses or peanut butter could make her lady parts whimper.

"I'll be on time for dinner." he added. "Maybe some pasta?"

She couldn't take her eyes off of his fingers, or his mouth. Gripping the edge of the island top, she tried to look away but his blue gaze and the slow, vibrating wave she felt working its way up her body, pinned her where she stood. "Sure," she managed.

He picked up the plate holding the sandwich and held it out to her across the top of the island. "Want some fruit or almonds?" He gave her a quick smile. "One of Lilah's popsicles?"

What she wanted was to run out of the front door, straight to the airport, and get on a plane back home to Baton Rouge. It was clearly a bad idea to agree to stay with him in his home but at least he didn't seem to notice her discomfort. She could squash these feelings for a couple of days.

Of course she could.

She hoped she could.

"No, just a sandwich is fine," she managed. She took the plate and sat on the bar stool beside Lilah, who was playing with the last two grapes on her plate. Trying not to watch Garrett, she took a bite of her sandwich. "Want to read a book after lunch?" Lilah nodded her agreement.

"I can read to her." Garrett leaned over to pluck the grapes off Lilah's plate and popped them into his mouth.

"Uncle Garrett!" Lilah said indignantly.

"Lilah!" he replied, grinning at her.

"Are you sure? I was going to take her upstairs and get her changed and read to her there so you can do whatever you want to do."

"You've had her on your own till now but we're in this together. Come on, kiddo." Picking Lilah up with one arm, he carried her, giggling, sideways and dropped down, placing her at his side. "What have we got here?" He picked up the book on top of the pile on the side table and reviewed the cover. "'*Harold and the Purple Crayon*'. How's that sound?"

"Good." Lilah wiggled up from his side, put one small hand on his wide shoulder for balance, and lodged herself on his lap.

Maggie felt another little twist in her stomach at the sight of Lilah nestled against Garrett's broad chest, his muscled arm curved around her. Turning, she picked up Lilah's plate from the island and then glanced back. Lucky little girl, tucked up against her uncle so contentedly. They would have a sweet relationship going forward from this time spent together. It felt good to be part of their beginning, but sad, too, that she wouldn't be part of their continuing story.

She caught Garrett glancing at her, too, so she gave him an encouraging thumbs up.

He winked at her and opened the book. "'One evening, after thinking it over for some time,'" he began in a low voice, "'Harold decided to go for a walk in the moonlight.'"

Maggie smiled at his rumbling tone of voice. With any luck, Lilah would nod right off. After putting Lilah's plate and glass in the dishwasher, she dug her phone out of her bag and joined them in the den. Plopping sideways in the leather chair adjacent to the sofa, she draped her legs over the armrest and stabbed her phone on to check her mail and messages. Yep. As expected, a deluge of texts from her girlfriends filled the screen. They'd been sending messages nonstop since she'd texted the group from the airport that she had flown to Denver. She read through the messages, grinning in amusement at the impertinent remarks and demands for information. After writing a group text designed to exasperate them even more, and another to her mom letting her know all was well, she hit send and looked up.

Garrett had stopped reading and was looking at her. When she met his eyes, he nodded down toward Lilah. She was already fast asleep, her head lolling against Garrett's chest. Maggie smiled and he smiled back and her breath hitched a little. If this was just a hint of what it would feel like someday, to have a child with someone she loved, she didn't know how she would stand it.

Garrett mouthed the words "Now what?" Chuckling, Maggie rose and pulled Lilah from his lap, eased her sideways onto the sofa and covered her with a throw. Garrett stood and stretched. Maggie couldn't help watching the flexing of his muscles. Mercy.

He silently tilted his head toward the great room. Maggie obediently followed him out of the kitchen area into the main living area. "How long do you think she'll sleep?"

"I'll wake her in a little while; otherwise she won't want to go to bed tonight."

He nodded. "Want to see the rest of the house?"

"A tour of your castle? Of course. Lead the way."

He led the way down the hallway and past his office, to another door on the left. She followed him into a large room with black rubber flooring and gym machinery and equipment. Like his office, one wall was nothing but windows, while the side walls were mirrored, and the back wall was glass with an opening that led to a stone steam room and a cedar-lined sauna. She opened the door to the sauna and inhaled the aromatic scent of cedar.

She'd never thought of steam rooms or saunas as being sexy but the mental image of Garrett, sitting on the bench, long legs splayed, with rivulets of sweat sliding down his skin, popped into her brain and she had to put her hand on the wall for balance for a moment.

Yikes.

Trying to regain her composure and praying her face wasn't beet-red, she ran her hand over a pile of the fattest, whitest towels she'd ever seen. Just two of these would be a whole laundry load. "Do you work out every day?"

He nodded. "Yeah. Some days here, some days at the facility. I have to try to stay in shape during the off season." He picked up a towel from the floor and tossed it into a hamper.

"When do you start back again?"

"Training camp starts the third week of July. You can use anything in here, if you want." Now Garrett was leaning against one of the machines, his crossed arms making his biceps bulge.

Great, now she was picturing him doing push-ups.

Maggie stepped onto the ramp of the treadmill to try to focus on the digital screen.

"Do you run?" He ambled closer and her pulse quickened.

"Only if something's chasing me." She stepped off again but he didn't move. He was just – right there. She had to edge her way carefully to avoid brushing against him. He sure wasn't making it easy for her to ignore her lecherous hormones. "I'm not really athletic."

"I don't know about that." He moved away to pick up hand weights and place them on a metal rack. "You were pretty fast getting to the water to save that little girl."

"Yes, and look what happened afterwards," she reminded him ruefully. "One short sprint and I almost passed out."

"I think that was more to do with shock than anything. I know it was frightening but if it hadn't happened, you wouldn't be here now."

Maggie glanced at him, confused by his remark. He only meant here now, helping with Lilah, right?

"So there's that," he added, squinting at something outside the window. He brushed his hands onto his thighs. "Come on, I'll show you downstairs."

She followed him out of the room, still mulling over his comment. He motioned to the third doorway off the hallway. "My room's there."

His room. Where he slept. She imagined him sprawled out in soft sheets, his head on a pillow. Was he a pillow hugger? Did he sleep on his stomach with his arms up, cheek resting on his forearm? Or maybe like she did, on his side with his gorgeous legs drawn up? What would it feel like, being the little spoon to his big spoon? With one of those corded arms wrapped around her waist, one of those legs draped over hers?

Gah.

Swallowing, she followed him back through the kitchen, past Lilah and down the back staircase to the lower level.

He opened a door to show her a media room that had three rows of theater seating and a wall-wide screen, and another to give her a glimpse of a richly paneled room with walls of empty wine racks. Finally he led her to an enormous room that literally rendered her speechless. She stood in the doorway and gaped.

"Yeah, it's a lot." Garrett shoved his hands into his pockets and hunched his shoulders. "The designer went a little crazy down here."

A pool table, foosball table, air hockey table, and along one wall, two freaking bowling lanes. A poker table, a blackjack table, a slot machine and, wait, was that a vintage Pacman arcade machine? Maggie edged farther into the room, still taking inventory. A horseshoe bar at the far end, a sectional sofa, one –, two –, no, *three* giant flat-screen televisions. There were several framed jerseys and two large cases of football memorabilia, and in between the cases – Maggie stopped in her tracks. A larger than life sized mural of Garrett. In his throwing stance, with his eyes focused downfield, arm cocked, about to unleash the football.

Like, so big.

Maggie looked at the wall, then back at Garrett.

He looked like he was dying. Eyes closed, shaking his head, rocking on his heels. "Don't say it. I know. It's ridiculous."

Maggie couldn't help it. It wasn't the mural as much as his discomfort. He looked like he wanted to disappear. She tried to suppress her amusement but a peal of laughter burst out of her despite her best effort to hold it in. Garrett's eyes snapped open, and his pained expression made her laugh harder. She dropped onto the sectional sofa and tried to stifle her merriment. "I'm sorry, I'm sorry." She flapped apologetic hands at him. "It's just – your face. Oh, Garrett, your face just now."

He dropped onto the sofa beside her, stretched out his long legs, crossed his arms, and gave her a mock glare. "Yeah, yeah, I know. You're not the first one to make fun of it. It wasn't my idea. It took me by surprise, too."

Her stomach hurt from laughing so hard. "Sorry, so sorry." She leaned over to pat his leg. "I wasn't making fun of it. Honestly. It just took me by surprise."

"You should hear what my teammates have to say about it."

Maggie drew her legs up beneath her and angled towards him. "Do they come over often?"

"We play poker down here once in a while. In fact, we're supposed to get together Friday night." He shot a glance at her. "Will that be a problem?"

Crazy to think she'd dropped into a world where professional football players came by for poker night. "Of course not. Why would it be?"

He uncrossed his arms and clasped his hands behind his head. "Means leaving you on your own with Lilah. I feel like I've been letting you down, not pulling my weight."

Maggie shrugged. "Not at all, and you'll just be down here if we need you. Since I leave the next day, it'll give me time to get my stuff together."

He frowned. "You leave the next day?"

"You said your sister's coming to get Lilah on Saturday. So I'll fly home Sunday."

"Yeah, that's right," he said slowly.

"What time is my flight home, anyway?"

"I haven't booked it yet. That way you can pick the flight you want."

"Garrett, if you wait until the last minute, it's going to cost another fortune."

He made a face at her. "Hardly."

She knew the cost of a last-minute ticket was nothing to him but to her it was stupidly extravagant. "I don't feel right about you spending so much on my airfare. And don't buy another first-class ticket. Economy's fine."

He looked at her like she was crazy. "Yeah, right. Economy? I don't think so. And we need to revisit your compensation. I'm paying you. It's not debatable."

That's where he was wrong. "You can talk all you want. I'm not taking your money."

"I wouldn't have asked you to come otherwise. It was part of the deal."

"Not part of my deal." For her, this wasn't a business transaction and she wasn't going to let him go all alpha on her about money. It was nice to be needed and at home she'd just be sitting on her rump feeling sorry for herself.

"Why are you being stubborn?"

She rolled her eyes at him. "Pot, meet kettle."

He looked partly amused, partly annoyed.

"Honestly, this is like a vacation for me. I'm glad I'm here and not home this weekend."

Saturday was her non-wedding day. Being here with him and Lilah was a godsend, really. First he saved her from fainting on the beach and now he was saving her from having to endure the weekend at home. He was her hero. And he was right there, so close. She felt so much appreciation suddenly that she gave in to the urge to give his chest a little pat. Yep. Hard as a rock. "In fact, I probably ought to be paying you. I mean, I'm staying in a freaking castle."

He opened his mouth to speak again. The pat on his chest had given Maggie a little false courage so she lifted a finger and lightly booped it against his mouth. "Nope. Not a word. I have spoken."

Chapter 9

After Lilah's nap, Maggie took her back outside for more pool time with the tiny hope that Garrett would join them. She wouldn't mind seeing him close up in his swimsuit, not even a little bit. She was a little concerned that he was purposely avoiding her, though, because after they'd gone back upstairs from the game room, he'd gone quiet again. Locked down like a vault.

Maybe she shouldn't have touched him.

She really shouldn't have touched him.

There was something wrong with her. She should still be grieving over her broken engagement instead of obsessing over patting Garrett Long's chest. Was this normal rebound stuff? Was she emotionally unstable? Or had she and Mason grown apart months ago and she'd been feeling more embarrassment than heartache?

All she knew for certain was that it was really hard to stop thinking about touching Garrett.

She and Lilah played in the pool until they were both tired and their fingers and toes were pruny. By the time she'd taken Lilah upstairs, given her a bath, and returned downstairs with her in her My Little Pony pjs, Garrett had come out from wherever he'd been closeted and was busy in the kitchen. He looked up briefly when they entered, his expression unreadable.

"Hey." She gave him a tentative smile and lifted Lilah to one of the bar chairs where she had crayons and a coloring book waiting.

He dipped his head in silent greeting and then turned away to do whatever it was he was doing with a skillet and garlic and olive oil.

O-kay. "Can I help?"

"I've got it."

She frowned at his back. "You sure?"

He nodded. "Yeah."

Awk-ward. Whether he was in a mood or not, the view from where she sat was still pretty spectacular. How did a grumpy man make chopping garlic and onions look so hot?

"Maggie, you color with me." Lilah tugged on her t-shirt sleeve.

Blinking, Maggie pulled another bar chair close to Lilah and sat beside her. "Okay, sweetie. Which page?"

Lilah flipped pages until she found one she liked. "Do the mermaid."

"The mermaid it is." Maggie kept her head down, concentrating on Lilah and the coloring book while Garrett moved around. He really did know what he was doing and it was sexy as hell. She peeked up once in a while to see him crumbling bacon, grating cheese, chopping vegetables for salad. All without a word. Once or twice she caught him glancing at her, too. And when that happened, she felt a zing straight to her lady bits.

Her lady bits were supposed to be on hiatus. Recovering from being dumped. Not cheerily waking up to wave hello to a man she'd only met a few days ago, no matter how attractive he was.

His silent streak continued on through a tasty but painful dinner, where he interacted with Lilah but avoided conversation with her despite her best efforts. Maggie was relieved when Lilah finished eating and she had an excuse to go back upstairs. She took her time putting Lilah to bed, reading aloud until Lilah's eyes began drooping.

So now what? Should she stay upstairs or go back downstairs?

It wasn't a hard decision. Garrett was downstairs. She was drawn to him, like an unfortunate magnet with questionable instincts. She'd just hang out quietly, minding her own business. The texts were still coming in fast and furious from her girlfriends, and there was always her Kindle to fall back on, although reading a romance novel was probably not the smartest idea.

He was at the sink when she returned, rinsing dishes and putting them into the dishwasher.

"Is she asleep already?"

He speaks!

"She was out before we got four pages into her book. The pool is going to be great for wearing her out."

"Glad it's getting some use." He took the pot from the stove top. "I don't use it much."

Who would have thought that a famous football player would be so – gorgeously domesticated? Maggie watched him at the sink, scrubbing and rinsing a pot. Mason had never offered to help her in the kitchen, much less do the washing up himself. Twat.

"When did you become interested in cooking?" She wasn't going to go down silent treatment road without a fight. She picked up a dish cloth and joined him by the sink.

"I had to learn when I was a kid."

"Had to?" She took the pot from the drain and began drying it.

"My parents owned a nightclub." He rinsed out the sink. "They were gone a lot. It was either learn to cook or go hungry."

She glanced at him, troubled by his matter-of-fact remark. She had taken enough psych courses in college to know that neglected children could grow up with a multitude of trust issues. It made his dislike of media a little more understandable. Also maybe his dislike of having basically strangers staying in his home.

"Ancient history now," he added indifferently. Pouring himself a glass of water, he turned to look at her and leaned against the counter. "You know where everything is now, so anything you want to do, you know, feel free."

Was he trying to hint that he wanted to be left alone now that Lilah was tucked in bed? She believed he was. It was probably hard for him, with his fondness for privacy, to have her so thoroughly underfoot, especially when she had a problem keeping her hands to herself.

"Oh, right," she said quickly. "I might sit outside for a little while."

"The hot tub's nice." He drank a sip of water, still eyeing her over the rim.

Oh hell no, she wasn't going to prance around in her swimsuit in front of him any more than absolutely necessary. "I need to call my folks. They're worried I've been coerced into a football groupie sex club."

He choked on his sip of water. "You're kidding, right?"

"Only a little. They're protective."

"Please call them. Right away."

Was it her imagination or had his mouth quirked into a tiny smile?

Garrett watched through the window as Maggie made her way to one of the chaise lounge chairs beside the pool where she sat down, cross-legged, phone in hand.

He was sure making a mess of his plan to keep her at a distance. It hadn't even been a full day and finding the right balance was way harder than he had anticipated.

And now here he was again, basically spying on her like he'd found himself doing in his office earlier. He had started off just glancing outside once in a while to make sure she and Lilah were okay, but every time he did, they were having so much fun that he had his chair turned around completely to enjoy the show. The best had been some kind of silly-jump contest, with Lilah trying hard to imitate whatever Maggie did from the side of the pool. He had laughed out loud a few times, all alone in his office. He didn't know which one of them was more joyfully uncoordinated. He'd been just about ready to give up and go outside to join the fun when he saw Maggie begin to dry Lilah off, and realized they were about to come inside. It was just luck that he was able to get his chair turned back around and grab some papers before Maggie showed up at the office door, looking so bright, so vital. She didn't need to know she'd completely distracted him.

The fact that she wasn't trying to get his attention made her all the more interesting. There had been a couple of instances when he was showing her around the rest of the house, where he found himself itching to get a little closer. Just a little. Catch a whiff of her scent. Brush against her arm. And if he'd expected her to gush over the house like the handful of women who had gotten a brief glance of it, he was way off. Maggie seemed more amused than impressed, and when they got to the game room and she saw that dumbass mural and lost it, he knew he was in trouble. How was he supposed to react to a girl who went into a fit of laughter instead of pretending to be awestruck?

Then when she'd touched his chest and then tapped his mouth with her finger? Fuck. Two tiny, insignificant actions and he'd gone hard as steel. He'd struggled to be still and prayed she hadn't noticed. He had known she didn't mean anything by it. And he wouldn't act on it if she did.

Well, he didn't think he would.

He couldn't.

She would end up expecting too much from him. As tempting as she was, as much as he might like getting to know her, or want to taste every smooth inch of her sweet body, he would end up disappointing her. She couldn't have made it plainer that she was all about long-term commitment and all that went with it.

Afterwards he went too far in the other direction, but he

needed space. Needed to recalibrate. Things weren't going as he'd planned. It should be easy to hold Maggie at arm's length. He was good at keeping his distance with women; it was second nature now.

But it felt messed up to ignore Maggie because she hadn't done anything wrong.

No, the problem was that she was doing everything right.

Had it been a monumentally bad idea to bring her here?

Maybe so.

He moved away from the window to flop onto the sofa and flick on the television. He could keep some distance by going downstairs to watch game film in the media room, leaving this space for Maggie, but the media room was soundproofed so he wouldn't be able to hear if she or Lilah needed something.

Who was he kidding? They wouldn't need him. He didn't want to go downstairs because he wanted to be close enough to watch her, to try to figure out what made her so damned appealing. He recalled the artless way she'd flung herself into the chair when he was reading to Lilah. Those long legs, draped over the armrest, were hard to ignore. Something on her phone had her smiling, and he wanted to know what it was. She'd tapped out messages and he wanted to know who she was texting. He wanted to see her photos, find out what kind of music she listened to.

None of that was any of his business.

He clicked through the multitude of channels, looking for something vaguely entertaining. Not even the sports channels offered anything that caught his interest. He picked up his phone and skimmed the news, a few sports blogs, and then scrolled through some Instagram posts. Inspiration struck; he searched for Maggie's account. He spent the next few minutes scanning her posts. There weren't many photos; just some random shots of scenery and a couple of funny memes, but there was one of Maggie and three other women, laughing and holding margaritas with a lake in the background. The other women looked nice enough but it was Maggie who glowed.

He set his phone aside and looked over his shoulder out the window again.

She was still sitting on the chaise lounge, holding the phone in front of her, apparently face-timing with her parents. Dude and Buddy were pestering her relentlessly, and she leaned over while talking to pet them. He saw her turn the phone so her parents could see them, too. He watched her expressions as she talked and listened; serious for a few moments, then laughing, then he watched her nod and blow two exaggerated kisses at the screen before touching the screen to end the call.

He sank back into the sofa, clasping his hands behind his head. What did it feel like to have that kind of relationship with a mother and father? To talk and laugh with them? He thought of his own parents, of their sick marriage, of all the drama and destruction. The old man was dead now, burning in hell if there was any justice to be had, and though it pained Emily, he had no desire to see their mother again. He'd pay for rehab or whatever else she needed, but he wouldn't visit her or forgive her. Some things were simply unforgivable.

Em had a kind heart, a caring heart, and she thought she'd wear him down one day. She was a great mom to Lilah, too, despite the fact she hadn't had any kind of role model. She insisted, every chance she got, that he would break the mold too but he'd made his peace with the fact he wasn't going to have kids. The crazy was going to stop with him.

It was turning out to be a little bit fun to be an uncle, though. More than he had expected. With Maggie here, he was a lot more relaxed. Lilah wasn't as intimidating as she had been as an infant. She was turning into a real little person, so animated, and her way of talking was ridiculously cute.

Kind of like Maggie. The stuff she came out with, like when she'd murmured something about his place needing a moat. He looked over his shoulder again, unable to resist, and saw that she was no longer talking on her phone. Now she was sitting on the edge of the pool, her legs dangling in the water, lavishing more attention on his goofball dogs.

She'd need a towel.

Minutes later, he stepped out of the French doors, walked toward her with a thick towel in hand, and was rewarded with a cautious smile. "Your dogs are absolute darlings."

"They're a disgrace. If someone ever broke in, they'd just wag them to death." He bent to place the towel beside her and then shoved his hands into his pockets, unsure of himself. He didn't really want to go back inside but maybe she didn't want his company anymore. He'd been pretty abrupt earlier.

She darted a glance up at him. "You want to sit for a minute?"

He did. He really did. He dropped to sit beside her. "Did you convince your parents that you're safe?"

"Yes." She gave him one of her smiles, not that he deserved it after being such a dick at dinner. "They didn't know what to make of me flying here like I did. Let's face it; it is a little bit crazy."

Was it crazy? He thought about it for a minute and winced. Yeah, it was. He was a selfish dipshit, accustomed to people doing what he wanted as soon as he wanted it. It was not a happy recognition. He'd barely met Maggie but he'd asked her to put her life on hold just to make his life easier. He was definitely a class-A dipshit.

And here she was, not at all put out. Cheerful, even. He slanted a sideways glance at her. She was easy with his silence, gently swinging her legs in the water.

"Well, I really appreciate you being here."

She leaned to bump her shoulder against his. "How could I not? You were practically crying. Most pathetic phone call I've ever gotten."

She was totally letting him off the hook for being an asshat earlier and it made him feel worse. "I wasn't far off, I can tell you."

She grinned at him. "Anyway, they're fine now. What's funny

is that my dad is a huge football fan so he;s torn between worrying about me and wanting me to get you to sign something. I should probably be mad at him for that."

"I'll sign anything you want," he said quickly. "Claire's probably got stuff in her office already. Would he like a jersey or something?"

"Are you kidding? He'd love it. He liked Dude and Buddy, too. He thinks you can always tell what kind of person someone is by the way they treat their pets, and your goobers look really happy."

His goobers. That was right up there with 'kerfuffle'. "So you grew up with dogs?"

"Oh, yes, one geriatric mutt after another. Their thing is adopting older dogs and then pampering the heck out of them. Right now they've got a one-eyed collie mix and a German shepherd with terrible hips." She grinned. "They didn't care for Mason."

"Your parents or the dogs?"

She laughed out loud. "The dogs, but turns out my parents weren't very fond of him either, at the end. He complained about the dog hair when we visited."

This Mason sounded more and more like a colossal douche to Garrett. "He sounds kind of fussy."

Maggie bit her lip. "I guess he is," she agreed hesitantly, and then more decisively. "Yes, he really is." She was quiet a moment. "He didn't like me to wear heels," she said suddenly.

"Why not?" Garrett recalled how great she looked in that short dress with those sandals. Legs for miles. What man wouldn't appreciate that?

"He didn't like me to be taller than him."

Insecure douchebag, he thought.

"He likes to wear those slim cut suits without socks," she continued, musingly. "But his ankles are too bony. He can't carry it."

That one made him smile. "What else?"

"And then he started being kind of a jerk to wait staff." She frowned. "And didn't tip enough."

Cheap asshole. "And?" he prompted her. "What else?" He wondered if he was enjoying this a little too much.

"His boss used to make snide remarks about me being a kindergarten teacher and Mason never really spoke up for me. He used to like that I was a teacher."

Brown-nosing coward. "You have a picture of him?" He wanted to see what this cheap, bony-ankled asshole looked like.

Maggie reached for her phone. "I deleted most of them but there might be one or two left." She scrolled through photos and stopped on one, enlarging it. "There he is." She handed Garrett the phone.

He looked at the photo of a self-satisfied looking guy wearing a prissy double breasted jacket and disliked him on sight. "Hm," he said noncommittally.

Maggie took her phone back, glanced at the photo, and hit the delete key. "Honestly," she began slowly, "he changed so much this past year that I really didn't know him anymore." She leaned forward and slowly swept a hand through the water. "He wanted a big family the same as me and we were together for so long that maybe I wanted to ignore the changes."

So the ex wanted kids, too. He knew that was important to Maggie and it was a good reminder that he needed to keep his distance. "Yeah?" He reclined back on his elbows and looked up at the night sky. "You said you were an only child. That's probably par for the course."

"You remember that?" She sounded surprised.

He remembered most everything she'd said since they met. "Yep."

She leaned back on her elbows, too. "I always thought having a brother or sister would have been wonderful. Tell me about your sister."

He smiled, thinking of Emily. "She's an emergency room

nurse. She and her husband Dan and Lilah live in Santa Fe."

"Younger than you or older?"

"Four minutes older but she acts like it's ten years."

She grinned. "Twins! So I guess you were close growing up?"

Garrett nodded. Their early years had been more of a survival challenge but they had endured it. Things changed when they reached their teens. And then that night that led to them to finally turn their backs on their parents together. It wasn't history he liked to recall, much less share.

Maggie touched his arm. "You okay?"

Her light touch brought him back to the present. He gave her a wry smile. "Yeah, sorry."

"I hope I get to meet her."

Did he want Maggie and Emily to meet? No. Em would have too many questions, like why he hadn't just called her for advice on how to handle Lilah. He frowned. Why hadn't he? Why had his first impulse been to call Maggie?

Simple. Because, despite his common sense, he'd wanted to see her again and Lilah was a great excuse.

"You're lucky to have a sister." Maggie sounded wistful.

"Hm," he said, noncommittally. "If she finds out I dragged you out here, she's going to give me a hard time." That much was true.

"She doesn't have to know how desperate you were," Maggie said teasingly. "We can tell her I barged my way in."

"She'll never buy it. She knows me too well."

Maggie gave him a questioning look.

He shrugged. "Let's just say I don't react too well to pushy people."

"Makes sense. I can understand that just from experiencing that crowd at the restaurant and the next morning when I left my rental."

"Was it bad?" He'd hoped she'd gotten away with no interference.

"Not too bad. I faked them out by acting like I was going to go out the back door to talk but then I sneaked out the front. My heart was pumping like I was trying to outrun a pack of wolves."

She'd hit on the perfect analogy for the media. "Good for you," he said, nodding. "What about at home?"

"Nothing I couldn't handle. I did get a call from one local reporter who was salivating at the idea of writing a story about how a local girl had captured the heart of the NFL's hottest quarterback." She slanted a grin at him.

She wasn't going to let that go. He shook his head in mock-annoyance. "If you don't stop bringing that up, I'm going to start reminding you all the time about that sneaky kiss you laid on me after our walk."

Maggie covered her face with her hands. "Oh, please don't. I'm still embarrassed."

Garrett laughed, and then they both fell silent for a few minutes. Maybe he shouldn't have brought up the kiss because now it was all he could think about, sitting here beside her.

"Anyway," Maggie said, "I don't know how you put up with the attention all the time."

"I was better at it when I was younger. I've lost a lot of patience the last couple of years."

"Because?"

Garrett hesitated. He wasn't used to talking about his issues. "It just never stops."

"Is it at least better during the off-season?"

He shook his head. "Not really. During the season it's mostly about the team and our games, and that's a requirement of the job. During the off-season the questions get personal. You saw that, at the restaurant."

Maggie nodded, her brow furrowed.

"I don't talk about personal stuff and most of the legit reporters know that but there's this one guy named Brent Buchanan who goes out of his way to be an asshole. I'm not sure what set him off originally, maybe me not agreeing to any interviews, but he really gets off on writing negative shit about me. And not just about football."

Garrett had locked down the demeanor and eye stare that deterred most of the unwanted media questions but Buchanan was a seriously slimy guy, always pushing a little harder, trying to get a reaction. Apparently tired of ragging on Garrett's professional abilities, he'd started digging into his background. Buchanan wanted a big story. It wasn't exactly a secret that he and Emily had left home at fifteen but Garrett could count on one hand the number of people who knew exactly why they'd left, and they were all trustworthy.

But the last time Buchanan showed up, when Emily was in town and he'd taken her to a team event, the asshole wouldn't stop shouting questions at both of them about their parents, and actually had the nerve to grab Em's arm. Garrett had seen red. He'd gone after Buchanan and it could have been bad but a couple of his teammates pulled him away before he could get his hands on him.

Fucking bastard, messing with Emily.

"I bet he's a sociopath with a huge inferiority complex," Maggie said firmly, bringing him back to the present. "And what better way to build himself up than try to tear down someone who is so much more successful? And I bet he looks like a toad," she continued. "He must hate you for how gorgeous you are."

Comments about his looks always made him uncomfortable but Maggie's matter of fact remark about Buchanan made him smile. The guy did have a passing resemblance to a toad.

"And he's probably got a textbook micropenis," she concluded.

Garrett burst out laughing. Her closing dig was the best thing he'd ever heard. He'd laughed more with Maggie the last few days than he had in months. "You're brutal, you know that? The things that come out of your mouth, Maggie."

"Sometimes my filter falls off," she agreed easily. "And you've probably noticed I ramble sometimes."

"Oh, really?"

She bumped him again. "Hey, I was thinking, now that you're in a better mood, maybe I can go back inside and, I don't know, watch a little TV?"

He dropped his chin, taking the hit he deserved. "Of course. Look, I'm sorry about earlier."

She scrambled up from the edge of the pool and used the towel to dry off her legs and feet. "I get that it's probably difficult, having me underfoot like this, but how about next time you say what's on your mind instead of going all Oscar the Grouch on me?" Offsetting her words with a smile, she slid her feet into her flip-flops and handed him the towel back.

He winced. Good on her for calling him on his bad manners. "Yeah, absolutely. And again, it was all on me. You're fine. I mean, I don't mind having you around. I, uh, like having you around."

He sounded like a fucking moron. Discomfited, he rubbed the back of his neck.

Maggie slanted an amused look at him. "Are words giving you trouble?"

Damned if he didn't like how she went straight from gently scolding to teasing him. "Is that something you say to your kindergarteners? Are you using teacher talk on me?" Offering her a grin, he swatted the towel around his legs, flipped it over his shoulder and then led the way back into the house.

"Maybe." She smiled up at him as she ducked under his arm in the doorway. Once inside, she dropped unceremoniously onto the sofa. He really liked the artless way she made herself comfortable. There was none of that affected posing he found so irksome. He sat on the sofa near her and picked up the remote. "I got the Disney channel for Lilah like you suggested."

She looked delighted. "You did? Does it have the movie 'Up'"?

"I don't know. We can look. What's it about?"

"You've never seen 'Up'?" Wriggling farther back into the

deep sofa, she drew her long legs up and wrapped her arms around them.

Those legs. He wanted those legs. Tangled in his sheets, wrapped around his hips.

He took a breath and tried to concentrate on what Maggie was saying.

"Oh, it's the best animated movie ever. The first part is amazing. It's this beautiful montage of Carl meeting Ellie and their life together and then it rips your heart out and stomps it into tiny pieces because Ellie dies and Carl is left behind."

Jeez. "Yeah, sounds fantastic," he said, making a face.

She nodded enthusiastically, completely missing his playful sarcasm. "There's a lot more to it than that; a big adventure with a little boy and a hilarious dog, but the beginning's just beautiful. Carl and Ellie were soulmates from the day they met, and they had these two chairs that they sat in and –"

He made a snoring sound and Maggie swatted at him. "Oh, okay, never mind." She tossed him the remote. "Find something testosterone-y with lots of guns and blood."

"No, go on. Tell me more about this adorable cartoon about dead old ladies."

Maggie laughed out loud. "You really shouldn't make fun of it without seeing it. I love that movie." Sighing, she rested her chin on her knees. "I want the whole soulmate, white-picket fence, his and her chairs side-by-side, till-death-do-we-part thing."

And there it was. The reminder he needed. That was exactly the reason he would be out of his mind to think of Maggie as anything more than a friend. He was not a white-picket fence kind of guy.

Chapter 10

Maggie woke early the next morning, surprised all over again to find herself in Denver. Lilah was still fast asleep, snug under her duvet, her arms clutching one of her stuffed animals. The room they shared was big and bright, with windows overlooking the front lawn of Garrett's pseudo-castle. Maggie rose to look out of one of the windows and saw a crew of men already at work, mowing and edging. She imagined there must be a housekeeper or maybe a team of maids to look after the interior on a regular basis, dusting that fancy dining room and washing the walls of windows. It was a beautiful home but she wouldn't want to live alone in it. That was apparently the way he liked it, though.

She slipped downstairs to look for coffee before getting dressed. She and Garrett had stayed up late watching an action film and she was in desperate need of massive quantities of caffeine if she was going to keep up with Lilah today.

Well, she hadn't really watched the film. The last couple of days had finally caught up with her. She'd fallen asleep less than ten minutes in. She'd only woken up when the credits were rolling at the end. Slumped down with his outstretched legs propped on the ottoman, Garrett hadn't offered any comment about the soft throw that was neatly tucked in around her, and she didn't ask. She'd just unwound herself from it, offered a sleepy good night and left him to go upstairs to bed.

Where she may or may not have indulged in a fantasy or two about the man downstairs before falling asleep.

Maggie cinched the belt around her short cotton robe and tiptoed down the stairs. She wondered which Garrett she would find this morning; the smiling one or the broody one. Yesterday he'd bounced back and forth between the two and, honestly, it was exhausting.

Rounding the opening from the great room into the kitchen, she faltered when she found him already in the kitchen. He was shirtless and barefoot, mug in hand, waiting for his coffee to finish dripping into his mug. He cast a sleepy look in her direction, his eyes moving from her face down to her bare legs and back up again.

Had he just checked her out?

Naah. No way.

"Mornin'." Yawning, he rubbed his chest. "Sleep ok?"

Maggie's mouth went a little dry. His dark hair stuck up in wild directions and the dark stubble on his face was eye-goggling. It was his pajama pants, though, riding low on his lean hips, that rendered her mute for a moment. Just the right amount of hair dusted his chest and swirled over his sculpted abdomen, and continued downward past the knotted drawstring.

Hormones she'd never met before performed a frenetic little tap dance complete with jazz hands.

She nodded wordlessly and then realized he wasn't looking at her. "Yes," she squeaked.

Grasping one elbow, he pulled his extended arm toward his chest, exhaling, then did the reverse. "Coffee?"

Those shoulders. Was he stretching on purpose? "Yes," she managed. He held out the mug and she edged forward to take it, and then rounded the island to sit on a bar chair. His back to her, he put another pod in the machine and opened the cabinet door above the coffee maker to withdraw another mug.

Sweet baby Jesus. The way his spine dissected the smooth, rippling muscles of his back? The width of his sinewy shoulders, that expanse of smooth, tanned skin, in comparison to the narrowness of his hips?

Bow chicka wow wow.

He glanced over his shoulder. "Lilah still asleep?"

And, mercy, the way his sleep pants were barely hanging on to the slope of his tight ass.

"Yes," she squeaked again, clutching the mug tightly with both hands. *Oh, for God's sake, pull yourself together.*

"That's good." Waiting for the cup to fill, he closed his eyes, tilted his head to one side, stretched, dropped his chin, and then tilted his head the other way. "Going to toss her in the pool again?"

Maggie held her mug to her lips, frozen, watching, only remembering to take a sip when he opened his eyes and lifted a questioning eyebrow.

"Uh huh."

He rotated his head some more, then extended one arm over his head, bent his elbow, grabbed it and pulled. The muscles in his triceps and lats bulged. He did it on the other side. Maggie took another sip of coffee but somehow managed to miss her mouth and coffee dribbled down her chin and onto her chest.

Oh, for God's sake. She swiped at her chin and brushed at her robe.

He looked at her, a smile lurking around his mouth. "Not a morning person?"

She wondered what he would do if she set the mug down and put her hands right on his chest. Not a pat. Just right there, both hands, right on his chest. She could actually feel her hands tingling as if they had a mind of their own and thought that investigating the contours of his six pack was a great idea.

"No. I mean, yes."

"I give up." His smile widened. "I'll wait until you've had your coffee to try again."

"Would you mind putting a shirt on?" she blurted.

He looked at her in surprise and then looked down at his chest. "Oh, sure. Be right back." He set his mug down and padded silently out of the room.

Was he grinning when he walked away? Maggie pulled out a barstool, sat, and hid her face in her hands Great, now he knew she couldn't handle being around his magnificent bare chest. Not embarrassing at all.

Lilah trudged in, dragging her fleece blanket and headed straight for the sofa. Maggie watched as Lilah climbed up on the cushions, curled in a ball and tugged the blanket up to her chin. Sweet little girl. She followed Lilah to sit on the edge of the sofa beside her. "Good morning, sleepyhead," she said, rubbing her back.

Lilah blinked at her. "I wanna go swimming."

"Okay. How about some breakfast first?"

Lilah nodded.

Garrett returned, wearing shorts and a Sooners t-shirt, and picked up his coffee mug. "Sorry for making you uncomfortable." He drank a sip and then eyed her over the top of his mug.

Okay, that time he did look at her legs, she was sure of it. Suddenly she was aware she was still just wearing a short robe over her pajama shorts and camisole. Flustered, she rose and cinched the belt tighter. "I'll take my own advice and get dressed, too."

After donning her bikini, a pair of shorts and t-shirt, Maggie returned, determined to be much more calm, cool, and collected and much less blithering idiot.

Back in the kitchen, Garrett was at the range, cooking eggs and bacon. Lilah was still content watching television.

"Fried or scrambled?" he asked.

"Whatever's easiest." She rinsed out her mug. Shirt or no shirt, it was amazing what seeing him just being handy in the kitchen did to her insides.

"Get the fruit out of the fridge?" He lifted bacon from the

griddle to a plate that already looked like it held two pounds.

Maggie opened the refrigerator. "What are your plans for today?" she asked, spying and removing a plate of cut melon and strawberries. "Aside from eating five pounds of bacon?"

He looked down at the plate of bacon. "It's just a pound."

"Still a lot of bacon." She swiped a piece and bit into it.

"It's an off-season vice. Don't tell anyone." He whisked eggs in a bowl, tossed in salt and pepper, and poured it into the skillet. "Anyway, I don't have anything in particular planned. I'll probably work out this morning, if you're okay with that, and I've got some guys coming out about some changes in my office, but otherwise, no real plans. Why? Is there something you'd like to do?" He flipped the eggs around and added some grated cheese.

"No, not at all," she said quickly, mesmerized by his easy skill. Granted, scrambled eggs didn't require gourmet training but Mason didn't even know where to find a butter knife. "It's just that I thought, with me here looking after Lilah now, you'd be busy doing whatever it is that you ordinarily do." Preferably in a room without wall to wall windows.

"I don't expect you to take care of Lilah all day by yourself. I just want some back-up so I can take a shower without worrying that she's shaving the dogs or getting into my liquor." Taking three clean plates out of a cabinet, he divided the eggs, bacon and fruit and set them on the island.

Maggie smiled at his examples. "Lilah wants more pool time so I can handle that if you want to do your workout." She really hoped he'd agree. His bare chest in the kitchen was bad enough; who knew what kind of stuttering fool she'd turn into if he was slathered with suntan oil.

"Yeah, okay," he said. "After the contractor comes and goes, I'm all yours." He flinched slightly. "All yours and Lilah's," he clarified.

"Right," she said quickly.

"Lilah, come eat your breakfast," Garrett said.

"No," came the small voice from the sofa. "Eat in here."

"She keeps forgetting I'm the alpha," he said in a low voice. "No, ma'am. Breakfast over here."

"So we can go swimming afterwards," Maggie added.

They heard a long suffering sigh, and Lilah rolled off of the sofa and trudged to the nearest bar stool. "Fine," she said, glaring at them.

He winked at Maggie. "Still the alpha."

After cleaning up the kitchen, Garrett headed to the workout room with good intentions but kept losing count of his reps. He'd watched outside the window, waiting for Maggie to discard her t-shirt and felt disgruntled when she left it on. Maybe she'd gotten a little sunburnt the day before. He banished the mental image of rubbing her down with lotion. When she climbed out of the pool, he realized that the wet shirt over her bikini looked pretty damn good, too. T-shirt or no t-shirt, it was hard to take his eyes off of her. She wasn't skinny with sharp points and angles or overly fit with muscles as hard as his own; she was curvy in an appealing, athletic way.

He thought about the last woman he'd dated, an actress doing a film in Denver. She'd said she was on board with keeping things light but it hadn't taken long for her to start talking about the future. Wanting to come watch him play, talking about the holidays. Major red flags. Even worse, she was obsessed with the whole social media thing; her status, her accounts, her followers. She wanted to go out every night and when he caught on that she was documenting every detail of their relationship for the whole world to see, it was easy to end it.

It seemed like the older he got, the harder dating became. He'd spent his twenties reveling in a never-ending parade of eager women but now that he was in his thirties, he was over it. So over it. The kind of woman that constantly turned up weren't interested in the human beneath the hype; they were only interested in the size of his paycheck and the fact he wore a well-known jersey on game day. Or worse, they were focused on matrimony, no matter how clear he was about keeping things simple.

It was just easier to be alone.

A noise outside interrupted his thoughts. Maggie and Lilah were standing side by side on the edge of the pool, holding hands, reciting the alphabet together loudly. At 'z', they cannonballed together into the pool and came up laughing. Maggie had a gift for sneaking little lessons into their play. He hoped she'd get her wish for a big family someday.

The thought wrenched his gut. Deciding to forego his weight regimen, he headed for the treadmill, but before he could even jab the program buttons his phone rang. Usually he'd resent the interruption in his routine but today he was relieved.

"Hey, Ty." Garrett sat down on the ramp of the treadmill. Ty Hurst was an old teammate and his closest friend.

"Hey buddy, what's going on? What's new?"

Garrett frowned. Ty never began a phone call like that. He always had something to say and usually got right to it. "Not too much," he said warily. "What's new with you?"

"I'll tell you," Ty began, "Eleanor's been worrying about something and she isn't going to give me any peace until I butt into your business and find out what's what."

Garrett saw where this was going. "You're talking about Maggie, aren't you?"

"Hell, I don't know what I'm talking about," Ty said. "Hang on a minute."

Garrett could hear Eleanor's voice in the background, apparently instructing Ty on what to say.

"Okay, honey," he heard Ty say. "If you'll just let me – well, here, then." Ty laughed into the phone. "Hold on, Garrett, the boss wants to talk to you."

Garrett felt another twinge of uneasiness. Ty's diminutive wife scared him a little.

"Hi, Garrett. I saw the photo of you and Maggie Parrish. What's going on with you two?"

There, that was exactly why she scared him. She was cute, like a bee, but would come at you with no hesitation. "Nothing's going on, Eleanor. We met in Florida and went out to dinner." He debated whether or not to add that she was there in Denver. It might sound more significant than it really was. "She's a nice girl," he added lamely.

"She's a very nice girl," Eleanor agreed. "But what I don't understand is why she's there with you in Denver when I thought she was getting married Saturday here in Baton Rouge."

Married Saturday? And how the hell did Eleanor already know Maggie was in Denver? "Uh," he said, his thoughts scrambling. "I hired her to help me look after my niece." Well, technically that wasn't quite true. He had meant to hire her but she hadn't agreed to let him pay her. Eleanor didn't need to know that, though.

There was a long silence on the other end of the line, and then Eleanor spoke again. "I'm confused. Is she not getting married anymore?"

"No, she's not."

"Is it because of you? What did you do?

"No! Nothing!" Garrett really wished it was still Ty on the line and not Eleanor. "They broke up before I met her. Anyway, how did you even know she's here?"

"Maggie's friend Toby told Allison who told me."

Allison was one of Ty's sisters. Garrett had forgotten how fast news traveled inside their family, and apparently, through Baton Rouge as well.

"I can't say I'm sorry to hear they broke up. I didn't like him very much when I met him. How's Maggie doing?"

"She's doing great taking care of Lilah, if that's what you mean." He knew that wasn't what she meant. "Do you want to talk with her? She and Lilah are outside but I can get her for you."

Eleanor sighed. "No, but I hope you're telling me the truth

when you say you're just friends. I like Maggie a lot, Garrett. Don't you dare break her heart."

"Come on, Eleanor. She's working for me." He hoped he sounded convincing.

"Is she staying for the visit to Greenbriar on Sunday?"

Garrett and Ty, along with a few other current and past Renegade players, were part of a group visiting a local retirement center for Father's Day. He rarely brought dates along to team functions but the idea of bringing Maggie along was appealing. He had a lot of misgivings about participating in something to do with fathers and having Maggie there might make it somewhat tolerable. "I don't know yet. My sister comes back Saturday so she may want to fly home Sunday."

"I see. Well, here's Ty again." Garrett heard more talking in the background between Eleanor and Ty, and then Ty returned to the line.

"Do me a favor, buddy. Eleanor really likes Maggie so don't do anything to make her come after you."

Garrett would never get used to the fact that the biggest and toughest defensive end in the history of the Denver Renegades franchise was a little bit intimidated by his tiny wife, but he didn't think he'd point that out. "Gotcha," he said. "See you soon."

He rose and stepped on the treadmill again, but the front gate alarm chimed before he pressed the start button. The contractor had arrived. Well, fine. He didn't want to work out anyway.

Chapter 11

After another full morning in the pool, Maggie led Lilah, swaddled in a towel, through the French doors and was startled to see a strange man in the living area by the kitchen. It looked like he was fooling around with the television over the fireplace. She knew Garrett had a meeting with a contractor about some renovation in his office but she didn't expect to see a stranger in this area of the house.

The man blinked when he saw her and dropped his hands to his sides. "Oh, hi," he said, moving away from the hearth. "You startled me there."

The feeling was mutual. She nodded at him, feeling uncomfortable.

He idled away from the fireplace. "I'm with Pete, the guy doing work in Garrett's office. I was just, uh, on my way to the truck to get a tape measure."

"I see," Maggie said, gripping Lilah's hand. But she didn't see. The den wasn't the direct path to the driveway.

"Yeah, I thought it'd be okay to just take a quick look around." He made a show of nodding and glancing around the room. "This is some place."

Lilah tugged on her hand. "Who's that, Maggie?" She

whispered her question. Judging from her big eyes, Lilah wasn't comfortable with his presence, either.

Maggie knelt to unwrap her from her towel. "Someone working for your Uncle Garrett," she whispered back.

"Yeah, some place," the man said. "It's not every day you get to see how the other half live." He idled a little closer and Maggie's skin prickled. "Big famous football star," he added somewhat caustically. "Pretty sick how much money he makes for just tossing a ball, huh?"

Maggie looked at him sharply. She didn't like his remarks or his tone and she didn't think Garrett would appreciate him wandering around his home. "Maybe you'd better go get that tape measure," she said, rising.

"Oh, sure. Is that your little girl?" He nodded toward Lilah. "She's cute."

Why was he asking questions about Lilah? Maggie was getting very bad vibes. "What's your name?" She tightened her grip on Lilah's hand.

"Chase." He stepped a little closer. "What's yours?"

"Chase, I think you'd better get back to work. I'm sure Pete is wondering where you've gone."

His expression darkened. "Yeah, right," he replied, turning on his heel. "Whatever you say, princess."

Maggie felt a little shaken, and wondered if she ought to tell Garrett about him.

"Maggie, I'm cold." Lilah tugged on her hand.

"Let's go get changed." She waited for the man to walk past them, to make sure he either went out toward the front door or back to the office. She wasn't leaving him alone in a part of the house where he had no business, no matter how uncomfortable he made her.

"Bitch," he muttered under his breath as he passed.

Maggie's breath hitched. Yes, she would definitely tell Garrett about him.

After outlining the work he wanted done in his office, Garrett waited while the contractor and his two employees took measurements, and then had to spend another half hour talking football before he could escort them out without appearing rude or impatient.

By that time, it was obvious Maggie and Lilah had already come inside for lunch, but there was no sign of them in the house or by the pool. He headed to the gym which had the widest view of the property, and through the windows he saw them by one of the big trees in the far corner of the property. What were they doing? Maggie was crouched down, with Lilah inside the circle of her arms, and they were both touching the bark of the tree.

Now they were looking up together, into the branches. Maggie pointed at something and Lilah nodded. He couldn't tell what they were looking at. What the hell were they doing?

They walked together to another tree and went through the same routine with the tree but this time they carefully pulled a few leaves from a low-hanging branch. Then they walked, holding hands, to another spot where Maggie leaned down to pick something up. He couldn't see what it was, but she showed it to Lilah. Lilah nodded, and Maggie put it in the pocket of her shorts before sitting down in the grass, right in the middle of the yard. Lilah dropped down beside her, and Garrett watched in bemusement as they stretched out and Maggie began pointing up at the sky.

He couldn't see what they were looking at in the sky, either. This was frustrating. He knew he should try harder to keep a little distance but suddenly he didn't care. Whatever they were doing, they were having fun, more fun than he was having by himself and it was time he pulled his weight on the babysitting front. In minutes he was across the patio and on his way across the lawn,

Dude and Buddy cavorting along beside him. Nearing the spot where they were still lying flat on the grass, he slowed down. Maggie lifted her head at the sound of the dogs, gave him a wave and sat up.

"Here's Uncle Garrett," she told Lilah.

"And Doo and Buddy." Lilah sat up and clapped for the dogs.

"And Dude and Buddy," Garrett agreed, reaching them. He looked up at the sky and still saw nothing. "What's going on out here?"

Maggie peered up at him, her hand shading her eyes from the sun. "We're on a nature walk. Want to join us?"

"We's been looking at stuffs," Lilah told him, imitating Maggie's head tilt and hand over her brow. "And we's gonna paint rocks and leafs."

"Oh, yeah?" It seemed that class was in full swing, right there in his backyard. "Where are these rocks and leaves?"

"Here's the leafs." Lilah clambered up to show him a small pile of leaves in the grass nearby. "And Maggie's got rocks in her pants."

Maggie and Garrett both laughed at Lilah's remark. He held his hand to her and tugged her to her feet. Her hand felt good in his, and he held it a fraction of a moment too long but she didn't seem to notice.

"In my pocket, to be specific." Smiling, Maggie dug into her pocket to pull out two smooth rocks. "We want to find some bigger ones." She turned to Lilah. "I bet Uncle Garrett can find some really good rocks for us."

Lilah hopped back and forth. "Yes! Find big rocks, Uncle Garrett!"

He was totally on board with rock hunting. "Okay, but only if you help me."

"I'll help!" she exclaimed.

"And Maggie, too," he added, turning toward Maggie. He smiled at the grass stuck in her hair and automatically lifted a hand to brush the bits away. Her hair was soft beneath his touch. He caught her brown gaze and couldn't look away for a long moment.

"And Maggie, too," Lilah parroted.

Lilah effectively broke the trance. Garrett cleared his throat and crouched down to brush grass from Lilah's hair as well. "But I have a question first. What were you looking at up there?"

Lilah lifted her arms to him. "Pick me up," she ordered him and he immediately obeyed. She put one little hand on his shoulder and pointed up at a cloud with the other. "That cloud looks like a bunny, see?"

Ah. Now he understood. He squinted at the cloud in question. "A bunny, huh?" He didn't see a bunny but who was he to argue? He pointed at another one. "What's that one look like?"

Lilah screwed her face in concentration. "It looks like a kitty!"

"See that one over there?" He pointed to another cloud and Lilah nodded. "That one looks like an elephant to me."

Lilah crowed with laughter as if he was the funniest person in the world. "No, not an efalunt!"

"Yes, an elephant," he insisted, putting her back on the ground, smiling. He looked at Maggie, who was smiling at him, her big, wide smile, and it sent a little ripple right through him. He took a breath. "All right then, let's find some big rocks. I think I know just the place."

Lilah put her hand in his and Garrett began to lead her away, toward the side of his yard where a creek bed ran parallel to the property. The rock-finding mission was underway.

An hour later, they were sitting at the table in the outdoor kitchen with the same bottles of paint that Lilah had used to paint the dogs, brushes that were too small for his hands, and a pile of freshly laundered rocks deemed suitable for the art project.

"What do you think of this?" Garrett held up a rock for Lilah's inspection.

Lilah cocked her head and squinted at the design he'd so carefully painted on the top of the stone. "What is that, Uncle Garrett?"

"It's a football," he replied indignantly. "Obviously."

Paintbrush in hand, Maggie leaned forward across the table to get a better look. "Are you sure that isn't the poop emoji?"

He mock-glared at her. "It's a football," he said sternly. "Anybody can see it's a football."

"You painted poop," Lilah chortled.

Maggie squinted at the brown design on the rock and then gave him a playful smile. "Thank goodness you're better at throwing them than painting them."

He grinned. If someone had told him that he'd have voluntarily spent an afternoon collecting muddy rocks and then washing them in the outdoor kitchen, he wouldn't have believed it. And now here he was, wielding a tiny paintbrush and being abused for his efforts. "Well, you paint a football, then. Let's see what you can do."

Maggie narrowed her eyes at him. "Are you challenging me?"

She was cute when she tried to be tough. "I believe I am."

She chose one of the bigger stones and bent over it with her paintbrush. Garrett smiled, noting her habit of biting her bottom lip when she was concentrating on something. "Ta da!" she said minutes later, holding it up for his inspection.

He took it and examined it. A perfect little football, complete with neat laces. "Not bad. This is mine now. I'm keeping it."

She looked pleased. "Here's a question for you; do you know what the shape of a football is called?"

She was even cuter when she was in teacher mode. Garrett raised his arm and waved it as if he were a student.

She tilted her head toward him, playing along. "Yes, Garrett?"

"A prolate spheroid," he replied smugly.

Maggie beamed at him. "Very good! And for that, you get a star." She picked up her paintbrush again, dipped it in paint, and leaned across the table to pick up his hand. Her head bent over, she painted a little lopsided star on the inside of his wrist. She was close enough for him to smell the fragrance of her hair. It would be so easy to tilt her head up for a kiss on those lips. To slide his hands into her hair, taste her mouth. Without thinking, he leaned forward slightly and curved his hand around her upper arm.

Maggie stilled, and lifted her eyes to his. For a long moment, he was hanging somewhere between her wary gaze and his good sense.

"I want a star, Maggie! Paint one on me, too," Lilah exclaimed, pushing her small arm between them.

Maggie sat down and he looked away.

"What color would you like, sweet girl?" Maggie asked her, swishing the paint brush in the cup of water.

Garrett didn't hear Lilah's reply. He was already up and on his way into the house, putting some much needed distance between himself and Maggie before she saw the effect she'd had on him. He was sure there was some game film or something he needed to study. Maybe a phone call to make. Anything to distract him from how badly he was failing at his simple plan to keep his distance.

Maggie made him hungry for the very thing he couldn't have; the kind of future that an undamaged man took for granted.

After bath time and settling Lilah into bed, Maggie took a shower and washed and dried her hair before changing into a comfortable old pair of leggings and a long sweatshirt. Garrett had made himself scarce since the early afternoon and she'd already decided she wasn't going to go looking for him. If he wanted to hang out with her, it was up to him. And if not, it was a nice night and she'd be perfectly happy just reading a book on her Kindle by the pool until she felt sleepy.

Dude and Buddy greeted her outside the French doors, wagging their tails madly, so she spent a few minutes lavishing them with attention before settling onto one of the chaise lounge chairs.

Then she heard the door open, and heard the dogs scrabbling to cross the patio. She kept her eyes on her Kindle, much like she'd done that day on the beach when he'd jogged past her.

"Hey."

Trying to ignore the way her heart kick-started when she heard his voice, Maggie turned her head to see Garrett ambling forward. He'd apparently taken a shower, too, because he was wearing different clothing; loose black athletic pants and a thin gray t-shirt, and his hair was damp and spiky.

"Hey." Geez Louise, he was something else to look at.

"Reading, huh?"

She held up her Kindle in answer.

He looked a little hesitant. "You going to make me watch a movie alone?"

That was exactly all she needed to hear. "Of course not." She felt like Dude and Buddy, ecstatic to have his attention. Now if she could just avoid wagging her tail on her way over to him, she'd be fine.

Garrett's shoulders relaxed a little. "Great." Leading the way inside, she settled on the sofa while he veered toward the refrigerator and withdrew two bottles of beer. He held them up, that damned eyebrow tilted in question. Maggie nodded so he crossed the room to the sofa where he dropped down beside her, only a couple of inches away instead of on the other end, where he'd sat the night before. He smelled wonderful, fresh and cool like toothpaste and Irish Spring soap.

Mason had read somewhere a self-confident, modern man should wear musky cologne so he had jumped right onto that bandwagon, even though she'd told him repeatedly the scent gave her a headache. Dimwit.

Dude and Buddy unwound themselves from their beds in front of the hearth and wagged their tails hopefully. "Oh, okay, come on up." Garrett patted the sofa beside him. Dude jumped up on to the end beside Garrett, and Maggie encouraged Buddy to curl up beside her. It was cozy, probably too cozy, being sandwiched together with the dogs as bookends, but she wasn't stupid enough to edge away. A vicarious thrill was still a thrill.

He twisted the top off one of the bottles and handed it to Maggie, then opened his own. "What do you feel like? Do you want to watch that depressing cartoon you were talking about?"

Maggie laughed. "I won't make you watch 'Up'. I wouldn't be able to be friends with you anymore if you hated it."

"Well, better not risk it then." Rotating through the channel listing, he paused. "Hey look. Order of the Phoenix."

She caught her breath. "Oh, yes, please!"

Damn, she was appealing. Too appealing. Flashing her big smile, wearing a sweatshirt with the text 'Straight outta pencils', delighted over a Harry Potter movie. He knew he was sitting a little too close, but any farther away and he couldn't smell her scent; something like vanilla or maybe it was almonds. Something tasty.

"You can't tell anybody about this," he said, leaning sideways and reaching over Dude to grab the throw on the end of the sofa. "It would ruin me." He handed her the throw. He knew she liked to snuggle beneath it. "Who's your favorite character?"

She pulled the throw up to her chest and drew her legs up beneath it, bumping his shoulder with hers when she did. "That's easy. Hermione, of course."

"Yeah? Me, too."

She tilted her head at him in question. "Not Harry?"

"Hermione was perfect. Pretty, smart, brave, and she could throw a mean right hook."

Maggie laughed. "And Draco never saw it coming."

"When I was a kid, I wanted to be one of the Weasleys. Cool family." He wondered if he'd be pressing his luck to put his arm on the sofa behind her head. He did slide down a little, ostensibly to prop his feet on the ottoman, nonchalantly edging his shoulder a little closer until it was touching hers. He felt like a teenager again, more aware of Maggie beside him than he was of the film playing on the screen. It was kind of fun, too. It had been a long time since he'd had to work so hard for such an innocent touch.

"I can understand that."

The tone of her voice made him uneasy.

"Yeah?" he asked carefully. "Why's that?" He wondered how much she knew about his background beyond his comment about why he'd learned to cook. He never talked about his parents and there wasn't much online about them because reporters were always reminded to steer clear of the topic. The creditable ones complied and he was quick to blacklist anyone dumb enough to push.

Like Buchanan.

She glanced at him and from the look in her eyes, he felt certain she made some assumptions about his childhood. "Who wouldn't? They're such a loving family."

"Yeah. I didn't have one of those. Kind of the opposite, actually."

Fuck, what was he doing?

Maggie twisted to give him her full attention. "I gathered that from your remark about having to learn to cook."

"Yeah, well," he said dismissively, wishing he could rewind the conversation to before the point he opened his mouth about families and wishing she wasn't looking straight at him with those big brown eyes.

"It's not something you talk about," she said softly.

That was an understatement. "No." he managed, his eyes trained unseeingly on the television.

"Okay." She sank back against the cushions again, a little lower, maybe even a little closer than before against his shoulder, and turned her attention back to the film.

Hmm. He was used to women pressuring him for more. More time, more attention, more emotion. Always more. But not Maggie. She didn't dig; she just accepted his backtracking with easy grace.

And she felt good next to him, warm against his shoulder. Just hanging out like this was such a new experience; one he could get used to, if things were different.

But things weren't different. He was still the same person, same baggage, and he had to quit sabotaging his own plan and remember that.

He'd remember it tomorrow.

Maggie's eyes were fixed on the wide screen as the movie played to the end but her mind was a million miles away. Sitting so close to Garrett was doing crazy things to her pulse and to her imagination. Mason hadn't been one for cuddling in front of the television, preferring to slouch in a chair alone, paying more attention to his phone than whatever program they were watching. Garrett, on the other hand, was built for snuggling against, and it was all she could do not to edge closer and burrow next to his shoulder. God bless Dude and Buddy for sandwiching them together in the middle.

As if he could read her mind, Buddy thumped his tail and pushed his nose under her arm for attention. "Yes, you're a good boy, aren't you? Yes, you are." Maggie stroked his huge white head, scratched his velvety neck.

Garrett glanced over and smiled. "Big doofus."

"I wish more people knew what great dogs they are. They're so misunderstood. Did you know that they were popular as nanny dogs for kids back in the day? And they make great therapy dogs?"

"Been Googling again?"

"So much knowledge at my fingertips," she replied, smiling. "What made you adopt these guys?"

"The team got involved with a fundraiser a couple of years ago for the local shelter and there were more pit bull mixes there than any other breed." He scratched behind Dude's ears. "These two guys were from the same litter. I took one look and that was it."

"Lucky little brothers."

"Yeah, I didn't even know I wanted dogs." The little grin he gave her was adorable. "Hey, want another beer?"

"Sure."

He rose and she watched him amble into the kitchen, admiring the way his thin t-shirt stretched over his wide shoulders. He wasn't overly bulky, just long and lean and ripply. He moved with a silky grace, light on his feet despite his size, like a stealthy tiger. She wondered if he moved the same way on the football field, in those bulky pads and tight pants. She guessed she was going to have to get the NFL package when she got home so she could watch him games. That would be weird, seeing him on television after seeing him in his own kitchen.

Thinking of the television reminded her about the man she and Lilah had run into earlier in the day. "I meant to tell you, when Lilah and I came in from the pool today, there was a guy in here. He said he was with your contractor."

He frowned. "What was he doing?"

To Maggie's silent delight, he sat back down in the same spot, maybe even a hair closer. He twisted the tops off of the bottles and handed her one.

"He said he was on his way to get something out of the truck and was just looking around." She decided not to mention his sarcastic tone or leering attitude. "He didn't stick around long after we came in." She drank a sip of her beer.

Garrett shook his head. "People are weird. I had to change my cleaning crew a while back because one of the employees was stealing my stuff and selling it on eBay."

Maggie gaped at him. "Are you kidding me?"

He laughed. "I wish."

"Like what?"

Was he blushing? He was! The tips of his ears were reddening. Maggie elbowed him. "Like what, Garrett?"

"Mainly clothes. T-shirts and stuff."

He wasn't telling her everything. T-shirts were not blush-worthy. She giggled. "What else?"

He glanced at her and then made a face. "Okay, underwear."

Maggie burst out laughing. "Your underwear? Were they clean or dirty?"

He looked stricken, like it hadn't occurred to him that they might have been dirty. This was too funny. Horrible, but funny.

"How much did they go for? And how did they prove they were yours?"

Dipping his chin, he rubbed the back of his neck. "I don't want to know."

Oh, now she had an idea. "Hey, maybe you could donate a few pairs for a school fundraiser? What do you think?"

He slid down and covered his face with his crossed arms. "That's a no, Maggie. Firm no." Lowering his arms, he shook his head at her and took a breath. "Oh, uh, Ty Hurst called today."

"Are you trying to change the subject?"

His ears were still red. "I am desperately trying to change the subject."

Maggie giggled again. "Fine, fine. What did Ty call about?"

"Eleanor got wind of your being here and was worried about you."

"What, did she think I'd been kidnapped? How did she even know I'm here?"

He shrugged. "Apparently you've got a friend who's friends with one of Ty's sisters."

Maggie smiled. "That's so typical. It's 'seven degrees of Baton Rouge.' Everyone knows everyone else's sister or mama or cousin."

"She warned me against breaking your heart."

Maggie glanced at him in surprise. He'd just tossed that comment off casually but the look in his eyes made her heart trip.

"Huh," she managed. Oh, well done. Brilliant response.

"Yeah. She's kind of protective of you."

That must have been some conversation. Why was she a topic? Her heart, in particular? What could have led Eleanor to warn Garrett not to break it? Was Eleanor worried that she might do something stupid like throw herself at Garrett and be rejected? Or did Garrett give Eleanor the idea that he might, maybe, possibly, see her as more than a co-babysitter? She had questions, so many questions, bouncing around in her brain but he didn't add anything else to the conversation to push her in one direction or the other so she made a weird "pffft" sound.

"I'm sure you told her I'm just here to help out for a couple of days, that we're just friends," she managed.

Was that the smart thing to say? What if he shook his head and said, no, they weren't just friends? The curious little moments from the past couple of days, coupled with the fact that she was sitting here, squashed against him, gave rise to a squiggle of hope that he'd say just that.

"I did." He tipped the bottle to his lips. "Not sure she believed me, though."

Well, that was less than helpful. Maggie felt dejected. "What else did she say?"

"She asked if you were staying through the weekend. They spend a couple of weeks near here in the summer and will be in town for an event on Sunday."

Was that an indirect invitation to stay longer? "What kind of event?"

"It's a Renegades community outreach thing for Father's Day. Some of the guys visit a local retirement home. Ty started it back when he was playing and he's been trying to get me to go for a while."

"It sounds like fun." Watching paint dry would be fun with Garrett, though, wouldn't it?

"Want to go?" he asked offhandedly, focused on peeling the paper label from the bottle in his hand. "We haven't booked your return ticket yet."

Maggie hesitated. Her disobedient hormones were shrieking *yes, yes, yes, I'll stay*, while her common sense was hissing that she needed to get back to her own world.

Common sense could be a real party pooper.

"I'd love to go." She smiled at Garrett and his answering grin had her pesky hormones doing a Puerto Rican style salsa.

Chapter 12

"No swimming today, kiddo." It was a gray, rainy morning and while he was sorry he couldn't enjoy watching Maggie and Lilah playing in the pool, it would give him a chance to be more involved. "I was thinking maybe we could go to the Children's Museum or the Aquarium. What do you think?" He shot a glance at Maggie, who was sipping her coffee while Lilah finished her breakfast, and was pleased to see her approving smile.

He could get used to seeing her every morning, her hair tousled and her eyes sleepy until her first cup of coffee kicked in. It was something to look forward to, especially since the nights were long. He wasn't getting much sleep; painfully aware of her sleeping just upstairs, imagining her beneath him in his bed, waking up with a throbbing erection.

Resisting her became more difficult every day. So what did he do? Oh, yeah, he invited her to stay longer.

Dumbass.

"But Maggie says we can have a tea party," Lilah stated with a chunk of cantaloupe in her mouth. "With my Bobbies."

He grinned. "Is that what you want to do?"

She nodded and speared another bite of melon. "Uh huh."

"A tea party it is, then." It was a little bit of a relief, knowing they wouldn't have to deal with the attention a public outing would bring.

"It might mean a little bit of mess," Maggie told him. "Do you mind if I borrow some things from around the house?"

"Borrow anything you want. How can I help?"

"It'll take a little while to set up. Why don't you do your workout and then come find us?"

Who would have thought he'd be more interested in putting together a tea party? He took his routine seriously but a couple of days of slacking off wouldn't set him back too badly. There was ample time to get back in it when Lilah and Maggie were gone.

He ought to be looking forward to that but he wasn't.

After just an hour he gave up on his workout. It was impossible to concentrate, knowing something fun was going on in his house and he wasn't a part of it. He took the quickest shower in history and then followed the sound of feminine laughter to the front of the house.

It didn't take long to find them. The dining room had undergone a complete transformation. The chairs were pulled away and there was a crazy patchwork of bed linens and blankets draped over the long tabletop, dragging onto the floor. They had built a fort. He grinned at the sight.

He could hear them talking underneath the table. Finding the entrance, he crouched down. "Knock knock." He used one finger to waggle the sheet that was serving as the door. "Can I come in?"

He heard Lilah's excited intake of breath. "Uncle Garrett's here," she whispered loudly to Maggie. "Can boys come in?"

"I think we can let Uncle Garrett in," Maggie replied in a loud whisper as well. "If he behaves himself."

"You can come in if you be good, Uncle Garrett," Lilah said. "Will you be good?"

It was ridiculous how much he wanted to be allowed inside. "I promise to be good."

"Okay, then," Lilah giggled and separated the sheets making up the opening. "We's having a tea party."

Garrett blinked at the sight beneath the table. There was the fleece throw from the den covering the rug and several pillows scattered around, fussy little pillows he recognized from the upstairs bedrooms. A couple of stuffed animals and Barbie dolls were propped up along the side, and Maggie and Lilah were sitting cross-legged in the center. Both were holding empty coffee mugs and little plates, but it was their attire that really made him pause. Lilah was wearing one of her little ruffled dresses, ruffled socks and had some kind of scarf tied in a big bow around her head, and Maggie was wearing her short flowery robe over a t-shirt and pink shorts, purple socks and had pulled her hair into two pigtails.

She looked hilarious. "A tea party, huh?"

Maggie held up a hand. "No, stop right there."

He stopped.

Maggie turned to Lilah. "He isn't dressed properly. He can't come to our tea party without party clothes. Tell him to go find his party clothes."

Lilah chortled. "You gots to wear your tea party clothes, Uncle Garrett."

"The sillier, the better," Maggie added. "Go wild."

Garrett couldn't wipe the grin off of his face. Asking Maggie to come help babysit had been the best idea he'd ever had, the dining room had never looked better, and if they wanted him to wear tea party clothes, he'd just have to go see what he could come up with.

Maggie was serving Lilah, the stuffed animals and dolls pretend party food when she heard Garrett outside the tent again. She needn't have worried that he would be upset with the way they'd destroyed his fancy designer dining room; his humorous acceptance had been as welcome as it was unexpected, and the look on his face when he'd been dispatched to change his clothes had warmed her heart.

"I'm back." He poked his head through the opening. "I want some tea. Let me in."

Maggie blinked and then grinned at the patterned wool beanie on his head, complete with ear flaps and long side tassels. "Come on in." And then burst out laughing as he crawled in on all fours, wearing a Hawaiian print shirt with a Santa tie and the most psychedelic pair of board shorts she'd ever seen. Combined with the beanie, he should have looked ridiculous but he looked big and masculine and far too appealing.

That beanie, though. Those ear flaps and tassels. What she wouldn't give for a photo of him in that hilarious thing. She couldn't stop laughing.

"Will I do?" He winked at her and settled beside her, cross-legged, his shoulders hunched and head angled so he would fit.

"Uncle Garrett!" Lilah patted his tie and laughed. "You gots a Santa Claus tie!"

Garrett looked at Lilah. "I do, and you've got red lipstick on." He looked at Maggie. "And so does Maggie."

Still grinning, Maggie dug a tube of lipstick from her robe pocket and lifted her eyebrows at Lilah. "Does Uncle Garrett need pretty lips, too?"

"No, he does not," Garrett said swiftly, giving Maggie a mock frown that made her laugh again.

"So where's this tea?" he asked Lilah. "Was I supposed to bring my own cup?"

Maggie handed him her empty cup. "Here you go."

"What about you?"

"I'm serving the party food," she explained. "Lilah, tell your uncle what we're having."

Lilah pointed at the empty saucers placed around on the floor. "That one's pancakes with chawberries, and that one's birthday cake and ice cream, and that one is got chicken nuggets with ketchup." She took a saucer and pretend-scooped up the imaginary food from each plate and handed it to Garrett. "Here. You gots to eat the pancakes first, but no tea yet because it's too hot."

There were apparently a lot of rules involved with pretend food. Garrett looked at the empty plate in his hand and back up at Maggie. "But shouldn't a tea party have real food?" he asked sotto voice.

"Not on your expensive rug."

"Baloney." He set his plate down on the floor. "Be right back." He crawled out of the tent, and Maggie tried not to notice his perfect rear, in those blinding board shorts, on its way out. Brief minutes later, he returned and began pushing food through the opening. A third coffee mug that said "blood of my enemies," a package of Oreos, string cheese, a bunch of grapes and a bottle of chocolate milk. Maggie laughed at the combination and Lilah chirped with excitement. Garrett wriggled his way back inside and gave Maggie a triumphant grin. "Now we're having a tea party." He settled again, hunched adorably in the space beside her.

"This probably isn't going to end well for your rug." She took the bottle and carefully poured chocolate milk into each mug.

"Who cares?" He opened the Oreo package with his teeth. "It's just a rug." He put a whole Oreo in his mouth and passed one to Lilah, who tried to put the whole cookie in her mouth as well.

"Don't eat like Uncle Garrett," Maggie told her quickly, elbowing Garrett in admonishment.

"Ow," he said, elbowing her back playfully. His knee brushed hers and Maggie shifted slightly so she could maintain that slight connection. It was amazing how such a small point of contact with his scarred knee gave her a thrill.

Like she was fourteen.

"Maggie, do it, too," Lilah said, her teeth blackened with Oreo dust.

Garrett held a whole cookie up to Maggie and she made a face but opened her mouth. Garrett carefully put the cookie in her mouth and she struggled to chew it, making both Garrett and Lilah laugh. “Mm,” she said, her lips pressed together. She didn’t want Garrett to see her with black Oreo dust in her teeth; it wouldn’t be nearly as cute as on Lilah.

“Good sport.” He smiled at her, a warm, indulgent smile, and her stomach did a little somersault.

“Watch me, Uncle Garrett.” Lilah plucked a grape from the stem and tossed it up to try to catch it in her mouth. It bounced off her face and she giggled.

“Let me try.” He retrieved the grape. “Open wide.” Lilah stretched her little lip-stick stained mouth open and Garrett gently lobbed the grape toward her.

“I caught it!” she chortled, mouth full of grape. “Do Maggie!”

“Can I do you, Maggie?” Garrett asked innocently, twisting toward her.

Maggie blinked at the blatant innuendo. Garrett’s face, dangerously near her own, wore an unexpectedly roguish expression.

“I think we’d both enjoy it if I – did you.”

She goggled at him, open-mouthed, her thoughts a jumbled chaos.

Then he gave her another smile, his eyes glinting with humor and, without looking away, he took another grape, brought it to her mouth and ran his thumb over her bottom lip. “Open up for me.”

Even with the silly beanie on his head, tassels dangling, his suggestive intimation sparked a zap of sexual awareness that shot from her toes to her fingertips and straight down to her core. She parted her lips without lucid thought and he tucked the grape inside her mouth. She held it in her mouth, frozen, and then finally remembered to chew and swallow.

“You did it wrong, Uncle Garrett!” Lilah protested. “You gots to throw it.”

Garrett reached for another grape, not taking his eyes off of Maggie. “I’ll throw them to you, but Maggie likes it when I do her like this.” He brought another grape to her lips. “Right?”

Maggie couldn’t look away from him. The corners of his

mouth tilting into a smile, he dipped his head down and dropped a light kiss on her mouth. It was just a whisper on her lips but it might as well have been a grenade to her lady parts.

This man, she thought fuzzily. This man and those lips. He tasted like chocolate and coffee, two of her favorite things in the whole world. And trouble. He really tasted like trouble.

He drew back a fraction and studied her face, his expression changing to something less playful. She saw his eyes darken and then he slanted his head and leaned forward for another kiss. Not quite as light as the first. Making her want to lean in, too.

"Uncle Garrett, you're kissing Maggie." Lilah giggled, breaking the spell. Maggie drew back, breath ragged, unable to stop staring at him.

"Yes, I am. I like kissing Maggie." Garrett eyed her mouth, then licked his thumb and scrubbed a little below her bottom lip. "Your lipstick's smudged. Can't have that." He popped the grape in his hand into his mouth, his eyes steady on hers.

She couldn't look away from him. Two little tiny kisses and one thumb-wipe and she was wrecked. Flattening her palms on the floor, she steadied herself. Last night, simply being snug against his side had been exciting enough. This was too much. Her panties, already smoking, might just instantaneously combust under the table and set the whole place on fire.

"My turn!" Lilah said, and Garrett turned his attention to her.

"Okay, here we go." He spoke in a completely normal voice. Maggie was sure if she tried to speak, it would sound like gibberish. "How many can you catch in a row?" He tossed one carefully and Lilah caught it, giggling. "Here comes number two."

It was suddenly stifling under the table.

"That's two," Garrett said to Lilah. "Let's go for three."

"I'll be back," she croaked, and twisted to her hands and knees, her eyes on her escape route through the opening. She needed air. Lots and lots of air.

Wincing, Garrett gazed at the side of the fort through which Maggie had escaped, and raked his hands through his hair.

He'd scared her away, literally.

When Lilah used her unfortunate phrasing, suddenly all he could think of was Maggie beside him, warm and playful and her pretty mouth, wide and stained red. He'd forgotten all about keeping his distance.

And kissing her, in front of Lilah? Jesus. Just a taste and he'd forgotten she was even there. Forgotten everything.

So much for staying detached.

"Can I have a string cheese?" Lilah asked him, tiring of catching grapes.

"Sure," he said distractedly. "Can you open it?"

"Mm hm." Lilah dipped her head, working on the plastic.

"I'll be right back. I'm going to check on Maggie."

"Okay," she replied.

Garrett climbed out of the fort, tugged the hat off of his head and adjusted his shorts. There was no hiding his arousal, from two pathetic, dry kisses. He needed a minute but he also needed to go find her and apologize. What could he say? Edging closer to her on the sofa was one thing, a kiss was something else.

Before he could decide, she returned with her purse in her hands, athletic shoes on her feet, and a wild look in her eyes.

She was leaving?

"I was wondering if maybe you could watch Lilah by yourself for a little bit?" She was talking fast, her color high. "I want to go to the store. Is there a store near here? A grocery store? Because Lilah and I might do some baking later, if that's okay. But I'll have to use your truck. Can I use your truck?" She took in a deep breath, twisting the purse strap in her hands.

She was in a state and it was his fault. He nodded and opened his mouth to reply.

"I'll be careful. I'm a good driver. You don't have to worry. But I need to go now because we need stuff."

She was rambling the way she did when she was flustered. Raising his hands, he tapped his right fingertips into his left palm. "Time out."

"For baking," she repeated weakly. "Cookies."

He wanted to put his arms around her, try to calm her, but he was afraid to get any closer. It would probably be the worst thing he could do at the moment. She was practically wringing her hands as it was. He felt like crap; it wasn't right to play games with Maggie. He took a cautious step in her direction. "I understand. You want to go to the store to get some stuff for baking."

"Yes." She pressed her lips together as if to staunch another flood of words.

He nodded again. "There's a Safeway just a couple of miles from here, and you can use the truck or the car, whichever one you want. There's a garage door opener and a control for the gate in each of them." Should he point out that she was wearing her bathrobe over her shirt and shorts? Or just let her go?

She nodded.

"Do you want me to come show you?"

"No," she said quickly. "I won't be long."

"You will come back, right?" He tried to pass his question off as a joke but it came out sounding serious. Probably because he was actually worried. The way she was looking at him, she'd be halfway to New Mexico in an hour.

She managed a weak laugh. "Of course."

He watched her turn and disappear through the great room and then he waited by the window in the dining room. A few moments later, he watched her ease his Porsche down the driveway at a snail's pace.

Lilah poked her little head out of the tent opening. "Where's Maggie?"

"She's going to the store. She'll be right back."

He hoped.

Maggie managed to find her way to the Safeway where she parked his frighteningly expensive car far away from other vehicles and then sat motionless for a few long moments, staring straight ahead.

What.

The.

Hell.

She clasped her hands on the sides of her face, which still felt hot. Okay, so she hadn't been sure about those small, unsettling looks and innocent touches since she'd arrived. They were so quick, so slight, that she kept convincing herself she had an overactive imagination to go along with her overactive hormones. She had actually enjoyed her little daydreams because that's what they were; make believe.

But there was no freaking way to mistake what had just happened under the table.

There was no mistaking a kiss.

Garrett kissed her.

Twice.

Maggie squeezed her eyes shut and dropped her head forward to rest on the steering wheel. The kind-of-maybe-almost-snuggling on the sofa, the accidental-on-purpose brushing of knees and shoulders – patting his chest like she was patting Dude or Buddy - it all seemed so harmless at the time but now she knew she'd been playing with fire. Garrett was mouth-watering when he wasn't even trying, with that face and that body and that voice, but when he focused all that boom-chicka-wow-wow straight at her?

Well, she wasn't ready for that.

Maggie lifted her head and pressed her fingers to her mouth. She felt like the proverbial dog that finally caught a car. What the hell did you do with a car once you caught it? You let it go, that's what you did, because a car could mess you up bad.

She sighed. She wasn't naïve enough to think Garrett was seriously interested in her. The women she'd seen with him in photographs were a whole different breed. A whole other species. Maybe it was because they'd been cooped up in his house, thrown together because of Lilah. He was getting restless. Maybe it was only natural. All that hotness had to go somewhere and there she was, wide-eyed, small-town, and underfoot. She couldn't get all discombobulated by that hotness or read anything into it. Once Lilah was back home and she was gone, he'd probably forget all about her anyway.

It was up to her to get them both back onto an even keel. No more sitting too close to him on the sofa, no more goo-goo eyes, no more hand touching.

Or knees touching.

Or shoulders touching.

And definitely, most definitely, there would be no lip touching.

Maggie touched her lips again. Her lips had really, really liked his lips.

For the rest of her short stay there was going to be a three-foot minimum distance between her and any of his perfect body parts. The 'easy target' sign was coming off and the 'friends only' sign was going on. She was going to keep her hands and eyes to herself. She had to get home in one piece.

Just get through the next two days and she'd be fine.

Heartened by her resolve, Maggie turned the key to start the engine, to return to his house.

It wasn't until she was out on the rainy highway again, with a white-knuckle grip on the steering wheel, that she realized she had forgotten all about actually going into the grocery store.

Standing sentry by the dining room window, Garrett gave a sigh of relief when he saw his car turn back into the driveway. Lilah had gone quiet so he bent to peek inside the fort and saw that she was engrossed in tea-related conversation with her dolls.

Rolling his tense shoulders, he headed for the kitchen. He needed to make amends. Kissing her had been an accident. A slip-up. Sure, he was attracted to her but she hadn't given him any indication she thought of him as more than a friend. The whole time she'd been gone, he'd tried to figure out how to apologize but he hadn't come up with anything remotely useful.

She was already coming down the hallway from the garage, slightly damp, grocery sacks in hand, when he reached the kitchen.

"Here, let me help you." He sprinted toward her to take the bags and place them on the island.

"Thanks." She carefully hung her purse and her folded robe on the back of one of the bar chairs.

"Find everything you needed?"

"Yes."

She wouldn't meet his gaze. "No trouble with the Porsche?"

"No."

He rubbed the back of his neck and drew in a long breath. "Look, I'm sorry about earlier. I shouldn't have done that. Kissed you, I mean." Like he needed to spell it out.

Maggie nodded silently and began taking items out of the bags and placing them carefully on the island top. Still not looking at him. Her unease was palpable.

He'd really messed things up.

"It won't happen again."

She finally looked at him, her brown eyes studying him for a long moment. "We're strictly friends," she murmured. "That's what we agreed."

He hated seeing her so withdrawn. "Yes, I know. It was wrong and I'm sorry." Had he ever had to apologize for kissing someone before? He didn't think so. But this was Maggie and he'd changed the game plan on her so it was up to him to make it right. He watched her put cold items in the refrigerator, carefully fold the bags and then arrange the rest of her purchases on the island in some order that apparently made sense to her. He waited. He realized he was holding his breath. He swallowed. "We're okay?"

Finally lifting her gaze to his, she rubbed the sides of her arms and gave him a small smile that didn't quite reach her eyes. "We're okay."

Garrett felt light headed with relief.

"On one condition," she added.

Anything. Whatever she wanted. "What's that?"

"Don't you aim anymore of that NFL's-hottest-quarterback magic sorcery at me again, all right? You keep that stuff bottled up on a shelf somewhere."

Now there was her real smile. Thank God. His tension disappeared and he felt downright giddy. He nodded vigorously. "Right. Got it."

"Okay, then. Where's Lilah?"

"Asleep inside the fort." He didn't want to remind her about the fort so he quickly changed the subject. "What's this?" He picked up a little bottle of what looked like candy.

"Sprinkles for cookies."

He picked up a tapered wooden stick. "And this?"

She made a face at him. "That's a rolling pin. You've never seen a rolling pin?"

"I was afraid it was a weapon." He swung it like a nun chuck. "You could take me out with this."

When Maggie burst out laughing, he felt like he'd thrown a Hail Mary for a winning touchdown.

"Give me that, you goober, before you hurt yourself." She took it from him and put it on the island.

Man, he was relieved he hadn't completely fucked things up. For a split second there, he'd felt like a little kid again, drowning in the helpless kind of tension that used to tie his guts in knots. He hadn't felt that way in years.

But it was good now. All good.

Grinning, he leaned forward, resting his forearms on the granite top. "What kind of cookies are you going to make?"

"You'll have to wait and see. Where are your bowls?"

He circled the island, opened a cabinet and pulled out a nest of mixing bowls. "Here."

"Perfect. Here, unwrap these for me and put them in the big one." She handed him a box of butter.

"Bossy." He tore the box open and began prying the paper off the sticks of butter.

"I heard that." She gave him narrowed side-eye.

"You were supposed to. I hope you're making a lot. Don't forget some of the guys are coming over tonight for poker." As soon as he said it, he realized it sounded like something a middle-aged husband would say.

"I remember. What time?"

He reached for another bottle of cookie sprinkles. "We start at eight so they'll start showing up a little before that." Unscrewing the top, he shook some sprinkles into his hand and tossed them in his mouth.

"Give me that." Maggie took the bottle away from him. "That's pure sugar. So what are you doing for snacks?"

"Snacks?"

She stopped arranging the groceries and looked at him. "Don't you have snacks for them? Do I need to go back to the store?"

Garrett felt warmth exploding in his chest. "I ordered some wings and stuff."

She nodded at him approvingly. "Good. Now, I know I saw a hand mixer somewhere."

"Been in my drawers?" That sounded bad. He straightened and circled the island to pull open a cabinet drawer. "This?" He held up a mixer.

"Yep." She took it from him.

"Wait a minute. I've got one of those big ones somewhere." He ducked into the pantry and came back out with a copper stand mixer that had been sitting in the same spot since he'd moved into the house. "Is this better?"

Maggie's eyes widened. "Oh my stars, that's the most beautiful mixer I've ever seen."

He laughed. "You can have it, if you want."

She made room for it on the top of the island and motioned for him to hurry up and set it down. "Don't think I won't take you up on that. Do you think they'd let me bring it as a carry on?"

He watched her unlock and admire the steel bowl, then examine the attachments. "You're more excited about a mixer than my car. There's something wrong with you."

She gave him a playful shove but then frowned and side stepped away from him.

Damn, he hated that she was uncomfortable messing around with him now.

"I was scared to death driving your car, especially in the rain."

"I was glad you took it instead of the truck. It's a lot easier to park."

She chuckled. "Especially when you park it at the farthest edge of the parking lot."

"Why'd you do that?"

She gave him a look. "I wasn't about to take a chance of bringing that thing back with a scratch."

"That's why you came back wet?" he frowned.

"Not very wet." She turned away to put the mixer bowl and attachments in the sink.

She had walked across a parking lot in the rain to avoid the possibility of a scratch on his car. A stupid car. Garrett looked at her, standing at his sink, in his house, in her pink shorts and purple socks, and those funny pigtails. He had to fight the urge to cross the short distance between them and gather her into his arms. He almost ached with it. It wasn't a sexual need, it was something else, something he couldn't define. All he knew was if he followed through on it, he'd destroy the easy rapport they'd managed to salvage. If anything was going to happen between them, she was going to have to make the first move.

He didn't want to think about how it would feel if she never made the first move.

God, he was fucked.

"I'm going to go check on Lilah," he said, his throat thick.

"Good idea," she replied.

He stood there a moment longer, looking at her, then turned and escaped.

Chapter 13

The front doorbell rang and Garrett was down in the game room so Maggie wiped her hands on a dishcloth and hurried to the foyer. When she opened the door, the solid wall of muscle filling the door was a bit startling and the five men crowded there looked surprised to see her, too. She recognized three of the five from the beach house and judging by their wide grins, they remembered her as well.

"Hey, look, it's our cheerleader," one of them said, eyes twinkling.

Maggie laughed. "Yep, that's me. Hi, guys. Garrett's downstairs already. Dominic, Wayne and Demario, right? Nice to see you again."

"Nice to see you, too," Dominic the Italian Elvis said, surprising her with a hug. "This is Matt Downey and Kris Thomas," he added, gesturing to the two other men. "They're big fans of the team, too." He winked at her.

"Saints or Renegades?" she joked, and they laughed. "I'm Maggie," she told Matt and Kris, shaking their huge hands. "Come on in."

"Didn't know you were here." Dominic's curiosity was evident.

"Just helping Garrett with his niece for a couple of days." She led them towards the kitchen and nodded toward Lilah, perched on a barstool at the island. She was smearing pink icing on a sugar cookie, her small face furrowed with concentration. "Lilah, these are some of Uncle Garrett's friends."

Lilah beamed at them, giggling when they took turns bumping fists with her.

"Maggie saved a kid from drowning," Wayne told Matt and Kris. "Just last week in Florida."

"Seriously?" Matt said.

"Cool," Kris added, nodding at her.

Embarrassed, Maggie changed the subject. "We've been baking cookies and now we're decorating them."

They came closer to the island and leaned over, eyeing the tray of cookies, bowls of tinted icing and bottles of sprinkles with interest.

"Help yourself. We baked a double batch so there's plenty."

"Can I try?" Demario nodded at the mess on the island with a hopeful grin.

Maggie smiled. "Sure. Here, I'll show you. Spread the icing on like this." She spread icing on a cookie with the back of a spoon. "Then shake sprinkles on before the icing hardens."

"I got this," Demario said, following her example. He picked up a cookie and carefully spread blue icing on top. The cookie looked tiny in his huge hand. He carefully shook blue sprinkles on top and then gave her a gold-toothed grin. Maggie nodded approvingly.

Matt picked up a cookie hesitantly.

"Do pink," Lilah encouraged him, licking icing off of her fingers.

In moments the men were circling the island around Lilah, vying for their choices of colors and ribbing one another good-naturedly over their results. Maggie was amused to discover that overseeing their efforts wasn't all that different from refereeing her kindergarten students.

"Give me some of those." Kris gestured toward the jar in

front of Wayne.

"Back off. I'm using them," Wayne leaned over to gently shake multicolored flower sprinkles onto his cookie. "Wait your turn, man."

Kris glared at him. "You got to share, dude." He reached for the jar, which Wayne swiftly moved out of reach.

Yikes, too much testosterone and not enough sprinkles. "How about the rainbow ones?" Maggie quickly pushed the bowl of rainbow sprinkles to him. Looking up, she saw Garrett standing just inside the kitchen, a look of amusement on his face.

"Hey, you." She waved a spoon at him. "We're decorating cookies."

He stepped closer, taking in the sight of his five oversized teammates bent over the island armed with spoons and cookies. "I see that."

"Hey, champ, check this out." Dominic held up a cookie for Garrett's review, and then bit it in half, grinning.

Garrett reached the island and shook his head at the icing in Lilah's hair. "Having fun, kid?"

She beamed at him. "Cookies are fun." She picked one up to show him. "This one I did. Eat it," she commanded, holding it up toward his face."

He leaned down and bit the cookie. "Mmm," he said, chewing. "That's a great cookie. You did a good job." He took the cookie and took another bite.

"Maggie teached me." Lilah returned her attention to the cookie she was working on, her little brow furrowed in concentration. "Maggie knows about cookies."

"She does, does she?" Garrett turned toward Maggie, cookie in hand. The warm smile on his face made Maggie's toes curl just a little. Her brain knew that holding onto the whole friends-only scenario was vital but her meddlesome hormones had taken that memo and tossed it in the shredder. She looked away and concentrated on filling a plate with cookies.

"So do you guys want to decorate cookies or play poker?"

"I don't know, man, these cookies are off the chain." Wayne grinned at him. "What you got downstairs that's better?"

"He'd better have a lot of Chivas," Matt said, stuffing a whole cookie in his mouth.

"Yeah, otherwise I'm sticking with Maggie," Dominic added, playfully putting his arm around her.

Laughing, Maggie stepped out of his embrace and passed the plate of cookies to Garrett. "Here, lure them downstairs with this, and I'll bring some more down in a bit."

Garrett shot a narrowed glance at Dominic and took the plate. "The food should be here any minute. It's paid for, just yell and I'll come up and get it."

"Got it," she said easily. "Y'all have fun."

He looked at Maggie, comfortable with his friends, comfortable in his kitchen, and felt like his grip on what was safe and what was necessary was slipping away.

Maggie stared at the photo on the Facebook post with an open mouth and unbelieving eyes.

No.

Not possible.

He hadn't.

He couldn't have.

But here was the proof, right here on social media.

A photo of a beaming Mason and his new bride.

His new bride.

After she'd tucked Lilah in bed and cleaned up the kitchen, she'd plopped down on the sofa with Dude and Buddy to catch up on messages and emails. She should've known something was up by the sheer number of texts waiting for her.

But this?

THIS?

So many thoughts were scrambling around in her head that she couldn't focus. She felt like she was being squeezed by some whole-body vise and everything around her fell away until all she could see was the photo.

Of Mason and the gorgeous, sultry woman he'd just started dating.

Of Mason's hand resting lightly on the woman's rounded stomach.

Mason's pregnant bride.

Mason's FREAKING VERY PREGNANT BRIDE.

After their usual evening of cutthroat poker, good-natured insults, and too much Chivas, his buddies were gone and the house was quiet. Poker night was always entertaining and normally he was a good host but tonight he'd been distracted. And glad to see his teammates finally make their noisy way out.

He headed to the kitchen to check that the back doors were locked before setting the alarm. The kitchen was neat as a pin, which must have taken some effort, considering the mess Maggie and Lilah had created earlier. The only remaining evidence was a final plate of cookies on the island, covered with plastic wrap.

He smiled, remembering the startling sight of his teammates fighting over candy sprinkles with Maggie handing out cookies and praise. He wasn't at all surprised at how quickly she had won them over. Anyone around her for even a few minutes got caught in her friendly orbit.

In fact, Dom had been a little too charmed. He didn't like it at all when Dom put his arm around Maggie in the kitchen, and when she'd showed up downstairs a little later with a second plate of cookies, Dom had fallen over himself trying to get to her first, laying on the compliments. He didn't want him eyeing Maggie like that. Dom might be a player now but he came from a huge Italian family that was all about marriage and children, right up Maggie's alley. And he knew, from personal experience now, that Maggie had a way of slipping under your skin and making you think about things differently.

No, he didn't want Dom anywhere near Maggie.

She hadn't seemed overly taken with him, though. In fact, when she came downstairs she'd seemed a little subdued, out of sorts. Un-Maggie-like. He'd wanted to find out if something was wrong but it was his turn to deal and the guys were ready so he couldn't follow her back upstairs like he wanted to. At the first opportunity, he'd jogged upstairs to check on her but all the lights were out.

And now he wouldn't see her again until morning.

It had felt different tonight, playing poker with the guys, knowing she was upstairs. He hadn't played worth a damn, either, to his teammate's delight.

He had the uneasy feeling that he was losing focus on more than poker night.

Just a couple more days and she'd be gone, and that was a good thing.

Well, it was supposed to be a good thing.

He didn't like thinking about it.

He worked the plastic off of the plate and snagged a cookie before continuing on his rounds. At the back door he noticed a light still on by the pool. He saw Dude and Buddy lying near the hot tub end next to a shadowy figure. He leaned forward and squinted.

Maggie, outside at this time of night? It was past two in the morning; she should have been asleep hours ago.

He quietly eased through the French doors. Yep, there she was. Sitting on the stone ledge above the hot tub, her feet dangling in the water. She was wearing earbuds and was armed with a spoon and a bucket of ice cream. He drew closer, quietly.

"…I wish I could live a little more," she was singing softly in a hiccupy, off-key voice, "look up to the sky, not just the floor – " deep breath – "I feel like my life is flashing by –" She nodded her head in time to the music only she could hear. "All I can do is watch and cry," she finished with a wave of the spoon, and then burst into tears.

What the hell? Something was really wrong. Was it his fault? He moved closer, feeling a little panicky.

Dude and Buddy noticed him and bounded up to greet him. Absently he reached down to pat them. "What's going on here, guys?"

Maggie's eyes opened. She blinked when she saw him and gave a little shriek. "Garrett!" She plucked the earbuds out of her ears and swiped at her face. "What are you doing?" She looked at him accusingly and the spoon slipped out of her hand and splashed into the hot tub. She looked down in horror. "My spoon!" And then back at him. "You made me drop it!"

She was – was she drunk? She sure sounded drunk. He saw the bottle of Baileys on her left side and it started to make sense. "I'll get another spoon," he said quickly. "Why don't you come inside with me?"

"Because I am very, very comfortable," she said stiffly. "And I don't need a spoon." She lifted the bottle of Baileys, sloshed a large amount straight into the container, set the bottle down and then lifted the container to her mouth.

Garrett watched in open-mouthed amazement.

"Mmm." She set it down at her side and swiped at her ice cream and Bailey's moustache with the back of her hand.

Well, if she wouldn't come inside, he'd stay outside. Toeing off his shoes, he hopped down to sit beside her on the stone ledge. Her eyes were red and puffy and the damp tracks down her cheeks twisted something inside him.

"What're you doing?" She frowned at him.

"Nothing. Let me try it." He nodded toward the container.

She looked at him suspiciously. "There isn't much left."

"Just one taste."

Grudgingly she handed it to him. He nodded toward the bottle. Sighing, she handed it to him as well. He sloshed another healthy amount in and swirled the alcohol into the remaining ice cream. What the hell. He lifted it and carefully drank from the container, too.

Well, damn. It was good. "Mmm."

She brightened like a star. "Right?" She reached for it.

He held it away from her. "I want the rest."

She looked like she wanted to argue and then slumped a little. "Fine. I stole it from you anyway, did you know that? From your liquor thing. And did you know you have so much ice cream in your freezer? Like, so much ice cream?" She held her arms out to show how much.

"I like ice cream." He tried not to smile.

"You like bacon, too," she said nonsensically.

He couldn't contain the smile any longer. "Yeah, I like bacon, too."

"Are you going to finish it or not?" She elbowed him, nodding toward the container. "'Cause I want it, if you don't."

"Yes, Maggie, I am." A spoon really would be useful, though. He peered down into the hot tub and decided against retrieving it. Dumping the rest of the Baileys into the carton, he swirled the contents together with a finger and sipped at the edge of the carton again. "So, you want to tell me what's going on?"

Her mood changed instantly. "No," she said haughtily. "I absolutely do not want to tell you what is going on."

Drunk Maggie was cute as fuck but he had to get to the bottom of this and make whatever it was better. "Why not?"

"I do not have to have a reason," she continued, her nose in the air. "You don't get to know everything."

"Come on, Maggie, tell me what's the matter. It can't be that bad."

She glared at him. "Fine. I'll tell you since you're obiously – obliously –" She huffed in annoyance at her inability to get the word out. "Since you're not going to shut up about it. How would you feel if the man you were supposed to be marrying, got married to someone else, on almost exactly the same day you were going to marry him?"

It took him a second to follow, and then he had it. "Mason got married today?" Careful, careful here. He knew he couldn't show any pleasure at the news, even though he wanted to pump his fist in the air.

"Yes!" she exclaimed. "And I don't even know why I care!" Her lower lip quivered. "Do you want to know why he dumped me, Garrett?"

"Do you want me to know why?" he asked carefully.

"I'll tell you why." Her eyes narrowed. "Because I wasn't exciting enough. He didn't feel sparks anymore. Sparks. He got married today, in a really big hurry, to someone who gives him sparks. I know, because tonight I saw pictures his stupid friends put all over Facebook. And do you know why they got married in such a freaking hurry?"

Garrett set the ice cream carton down carefully.

"Because she's pregnant!" Maggie announced furiously, her hands fisting. "He was cheating on me before we broke up! Can you even believe that? Can you? I don't want him, the stinking bastard. But it's not fair. Why should he get to have a baby? I'm the one who wants a baby. I don't want him, I really don't, and I don't want his baby because he's a stinking bastard but I am really, really, really mad! And this all makes me feel like such a loser." She drew in a rattling breath. "I'm mad, and I'm boring, and I'm a loser." She sat forward, hunching her shoulders, her expression the definition of dejected. "I hate feeling like this."

Where did he even begin? "You're none of those things," he began comfortingly, putting his arm around her shoulder.

"Don't do that," she warned him, shaking him off. "Keep that

– that – hottest quarterback stuff away from me, remember?"

He had to turn almost completely around for a second to hide his smile. "Well, you have every right to be mad, and that's okay. But you're not a loser and you're the least boring person I know."

She crumpled like a tissue and leaned into him. "No, I'm not, Garrett. I'm so boring." Tears welled up in her eyes. "I've never done so many things."

He loved the feel of her next to him and he wished he could wipe those tears away but he was afraid to do anything to set her off. "What are you talking about? The very first day I met you, you saved a little girl's life. What about that?"

She waved his remark away. "I've never gotten a ticket, I've never smoked marijuana, I've never stayed out all night, I've never played strip poker, I've never danced on a table top, I've never even gone to the movies by myself. I'm so lame."

"Do you want to play strip poker?" He was teasing her, of course he was, trying to make her laugh, but he'd be lying if he didn't admit the idea of playing strip poker with Maggie was enticing. Stupid, reckless, dangerous, but pretty damned enticing.

She stopped and looked at him. "No! Yes! I don't know! What are you talking about?"

"Strip poker. We can cross that one off your bucket list tonight." He waggled his eyebrows at her.

She looked at him for a long minute and then giggled. "No, we can't do that."

That drunken giggle had to be the best thing he'd ever heard. "Why not?"

"Because that would be very, very, very dangerous." She poked his chest with each "very."

He rubbed his chest with his free hand. "Why would it be very, very, very dangerous?"

She looked worried, and then giggled again. "Okay, I'll tell you why. Because I have the –" she broke off.

"You have the what?" he asked.

She shook her head vehemently. "No, I can't tell you."

"Of course you can tell me. What do you have, Maggie?"

She bit her lip. "It's a secret," she said in a whisper.

He bent his head closer toward her. "Tell me," he whispered back. "I can keep a secret. Please."

She squinted at him for a long moment, then leaned toward him and put her lips by his ear. "Remember today? Under the table? When you kissed me?"

He wasn't likely to forget. Even now, just thinking about it, made his blood rush south. "What about it?"

"I had the hots for you so bad." Her breath was warm in his ear. "So bad. Like, you wouldn't believe how bad. But it would ruin everything if you knew."

Garrett choked back a laugh and she blinked, and then looked at him in abrupt, momentarily sober horror. "Oh my God," she managed. "OhmyGodohmyGodohmyGod." She struggled to stand up. She made it to her feet and backed away from him, swaying slightly.

"Wait, Maggie." He hopped up. "Wait a minute, please."

Her eyes huge, she was still mouthing "oh my God" but no noise was coming out.

He held his hands out. This was huge. He couldn't let her get away. "Wait, listen –"

She turned on her heel and sped toward the house. By the time he reached the door, he could hear her stumbling up the staircase, and by the time he jogged up the stairs, she'd closed the door to the room she shared with Lilah. He had no doubt she had also turned the lock.

He stood there, outside the door, and grinned.

Maggie had the hots for him.

Chapter 14

Maggie woke painfully; her eyes crusty, her mouth sour, and her head aching like someone had wrapped it with rubber bands like one of those watermelons on YouTube. She carefully moved her hand toward the bedside table and felt for her phone. Bringing it to her face, she squinted against the light to check the time.

Oh dear Lord. It was almost noon. Who was taking care of Lilah?

Garrett.

A wave of horror swept over her as she recalled the night before, and she moaned, clamping her pillow over her face. Had she really told him that she had the hots for him? She had actually used the words 'the hots'? She moaned again, a long, self-loathing, stomach rumbling moan.

How could she ever face him? Could she pretend she had no memory of her confession? Would he let her get away with that?

Thank God his sister was coming back today. Could she pack her bag and call for an Uber and sneak out of the house? Could she escape before she had to face him?

Her stomach heaved, her eyes widened, and she stumbled out of bed and lurched to the bathroom, where she spent the next few minutes draped over the toilet.

She deserved to be sick.

She had been so distraught when she saw the photos of Mason and his pregnant bride online. She had felt alone and sad and angry, but to snoop through Garrett's liquor cabinet and drink an entire bottle of Baileys – with a carton of Blue Bell vanilla no less – and to be discovered outside wailing along with Adele; well, that alone would have been more than enough humiliation, but the rest of it – the drunken confession whispered in his ear – it was the most horrific humiliating thing she'd ever done. It brought a new universe of meaning to the definition of horrific humiliation.

How was she ever going to face him?

She huddled there a few more minutes, resting her hot cheek against the cool porcelain, trying to come up with a plan. She would clean herself up, go downstairs, and pretend it was all a big joke. Remind him that he was the NFL's hottest quarterback and it was to be expected that she'd eventually collapse in the face of his legendary appeal.

Or should she just admit it was true, but explain that she didn't have any expectations. Because she didn't. He was like the sun and she was like Pluto. Poor Pluto, so small and insignificant it wasn't even considered a real planet anymore. Or like oil and water. Oil and water did not mix, everyone knew that. Even if oil was tall and golden and gorgeous and had an eyebrow that could do tricks. Oil and water could only be friends.

Shuffling back into the bedroom with her hands pressed to her temples, she spied a bottle of water on her bedside table, along with a package of Advil. She blinked at it. Great, just great. Garrett must have slipped into her room at some point and left them for her, and God only knew what she had looked like. Snoring, drooling, starfished across the bed like roadkill. Probably all of the above.

After taking a long shower and getting dressed very slowly, very gingerly, Maggie was as ready as she would ever be to venture downstairs. She could hear Garrett and Lilah in the kitchen; Lilah's high pitched chatter and Garrett's low pitched replies. She edged into the room to see Garrett presenting Lilah with a bowl of orange slices.

"Did I do it right?" Just the sound of his voice sent quivers down to her toes.

Lilah touched an orange slice with one finger and beamed at him. "Yes," she said, with the air of a princess granting a favor to a peasant. "Just right."

"Thank you, kiddo." He bent to drop a kiss on the top of her head. Turning to toss the peelings into the trash, he spied Maggie creeping into the room. "Hey Maggie," he said casually. "We've just had lunch."

"Maggie!" Lilah crowed. "Uncle Garrett's done me an orange." She popped a wedge in her mouth. "Mmm."

"That's nice," Keeping her head down, Maggie slid onto the bar chair beside Lilah. Dude and Buddy bumped one another vigorously to try to get closest to her. "Good boys," she murmured, patting them on their massive velvety heads.

Wordlessly, Garrett withdrew a sports drink from the refrigerator and handed it to her.

"Thanks." She unscrewed the bottle and lifted it to her lips, looking anywhere but in his direction.

"When you finish your orange, you can go watch cartoons," Garrett told Lilah. Maggie smiled in spite of herself as Lilah crammed the last two orange slices in her mouth and sped over to the sofa.

He followed her, turned the television on, and then returned to prop a lean hip on the bar chair that Lilah had vacated. Close to her. Very close to her. "So," he began casually, "how do you feel?"

Finally glancing up, she found him smiling just the tiniest bit. "Like death," she murmured, looking away again, studying the bottle in her hands.

"Sorry to hear it." He straightened. "You'll feel better after you eat something. Maybe a nice greasy cheeseburger?"

Closing her eyes and dropping her head down, she swallowed and held up a hand to stop him talking.

She heard a low huff of amusement, then felt him move and then his big hands slid onto her shoulders. She froze, stiffening when he swept her hair to the side, and even more when he began kneading her neck and shoulders, squeezing and digging into her muscles. He had magic fingers. Magic eyebrow, magic fingers. He probably had a magic –

No. Not going there.

She dropped her head forward and it was all she could do to press her lips together to keep from moaning, especially when he applied pressure in little circles with his palms. Mercy. Her goosebumps had goosebumps. And then, oh dear Lord, he pushed his fingers through her hair and rubbed the back of her skull with his thumbs. This time a little moan did escape because it felt so freaking amazing. She felt him hesitate for a moment, then continue for another few moments before giving her shoulders one last little squeeze.

"Better?" he asked casually, as if his big old warm hands hadn't just reduced her to mush. She blinked at him and nodded. She did feel better.

"Finish your Gatorade. That'll help."

Obediently she drank the rest of the sports drink.

This was torture. Well, not the massage, that was heaven, but the way he was acting normal. Was he going to pretend last night hadn't happened? That he hadn't heard her humiliating confession? Could she be so lucky?

"Emily called." He put Lilah's lunch plate into the dishwasher. "She should be here in a little while. I've been gathering up Lilah's toys and stuff. Are you up to picking up her stuff in your room?"

Maggie felt an easing in her chest. Maybe he wasn't going to bring it up. Maybe they could pretend she'd never said a word. "Of course," she said. "It won't take long."

He gave her a brisk nod. "Great." He opened the refrigerator, took out a bottle of water, and passed it to her. "Keep hydrating. Got to get all that ice cream out of your system."

Maggie shot a quick glance at him and he winked.

Gah.

"But I don't wanna go!" Lilah wailed. "I wanna stay more with Uncle Garrett! I wanna go swimmin' some more with Maggie!"

Garrett couldn't help laughing. It seemed that Lilah was about to repeat her award-winning pink demon performance, but his sister would have to deal with it. It was nice to be on the flip side of the tantrum this time.

He was happy to see Emily, but he'd be even happier when she and Lilah were on their way back to Santa Fe. He wanted to focus on Maggie. He hadn't been able to go to sleep after her confession. He'd tossed and turned, reminding himself of all the reasons he couldn't get involved with her. But the next thing he knew, he was upstairs slipping inside the room she shared with Lilah. Just to leave some pain reliever and water, just to make sure she was okay. She'd still been fully dressed, face down on top of her covers. He'd carefully worked the covers over her and then just stood there a few minutes, watching her sleep and wondering what in the world he was going to do with her.

Maggie, who had burst into his life and lit it up with her personality; Maggie, who charmed everyone lucky enough to land in her path.

Maggie, who was doing her best today to avoid meeting his gaze.

He knew she was agonizing over her tipsy confession, worried about what he was going to say or do in response. He didn't know what he was going to do. His plan to keep his distance had exploded in his face. They didn't want the same things but he was tired of fighting the way he felt about her. Knowing that she was attracted to him changed the game but he didn't know the playbook. He knew a hundred ways to brush women off, but he didn't have one good idea of how to coax Maggie closer without freaking her out in the process.

She'd sure freaked out last night. All he had to do was think about her horrified expression and those silent "oh my God's" stuck on repeat and he couldn't help grinning.

"You stop that right this minute!" Emily crouched to wrestle with her daughter who was now clamped onto Maggie's leg like a sloth. "If you don't stop, we're leaving all your new things here and Uncle Garrett's going to find some other nice little girl to give them to."

Lilah closed her mouth and glared suspiciously at her mother.

Garrett exchanged an amused glance with Maggie. "I'd never do that, kiddo," he told Lilah. She beamed at him.

"You're not helping." Emily tried not to smile. "All this stuff! I don't know if all of it will even fit in the car. Are you sure you don't want to keep some of it here for the next time you babysit?"

"I'll buy her new stuff next time she comes." He hunkered down and held his arms out to Lilah.

Emily's eyes widened. "I was joking! Do you mean you'd babysit again?"

"Absolutely." He was pleased when Lilah let go of Maggie and let him pick her up. He loved how she patted his cheeks every time she was close enough to his face. He gave her a little boop on the nose and she giggled.

Emily gaped at them, and then at Maggie. "You heard it, too, didn't you?"

"I did." Maggie smiled.

"And the pictures," Emily said, gesturing to her phone, referring to the photos that Maggie had just sent to her. "They're wonderful! Thank you so much for taking them."

Garrett hadn't realized that Maggie had taken photos during the past three days; Lilah splashing in the pool, painting rocks, petting the dogs. It hadn't even occurred to him. He gazed at her, thinking of all the thoughtful little things she did all the time. He noticed Emily eyeing him with interest. "I'll take this stuff out," he said hurriedly, putting Lilah back on her feet. "Want to help, Lilah?" He picked up the two totes crammed with playthings. "Is your car unlocked?"

"Yes, and the keys are on the console." Emily said. "And Garrett? Would you mind starting it and listening to the engine for a minute? I heard a funny sound a couple of miles back."

He frowned. "What kind of sound?"

"A squeaky sound," she replied. "It sounded like it was coming from the front."

"Okay." He turned and left the room, arms full, Lilah skipping next to him.

Emily turned to Maggie as soon as Garrett was out of earshot. "That'll keep him busy for a minute. I wanted to talk to you. What in the world have you done to him?"

Maggie blinked. "What do you mean?"

Emily beamed at her. "He's so happy!"

"I think he really enjoyed spending time with Lilah," Maggie said uncertainly.

Emily shook her head. "No, well, yes, I hope he did. But that's not it." She took Maggie's hand. "Garrett's been closed off for so long. He's finally opening up again. He's relaxed. He's smiling and laughing. You have no idea how long it's been since I've seen him laughing."

Maggie bit her lip. "I don't think it has anything to do with me."

"I think it has everything to do with you!" Emily insisted. "I know it's none of my business, but are y'all –" She lifted her eyebrows suggestively.

Uh oh. She didn't know what to say. "No, we're just friends." Emily didn't need to know about those two tiny kisses.

Emily didn't look convinced at all.

"Really," Maggie added.

"I see the way he looks at you." Emily crossed her arms. "I've never seen him look at anyone like that before. You do like him, don't you?"

This was the weirdest conversation. "Of course I do. As a friend," she clarified.

"Do you already have a boyfriend?"

"No," Maggie said faintly. "I was engaged until just recently, though. Really recently."

Emily nodded but continued to study her. "Well, I'm glad you're not anymore."

Maggie blinked.

Emily grimaced. "I mean that in a good way."

Maggie wished really hard that Garrett would return and save her from this conversation. "He's lucky to have you for a sister," she deflected.

Emily was un-deflectable. "I'm lucky to have him for a brother. He's the best, but I'm sure you can see that for yourself. I think you make a great couple."

Maggie gaped at her. This conversation was really going off the rails. Garrett really, really needed to come back inside. Or else she needed to escape.

"I just remembered," she said quickly, "Lilah's swimming suit is hanging in the laundry room. I'll go get it."

Garrett closed the front door and turned toward Maggie. "So." His gaze was fixed on her.

"So," Maggie repeated awkwardly. The air between them in the foyer suddenly felt thick and she couldn't breathe properly. "Emily's nice."

"Emily's great." He took a step towards her and propped his arms on the balustrade. "I was thinking, now that it's just the two of us and the weather's nice, how about a lazy grown-up afternoon by the pool? Or would you rather go someplace? See a little more of Denver than just my house?"

Maggie twisted her hands together. Going someplace would involve other people, which would be a very good thing. Lazy pool time would involve a shirtless Garrett and possibly the application of suntan lotion.

"Lazy pool time sounds nice."

"Great. I know a place close by that makes great burgers so I'm going to run pick up some lunch for us. It won't take long. We'll eat by the pool. Sound okay?"

"Will you be safe from people bothering you? Would you rather I go pick them up?"

He flashed a grin that curled her toes. "Yeah, I'll be safe. You just relax and I'll be right back." He started off toward the kitchen and was soon out of sight, but then he called back to her. "Do you want me to get some more vanilla ice cream and Baileys?"

Oh, crap. There it was. "No, thank you," she called back.

"Just checking."

Maggie could hear the grin in his voice. Hurrying to her room, she changed into her bikini, and then debated for way too long about whether or not to wear a t-shirt, and then she'd rushed to shave her legs, and then wondered if she should wash her hair but decided that was stupid because she'd only be getting it wet again. She had just redone her ponytail for the third time, located her sunglasses, and swiped on a bit of waterproof mascara when she glanced out of the window and saw him easing back down the driveway, so she rushed downstairs and out the French doors to make it appear she had been lounging casually since he left. Like she wasn't freaked out at all at the prospect of pool time alone with him.

She didn't know why she was going to all that fuss and bother, she really didn't. Nothing was going to happen.

Her heart was still thumping like a bass when she heard the door open. She opened her eyes as if she'd been dozing and then sat up in what she hoped was a graceful manner.

And, oh, my, God. Thank goodness she was already sitting down.

Garrett was heading toward her, wearing black sunglasses and low slung black swim shorts that left very little to the imagination. He was all tousled dark hair, wide shoulders, chiseled abs, and long legs. As if that wasn't enough to make her mouth go as dry as sandpaper, the flat plane of his belly angling in toward his pelvis was hammering the final nail in the coffin of her fortitude.

She just couldn't look at him. That's all there was to it. Shakily she reached for her sunglasses and slipped them on. She wished they were the reflective state trooper kind that would let her gawk at him without his knowledge.

Carrying a paper bag in one hand and two bottles of water in the other, he stopped beside her. With a particularly interesting part of his anatomy exactly at eye level.

"Hey."

"Hey." The voice of her imaginary sexy-evil twin replied in a throaty Scarlett Johannsen voice. Her actual response came out sounding much more like Minnie Mouse.

"Hungry?"

"Starving." Make that Minnie Mouse being strangled.

He set the two bottles on the ground and sat on the chaise beside her. "You're in for a treat." He dug into the bag. "I don't get these often but sometimes nothing else will do." He pulled out a burger wrapped in white paper and handed it to her. "Check that out."

Maggie unwrapped the paper and sighed at the sight of the enormous cheeseburger with all the trimmings. It smelled divine. Yes, yes, and yes. She took a big bite. "Mmm," she said, nodding at him.

"Right?" He grinned at her and sat back on his chaise, stretching his long legs out before unwrapping his own burger. "Good for what ails you."

Was that another sly reference to her drunken state last night and hangover this morning? Maggie shot a sideways glance at him and was dismayed when he winked at her. She knew she'd eventually have to address the horror but she wanted to put it off as long as possible.

"Got fries, too." He shook the bag toward her and she reached in obediently. He put the bag on the ground between them and took a bite of his burger. "Yeah." He nodded with satisfaction. "This is all right. Sometimes needing to eat healthy all the time sucks."

Maggie reached into the bag for another French fry and bumped into his hand, reaching in, too. She picked up a fry only for him to steal it from her fingers. "Hey." She glared at him.

He pulled it out of the bag and ate it, grinning.

She reached in again, and he did the same thing. So that was how it was going to be. It made her smile. "You're doing that on purpose. Stop it."

"You stop it. You're committing a French fry neutral zone infraction."

"What does that even mean?"

"It means if you do it again, there's going to be a penalty."

"What kind of penalty?"

"Do it again and find out."

Maggie studied him, noting the glint in his eyes, and wondered if she had the nerve to call his bluff. She slowly reached her hand into the bag, keeping her eyes trained on his. He moved his hand into the bag just as slowly. She felt around for a fry and tried to pull it free, but he clamped onto it and tugged. Maggie laughed as it broke into two pieces. "Look what you did." She showed him the broken bit of French fry. "That's encroachment, isn't it? Or off-sides or something?"

He put his half fry in his mouth, put his burger aside and stood up, his eyes fixed on her.

"What are you doing?" A shiver ran up her spine at his stance, perfectly still, one hundred percent honed in on her. So that's what a quarterback looked like the instant before the snap. *Yikes.* Keeping her eyes on him, looking over her shoulder, Maggie turned and slowly eased her legs off the far side of the chaise.

He moved closer, stealthy and focused.

Maggie couldn't wipe the grin off of her face if she tried. She carefully set her burger down, stood and took a step to circle around the ends of the chairs. "You keep away from me."

He shook his head. "You were warned." Lunging toward her so quickly that she didn't have time to react, he caught her around her waist, picked her up and pivoted toward the pool.

"Unsportsmanlike conduct!" she shrieked, and then they hit the water.

Maggie came up sputtering and laughing, and reached out for the edge of the pool. Garrett was already there, his hair slicked back, grinning at her. "That was mean."

"That was fun," he corrected her, shaking water from his hair.

"Yes, it was." She stretched her arms along the edge of the pool. "You're fun. I'm going to miss you when I go home."

It hit her hard to realize how much she was going to miss him. It felt so easy and natural here, like it was where she belonged. She smiled at him, at his stupidly handsome face, emotion suddenly thick in her throat.

His expression changed so swiftly that she caught her breath. He was studying her with such intensity, as if he were memorizing her. His gaze dropped to her mouth for a long moment and then he blinked and gave her a half smile before pushing away from the edge to swim to the other side of the pool.

Pulling in a shaky breath, Maggie took the opportunity to climb out of the pool and return to her chaise. She watched him swim a couple of laps, slicing through the water. He hoisted himself out and dried off. That proved too much for her; those lean muscles rippling as he toweled off. She focused on her burger. It didn't take long for them to finish eating, both of them subdued. After crumpling the sandwich paper into a wad and dropping it into the bag, Garrett lowered the back of his chaise to a flat position and clasped his hands behind his head.

"No swimming for thirty minutes." He tipped his sunglasses onto his nose.

Maggie tried not to stare at his bulky shoulder muscles and washboard abs. "An hour." She sat up to release the latch on her own chair. "I always heard it was an hour."

"Such a know-it-all. An hour, then."

Maggie was glad he was teasing her again. She pressed the latch on her own chair but it wouldn't release.

"Are you having problems?" He raised his sunglasses to peer at her.

"Your chairs are stupid." She tried it again.

He sighed and sat up. Leaning over, he flicked the lever on her chair and it dropped with a noisy bang. "There. Now try to be quiet. I'm going to sleep."

Maggie bit back a laugh. He had changed so much in just a few short days from the somewhat stoic man she'd first met in Florida. She thought about what Emily had said, and wondered if there really was something to her remark about his new openness. The notion that she might have something to do with it was lovely. It was more likely that they were just more at ease around one another than they had been at the beginning, especially now that they were on the same friends-only page.

Friends only. Like they'd agreed, and then re-agreed after the tea party kiss incident.

It was pointless to consider anything else, no matter what her squirming lady parts said.

She wriggled around on the chaise until she was comfortable on her stomach, facing Garrett with her head resting on her crossed arms. If it weren't for the fact that she couldn't seem to stop sneaking glances at his long, lean, mostly bare body and that she couldn't seem to pull in enough air to breathe and that the warm sun on her skin was nothing compared to the heat sliding through her veins and pooling in her lady bits, it would be a perfectly pleasant, relaxed afternoon.

Maggie had fallen asleep so now he could gaze at her all he wanted. It was killing him, being this close to her, close enough to see her thick fringe of eyelashes, the light dusting of freckles on her shoulders, the flyaway hair trying to escape from her ponytail. Mere inches away from her curvy, tanned body in that little red bikini. He loved looking at her, studying her when she wasn't paying attention.

It was a good thing she was asleep, too, because he was growing hard and there was no hiding it in his swim shorts. He willed himself to relax, for his blood to cool, or else he'd have to jump back into the water and swim a few more laps.

He really wanted to talk about last night, about her staggering confession, but he was damned if he knew how he was going to do it. He was trying to wait her out, see if she would bring it up. So far she had successfully avoided the subject. He didn't want to push her. If he'd learned anything the last couple of days, it was that Maggie could be skittish.

He wasn't good at being patient, and time was running out. He closed his eyes and drew in a deep breath.

Was he even sure he wanted to push the subject? Maggie might be attracted to him but she was still a forever kind of girl and he was still a here-and-now kind of guy. All the talent and fame and success in the world couldn't help him where she was concerned. He couldn't offer what she wanted.

He flung an arm over his face and swallowed.

Maybe she had the right idea. Just leave it alone. He didn't want to be the next guy to hurt her. If she didn't bring it up, neither would he. She'd come to Denver to do him a huge favor and he wasn't going to complicate either one of their lives with changing the rules now.

Chapter 15

Garrett was usually happy to see Ty and Eleanor when they came to Denver, but would this meal ever end? Shifting slightly in the booth beside Maggie, Garrett glanced surreptitiously at his watch.

When Ty phoned earlier to invite them out to dinner, he would have gladly turned him down without a second thought but he wanted Maggie to have a say since she'd hardly been out of the house since her arrival. He was kind of bummed when she'd seemed delighted. Did that mean she was tired of being alone with him? He wasn't tired of being alone with her.

Watching her interact with Ty and Eleanor was fascinating, though. In the past when he brought other women to meet them for a meal there had been awkward lulls because his date either wasn't interested in engaging or monopolized the conversation. With Maggie and her bright interest in everything around her, the conversation never flagged. He'd even learned some things about Ty and Eleanor and their family that he hadn't known before.

That was Maggie for you. Shining her light on everyone she met. He'd spent a major part of the evening just looking at her, how she leaned forward when she was listening to Ty or Eleanor speak, the expressions she made when she tasted her food, and then there was that blissful little moan she gave when she tasted her dessert. That particular little noise had shot straight to his dick.

Luckily, Ty and Eleanor weren't the kind to go clubbing after dining out, and the bill had already been paid, so if they could just get through dessert without any more little moans, they could say their goodbyes and he'd have her to himself again.

For one more day.

"Want some?"

He looked at her, sitting close enough for him to smell her perfume. She was holding up a spoonful of cheesecake. He leaned closer to try it, and nodded. "That's good." He took the spoon from her to scoop up another taste. "Good choice."

She beamed at him. "Right?"

Garrett took a risk and squeezed her knee under the table. It would be nice to be able to keep his hand there, on her smooth, warm skin, to slide it up her thigh, bare under the skirt of her dress–

He took a long drink of water and willed the blood to abandon his dick and return to his brain.

"Well, this was fun." Eleanor pushed her own dessert plate back. "But this pregnant mama needs to go to bed."

Ty leaned over and kissed the top of his wife's head. "Well, you guys heard the boss."

Garrett glanced down and was relieved to see he was fit to leave. He and Maggie might have been able to maneuver their way quickly enough to the exit, but he and Ty together were hard to miss and it was inevitable that they were stopped a few times along the way for autographs and photos. He did his best to keep smiling as they worked their way toward the exit where Maggie and Eleanor patiently waited. Finally they were outside. Goodnights were exchanged and then they were on their way to his car.

"You were quiet tonight." Maggie clipped her seatbelt over her lap. "Is everything okay?"

"Absolutely." He started the engine and backed out of the parking space. "Did you have a good time?"

She nodded. "I like them both a lot. I can see that you and Ty are close."

"He's like a brother to me." Garrett pulled onto the road. "I wouldn't be where I am if it weren't for him."

"Really?" Maggie studied him.

He hesitated. He hadn't really meant to say that.

Maggie picked up on his long pause. "You don't have to explain," she said quickly.

The way she retreated whenever she thought she'd dug too deeply made him wince. "No, it's fine. It's just hard to think about what an immature prick I was when I was first drafted. There's a world of difference between college and pro. I had the skills but I didn't have the emotional maturity to fit in. The quarterback is a leader but I didn't trust my coaches or my teammates, and I made lots of stupid decisions. Then I got traded to Denver. I was pissed about being traded, on top of everything else, so friends were few and far between. Then one day, I pissed off the wrong person." He gave her a half smile. "Can you guess who?"

She smiled back at him. "Ty?"

"Yeah. First he very calmly broke my nose, and then he tossed me into his truck and drove me to his house where he sat me down and explained that my behavior was unacceptable and wasn't going to be tolerated any longer."

"He broke your nose?" Maggie looked horrified.

Garrett smiled ruefully at the memory. "It got my attention. I deserved it. From that day on, he started mentoring me, keeping me focused, keeping me out of trouble. I learned more about being a leader on the field from him than I did from anyone else. I didn't make it easy for him but he never gave up on me."

"He saw more in you than you saw in yourself."

Garrett looked over at her, surprised by her words and by the change in her tone. Her head was turned sharply away from him, as if she was looking out of the side window, and her hands were clasped tightly in her lap.

"Maggie?"

She didn't turn toward him.

"Hey." He lifted a hand from the steering wheel to touch her shoulder. She shook her head, still averting her face. He felt a twinge of apprehension. "What is it?"

She glanced at him and he saw her eyes were glistening.

"What is it?" he asked again, alarmed.

"I'm sorry," she said in a tight little voice. "It just pains me to think of you hurting like that."

His heart thumped. "You do understand that I was the asshole in that situation, right?"

She gave him a tiny, lop-sided smile. "Yes, I understand that. I'm thinking about what led you to that behavior in the beginning. I'm thinking about that little boy trying to cook dinner for his sister; how hard he's worked and how far he's come."

Garrett gripped the steering wheel tightly. How did she do that? How did she reach right in and see inside him? Now he was the one who couldn't look at her.

"Friends can hold hands, right?" she asked quietly beside him.

He reached out swiftly to capture her hand and held it carefully, on the dividing console, like a fragile trophy. He didn't trust himself to speak, and she turned her face toward the side window again, and he didn't let go until they reached his driveway.

Kicking off her shoes, Maggie sat down on the edge of her twin bed and covered her face with her hands. This was getting to be too hard. She should have stuck with her original plan and booked her flight home for tomorrow, not Monday. She needed to go home.

When Garrett told her the Hursts had invited them out for dinner, she thought it would make things easier. Give her something else to focus on for a little while, because spending all afternoon with him by the pool had been an exercise in both delight and frustration.

And a little bit of fear, too. She was afraid that, at some point, he was going to bring up last night's humiliating confession.

But he never did. And she didn't know if that was a good thing or a bad thing. She didn't know how he really felt about her. She wasn't sure how she really felt about him. They were calling it friendship but it felt like something else.

Was it because they'd been living in one another's pockets for the last few days? If she gathered up the courage to consider that it might be more, what possible difference would it make? She still had a life in Louisiana and dreams of marriage and children. He was still a larger-than-life professional athlete here in Colorado, adamantly opposed to commitment.

They'd been living in a little bubble, here in this house, but it wasn't the real world.

And they'd only known one another for nine days.

Nine days.

Maggie flopped backwards onto the bed and sighed.

Ten days ago she had been heartbroken over Mason. Mason! Who was less important to her now than a gnat in the wind.

And if she was that fickle, how could she trust anything she felt for Garrett?

She and Mason had drifted apart; she could see it now. But even in the beginning when things were good between them, when they made one another happy, it wasn't anything like how she felt with Garrett. Weak knees when he smiled. Breath catching when he winked. Blood thundering when he touched her.

Sharing a spoon tonight for dessert? Damp panties.

She'd hoped the distraction of dinner with Ty and Eleanor would give her a little clarity. She thought it would put their situation into perspective. But it hadn't helped at all. In fact, it had made matters worse. It felt so natural to sit beside him at the table, like they were a real couple.

And on the way home, when he'd shared some of his history

and his relationship with Ty, she'd gotten a glimpse behind his words and understood there was so much more to him than she would ever know. Dark things that still had power over him, things he kept closed up inside. She'd been overwhelmed with an inexplicable yearning to know more.

She'd taken a risk when she'd asked to hold his hand but she'd been so desperate to touch him. She didn't know what he was thinking, but the fact that he responded so quickly, and held her hand so tightly the rest of the way home, was like a song in her heart.

She was crazy about him.

And not because he was Uhtred and Thor and Wolverine and Aragorn all rolled into one, like some world-ending cosmic accident of masculine strength and beauty. Because he was thoughtful and kind and funny and he was a closet Harry Potter nerd. And sometimes he was mysterious and broody and that was pretty hot, too. And he loved dogs and he could cook and when he smiled at her, everything was right in her world.

He was everything but the white-picket fence.

Garrett eased toward the staircase and propped his arms on the balustrade. She'd been up there for a while now and he wasn't sure what to do. When they'd come inside from the garage, she had murmured something about changing clothes and that was the last he'd seen of her.

He wanted her to come back downstairs. "Maggie?" He took a couple of steps up the stairs. "Maggie?"

He heard a door opening. "I'm coming down," she called.

"Okay." He backed down the steps and returned to the den. He was opening the door for the dogs when she rounded the opening into the kitchen. Her face was scrubbed clean and she was barefoot in clingy yoga pants and a long, soft looking top with her hair piled on top of her head in a messy knot. She looked fresh and natural and perfect.

She was everything good, and he wasn't right for her.

"Hey." With one hand he rubbed at the little ache in his chest while the other was still on the door handle even though Dude and Buddy were already halfway across the room in her direction.

"Hey yourself." She leaned to pet the dogs.

"Thought maybe you fell asleep." He belatedly remembered to shut the door.

"And miss movie time? No way." She flashed her big smile at him. "Can I give them a treat?"

"Sure." He watched her open the pantry door and reach for the treat jar. Dude and Buddy danced around her as she fed them. It did something to his gut to see how at home she looked, how she knew where he kept things.

"Such good boys. I'm definitely going to adopt a dog as soon as I get home. If I'm lucky, I'll find one like these guys. My own little velvet hippo."

He felt that sharp pang again, the one he felt every time she mentioned going home.

Crossing the room to the den, she scooped up the fleece throw and sat down on the end of the sofa. Not in the middle like the other night. She was letting him know he had to keep his distance.

He had an idea. It was risky, and he couldn't believe he was willing to go to such cheesy lengths just to be close to her, but it was worth a shot. He put a hand on the small of his back and stretched a little, and rolled his shoulders for good measure, all the while making a face.

"What's wrong?" Maggie asked, her brow furrowed.

"I think I pulled something." He winced a little more.

She looked horrified. "From picking me up and throwing me in the pool?"

Damn, he didn't want her to think that at all. "No, it was

aching a little yesterday." He rolled his shoulders again. "I just need to lie down." Picking up a throw pillow, he sat on the sofa and sank back in her direction. Stretching his legs down the length of the sofa, he pushed the pillow behind his head and onto her lap.

There. "You don't mind, do you?" he asked straight-faced, looking up at her face, her mouth in a perfect "O".

"Uh –"

"It helps to have my head raised a little," he lied, lifting his arm to point the remote at the television. "I feel better already. Okay with you?"

"Yeah, okay. If it helps. Sure."

Fighting not to smile, he began flipping through the movie selections. "Hey, look, the Harry Potter marathon is still going on. The Order of the Phoenix just started."

What special hell was this? It had happened so fast. She hadn't even had a chance to get up and give him the whole sofa. What the crap was she supposed to do with her arms? Well, she could prop her left arm up along the arm of the sofa, but the right arm was the problem. In a perfect world, she'd be playing with the spiky dark brown hair that was covering the head that was resting on the pillow in her lap.

In her freaking lap.

Or stroking the wide shoulder that was connected to the neck of the head in her lap.

In her freaking lap.

She couldn't lift her arm high enough to rest along the back of the sofa, she couldn't wedge it behind him, and she certainly couldn't continue to hold it aloft, either.

Garrett shifted a little, more on his side, to see the television more easily.

She looked down at him suspiciously. He sure moved

smoothly for someone in pain. "Did you take anything for your back?"

He blinked. "I will if it doesn't ease up."

"Mm hm." She wasn't completely convinced he had a back ache at all.

"Ow," he said, as if he had read her thoughts, and he shifted a little more. "Did you know that J.K. Rowling had to tell Alan Rickman her plan for the ending before she'd even written all the books?"

"I did know that." Maggie was still contemplating her right arm.

"Maggie, just relax and put your hand somewhere. I'm not going to bite it off."

She swallowed and carefully placed her hand on the top of his shoulder. It was hard and warm beneath the thin t-shirt.

"Did you know Severus Snape was the only Death Eater that could conjure a Patronus?"

If she wasn't so flustered, she'd be amused at his knowledge of Potter trivia. "I did not know that."

"Yep."

With his attention angled towards the screen, Maggie kept her head up but slanted her eyes to study his body, so nonchalantly stretched down the sofa. The width of his shoulders, the length of his back, the silky shorts clinging to his lean hips, the long, muscular legs and bare feet. He had such nice feet. Was she developing a foot fetish? She could feel her heart pounding in her chest. She couldn't seem to regulate her breathing.

This was torture.

Oh, God, it was the most wonderful, awful torture.

Her fingers were actually twitching to slide through his hair, touch his ear, trace his profile. She wondered what Garrett would do if she actually –

"Did you know that J.K. Rowling is the richest author in the world?"

Maggie stifled a nervous giggle.

"What?" Garrett turned his head to look up at her.

"Nothing." She was glad he'd interrupted her dangerous train of thought.

"Is my trivia distracting you from the movie?"

Yes, that was it. It was his trivia that was distracting her. Not his head in her lap and his perfect male body calling a siren song to hers. "A little."

"I'll be quiet." He turned his face back toward the screen.

He knew he should be ashamed but it was heaven lying on the sofa with his head in her lap. She smelled so great. He could feel her breath, rising and falling, and her hand, lightly resting on his shoulder. It had been hard not to laugh when he saw her from the corner of his eye studying her own arm, trying to decide what to do with it.

He wondered what she'd do if he feigned falling asleep. What the hell. He closed his eyes and wondered how long it would take before she glanced down, and whether she would be suspicious or would fall for it. He couldn't wait to see what she would do.

He decided to give it a few minutes, just for fun.

Fun. Who'd have thought it?

With his eyes closed, he tried matching his breathing rhythm with hers. He wanted to peek up at her but he kept his eyes closed and started feeling more relaxed than ever. This was great. He could do this every night.

"Garrett."

"Hmm?"

"Garrett. Garrett. Wake up."

Someone was gently shaking his shoulder. Garrett opened his eyes. He was stretched out on the sofa, his head still on the pillow in Maggie's lap, but he was burrowed more deeply into it, and his right arm was flung across her legs.

"Maggie." His blinked, his mind fuzzy. "I fell asleep. Is the movie over?"

"It's over, and Half Blood Prince is over, too."

He sat up, swinging his feet to the floor. "Are you kidding?" He rubbed his eyes with the palms of his hands. "You've been sitting here, trapped, the whole time?"

She nodded, tossing the pillow from her lap to the other side of the sofa. "I dozed off, too."

He stared at her and struggled for words. He'd wasted the whole evening. He never thought he'd go to sleep for real. He never, ever dropped off to sleep like that.

He'd wasted the whole evening. "What time is it?"

"Almost one."

Son of a bitch. He rose and curved his hands on the back of his head in frustration.

Maggie tried to rise, but collapsed back down onto the sofa with a breathless 'oof.'

He frowned. "You okay?" Holding out his hand, she took it and he towed her up.

"My leg's asleep." Smiling sleepily at him, she twined her fingers together, inverted her arms and stretched forward.

Working the knots out from being trapped beneath him. He was an idiot. "I'm so sorry. You should have woken me up hours ago."

"I didn't mind," she said cheerfully, stretching her arms over her head. "How does your back feel?"

He winced at her concern for his imaginary backache. He was an immature asshole. "A lot better."

"I'm glad," she said, yawning and rolling her head in a circle.

"Here, let me." He turned her around and massaged her shoulders like he had done that morning. She was so close, her skin so soft, the top of her head just an inch or so from his chin. He inhaled and caught her delicious scent.

"Mmm." She dropped her head forward. "Feels good."

Her knot of hair was slipping down, her slim neck exposed. She had a little freckle just behind her right ear. He managed to resist the urge to bend down to kiss it but he couldn't resist moving closer, pressing his body against her.

Just like that, he was hard. Obviously, blatantly hard. Impossible-to-miss hard. Painfully hard. He didn't know what to do. He knew what he wanted to do. He wanted to lay Maggie back down on the sofa and peel her clothes off and kiss and stroke and lick her to an orgasm or two, and then fuck her until they were both breathless and came again together, then carry her into his room and do it all over again.

His hands stilled on her shoulders and he had to edge away from her so she wouldn't feel his dick prodding against her back.

Maggie yawned again, and without turning around, lifted her right hand and patted his hand, frozen on her left shoulder. "I'm off to bed. Night night."

"Goodnight," he replied hoarsely, watching her trail through the kitchen and out of sight.

He was so fucked.

Chapter 16

The very first thought that came to her mind when Maggie woke up was that it was her last day with Garrett.

She reached for her phone to check the time. Barely six a.m. Her flight tomorrow was at nine in the morning. Twenty-seven hours. That's all she had left.

No time to waste. She hadn't slept much on the sofa while the movies played, and she hadn't been able to fall asleep in her bed, either. Knowing he was just downstairs, alone in his bed, too, was more conducive to unrealistic fantasies than to a good night's rest.

But last night was a memory she'd hang onto for the rest of her life. As long as she lived, she didn't think she'd forget how it felt, how he looked, sprawled across the sofa with his head on her lap. It was a humdinger of a memory, one that still made her insides feel like lava. Oh, the chances she had taken. Once she felt convinced he was truly asleep, she had caved in to the temptation to touch his hair. She'd tested the texture between her fingers, all the while keeping her eye on his face to make sure he didn't stir. When he kept sleeping, she smoothed it one way, then another, and then even twined a bit of the longer strands around her finger. She'd lightly traced his eyebrows, felt the scratch of his light stubble, and she even touched his neck to feel his pulse. It was slow and strong, and her body reacted with a heightened pulse of its own, coiling all the way down to her toes.

The movie played on, ended, and another one began, and she had continued to watch him sleep.

It wasn't creepy at all, right?

Maggie closed her eyes, embarrassed.

And then he'd stirred, and she'd frozen. He turned a little more to the right, settled more deeply into the sofa, drew his right leg up into a bent position, and curved his right arm across her legs. He murmured something into the pillow, and then all was quiet again. That was when she'd finally dozed off, too, only waking up when the credits were rolling on the second film.

The way he'd bounded up, after she finally had to wake him, made her suspicious that his back had never bothered him at all.

But she would never complain.

In minutes, she was dressed in shorts and a t-shirt and on her way down the stairs. She made a cup of coffee and looked out the window to see Garrett sitting on one of the chairs near the outdoor fireplace. He looked like he was in deep thought, head down, his forearms resting on the tops of his thighs, hands clasped together. A cup of coffee sat on the tabletop and Buddy and Dude were at his feet.

Crossing the room, she eased the door open and stepped outside. He lifted his head immediately and offered a pensive smile. "Morning." Dude and Buddy rose and wagged their way toward her.

"Morning," she replied, patting them in turn.

Garrett leaned over and pulled a chair away from the table for her. "You're up early."

Nodding, Maggie sat and wrapped her hands around the warm mug. "You, too."

"Couldn't sleep," he said briefly.

"Me, either." Maggie avoided his quick glance and

concentrated on sipping her coffee. They sat in silence for a few minutes.

"About today," he began, and then hesitated.

She looked at him questioningly.

"This thing at the retirement home. What do you think about maybe not going? I was thinking we could take a drive up to Grand Lake instead."

Maggie didn't know if she could survive the delicious stress of being in a closed vehicle with him all day. It was hard enough just being in the same house. "Didn't you say you'd be there?"

He rubbed the back of his neck. "Well, yeah, but it's your last day and you've barely been out of the house."

Because being alone with him inside his castle had been really terrible. Maggie took another careful sip of coffee.

"It's going to take a big chunk out of the day," he added.

"I think that if you said you'd be there, you need to be there."

He sighed. "Yeah, I guess so."

"I think it'll be fun. Will I get to see old ladies throw their granny panties at you?"

He huffed in amusement. "It's your job to make sure they don't."

"I'm not getting between you and your cougars. I don't want to go home with a black eye or bruises from wheelchairs trying to run me down."

"You could probably outrun them."

"I should hope so," she grinned.

Garrett gazed into his coffee mug. "If you stayed a little longer, we could go to Grand Lake tomorrow."

No, she couldn't stay any longer. Every additional day with him challenged her resistance. She didn't want to go home more ruined for mortal men than she already was. She would take this one last day and then return to the real world. She shook her head. "I have to go home, Garrett."

He frowned.

"Hey." She jabbed him lightly. "Don't be cranky. Lilah's gone and you don't need me anymore. You've got to get back to business, too. Shouldn't you start practicing your spirals or fancy footwork or something?"

"My spirals are fine, thanks, and training camp doesn't start for another month. And you said school doesn't start until early August."

She was surprised he remembered. "But teachers have to be back mid-July."

"Still almost a month away."

If she wasn't careful, he'd talk her into it, but then she'd be worse off than she was already. She rose and put her hand on her hip. "Are you hungry? I'm hungry. Let's go inside and I'll fry eight pounds of bacon for you." As diversionary tactics went, it was pretty lame but it was all she had.

"It was only a pound," he finally said, rising. "And you and Lilah ate half of it."

She locked her arm through his because she couldn't help herself, and led him inside. "Lilah had one slice and I had two. Keep eating pork like that and you won't be the NFL's hottest quarterback anymore."

He squeezed her arm. "Careful or I'll take you to the airport right now."

It was an idle threat and they both knew it.

It was his last afternoon with Maggie and they were wasting precious time at Greenbriar Retirement Home. Garrett wondered how many more games of bingo he had to get through before he could grab her and make a run for it.

Pasting a smile on his face, he turned the lever on the wire bingo cage on the table in front of him and withdrew a ball from the chute. "B7," he said loudly, before placing it in the master board. He glanced across the large room filled with people seated at long rows of tables. He wasn't sure how he'd been designated the game caller, but he'd been giving it all he had.

"What was that?"

"What did he say?"

"He said 'B7,' several participants repeated.

"Speak up, son!"

It was the same thing every single time he called out a letter and number, going on five games now. He caught Maggie's eye across the room, where she was sitting beside an octogenarian in a wheelchair. She gave him a private, amused smile that helped him relax a little.

Funny how she could do that.

"B7," he repeated, even louder than before. He had to call bingo almost as loudly as he had to call plays on the line of scrimmage. He was going to be hoarse when it was over. If it was ever over.

While he participated as often as possible in team-sponsored community events, today was testing his patience. It was bad enough that the clock was ticking down on his afternoon with Maggie, but Father's Day wasn't exactly dear to his heart. Mixing with families who were happy to spend time with beloved fathers and grandfathers made him uncomfortable. Bitter, even.

"N30!" he called out.

They'd been there since mid-morning. A special brunch had been served and the arts and crafts project had concluded. The last activity on the agenda, bingo, was in full swing. Soon it would be over, and not a moment too soon.

"Bingo!" A tiny blue haired lady waved her arm in the air. "I have bingo!"

After it was confirmed that she did indeed have bingo, Garrett carried the prize to her and hunkered down so that the staff could take a photograph. By now he'd posed for photos with practically every resident and all of their family members, every staff member and all of their family members, the other players, and even a pair of emergency medical technicians who had come to take someone to the hospital. He only hoped the resident who needed to go to the hospital hadn't stroked out or something while the EMTs got their stupid photo.

His smile was wearing thin.

After a couple more games, one of the staff members approached him. "I'll take over for you now, if you'd like." Garrett nodded his thanks and edged to the side of the room. One step closer to the door and freedom. Looking over the room at all the frail bodies and lined faces, it struck him that the residents had been young and vital once. The day would eventually come when he couldn't play anymore, and then what would he have? No football. No Maggie.

Ty joined him and elbowed him in the ribs. "Look. Maggie's made a conquest."

Trying to shake off his mood, Garrett followed his gaze and saw Maggie sitting beside a wizened little man in an electric wheelchair wearing a Renegades baseball cap on his head. They were deep in conversation. Maggie had one of the gentleman's hands pressed between her own.

"That's Arthur. He's been here a few years. He's a cranky old bastard but he has some great stories. He doesn't usually stick around long at these things but Maggie seems to have charmed him."

"That's Maggie for you." Garrett watched her give the old man a kiss on his cheek. Lucky old bastard.

"Hey, you know, I'm glad you finally agreed to come to this. It hasn't been too bad, has it?"

"Not too bad." Ty didn't need to know how ready he was to get away.

Ty crossed his arms in front of his chest and gave him a sideways glance. "So what's the story with you and Maggie?"

Garrett glanced at him. "What do you mean?"

Ty frowned at him. "Give me a break. You're crazy about her."

Garrett sighed. He wasn't going to lie to his best friend. "Yeah."

Ty elbowed him again. "That's great, Garrett."

"It would be if we wanted the same thing, but we don't."

Ty frowned. "What are you talking about?"

Grimacing, Garrett shoved his hands in his pockets, his gaze fixed on Maggie. Now she was talking with a little old lady who was sitting alone, looking like whatever the lady was saying was fascinating. "You know what I mean. She wants what you and Eleanor have. Marriage, a lot of kids, a happy ever after."

Ty sighed. "This is about your father, isn't it? You're still hung up on that?"

Garrett didn't bother to answer. When he'd gotten word that his father had died, Ty was the one who found him in a bar near the training facility. He'd taken him home, sobered him up, and then insisted on going with him to Oklahoma for the funeral. Garrett hadn't wanted company, hadn't wanted anyone to see what he came from, but Ty, being Ty, wouldn't take no for an answer. He had dug and pried until Garrett gave up and explained exactly why he was so glad the bastard was dead.

"Hey, buddy, you're not your father. We've talked about this. You're your own man."

It was a waste of time talking about it. "It's in my DNA. Better to accept it and roll with it."

"You really piss me off when you spout that crap." Ty glared at him. "You're going to just let her go back to Baton Rouge, then?"

He had no fucking idea what he was going to do about Maggie. Time was almost up. "It's complicated."

"Well, uncomplicate it, genius."

Garrett didn't hear him. He was watching that manwhore Dominic Moretti ease his way toward Maggie, a shit-eating grin on his face. Eyes narrowed, muscles tensing, he watched Maggie smile back at him, watched Dom give her a hug.

Hell, no. Time to interrupt that crap.

"Boy!"

Garrett felt a whack on the back of his leg, and spun around, frowning. The wizened man in the electric wheelchair had rolled up silently next to him. He was holding his cane like a bayonet, ready to hit him again.

"Hey, Arthur." Ty put his hand out. "Good to see you."

Arthur swatted Ty's hand away with his cane. "You, go away," he told him. He pointed his cane at Garrett. "You, come here."

"All righty, then. I think I'll go away." Ty winked at Garrett and ambled off.

Garrett watched Maggie say something to Dom and then turn away, leaving him standing alone, looking a little baffled. His breath eased up and he felt a little less murderous.

"You!"

Trying to smooth his scowl into a smile, Garrett hunkered down to Arthur's level. "Yes, sir?"

"I want to talk to you." The man jabbed his cane at the nearest chair. "Sit down."

Garrett sat and slid the chair a little closer. "What can I do for you?"

"You can't do a damned thing for me," the man said grumpily. "I'm going to do something for you."

"Okay." Ty hadn't been kidding when he said Arthur was cranky.

"You see that girl over there?" Arthur jabbed his cane in Maggie's direction. "That girl in the green dress?"

Now Maggie was collecting bingo cards and markers, her long dress swirling around her legs. "Yes, sir, that's Maggie Parrish."

"I know her name! I want to tell you something about her."

Garrett leaned closer to him. "What's that?"

Arthur narrowed his eyes at Garrett. "That one's special."

Garrett watched Maggie stop to speak with a pair of elderly women, that wide smile of hers blooming on her face. He could tell she had complimented one of the women on her earrings, because the woman brightened, touched her earrings and then patted

Maggie on the arm. "Yes, sir, she is."

Arthur jabbed him. "Look at me."

Garrett looked at him, and wondered if he could get the cane away from him for the length of their conversation.

"That girl there tells me you and she are friends." He spat out the word 'friends' like it tasted bad.

"Yes, sir, that's right."

He gave Garrett a disgusted look. "Are you stupid?"

Arthur didn't pull any punches. Garrett shook his head. "No, sir."

"Because you'd be stupid to let that one get away."

Garrett looked over at Maggie again. She was all over the place, like a butterfly flitting from person to person. Now she was talking to Eleanor and Ty, and as he watched the three of them turned and grinned at him. He hoped Arthur didn't hit him while they were looking.

Arthur whacked him on his knee.

"Listen to me, boy. It wasn't that long ago when I was your age, maybe younger, and I met a girl that was special like that one." He breathed wheezily.

"That so?"

"Don't interrupt when I'm talking!"

"Yes, sir." Garrett leaned forward, propping his forearms on his thighs, hands clasped together.

"She said she only wanted to be friends, and she was going with some other fellow, but he wasn't good enough for her. Hell, I wasn't good enough for her, but I didn't let that stop me. I chased that girl down with everything I had in me, and I want you to know that when I caught her, I married her before she could blink, and we were married sixty-seven years."

Garrett gazed at Maggie, laughing with Eleanor at something Ty must have said, and felt another whack. "Pay attention!"

He was going to have bruises.

"So you know what you gotta do, don't you, boy?"

"I've got to chase her with everything I've got," Garrett answered slowly.

But Arthur didn't understand. It wasn't that simple. What was the point of chasing her when she wanted more than he could give her? She didn't want the superficial things like his celebrity status, his money, his lifestyle. She wanted marriage and a big family. That wasn't going to happen, not with him.

And she'd be gone tomorrow. He'd be here, knocking around by himself again.

To his surprise, he felt Arthur's thin hand cover his clasped hands. "That's right, boy, that's what you've gotta do. And don't fuck it up. Now get out of my way."

Garrett rose and pushed his chair back so Arthur could glide away. He crossed the room again, joining Eleanor and Ty. "Where's Maggie?"

Eleanor and Ty exchanged knowing smiles.

He was irritated that they thought he was funny. "Shut up. I'm ready to leave and I can't leave without her."

"We didn't say anything," Ty replied with a grin. "Did we say anything, Eleanor?"

"We can give her a ride home," Eleanor chimed in. "You can go on if you want." She winked at her husband.

He wanted to hit something.

"Okay, okay," Eleanor laughed. "She's over there." She nodded toward the back of the room.

Garrett followed Eleanor's gesture and saw Maggie sitting at a table near the door, talking to a man in a Kansas City Chiefs windbreaker. Garrett couldn't see his face but there was something familiar about him. The man turned and glanced around the room, and Garrett stiffened. It was Brent Buchanan, the freelance sports writer who'd made a career out of trash talking him. The one who wouldn't stop digging into his past.

Talking with Maggie.

"What the fuck is he doing here?" Garrett jerked his head

toward Buchanan. "I didn't think the media was invited." He drew in a jagged breath when he saw Buchanan touch Maggie's arm.

Ty followed his narrowed gaze. "I didn't think they were, either."

A staff member moved past and Ty flagged her down. "Excuse me, miss. What's that reporter doing here?"

"Mr. Buchanan? He's not here in an official capacity. He's related to one of our residents."

"Fuck that." Garrett started across the room.

Ty caught his arm. "No. Let me."

Garrett tried to shake him loose.

Ty tightened his hold. "No, Garrett. I'll get Maggie. You stay here. Buchanan will try to start something with you."

"Fine," he bit off. He watched Ty cross the room and lean down toward Maggie. She looked up and nodded at whatever he said. Buchanan put his hand out to Maggie. Garrett watched, jaw tight, as Maggie shook his hand and then rose and turned to follow Ty.

Buchanan glanced over his shoulder, straight at Garrett, and gave him a greasy smirk.

Garrett felt rage flood through his veins. Why was he really here? What possible reason could he have for talking to Maggie?

Maggie appeared at his elbow. "Hey, are you okay? Ty said you needed me."

He broke his locked gaze with Buchanan and looked down at Maggie. "Why were you talking with him?"

Maggie blinked. "Who? The man just now?"

"Yes. You know who that is?"

Maggie shook her head, frowning at his tone.

"That's Brent Buchanan."

Maggie's eyes opened wide. "That's micropenis?" She looked over her shoulder, and Garrett gritted his teeth when Buchanan gave her a little wave. She turned back to Garrett. "What's he doing here?"

"That's what I'd like to know. What did he say?"

Maggie looked worried. "Nothing really. We talked about how nice this place is. He asked if I worked here and I told him no, I was here with you."

"Then what?"

"He asked how well I knew you and then Ty came and got me."

Garrett drew in a deep breath, his eyes still fixed on Buchanan, who had turned to speak to one of the retirement home employees.

She touched his arm. "That's all there was to it. Are you okay?"

No, he was a seething, twisted mess. There was something up with Buchanan showing up like this. No way he was here just to visit a family member. "Yeah. You ready to go?"

"Is it over?"

It was for him. He nodded, his eyes still on Buchanan.

"I'll just go get my purse."

By the time Maggie returned, Buchanan had left the room. Garret walked ahead of Maggie toward the foyer of the center, glancing around to find him. The bastard was obsessed with digging up shit on him and the idea that he would have the fucking nerve to talk to Maggie was more than he could take.

There was no sign of him inside. Garrett stalked through the front doors, still searching, and was a few yards into the parking lot before he realized he'd left Maggie behind. He turned to see her hurrying to catch up, a worried expression on her face.

He drew in a big breath and waited for her. "Sorry."

"No problem. You sure you're okay?"

"Of course."

He wasn't okay. Fucking Buchanan. Just the thought of him, on a good day, was enough to set his teeth on edge. He didn't belong at the Renegades event today. It was impossible to believe it was just a coincidence.

"Everyone was so nice. I really enjoyed it. Do you think you'll do it again next year?"

Next year, when she wouldn't be there to charm the socks off every person she met? The next year when, if Arthur was still alive, he'd get beaten with a cane for showing up without her?

"Probably," he lied, to appease her. She wouldn't know if he went or not. She'd be living her life a thousand miles away.

They reached his car and he opened her door. "That's good." She slid into the seat. "I could see how excited they all were to meet you."

"If you say so." Closing her door a little harder than necessary, he strode around to open his own door and dropped into the seat.

She eyed him as he started the engine. "You're in a bit of a mood, aren't you?"

Hell, yes, he was in a mood.

Having to parade around like a performing circus monkey tended to put him in a mood.

Having Dom sniffing around her put him in a mood.

Having an old man give him impossible advice he hadn't asked for put him in a mood.

Having Ty and Eleanor exchanging stupid glances at his expense put him in a mood.

Having fucking Buchanan show up and have the unspeakable gall to touch her put him in a mood.

All of that, and then having only a handful of hours left before she left him to go back to Baton Rouge put him in a goddamn fucking mood.

"I don't know what you're talking about." He backed out of the parking space with a screech.

"You just seem a little tense."

"I'm not tense at all."

"Said the very tense man," Maggie murmured.

"Hilarious. There's nothing wrong with me." He pulled out on the road in front of another vehicle. The other driver blew their horn and he flipped them off.

Maggie frowned at him. "That wasn't nice."

"Sorry." He wasn't sorry at all.

Maggie crossed her arms and made an "hmph" noise.

"What was that for?"

"What?"

"That noise you just made. If you have something to say, then please, by all means, say it." He knew he was being a dick but he couldn't seem to help himself.

"I'll wait until you've come down from Cloud Grumpy Pants."

He blinked. "What?"

"Cloud Grumpy Pants."

He glared at her. She was casually examining a fingernail.

"Are you seriously using kindergarten tactics on me?"

She shrugged. "Are you acting like a kindergartener?"

Swerving across two lanes, Garrett whipped the car into a parking lot, slid into a space and killed the engine. He twisted in his seat to face her.

"I am not acting like a kindergartener, Maggie."

She examined another fingernail.

"Maggie." He willed her to look at him but now she was inspecting a third fingernail. "Cloud Grumpy Pants?"

"That's what I said."

He felt an unwelcome twinge of amusement. "Maggie."

"Hmm?"

"Would you please look at me?"

She looked at him, her expression unruffled.

"Cloud Grumpy Pants?"

"You heard me the first time. Repeating it over and over again isn't going to change it."

Damn it, he was losing his bad mood.

She pressed her lips together, to try to hide the edges of a smile.

He was ruined. He was screwed. He was lost. He was completely, utterly lost in the delight that was Maggie. He would never know what to expect from her. He felt his frustrated fury evaporate, a grin slipping across his face. He burst out laughing.

Maggie started giggling and then she started laughing, and then she snorted which was the funniest thing he'd ever heard in his life, and he laughed until his chest hurt. Finally they composed themselves and wiped their watering eyes.

He wanted to reach over and grab her and pull her over the console into his lap and kiss her until neither one of them could breathe.

Instead he pulled in a long breath and blew it out again.

"Let's go home." It was time to talk about her tipsy confession. He had a confession of his own to make.

He had one evening left to chase her with everything he had.

Chapter 17

Maggie felt light as a soap bubble after Garrett's good humor resurfaced. It had been touch and go for a few minutes, especially when he'd gone all Arnold Schwarzenegger in True Lies on her, screeching across the highway and skidding to a stop in the parking lot. Bringing up Cloud Grumpy Pants had been a big gamble. At first, it seemed like her attempt to coax him into a better mood was going to backfire spectacularly. It didn't always work with her kindergarteners either, come to think of it. Sometimes they were so set on having a tantrum that nothing could sway them. But, thankfully, once she saw the corners of his lips twitch, she knew she had him.

And if there was anything more appealing than the sight of Garrett with his muscles straining against the fabric of his sexy-tight dress shirt, draped over the steering wheel, laughing until his eyes were watering, she didn't know what it could be.

She wasn't completely sure what had instigated his bad mood. Obviously he'd been pretty ticked to discover Brent Buchanan at the event. She didn't know what his motive was in striking up a conversation but she was glad Ty had interrupted when he did.

It had been quite an education watching Garrett adeptly handle the furor that erupted when they arrived. The small crowd at the restaurant in Florida and at the restaurant with the Hursts' had only been a small taste of what she had witnessed today. Here in Denver, he was revered like a god. The public Garrett was bigger than life, accustomed to the fawning adoration of his fans. It was hard to reconcile this polished Garrett with the playful man swinging a rolling pin like a nun chuck.

She'd felt inadequate there, invisible. She had been happy to step aside, watching from a distance as he smiled, shook hands, signed autographs, talked football, and bent down for countless photos.

Just another reason for her to get back home, back to normal, where gods were thin on the ground and she felt like herself.

The first item on the agenda had been to help serve a special Father's Day brunch to the residents. When a cafeteria employee handed Garrett a long bib apron, he'd searched Maggie out and held it up slightly to show her, mouthing the word "help." But it wasn't her, or Eleanor, or the other significant others that were the attractions of the event, so she hung back and made herself useful in other ways while he and the other players filled plates. When the arts and crafts project got underway, Garrett tried to include her as he circulated, but she was no match for the eager fans who wanted his attention, so she edged out of the way and instead, visited with the residents. She liked elderly people as much as she liked children so it was no hardship at all.

When they arrived back at Garrett's house, he parked by the front door. She glanced at the dining room as they passed through the foyer and realized it was still in total disarray.

"After I change, I'm going to get your dining room back in order." She nodded toward the blanket fort. "Put all the pillows and stuff back where they belong."

"No, don't. I like it a lot better like that. And when I get Lilah again, it'll already be set up." He started through the foyer, toward the kitchen, tossing his keys from hand to hand.

The idea that he was thinking about babysitting Lilah again put a big smile on Maggie's face. He had certainly gained a lot of confidence on the uncle front since that panicked telephone call. Following him into the kitchen, she hung her purse on the back of one of the bar chairs.

"Anything special you want to do tonight?" He opened the back door to let Dude and Buddy inside.

The last night. Tomorrow at this time, she'd be back home. He'd be here, she'd be there. Where they belonged. Like they'd never met. Maggie turned away so he couldn't see her face. "Like what?"

"Anything you want."

She took a deep breath and faced him again, hoping her distress was hidden.

He leaned against the island and studied her. "Dinner someplace nice, maybe a movie, maybe there's somebody good at the comedy club."

She didn't want to go anywhere. She didn't want to share him with anyone. If they left the house, he'd have to be Renegades quarterback Garrett Long and she'd be invisible again. What she wanted was to shut all that out for one more night and make a few more harmless little memories to recall when she was home, alone, and thinking of him.

"Do you mind if we just stay in?" She leaned to tug one shoe off. "Maybe order a pizza? Watch Deathly Hallows?"

His smile made her heart flutter. "Sounds perfect. You're perfect."

She blinked at his comment. "Hardly," she managed. "Just lazy." She pulled her other shoe off and sighed.

His smile broadened. "What do you like on your pizza?"

"No anchovies, pineapple, or mushrooms."

"Got it. Go change and get back down here so we can start the movie."

"Be right back." She hurried upstairs and stripped off the dress and tugged on a pair of shorts and a t-shirt, looking forward to Garrett's expression when he saw the design on her shirt.

She wasn't disappointed. When she got back downstairs, he had already changed into shorts and a t-shirt, too, and stopped in his tracks when he saw the gold New Orleans Saints logo on her black shirt.

"Aw, hell no." His outraged expression was comical. "Are you kidding me? That is completely unacceptable."

Biting back a smile, she took the hem of her shirt in her fingers and held it out to admire the logo. "It's my last clean shirt."

"Absolutely not. Not in this house." He turned on his heel and disappeared, and returned moments later with a Renegades jersey. "Here. Take that off. Wear this instead."

She took it and examined it while he watched. It had his name and number on the back. She loved it. He didn't know it yet but it was going home with her and she would treasure it forever.

"Nice." She glanced back at him and his playfully narrowed eyes made her feel reckless. She tugged the Saints shirt over her head, right there in front of him, and pulled the Renegades jersey on. It wasn't that big a deal, really. Her sports bra covered a lot more than her bikini top. She smoothed the fabric, loving how big it was, how dainty it made her feel. She glanced back up at Garrett, her Saints shirt in her hand.

He was motionless. His playful expression was gone. His gaze was hot, his lips parted.

Oh Lordy. Maggie swallowed. "Better?" she managed.

He blinked, dropped his gaze and turned away. "Yeah." He sounded a little hoarse. She watched him open the refrigerator, stare inside it for a moment, then finally take out two bottles of beer.

"Did you order the pizza?" Her own voice sounded weird, too.

He nodded, keeping his back to her as he closed the refrigerator door.

She folded her Saints shirt and placed it on the island. The air felt thick and she wondered what on earth had possessed her to flash him like that.

"So who are you going to pull for when we play?" He finally turned to look at her, his expression easy again.

She bit back a smile at his question. "Did you order the pizza?"

He rounded the island and handed her a bottle. "Maggie. Who are you going to pull for?"

"Did you remember I don't like mushrooms?" She was having a hard time not grinning.

He lifted his magic eyebrow and put his hands on his hips. "Want me to throw you in the pool again? Because you know I will."

"Please tell me you didn't order pizza with mushrooms."

The corners of his mouth forming an almost imperceptible smile. "Last chance, Maggie."

"Okay, okay." She held up her hands. "I'll pull for the Renegades, although my parents will disown me and none of my friends will ever speak to me again. Happy?"

He twisted the cap off his beer bottle and drank a long swallow. "Happy." He pulled a bar chair away from the island and propped a hip on it. "Very happy," he said again, in a different tone, gazing at her. Maggie felt a tingle chase down her spine and found it hard to look away from his intense gaze. He drank another swallow, pulled another chair away from the island and patted it. "There's something we have to talk about. Come sit down."

Maggie had the uneasy feeling she knew where this was going. She sat slowly.

"Friday night," he said succinctly, eyeing her over the rim of the bottle.

Damn, damn, damn. It seems her wish to never discuss Friday night was not going to come true.

"While we've got this one last chance." He rubbed the back of his neck. "I've been hoping you'd bring it up yourself, but you haven't, so –"

Crap, crap, crap. She tried for a nonchalant, playful tone. "Oh, you mean the stuff I said when I was drunk."

He nodded.

"You mean when I said I had the hots for you? Who even says that, – 'the hots'? Ugh, and all that Baileys. All that ice cream. It tasted great at the time but, I'll tell you, it wasn't so great the next morning. I was so sick. Like, hugging the toilet sick. I will never, ever do that again." Oh, God, she couldn't shut up.

He pinned her with his gaze. "Was it true?"

She tried to laugh and it came out like a helium-inspired nervous witch cackle. "I was so drunk, Garrett."

"Was it true?"

There was no dodging the bullet. She covered her face with her hands. "Yes, of course it was true," she said, her voice muffled. "Show me a woman with a pulse who doesn't have the hots for you, Garrett. That would be the real shocker."

He put his bottle down on the island. "Well, here's the thing, Maggie. I feel the same way."

Maggie peeked through her fingers. He looked totally serious.

He pried her hands from her face and chafed them between his own. "Why else do you think I don't want you to leave tomorrow? I want to see what this is, where it goes."

She looked down at her hands inside his, and back up at his face. "But I thought – you said – we're just – you mean that when we were having the tea party, when you – that kiss – you apologized and said – Maggie trailed off.

He shrugged. "I know what I said but it wasn't true. I only said it because you freaked out."

Maggie gaped at him and grasped onto his last comment. "I did not freak out."

That eyebrow lifted in amusement. "Maggie, you ran out of the house in the rain wearing your bathrobe."

"Okay, I freaked out a little." She waved a dismissive hand. "But that kiss came out of the blue and now you're telling me – what exactly?"

He rose and stepped closer, bumping her knees. Way, way

inside her personal space. So close she had to tilt her head back to see his face. Any closer and she'd have to part her knees.

"That I've got" – he shook his head slightly. "Feelings for you." He put his hands on her upper arms and stroked her skin with his thumbs. It felt delicious.

"You've got feelings for me," Maggie parroted. Her knees, traitorous joints, parted of their own accord. She had absolutely nothing to do with it.

He edged closer. "Yep, kind of simmering since you got here. Maybe since Florida." He looked away, narrowing his eyes thoughtfully. "Maybe since that dress. No, maybe even before that, when you did that 'go Renegades' thing." He dropped his gaze back to her face. "I don't know, it's hard to say. You're tricky. You kind of snuck up on me."

"But we've only known one another for a few days," she managed weakly. "Less than two weeks."

He shrugged. "Maybe sometimes that's all it takes."

Maggie needed to make sense of it but his big, warm hands going up and down her arms were making it hard to think. "Don't you think probably it's just because we've been together a lot since I came?"

"Maybe that sped things along, but so what? Having you here, being around you," He lifted a hand to gently twist a bit of her hair around his finger. "You've got such a brightness in you. You make me happy." He curved his hand along the side of her neck. "Really happy."

Maggie caught her breath.

His hand curved around her neck. "I didn't think there was anyone like you out there."

His words were shattering, thrilling. "Why are you telling me all of this? When I'm leaving tomorrow?"

"Because I can't let you go without knowing how I feel. Why I want you to stay." He edged a little closer, his hips nudging her thighs open a little farther, and slid his hand up into her hair and she couldn't help leaning into that big, warm palm. "Stay a little longer, Maggie. Please?"

Oh, God. Her head was spinning. "I have to think."

"Okay." He dropped his hand from her arm to her thigh and edged the final millimeter closer. She felt the warm, hard bulge in his shorts nudge the seam of her shorts and her breath quickened. That one hand cupping her head, the other one slipping beneath the hem of her shorts, his eyes on her mouth.

He was coming for her.

She was in heaven.

She was in terrible trouble.

She had to think but she couldn't think straight. Squeezing her eyes shut, she put her hands on his chest, pushing him away and clamping her legs closed. "No. That's not fair. I can't think with, with, with all that," she gestured at him, flapping her hand up and down. "With you, with that –" she pointed at his shorts and grimaced. "Not fair, just not fair."

Garrett gave a half-laugh, half-groan but backed up to lean against the island beside her. "I'd say I'm sorry, but I'm not."

"Be quiet for a minute." She covered her face with her hands, took a couple of deep breaths. In through the nose, out through the mouth. She waited for her heart to slow to a normal rhythm. And for her brain to function. She tried to make sense out of the last few minutes. She peeked through her fingers to find Garrett studying her. Silently, patiently. Garrett freaking Long, who had feelings for her. Who wanted her to stay a little longer. She wasn't sure what that meant. Stay for something casual? Until school started? Until his football season started? She didn't do casual. And he didn't do serious. A month ago she was engaged to someone else. Because she wanted marriage. And children. The whole domestic enchilada. Garrett didn't want marriage. He didn't want children. But he had feelings for her, and he was wonderful. Smart, funny, gorgeous. And so freaking hot. Those eyes, those legs. That bulge in his pants, well, damn. No. No, his penis wasn't a factor.

Her lady bits didn't have a say.

He had feelings for her.

But he didn't want marriage or children.

Maggie sighed into her hands. She had to remember that. Despite everything else. So much else. So this was going to be difficult. Maybe the most difficult thing she'd ever done.

Dropping her hands, she drew in a long, shaky breath and raised her face to Garrett. He was leaning casually, arms loose by his sides, but his expression was taut, as if he had heard all her whirling thoughts and already knew what she was going to say.

Maggie wrapped her arms around herself and went straight to it. "Do you remember the first day we met, when you told me that you don't see yourself ever getting married or raising a family? Do you still feel that way?"

Please say you've changed your mind. Please say you've changed your mind. Please –

She saw the change in his eyes immediately, like the closing of a window, shutting out the light.

"Yes." His tone was flat.

That was that. Maggie swallowed. "I'm never going to change my mind about wanting those things."

She saw the muscle working in his jaw before he spoke again. "Do you think maybe knowing why I feel the way I do would make any difference?" he asked quietly. "About kids? It's not just a random preference. I have a good reason."

She hugged herself tighter. She really did want to know why. She knew he wanted her to say yes, it would make a difference. She wished she could, but no matter what his reason was, she had to be true to herself. She tried to choose her words carefully. "I'm sure you do. Understanding wouldn't change what I want. I'm not the kind of girl to have a fling and then go home like nothing ever happened. I'm not built that way."

He studied her for a long moment, opening and closing his hands restlessly and then looked down and sighed. "Yeah, I guess you're right." Looking back up at her, he tried to smile at her.

"Yeah, you're right. Good thing one of us has some sense."

Maggie swallowed.

"You know, your honesty is one of the things I like best about you," he said quietly. "I trust you, Maggie. I don't trust a lot of people."

"I like so many things about you," she replied thickly. "I'm going to miss you so much." She felt tears well up in her eyes. "But if I stayed, I'm afraid we'd end up disappointing one another. I don't want that."

"I don't, either. Come here." He stepped forward.

She stood, slid her arms around his waist and rested her cheek on his chest. She could hear his heart beating. She thought hers might be breaking.

"Movie time? One last time?" he asked, his voice rough.

Unable to speak, Maggie nodded.

Garrett pulled the truck up to the curb at the drop-off area and turned off the engine. "Wait there," he told her. He collected her duffle bag from the back seat, and then circled the hood to open her door. Maggie hitched her purse over her shoulder and slid down out of the truck.

This was it. She was about to walk away, board a plane, and return to her own life. Why did it feel like she was making a terrible mistake?

There were so many little moments she'd remember from her scant few days with Garrett, but last night would be engraved on her heart for the rest of her life. They'd both made a herculean effort to move past the difficult conversation. They'd shared pizza and watched both Deathly Hallows movies. She'd never actually cried during the two films before, but every little tragedy had her weeping like a baby, and she hadn't resisted when Garrett pulled her onto his lap and into his arms so she could cry against his chest. She figured they both knew she was overwrought over more than Dobbie's death or Snape's love for Lily but there was no point in talking about it anymore. She held his hand and he rubbed little circles on her back, and when the second movie ended, neither one of them made a move to get up and head to their separate rooms so they just - didn't. They both fell asleep eventually, and by the time daylight crept through the windows, she was still tucked inside the circle of his arms.

There hadn't been much conversation this morning. She'd left him to go upstairs and pack her things, they'd shared a quiet cup of coffee, and now they were here at the airport.

He was standing only inches away, blocking her path to the automatic doors. She looked up and found him gazing down at her.

"So I guess this is goodbye, then." His face was taut, lips barely moving when he spoke.

"I guess so." She tried to smile up at him but it was probably more of a grimace, and she had no idea what to say. *Thank you? Text me? Will I ever see you again? Have a good life?* She drew in a deep, rattling breath and stepped forward to lean against him, just one more time, resting her forehead against his warm chest. She felt him stiffen for a split second but then he wrapped his arms around her in a tight embrace. She slipped her arms around his waist and clung to him for several long moments, listening to his heartbeat. Then she stepped back. She was cold, her eyes were stinging, and she could barely swallow past the lump in her throat.

"Thanks for everything."

"It was fun," she managed, and winced at the absurdity of her statement. She picked up her bag and offered him a small smile, willing the tears to stay put until she was out of sight. "Take care of yourself." She turned and started walking toward the doors that slid open at her approach.

Don't look back. Do not look back.

On unsteady legs she started in the direction of the escalators but took a detour into a ladies room where she closed herself in a stall and let the tears flow. They didn't lessen. Instead they degenerated into heaving, snotty, hiccupping sobs to the point where someone on the outside of the stall asked if she was okay.

She wasn't okay – far from it – but she couldn't wail in there forever so she slipped out, trying to ignore the curious glances.

Garrett watched Maggie walk through the sliding doors. Away from him. He felt pressure building in his chest.

"Hey, buddy, you gotta move."

He watched her stop, her head down, as she adjusted her grip on her bag.

"Hey, buddy. Come on, move it."

Garrett blinked and turned slowly to see an orange-vested airport employee walking toward him. The man's eyes widened when he recognized him, his scowl turning to a wide grin. "What the – hey, man!"

Garrett gave him a blank nod and looked back through the glass, searching.

Maggie was about to be swallowed up in a group of travelers.

"Dude, it's so cool to meet you!"

She was almost out of sight. He could just make out her shoulders, her hair.

"Hate to ask you to move, for real."

She was gone.

"It's okay," he managed, clenching and unclenching his hands.

"Do you think I could get a selfie real quick first?" The man was already fiddling with his phone. "We're going to have a great season this year, right?"

"Right." Garrett rubbed his face and slid his hand around to the back of his neck, gripping hard. He tried to smile for the photo, shook hands and then kept smiling and nodding although he wasn't registering anything the guy said. Finally he was back in his truck and he eased out of the corridor.

So that was that.

Heading up Peña Boulevard, he glanced at a plane gaining altitude on his right. Maggie would be boarding a plane like that soon, heading home to Louisiana.

Fuck.

What had he done? He'd left it too late, made a bad call, waiting until last night to get serious with her. He'd wasted so much time. What had he been thinking? He'd had two full days after she dropped her drunken bomb that she was into him to figure out how to fix things. What was he – so fucking irresistible that he didn't have to lift a finger to convince her that he was right for her? Did he think she'd forget her reservations and take a chance on him without him doing everything he could to convince her he'd make her happy? This was Maggie. She was different. If he wanted Maggie, he'd have to work a hell of a lot harder. She wasn't about the hype. She was real. Sweet, funny, honest. Just hanging out with her made him happier than he could ever remember. And last night he'd finally gotten his hands on her, was so close to tasting her, showing her what she meant to him, only to have her slip away again.

It was simple. He hadn't tried hard enough.

Not nearly hard enough.

He jerked the wheel to the shoulder on the right and slammed on his brakes, breathing hard.

He wasn't a fucking quitter.

He was going back for her.

Adrenaline surged through him like a charge of electricity. There was an emergency turnaround a little farther ahead but to hell with it. He yanked the steering wheel to the left and cut across both outgoing lanes toward the wide dividing median. It was a jarring ride but he didn't slow down. Luckily there wasn't a lot of traffic on the other side so he skidded back onto the road and punched the gas, heading back to stop her.

Maggie found her way to the escalator and stepped on ahead of a crowd of boisterous teenagers. When she stepped off, she moved to the side and set her bag down to wait for them to go around her because they were entirely too happy. Once they were out of sight, she sighed, picked up her bag and put herself back in the flow of travelers.

"Maggie!"

The sound of someone calling her name cut into her heartsick fog. Confused, she turned.

Garrett was at the top of the steep escalator, and the breath left her lungs with a whoosh. She dropped her bag and steadied herself with a hand on the wall as he began jogging down the moving steps, swiftly sidestepping other travelers, oblivious to the rising buzz as people began to recognize him and move out of his way. His scalpel-sharp gaze never wavered from her face, his expression grim.

When he reached the bottom, before she could even string together a coherent thought, he was in front of her, against her, sliding a hand onto her waist, jerking her against his tall frame, and with his other hand he cupped the back of her head to yank her mouth to his.

And his kiss, oh, his kiss. Hard core, frustrated, fierce, delicious. His hot tongue explored her mouth like he was starving, like he was desperate for something only she could give him. Maggie felt the wall behind her back, felt him pressing against her. His hand tangled into her hair, clenching the strands in his fist as if to hold her captive. She could feel his erection against her stomach, could feel his body humming with tension. She knew he was fighting to keep from grinding against her. Maggie pushed her fingers through the thick silk of his hair, scraped his scalp with her fingernails and then slid her hands to his face, curving around his angled jaw, the slight stubble rasping against her palms. She heard him groan against her mouth, a low guttural sound, and it made her shudder, made her body pulse helplessly. It was an out-of-body experience. The steadily growing desire she'd tried so hard to ignore over the past few days and the angst of their last evening only needed one turbulent touch to ignite a firestorm. Their tongues stroked and plunged in a dueling parry and thrust. Maggie lost all sense of where she was, of the people moving around them, of the bustle and noise. There was just Garrett, his mouth hot on hers, his body hard, pressing against her in the middle of the airport, and the need that had exploded between them both.

He broke off the kiss and she clung to him, disoriented, her breath shallow. He tipped his forehead against hers and held her close for a long moment, his breath ragged. She could feel the muscles clenching along his jaw line, his pulse beating fast, in time with her pounding heart. "Don't go, Maggie," he whispered hoarsely, his breath making her shiver. "Please don't go."

His words slid into her heart like a silk dagger, bleeding all her reservations away. How could she leave? If she did, she'd regret it the rest of her life. It was crazy how happy she'd been the last few days. She only had one thought, only one choice.

Never mind all the problems, like the miles between their vastly different lives or the fact he wasn't the marrying kind. She'd grab onto this once-in-a-lifetime interlude with both hands and an open heart and, when it was over, she'd go home, dust herself off and get on with her life.

"Okay," she whispered back. There was no other response. She knew if she got on the plane, she'd never see him again. She couldn't imagine not ever seeing him again.

He tipped his head back, his gaze piercing. "What did you say?"

"I don't want to go." She knotted her fists in his shirt, pulling him harder against her. This felt right. It felt inevitable. "I don't."

Garrett expelled a harsh breath and then pressed a swift, hard kiss on her mouth. "Come on." He clamped one arm around her waist and picked up her bag with the other. Oblivious to the rising interest of people around them, calling his name and pointing phones in their direction, he held her tight against his side and hurried her to the up escalator. He kept her close as he sped her through the building and back out of the automatic doors where his truck was double parked. He opened her door, she climbed back in, and she watched, still dazed, as an airport employee tried to flag him down. The guard did a double-take when he recognized Garrett.

"Back again so soon?" he called.

"Yeah, sorry," Garrett called back, waving his apologies. He opened the back door, flung her bag into the backseat, and then jumped into the driver's seat.

"Buckle up."

Maggie fumbled with her seat belt as he started the engine. She grabbed the armrest as he pulled the truck out a little too swiftly. She heard a couple of annoyed horns sound behind them but Garrett didn't flinch. Leaning forward, his attention was focused, weaving between the stop-and-go traffic ahead of them.

She couldn't take her eyes off of him. He kept glancing at her as if he wasn't sure she was really there. He reached his hand out and she took it, twining her fingers through his, joined on top of the console.

"What just happened?" she asked finally.

He shot another glance at her and shook his head slightly. "You –I couldn't go back home without you, Maggie."

Maggie's heart gave a happy thump, an over-the-moon thump. "Well, it wasn't fair, what you did back there, just so you know."

He looked worried. "What I did?"

"Yes. You unbottled it again. After I specifically told you not to."

He frowned, confused.

She squeezed his hand. "Your hottest quarterback magic sorcery. That stuff's lethal."

He laughed out loud, the best sound Maggie had ever heard. He lifted their clasped hands and pressed kisses on her knuckles. "I play to win."

Chapter 18

Maggie didn't think they would ever get back to his house. It was only thirty miles, but between the traffic and her impatience, it was interminable. They didn't speak. She knew what was going to happen when they got there and her skin felt like tinder, ready to catch fire. Her heart was thumping like a drum and she was holding onto his hand like it was the only thing tethering her to reality. Garett was driving with his left hand, and when he was forced to slow down or stop, he tapped his fingers restlessly on the steering wheel. Once, at a red light, he reached over and caught her face, his kiss hot and wet and demanding, robbing her of her senses, until the driver behind them blew their horn. When they finally turned into his driveway, he didn't take the time to pull the truck around back to the garage. She was opening her door before they had even come to a complete stop because, if he thought she was waiting for him to do his gentlemanly thing, he was crazy. She jumped out of the passenger side, on his heels as he strode to the front door.

"Hurry up, hurry up, hurry up." She gave into the temptation to squeeze his gorgeous ass as he put the key in the lock. Oh my God, it felt just as firm as it looked. Bitable.

"I'm hurrying," he answered with a half-laugh, half-groan.

Yanking the door open, he grabbed her hand, pulled her inside and kicked the door closed. Maggie pushed him against the back of the door, reaching for his face, that gorgeous face, that hot mouth.

He slid his hands to the back of her thighs and hoisted her up, then pivoted and pushed her against the wall. Maggie locked her legs behind his waist and whipped her arms around his neck, and their mouths slammed together again. His big frame pinned her to the wall. He clamped one hand to the back of her neck and angled her head to make the kiss harder and wetter. His flavor overwhelmed her senses. He was the best thing she'd ever tasted and she couldn't get enough. He nipped at her bottom lip, then licked it, sucked on it. She bit him back. His growl of approval sent lust through her.

She squirmed against his lean, hard body, shivering at the friction of his stiff length against the seam of her jeans. Groaning, he dipped his head to lick and kiss the sensitive curve between her neck and shoulder and cupped her ass, squeezing as he flexed his hips into her. He rocked into her in a dirty rhythm that teased and tormented her and felt wonderful but wasn't enough, not nearly enough. She arched against him. He ground harder, nibbling his way up to her ear, sending shivers down Maggie's spine. She was going to melt into a puddle at his feet. The friction from his thrusts against her center was inciting her to madness. She wanted the barrier gone.

She uncurled her legs from his hips and slid down to stand on shaky legs. But before she could reach her goal, he caught the hem of her shirt in his hands and stripped it off, over her head, then unclasped her bra before she had time to think. She didn't want to think about how quickly he'd managed it, how practiced he was. It didn't matter. All she cared was that it was one more piece of clothing discarded. He looked down at her bare breasts, his eyes narrowed, and made a deep rumbling noise that she felt to her toes.

His big, warm hands cupped her. He made a strangled moan of

appreciation as he palmed their weight, shaped the curve with his fingers, swept his thumbs over the tips. Maggie jerked against him, arched into his hands, hissing with pleasure. Dipping his head, he laved one, then the other. Her head lolled backwards. His mouth, licking, nibbling, sucking; his hand, stroking and teasing one breast, then the other. Could she orgasm just from this? It seemed likely.

Very likely.

Oh, my.

Maggie leaned against the wall limply as he continued his assault on her breasts. She grasped his head and scraped his scalp with her nails, skimmed her fingers through his hair, reveling in the thick, soft texture and the sounds he made.

He straightened, his eyes dark and hooded, and captured Maggie's face between his hands.

"Maggie," he murmured hoarsely. "God, Maggie."

"Yeah," she managed. "Me, too."

He choked out a laugh, then slid his hands beneath her and lifted her again, one forearm under her ass and the other banded around her back. He strode through the great room and down the hallway to his bedroom.

"This is happening," Burying her face in his neck, she gave him a lick and a little bite and he laughed.

"Hell yeah, it's happening." Reaching his room, he crossed to his bed in a few long strides, bent to deposit her on the bed, and pulled one of her shoes off, then the other. "I've imagined you in here, in my bed every night. Every fucking night. I've jacked off so much since you got here I'm surprised I'm not chafed." His voice was low, his explicit confession sending another river of roiling lava through her veins.

Maggie felt a heavy, aching pulse throbbing low in her stomach, between her legs. "I'm sorry?" She wasn't, though. Not at all. The mental picture of Garrett stroking himself to orgasm, thinking of her, was crazy electrifying. "I fantasized about you coming up to get me." She scrambled to her knees to grab his shirt front. "Get this off." She tugged it upwards. He reached behind his head and pulled it off in one sweep, then toed his shoes off, kicking them away.

Finally, finally, she could put her hands all over his chest. Follow the grooves and swells of his muscles, touch the swirls of hair, lick and tease his nipples. She reached for him, needing to trail her fingers along the V that disappeared into his low slung jeans, but he gave her a little nudge to lie back down so he could tug her socks off, too.

"That red bikini. Are you kidding me? Thought I was going to asphyxiate the first time I saw you in it."

Maggie shivered when he kissed the arch of one foot, then he slid his hands up her legs to slide the zipper down on her jeans. She lifted her hips and he skimmed them down her legs. Tossing them on the floor, he stood and shook his head. "You're so beautiful, Maggie. And your legs," he said reverently, smoothing a hand up and down the length of one. "If you knew the things I've been thinking about doing with those legs."

Her pulse skyrocketed. It was thrilling to know he'd been fixated on her legs. Nice to know there was some parity. "I hope you're interested in doing things with other parts, too." She was breathless at the sight of him, his ripped chest rising over her.

"Oh, yeah." His voice was rough as he bent a finger under the lace edge of her thong to tug it off. "Lots of other things." He crumpled the thong in his hand and lifted it to his face, inhaling her scent.

Ohmygod. Hottest. Thing. Ever.

He dropped them on the floor, and Maggie watched, eyes wide, as he unzipped his jeans and slid them down the length of his perfect long legs, and he was standing before her in just a pair of snug, black briefs.

He took her breath away. In the morning light, he looked golden. His body was beautiful, from his ridiculous face, to his wide shoulders, sculpted biceps, shallow navel, and golden hair arrowing down to his briefs.

He hooked the band of his briefs and peeled them off, too.

Maggie's mouth went dry at the sight of his cock. She swallowed, her eyes wide. It was beautiful, but it was also freaking huge.

She blinked and lifted her gaze to his face, to his blue eyes, at that hint of a roguish smile at her expression. Her eyes dropped down again, making sure she wasn't hallucinating.

No, she was not.

She realized she'd been holding her breath.

"You don't look chafed to me," she squeaked, and was rewarded with a quirk of his lips. He yanked open the drawer of his bedside table and dug around swiftly, frowning until he found what he was looking for. A condom, Maggie realized, grateful that he was still cognizant enough to think of protection. He tore it open with his teeth and she watched, mesmerized, as he rolled the condom onto his cock, and then gave himself a couple of slow, fisted pumps, his eyes locked onto hers. Maggie's stomach did a double reverse somersaulting flip.

"Garrett," she hissed, clenching and unclenching the sheets in her fists.

His eyes glittering at her response, Garrett placed a knee on the bed and stalked up her body. Maggie's eyes fluttered from the sensation of his form moving over hers, hard and warm. He braced himself above her, his legs bent on either side of her hips and gazed down at her. She was sure she could lose her mind looking straight into those blue eyes. She would gladly take that chance. He moved one knee in between her legs and then the other and she wrapped her legs around him with a breathless sigh, gasping when his hard length pushed against her throbbing center. His mouth covered hers again as he moved inside the cradle of her thighs, rolling his hips, nudging her. His tongue swirled, demanded. He copied the thrust of his hips, robbing her of her ability to think. And it was just as well because the spark flared scorching hot.

"Maggie, I want to go slow but I've got to – I need to –" he groaned tautly against her mouth.

She understood. She didn't want soft caresses or sweet exploration. She needed him inside her, too. Urgently. Nothing else mattered. "Yes. Now." Her voice sounded strangled. She gripped his hips, sliding her hands to his ass, squeezing, biting into his flesh with her fingers, encouraging him.

His gaze locked onto her, Garrett reached a hand down to guide his crown to her center, stroking down the length of his shaft once, twice, parting her. He thrust hard, burying himself in her in one fluid motion. Huge, hard, hot. Burning. Arching helplessly, Maggie gasped at the overwhelming, foreign fullness, waiting for her body to loosen, to accept. Garrett held still and they panted against one another for a long moment.

"You feel like fucking heaven," he hissed, his forehead resting on hers. She couldn't speak, but she nodded, her hands moving to grip his wide shoulders. "Are you okay?"

She was so much more than okay. "Yes." She clenched him inside and felt him tense, heard his breath hitch. "Yes," she breathed, capturing his lips. "So good."

Plundering her mouth, he braced one hand on the headboard and wrapped his other arm around her shoulder. "Hold on, baby."

Those three stark little words made her shudder.

The rhythm of their bodies took over, first with slow, torturous, sinuous, rapturous thrusts, and then his strokes grew faster, harder. Hot and demanding, the heat of his skin, his sultry, potent scent, the intimate sound of their damp flesh slapping – the sensations were overwhelming. The pleasure swelled into a wave that threatened to steal her ability to think.

"Garrett, please." She was at the edge of something so huge, something she'd never approached before.

He let go of the headboard and brought his hand down between them, applying delicious pressure to the sensitive bundle of nerves at her center. He rubbed and swirled as he continued thrusting, his fingers sliding in her wetness. She made incoherent noises at the escalating trembling in her core. Sighs, moans, words that made no sense but spurred him on.

He thrust again and pinched her nub and she shrieked as she shattered into a million pieces, shuddering violently, her arms tight around his shoulders. He slowed his thrusts to match the endless rippling as she rode out the orgasm. She felt him inhale a rough breath and hold it, drop his head back, his throat exposed to her, heard him groan her name through clenched teeth. On and on, his eyes squeezed shut. She murmured to him, senseless words, until he breathed again, dropped his forehead down to hers. He slid his arms around her and somehow flipped their positions. She was a limp heap on top of him, both of them sweaty and gasping, arms tight around one another.

Devastated and depleted, Maggie dropped her head onto his chest, letting her hair fall to hide her face. She squeezed her eyes closed against the tears. It had never been like that for her. He had taken her apart and put her back together, and she wasn't the same anymore.

Sweeping her hair back from her face, Garrett tilted her face up, his gaze searching, and spied the wetness on her cheeks. "Baby," he murmured, grazing the tears away with his fingertips. "Maggie."

"I think you broke me," she managed, stroking his corded arms, his broad shoulders, his warm, delicious neck. She studied the chiseled lines of his face. His thick lashes, his eyebrows, the scar on his chin. It was his lips that made her sigh and she traced them with her finger.

"Back at you, sweet baby," he murmured. She tucked her face into the hollow between his neck and his shoulder, overcome by his endearment. He slipped a hand to her cheek, pulling her face back up to his and nuzzled the dampness on her cheeks. He pressed kisses on her eyes, her forehead, her nose and then slanted his head to kiss her mouth. "I'm sorry," he murmured.

Toying with his hair, Maggie huffed in amusement. "Are you

honestly apologizing to me?"

He smiled against her mouth. "I'm better than that. You'll see."

Maggie's breath hitched. Better than that? She didn't know how, but she couldn't wait to find out.

Waking up in bed with Maggie tucked against his chest had to be the best damn feeling in the whole fucking world. Maybe only second to finally getting her into his bed. Garrett looked down at her, a long smooth leg draped over his thigh, an arm curled over his chest, her face, almost hidden by her hair, pressed in the dip between his shoulder and his neck. He still could barely believe it. He'd come so close to never knowing what it felt like.

It felt like nothing he'd ever known.

It still made his guts coil just to recall watching her walk away from him at the airport. Thank God he'd turned around. Thank God he hadn't been too late. When he'd caught sight of her from the top of the escalator, he couldn't get down that escalator fast enough. The tears on her face had sacked him and at that point it didn't matter if he was making a scene in the middle of the airport, if there were a hundred people crowding around or a hundred cameras pointed at them. All that mattered was Maggie, that she was still within reach and he had one more chance to keep her.

His arms tightened around her as he relived that kiss. He'd been desperate. He'd taken everything he felt, everything he wanted, and everything he wanted to give her and poured into that kiss. What was fucking amazing was how she'd almost scorched him with her response. His Maggie, blazing and desperate.

The fear was still there, though, threatening to choke him when he asked her not to go. And when she nodded, her cheeks wet with tears, the relief he felt had almost brought him to his knees.

Maggie breathed something incomprehensible and then squirreled closer, sighing. He felt a wave of emotion and closed his eyes.

The drive home from the airport had been both the best and worst thirty minute ride of his life. He had been unable to stop glancing at her to see if she was showing any signs of doubt or having second thoughts. She had held onto his hand with a vengeance, making frustrated noises that went straight to his groin when they hit traffic or a red light.

Maggie's hand uncurled on his chest and slid around to curve onto his arm. He debated whether to hold still and savor the moment or to let another part of his body dictate how to respond. They'd been at it for hours, with intermittent recesses – yeah, she called them 'recesses' – for food and sleep. He'd never spent a night like that before, ever. His sassy, Southern girl was every bit as enthusiastic in bed as she was in every other way. He'd known it was going to be good, but it had been mind-blowing. He had needed to make it as good for her as he possibly could, and then her pleasure became his pleasure. It just grew exponentially, each time better than the last.

And it wasn't just hot; she made it fun. Crazy, silly fun. Lots of laughing and tickling. The unexpected things she said that cracked him up. They'd tried having a picnic in bed at one point but that hadn't worked out. Well, it had, just not the way they'd planned. All it took was one charged look and then the laughter stopped and they were a desperate tangle of arms and legs and hands and mouths. And there you were, with twisted sheets and melted ice cream and Oreo crumbs everywhere.

And he did mean everywhere.

Grinning, Garrett pressed a careful kiss on top of Maggie's head. Being with her was a crazy-ass combination of lust and laughter. He was in it for the long haul. They had stuff to work out but he wasn't giving her up.

Maggie murmured something else in her sleep and apparently

she was speaking directly to his dick because it was definitely responding.

What to do, what to do. Let her sleep? Nibble on her again, up and down, between her sweet thighs? Make her gasp his name, melt in his hands?

She stirred again, blinked, and buried her face deeper into his neck to draw in a deep breath.

He chuckled. "Are you smelling me?"

She giggled. Wriggling down, she stuck her nose in his armpit and inhaled deeply. He rose up on one elbow and brushed the hair from her face, looked at her shining brown eyes. "There's something wrong with you. Something seriously wrong."

She gave him a smile that made him catch his breath, and then she frowned.

"What? What is it?"

She reached under the covers, feeling around for something, and then withdrew her hand to show him the crumbled half of an Oreo. "Breakfast."

"No, baby." Shaking his head, he rolled on top of her, and then shimmied down, detouring for a few minutes at her perfect breasts, then spread her beautiful long legs and hitched them over his shoulders. "Breakfast."

Chapter 19

Maggie looked at the plate piled high with bacon and sighed. "I think that's enough, don't you?" She was sitting on top of the island, swinging her legs, wearing one of Garrett's Renegades t-shirts and a pair of his boxer shorts rolled over at the waist.

"What are you, the bacon police?" He looked at her over his shoulder, an eyebrow cocked. He put the cooking fork down to push his way between her knees and slide his hands beneath her shirt. "I only eat it during the off season. Leave me alone."

All he had to do was tilt that eyebrow and she was a goner. His big warm hands felt so good and now she knew they were skilled at a lot more than just launching a football. But she was hungry. "Feed me," she said, slapping his hands away. "I require sustenance."

He picked up a piece of bacon and put it in her mouth, then slid his hands into the boxers, kneading her ass. "I want this." He tugged her closer, nuzzled her neck.

"You can't have any more of this until you feed me." She made a lie out of her own words by hooking her ankles around his hips and pulling him closer. God, she couldn't get enough of him. She'd actually thought she'd had good sex before. She was wrong, so very wrong. This man was gifted in more ways than one. His stamina was the stuff of legends. And he had skills. Oh, boy, did he. She shivered just remembering his mouth, his tongue, his fingers, all up in her lady business, reducing her bones to Jello.

She giggled and fed him a piece of bacon, laughing when he nibbled her fingers.

And with him, she was fearless. She trusted him completely and reveled in the moments when she took him apart, too. Every time they came together it was more powerful, more heightened. She didn't think it was just her, either. She saw it in the way he took her with such hunger, held her with such tenderness, how he wrapped himself around her when they slept.

Plus if there was a Super Bowl for best kissing, he'd have giant rings on every finger. She could kiss him for hours.

Desire pooling, she looped her arms around his neck and pulled him in for one of those kisses. A deep kiss, a drawn-out, breathless, tongue-fondling kiss, the kind that made her forget all about needing food and him forget all about the bacon sizzling on the stove.

The bacon sizzling on the stove. Burning, more like. She pushed him away and he looked puzzled at her wrinkled nose, then realized why. "Shit." He turned back to the stove and grabbed a hot pad to take the skillet off the flame. "Woman, you made me burn the bacon."

"I think six pounds is enough, anyway." She stole another slice.

"It's just a pound." He gave her a mock-glare and dumped the burned strips into the trash.

Maggie laughed. "You ought to be the spokesperson for the National Pork Board."

"I'll tell my agent to get right on that. Want eggs?"

"No, six pounds of bacon is plenty on its own."

"One pound minus the burnt pieces. I'm glad to know my evil plan is working." He picked up the plate and carried it to the den.

"Tell me about this evil plan." Maggie hopped off the island and followed, her eyes on his booty.

He sat on the sofa. "To turn you to the –" he waggled his

eyebrows. " Pork side."

She burst out laughing. His Darth Vader impression was beyond terrible. What a weirdo. How had he managed to hide his goofy streak for so long? He had come a long way in just a few days. She loved it so freaking much when he was silly. "That has got to be the worst joke I've ever heard in my entire life. I can't wait to tell my father. He'll love it."

"Tell me about your dad." Sitting back, Garrett made a 'come here' motion. Maggie didn't need further invitation. Taking the plate from him, she curled up on his lap sideways and put a piece of bacon in his mouth.

"He's just the best." She ran a fingertip over his magic eyebrow. He arched it for her and she laughed and kissed it. "He looks very proper and distinguished, but underneath he's a big kid with the goofiest sense of humor. He makes me and mom laugh all the time. What about your dad?"

Garrett went still and Maggie faltered.

"Sorry," she said quickly. "I know you don't talk about your parents."

He blinked as though he'd been far off someplace else and then turned to her with a serious expression. "It's okay. I'll tell you about them if you want. I'll tell you anything you want to know."

His words took her breath away. This was a part of his life that she knew he didn't expose to anyone. Maggie put her hands on his scruffy cheeks and kissed him. She loved that scruff. "It's okay, really."

"You need to know. It's why I don't ever want kids."

Dread curled its way down her spine. She knew they would have to address the elephant in the room at some point, but she wasn't ready. And she was afraid of what he was going to tell her. She didn't want to fail him, to respond in a way that would make him regret confiding in her.

He took the plate and rose slightly, as if she was a feather on his lap, and reached to place it on the ottoman. "So, my parents," Sighing, he captured her hand and twined his fingers through hers.

"My parents should have never had children." Hesitating, he gave her a pensive half-smile.

"Garrett, you really don't have to –"

"Nah, it's okay." He kissed the inside of her wrist. "It's just hard to know where to start."

She lifted her free hand and smoothed his tousled hair. "Take your time."

He nodded. "Okay, so my father had issues." He snorted and shook his head derisively. "Serious issues. Em took a boatload of psych courses in college and she's pretty convinced he had both borderline and narcissistic personality disorder. Apparently they can go hand in hand. Together, let me tell you, awesome combination."

Maggie pressed another kiss on his wrist.

"She gave me tons of stuff to read. She's probably right, but you don't care what it's called when you're a kid. And you're sure as hell not equipped to deal with it."

"Of course not," she murmured.

"I can't remember a time as a kid when I wasn't afraid of him. He'd go into a rage over nothing so we were always walking on eggshells. I can remember lots of times when we were young, maybe even younger than Lilah, hiding together in a closet until he was asleep or left the house."

He trailed off, and Maggie stroked his cheek. "What about your mom?" she asked hesitantly.

He made a noise. "She just kind of checked out as far as motherhood went. Alcohol, sedatives, oblivious to everything. I told you they owned a nightclub, right?"

She nodded.

"Yeah, worst possible lifestyle. Alcohol, drugs, lots of opportunities for screwing around. They never said no to any of it. At the nightclub he could be the big man, important, you know? And he liked having a beautiful wife who other men admired, who did whatever he told her to do, even if she could barely stand up half the time."

Maggie's heart hurt. How old had he been when he started figuring all this out? Seeing what was going on, realizing it wasn't normal?

"Now he liked it when I started getting attention playing ball because it made him look good, feel important. That was when he started really coming down harder on Emily. I started doing whatever I could to be someplace other than at home, and I could get away with it because of football, but Em –" he broke off and closed his eyes. "I messed up. I should've taken better care of her. She was stuck there, bearing the brunt of his crazy-ass temper, all his criticism and manipulation. Our mother was no help." He rubbed his jaw, smiling wryly. "Em was tough, though. Tougher than me. She would do some of the craziest shit just to mess with him. He'd go nuts. He never did manage to break her down. Probably wasn't the best idea, fucking with him, though, because pretty soon shit got real." He fell silent for a minute and Maggie could feel sudden tension in his body.

"That's enough." It pained her to see him struggling. "You don't have to –"

"I want to. It's important that you understand." He tilted his head back and closed his eyes. Maggie stroked his jaw. She laid her cheek against his chest. He wrapped his arms around her and rested his chin on top of her head. They sat there a moment, silent, entwined. Maggie hoped he could feel her love.

Because she did love him. This was more than a crush. More than happy hormones. What she had felt for Mason was nothing compared to the sea of emotion she felt for Garrett. Making love with him brought her to tears almost every time. It was like he filled up spaces in her that she didn't even know were there.

She felt him take a deep breath. She smoothed her hand up and down over his warm chest to the bulk of his shoulder to his jaw where his muscles were clenched.

"So now we're in our teens. Like I said, I stayed away as much as I could, but one night I went home unexpectedly. When I went upstairs, he was in Emily's room." He said it fast, then stopped and cleared his throat.

Maggie's heart thumped and she looked up at him in horror.

He saw her expression. "Yeah." He nodded slowly. "Yeah. It was messed up."

"Oh, my God," she whispered.

He nodded again, his expression stark, his eyes distant. "I was in time, though. Pretty close, but, yeah, just in time."

"Emily?" Maggie prompted.

"Em was – she was okay. Well, you know. She was freaked out, she was fighting him, but, yeah, she was – he hadn't –" He shook his head, grimacing. "So, anyway, by that time I was bigger than him. I went after him."

Maggie couldn't take her eyes off his face.

He let go of her hand to rub the back of his neck.

"I hope you hurt him," she said softly.

He squeezed her. "I did. The element of surprise, you know. And the fact his fucking pants were down. I beat him to a bloody pulp. Broke his nose, cracked his jaw, couple of his ribs."

"Where was your mother?"

He scoffed. "Passed out downstairs at first, then I guess she heard us because next thing I knew, she was hitting me, screaming at me to stop." He blew out a breath. "Didn't want me to hurt him, I guess. Never mind what he was going to do to Emily. Some mom."

Maggie felt wetness on her cheeks.

"The next day I went back while they were at the club to get our stuff. We were never going back. And would you believe it, the bastard had the fucking balls to show up at my next game, acting like nothing had happened." Garrett made a disgusted sound. "I went after him again but my coach knew what was going on. He got between us and pulled him off to the side and said if he didn't go and stay gone, he'd file charges. The bastard tried to tell him it was me who tried to rape Em. Can you believe that shit?"

Maggie had no words. "He accused you?"

He nodded.

"Did you? File charges?" she managed.

"No. That would've made it worse for Emily. It was bad enough what he tried to do, but to have it made public," he broke off. "We couldn't put Em through that. All Em and I wanted was to get away from them. The threat of ruining his fucking reputation was enough to stop them from making any trouble. He had to keep up appearances, you know, be admired. That's what he cared about. He wasn't going to mess with that."

"How old were you?"

"Fifteen."

Maggie's breath hitched. When she was fifteen, she was focused on getting a smartphone. Garrett was protecting his sister from being abused.

"Where did you go?"

"We stayed with a family in our neighborhood. Nice people. They took us in, no hesitation."

"And Emily? Afterwards?"

"Counseling. She's good now. Like I said, she's tough." He sighed. "I should have been there more. I shouldn't have stayed away, leaving her alone."

She smoothed the fabric of his shirt on his chest. "You were a child, Garrett."

"No, I let her down. It's a fucking miracle I went home that night. If I hadn't –" he broke off again.

"I bet Emily doesn't think you let her down. She loves you so much. She told me so."

He was silent.

"And you? Did you have counseling, too?"

"Nah, I didn't need it. I got my therapy on the football field."

Maggie's heart broke a little more. You didn't overcome a lifetime of abuse from playing sports. Not at any age. He'd been his sister's hero and gotten her the help she needed, but he had been bottling up his emotions about it ever since. "What happened to them?"

"My mother's still alive. My father died a while back. I went to his funeral because I wanted to make sure the bastard was dead. That was a shitshow, let me tell you." He shook his head. "My mother saw me, started crying and grabbing onto me, going on about how I was just like him, how much she missed him." Garrett gave a bitter laugh. "She always said that. 'Just like him.'" He shook his head. "Gee, thanks, mom."

Now Maggie understood his aversion to marriage. He had grown up trying to survive in the shadow of the worst example. She thought about the fifteen-year-old boy he had been, protecting his sister, burying his pain, fighting his way out of neglect and abuse to become the strong, sensitive person he was now. Her heart swelled with love.

"So there you have it," he said. "Two psychos for parents. Well, one psycho and one alcoholic-slash-drug addict. Talk about a fucked-up gene pool."

And now she also understood why he didn't want children. It all made perfect, terrible sense.

He looked down at her and his expression softened. "Are those tears?" He lifted a hand and stroked her cheek, his thumb tracing the path a tear had taken.

"Shh." She straddled him, shifting on her knees and gripping his shoulders to get closer. She wanted to hold him as tightly as she could, with all of her strength. She wanted to comfort the confused little boy, the fierce teenager, and the amazing man who kept the secrets and carried the scars.

"Maggie," he breathed, lifting her easily to position her exactly where he wanted her, astride the thickness in his silky shorts. "You make me …" His voice faded as words failed him.

"Shh." He'd given her his trust, shared the painful history he kept hidden, and she needed to show him she understood the significance of his gift. Leaning forward, she took his face between her hands, smoothing the dark hair away from his temples. "Close your eyes." He obeyed, thick lashes skimming his skin, and his male beauty took her breath away. She kissed his forehead, his closed eyes, one, then the other, and used her hands to tilt his head and press a kiss to his lips.

It was a soft kiss, a tender kiss, but it had the impact of a match to gasoline. Sharing his story had come at a cost and with a guttural, masculine groan, Garrett sat forward, one arm clamping her against his chest, the other fisting in the back of her hair, kissing her like he was starving. Maggie wrapped her legs around his torso, sank her hands into his silky hair, meeting and matching the thrusts of his tongue, grinding down on the hard length of his erection. The kiss went on and on until they were both panting, need throbbing and heat pulsing between them like a live wire.

Desperate to get closer, to feel more, Maggie reached for the hem of his shirt and yanked it upwards. There could be no barriers. She needed to feel his skin, smooth and warm, under her fingertips, to inhale his scent, to match her delirious heartbeat with his.

Garrett broke away from her long enough to seize the fabric and yank it off. He drew her shirt up and over her head, lifting his lips only long enough for it to clear her face and then his mouth returned, hot and hungry. He ran his hands over her rib cage and cradled her breasts, teasing the peaks with his fingers, his lips, his tongue. Maggie ground down on him, scraping her fingernails across his shoulders and down the hard muscles of his biceps. Still yearning for more, she tried to slip her hand down beneath the band of his pants to grasp his hard cock.

Garrett gave a hoarse groan. Standing without warning, he put her on her feet and then with one easy movement, lifted her over his shoulder. Maggie squeaked, astonished at being upended so easily and carted through the house at such a pace, secured only by one large hand on the backs of her thighs.

Reaching the bedroom, he lowered her to the bed and followed her down. Caging her with his arms and legs, he brushed her hair from her face and gazed at her, his eyes dark and hungry.

Maggie's breath hitched. He dipped his mouth to hers for another long, desperate kiss before rising to his knees to pull her shorts down and toss them to the floor. Her limbs heavy with desire, Maggie watched him slide down her body, clutching the sheets with her fists as he nuzzled and licked and sucked her aching center. Trembling as he murmured nonsensical praise, panting as he worked his fingers in and out, until she was drowning in sensation. She gasped when he pressed her thighs farther apart, baring her relentlessly, stroking and plundering with his tongue. "Yes, yes, yes, Garrett. So good," she managed, her voice thready. Delirious from the building sensations, she arched her back and flung her arms over her face, rocking her hips against him. "So close. So close."

Garrett stopped and stood, kicked off his pants and then lunged for the drawer of the bedside table. Panting, Maggie fisted the sheets again, watched the muscles in his jaw pulsing as he tore the foil packet and rolled the condom down the length of his rigid cock. He straightened and looked down at her, and she could see his thighs trembling, his chest heaving with barely contained emotion. Shuddering, she reached for him and he pulled her to the edge of the bed and flipped her around, onto her elbows and knees. He gripped her hips and drove into her in one deep, desperate motion. Bending over her back, he began thrusting, pumping hard and fast, hitting a sensitive spot she didn't even know she had. It was fierce and primal and she felt her climax building again, even higher, but before it sent her over the edge, he pulled out and suddenly she was on her back again. He was between her thighs, gripping and lifting her hips, pounding into her again, faster and harder. Overwhelmed, Maggie squeezed her eyes shut, lost to the heat coiling inside her body.

"No, look at me. See me," Garrett rasped hoarsely, clasping a hand around her jaw. The raw emotion in his eyes pushed Maggie over the edge and she shrieked, spasms sweeping her, blurring her vision. Garrett watched her, his jaw clenched as she writhed and moaned with pleasure, and then his breath caught. He stiffened, the cords in his neck tight, and gasped her name. Maggie clung to him, her arms wrapped around his neck and her legs tight around his hips as his body jerked and throbbed inside her.

Damp and spent, their breath ragged, they clung to one another for long moments and then he rolled over, taking her with him, keeping their connection. One warm hand spanned her ass, holding her tight, and the other cradled her head to his chest. Maggie thought she could probably stay that way forever, sprawled over him like a jellyfish. It might take forever for her panting to stop.

"Maggie." His voice was a low, satisfied rumble.

"Hmm?" No way she could form real words yet.

He shifted slightly, moving her to his side, and lifted up on one elbow to look at her. Trailing his fingers over the dip of her waist and slope of her hip, he gave her a look of such unabashed tenderness that Maggie had to swallow.

"What are you doing to me?" His fingers were gently sliding through her hair, grazing her scalp.

"I'm just loving you." The words were out of her mouth before she could stop herself.

He stilled instantly.

Oh no. Maddie felt paralyzed, pinned by his gaze and afraid of his reaction. It wasn't as if she'd actually said 'I love you' even though that was what she meant. He didn't need to know how quickly and deeply she'd fallen for him. Confessing to have feelings was one thing, but labeling it as love right out of the gate was madness. Nobody fell in love that quickly. He'd think she was crazy. He might be right.

"You know what I mean," she equivocated nervously. She felt awkward and couldn't meet his gaze. "I'm having such a good time making love with you." That didn't sound right and it was also the understatement of the millennium.

Garrett continued to study her.

She tried again, with growing anxiety. "I love being with you.

Here in Denver."

For the love of all that's good, please shut up.

Feeling exposed in more ways than one, she rolled away and sat with her back to him, tugging at the sheet so she could hide in it.

She felt the bed shift, and before she could look over her shoulder, he'd moved behind her, his long legs on either side of hers, one hand snaking around her waist to hold her snugly against his chest, the other tugging the sheet away to caress her breasts. She felt him drop his chin on her shoulder, and felt his breath at her ear as he nestled her within the warm curve of his body. "I'm loving you, too, Maggie," he said, nibbling at her ear.

Wait, what? She gasped at his words.

"Here in Denver." and she could feel his chest shaking with laughter. "The things you say." She felt him shake his head.

Oh. He didn't take her seriously. That was good, right?

She had no idea anymore.

Chapter 20

"Ready?" Garrett dropped his duffle bag on the kitchen floor next to her battered old pink camo bag.

Almost." Perched on one of the bar chairs, Maggie pressed the send button on another upbeat text to her mom and dad. They weren't helicopter parents but she knew they were worried about her recent un-Maggie-like decisions and would be relieved when she returned home.

Closing the distance between them, Garrett slid a hand around her cheek, tilted her face up and captured her lips. Maggie stood, savoring the way he caged his arms around her, pressing her into his chest. This was her place, inside his embrace. She deepened their kiss, ran her hands beneath his shirt and grazed her fingernails down his wide lats, to his sculpted V shaped abdominal lines, and lower where his erection strained against the fabric of his jeans. Groaning, Garrett shifted against her, breaking away from her mouth to nibble at her ear, lick the pulse point at her throat.

"Morning!" Garrett's assistant, Claire, called from the hallway to the garage.

"Damn," Garrett muttered, pressing his forehead against hers. Maggie lifted her hands to his temples and pressed a quick kiss on his mouth.

"Just as well," she breathed. "Or we'll never get on the road."

He huffed in amusement. "You're right." He adjusted himself and moved to the far side of the island. "Hey, Claire," he called. "Come meet Maggie."

Maggie felt a little nervous about meeting his long-time assistant. Garrett spoke with her on the phone often and from what she could glean from his side of the conversations, Claire was the warm, motherly type who wasn't afraid to scold him when he was being difficult and ran interference for him like a well-seasoned left tackle.

Claire came into view and Maggie knew at first glance that she would like her. She looked anything but motherly, though. She was short and slender, with spiky blonde hair and she was beaming from ear to ear.

Garrett waved at the air between them. "Maggie, this is Claire. Claire, meet Maggie."

Claire came forward, her smile huge, and gave Maggie a big hug. "I can't tell you how happy I am to meet you, Maggie."

Maggie squeezed her back. She loved huggers. "Me, too."

Claire headed for the coffee maker. "I didn't think I'd get the chance, though. I thought you guys were leaving early this morning?"

Maggie hoped she wasn't blushing. Their original plan was to leave by nine a.m. for Grand Lake but getting out of bed and getting dressed was harder than expected when they couldn't keep their hands off one another.

"Yeah, we meant to." Garrett winked at Maggie. "Had a tough time getting out of bed."

He just said that. Out loud. And yes, she was definitely blushing.

Claire blinked and her grin widened. "Okay, then." She dropped a pod in the coffee maker and then dug her phone out of the back pocket of her jeans. "Well, I hate to be the bearer of bad news when you're having a nice morning but I've got something to show you." Tapping her phone on, she held it out to Garrett.

He looked at the screen and shrugged. "Oh, well."

Claire's eyes opened wide. "'Oh, well'? That's it?"

He shrugged again. "Better show Maggie." Reaching into the refrigerator, he held up a bottle of green tea to Maggie questioningly. She shook her head, anxious about Claire's bad news.

Claire held the phone out to her. She took it and inhaled sharply. It was a photo of her and Garrett in the airport. Yikes. It looked – not PG. He had her flattened against the wall and they were tangled together like a twisty knot of wire. The caption read "Renegade quarterback Garrett Long makes a play for Maggie Parrish at Denver International Airport."

Maggie's heart thumped. They printed her name. *Ohmygod* they printed her name. She lifted her horrified gaze and found Garrett watching her. "It was inevitable, babe." He drank a long swallow of his drink and rounded the island to slide an arm around her waist. "Nothing to worry about."

She stared at him, astonished. Who was this man? Surely not the man who despised having details of his private life heralded on the Internet. Why wasn't he upset?

From Claire's reaction, she was wondering the same thing. "It just showed up on TMZ this morning," she said. "I'm guessing 'no comment', right?"

Garrett drank a long gulp of his tea. "Yep." He pressed a kiss on Maggie's still-surprised mouth. "What? You're not embarrassed to be linked with me, are you?"

She made a face at him. "Of course not, but this is –" It was pretty damned personal is what it was, his kryptonite, and he was so calm. "You hate being in the news."

He looked thoughtful. "Yeah, I do, but this is different. I don't mind." He didn't elaborate.

Maggie caught Claire's comically raised eyebrows, her disbelief at his casual response. Then Claire looked at Maggie again and the sudden smile on her face expanded into a big grin.

She scrolled past the photo, down to the article. It was short, just a blurb, but it mentioned that she was from Baton Rouge. "My folks are going to freak out." And her friends, and her colleagues. She dug her phone back out of her purse. Messages and voicemails were already coming in. She showed the screen to Garrett. He looked at it and squeezed her against his side.

"Just give your folks a call and don't worry about any numbers you don't know. Claire will put something out that'll direct questions to my publicist. I'm going to put the bags in the truck and go get gas." He kissed Maggie again. "Be right back."

She and Claire watched him amble away, through the door to the garage, and then Claire turned to her. "Who is that and what did you do with the real Garrett Long? The one who gets dark and twisty when he makes the news?"

Maggie shrugged helplessly, pulling the article up on her own phone. She was still trying to figure out how to explain the photo to her mom and dad.

Claire pulled out a bar chair and perched on top of it. "Are you okay?"

Maggie tried to smile but she was feeling a little sick to her stomach. "A little worried, honestly."

Claire looked sympathetic. "I can imagine. Garrett's used to dealing with press so try not to worry about it. We'll handle it."

Maggie nodded, then drew in a deep breath and turned her attention to Claire. "He's told me nothing but nice things about you. He said you've worked with him for a good while."

Claire nodded. "Going on six years, but I've known him since we were kids."

Garrett hadn't mentioned that. "Really?"

"Yes. We lived in the same neighborhood, growing up. I'm two years old than him and Emily. My brother, Jim, is two years younger."

Maggie made the connection. "Wait. Was it your mom and dad who looked after him and Emily?"

Claire's eyebrows lifted. "You know about that?"

Maggie nodded.

"Wow. A lot has happened in the last two weeks, hasn't it? I mean, I could tell, just over the phone, that something was different." Claire shook her head slowly. "I've honestly never seen him so relaxed."

Was she blushing again? Maggie's face felt hot. She needed to stop thinking about the bone-melting ways they'd 'relaxed' one another all night long. "So I bet Garrett keeps you really busy, huh?"

Maggie could tell by Claire's grin that her abrupt change of topic didn't go unnoticed. "Crazy busy. There's never a dull moment, that's for sure. I do everything from answering his mail and managing his schedule to making sure Dude and Buddy don't run out of food." She eyed Maggie over the top of her glass. "So now I'm going to switch over to big-sister mode. Did you know that you're the first woman Garrett has ever invited to stay here in his house?"

Maggie blinked. "Uh, no, I didn't know that. We haven't really talked about his past relationships."

"Relationships," Claire snorted. "It would be a stretch to call what Garrett's had in the past 'relationships.'" She clasped her hands together. "I know you met at the beach but I had no idea he'd invite you to come here and stay with him."

"He was struggling with Lilah and called me to ask if I could come help look after her."

Claire gave her a sly smile. "Sounds a little shady to me. There were plenty of people here who would have been happy to help him; me or my parents, for example."

Maggie shrugged helplessly. "If you're looking for a plausible explanation, I really don't have one. I'm as surprised as you are. We didn't plan it. Things just escalated."

"I'll say," Claire replied, a mischievous grin on her face. "To the point that Garrett doesn't mind having your picture together pop up in the news. That's a first. A huge first. So huge I don't really even know what to make of it, but if I had to guess, I'd say it means he's really serious about you."

Maggie's stomach tumbled. They hadn't had any real conversation about the future and she didn't want to make assumptions.

"Emily called Saturday to rave about you. When she said Garrett was smiling and laughing, I told her not to lie to me."

Garrett had certainly been reserved when they first met, but he'd still had a wry sense of humor. "He's not that bad, is he?"

Claire raised an eyebrow. "He can get pretty cranky during the off season. We try to get him to get out of the house and do things, go places, but he's more of a hermit every year. He'll go to the facility and work out or to his lake house, but that's about it. I was so glad he went to Florida with Dominic and the others. Especially now, since that's where he met you. We'd almost given up hope of him meeting someone nice."

Maggie traced her finger along a swirl in the granite island top, feeling awkward about the conversation but dying to hear more. "I'm sure he meets tons of nice women. I've seen the photos online."

Claire sighed. "If by nice you mean the kind of women who don't see anything but his face, his fame, and his paycheck, sure."

Maggie smiled. "His face is awfully pretty."

Claire snickered and then fell serious. "I still see the skinny boy from down the street who needed a haircut and a good meal." She reached to pat Maggie on the arm. "I'm still a little shocked that he opened up to you like that. It just goes to show how good you are for him. How soon do you think you might move to Denver? Before the season starts?"

Claire was getting way, way ahead of herself. She and Garrett hadn't talked about the future at all. Maggie had been trying desperately hard not to think about it. There was something to be said for pretending the outside world didn't exist, or was at least in a holding pattern.

Claire must have read Maggie's expression because she drew in a flustered breath. "Oh, sorry, I didn't mean to be so nosey. It's just that, well, I'm nosey."

Maggie offered a weak smile. "It's early days yet."

"Of course," Claire said. "I understand."

"I'm going to give my folks a call before he gets back, if you don't mind." And try to explain why she'd been photographed in a public place trying to climb a man they'd never met like a tree.

"Would you rather… sing like Adele or cook like Gordon Ramsay?"

Maggie laughed. She and Garrett were walking hand in hand along the sidewalk in downtown Grand Lake. She was in love with the picturesque Western-style town, set against the background of the Rocky Mountains, where the locals were laid back and didn't seem terribly phased by Garrett's appearance. There were the occasional requests for photos and autographs but on a whole they were left alone and Maggie enjoyed seeing Garrett much more relaxed because of it.

"As you may recall from my drunken concert, my singing skills are right up there with Adele already so I guess I'll go with cooking like Gordon Ramsay."

Garrett lifted their joined hands and pressed a kiss on Maggie's fingers. "I'm surprised dogs weren't howling all over the neighborhood that night."

"Rude." She bumped him with her shoulder and he dropped her hand to put his arm around her shoulder.

She loved being tucked under his arm.

He grinned down at her. "What've you got for me?"

She reached up and waggled the brim of his OU baseball cap. "Okay, would you rather… never be allowed to eat bacon again or ice cream?"

Wincing dramatically, he pressed his free hand to his chest. "Oh, that one hurts. Gotta think about that one."

They'd been playing the 'would you rather' game off and on all morning, starting off in the shower together, while paddle-boarding on the lake and over their lazy lunch. Turning the corner on their way back to his truck, they continued past a park where a handful of boys were playing a pick-up game of football.

"Look." Maggie nodded in their direction. "The one holding the ball is wearing your jersey." They slowed to a stop and watched the boy step back and throw the ball toward the far end of the lot, a pack of boys scrambling to try to catch it.

"His stance is off," Garrett murmured. "He needs to keep his arm in tight and use his legs to propel his body forward."

Maggie nudged him. "Why don't you go show him?"

He glanced down at her. "Yeah?"

She made a 'duh' face at him. "It'll be fun. I'll find someplace to sit and watch."

He gave her an adorable grin and dropped a kiss on her mouth before ambling across the lot. Maggie smiled as, one by one, the boys began to notice his approach, going perfectly still for a moment before jumping up and down and shoving one another in noisy excitement. She found a shady spot and sat cross-legged on the ground, watching Garrett talk to them for a few minutes before sending all but the young quarterback down field. He demonstrated his stance a few times, talking to the boy as he moved, and then dropped back and launched the ball toward the waiting receivers. The ball was returned and Garrett handed it to the boy. After he threw it a few times and Garrett was satisfied, he gave him a fist bump. Finally each grinning boy took a turn catching one of his passes and then one of them ran to dig a phone out of a backpack.

Garrett turned from the boys to wave to her. Scrambling up, she dusted off her jeans and crossed the lot.

"That your girlfriend, Garrett?" one of them asked.

"She's pretty," another one piped up.

"Yeah, she's pretty, Garrett!"

Garrett grinned at Maggie. "Yep, that's my pretty girlfriend, Maggie. Think you can take a picture for us, Maggie?"

Maggie's heart thumped so loudly she put a hand to her chest.

Girlfriend.

That was just a little bit crazy but she thought she could live with it.

"Don't flip me out of this thing." Maggie grinned up at Garrett as he sat carefully on the edge of the double hammock on the deck. He rocked it a little, making her squeal and dig her fingers into the knotted ropes, before easing down beside her and sliding his arm beneath her neck.

"Mm, nice." He pulled her closer. She turned sideways and traced his profile with her finger, and caught her breath when he caught her hand and pressed a kiss in her palm. "You having a good time?"

What a question. She was cuddled up with this sweet, sexy man in a hammock under a clear blue Colorado sky, as contented as a kitten napping in the sunshine. "I'm having the best time," she replied, latticing her fingers through his. She loved his hands, his broad palms and his long, tanned, talented fingers. "I love it here."

Resting their joined hands on his chest, he hummed his approval. "Wait until you see it in wintertime."

His casual remark caught her off guard. First he'd called her his girlfriend and now he was looking months ahead. She didn't know what to make of it. They hadn't really had a conversation about the future. When he'd come back for her at the airport, she'd pushed common-sense-Maggie to the side and let flying-by-the-seat-of-her-pants-Maggie make the dangerous decision to go back home with him, aware it would be a short-term involvement . She didn't have any expectations. For once in her life, she'd decided to just live in the moment. No promises, no regrets.

She certainly hadn't allowed herself to think about Garrett in terms of the future she wanted for herself but now he seemed to be thinking ahead and that raised a whole new crop of questions. The answers to those questions would determine whether she'd see Grand Lake in the winter with him.

Might as well go there.

"I liked watching you throwing the football with those boys today." She'd been thinking about it all evening, how patient and kind he'd been. How natural he'd looked with them.

Stroking her thumb, he nodded. "That's the best kind of fan interaction, you know. Random, no fuss. Just kids being kids and having fun playing."

"They'll certainly never forget it."

"Hmm."

"Have you – have you ever thought about what it would be like to have a son to toss a ball around with?"

His hand stilled and she felt his entire body tense.

"I think you'd make a good dad. That's what I thought about, watching you with them. I thought the same thing when we were looking after Lilah."

She watched him wince.

Yep, she'd gone there. All the way there.

He was silent for a long moment before blowing out a breath and speaking. "Being good with random kids occasionally is one thing, Maggie. Having kids is another." He let go of her hand and pinched the bridge of his nose as if he were warding off a headache. "I know it's not what you want to hear but I meant what I said before. I'm not interested in having children and I'm not ever going to change my mind."

It was true. He'd said it the very first day they'd met.

"And you know why I feel that way." he added bleakly.

"Because of your parents," she murmured.

"Exactly." He sat up and swung his legs out of the hammock, sitting in it with his back to her. "No way I'm cursing an innocent soul with their berserk shit."

"It's not all just genetics, you know."

He sighed. "Yeah, I know. I've done the research, believe me, but you can't understand what it feels like, knowing you're carrying a whole cesspool of crazy around inside you."

Maggie rubbed his back, relieved when he didn't pull away. "I could have the same concern about my parents," she offered slowly, wondering if her own circumstances might help him reconsider.

He frowned at her over his shoulder. "What are you talking about? You said your parents are great."

"They are. I'm talking about my birth parents." She hadn't intentionally kept the fact she was adopted from him; it just wasn't something that someone trying desperately to live in the moment would bring up.

He looked dumbstruck. "What?"

Maggie shrugged. "I'm adopted so, as far as I know, I could be carrying around crazy genes, too."

"I had no idea," he managed, rising carefully.

She swung out of the hammock, too, and moved to lean against the railing of the deck beside him "It's no big deal. It just hasn't come up. My folks adopted me when I was a newborn. My birth mother was a heroin addict who checked herself into a clinic when she discovered she was pregnant. I was born addicted to methadone. I have no information at all about my birth father."

It was obvious from his expression that Garrett was having trouble wrapping his head around her casual announcement. "You're not worried about what you might pass on to your kids?"

She shook her head. "No. Nobody knows how their children will turn out. I've seen parents who do everything perfectly end up with troubled kids, and terrible parents end up with fantastic kids. Like you," she added. "Look at how you turned out despite your background."

"But if you were worried," he pressed, the frown creasing his forehead.

Maggie struggled to break her perspective down to its simplest form. "I would have faith," she said finally. "My parents taught me by example."

Garrett rested his forearms on the railing, hands clasped together, his head down. "So did mine. That's the problem."

Her heart hurt for him. No matter how badly she wished things were different, she wasn't going to dismiss his feelings or try to change them. As he said, he'd been open from the beginning. If all they had were a few golden days of summer, she'd make sure they both had nothing but good memories of one another when it was over.

"Hey." Tugging him away from the rail, she slipped her arms around his waist and laid her cheek against his chest. "I'm sorry I brought it up. It's okay. It's fine. Let's forget about it."

His arms enfolded her, pulled her against the hard length of his body. "I'm sorry, Maggie."

She raised on tiptoes to kiss him. They might not have a future but they had a right-now and she was going to make the most of it.

She'd pick up the pieces of her heart when she got back home.

Garrett stepped through the sliding doors to the deck overlooking the water. It was their fourth day on Grand Lake and he never wanted to leave. Except for that uncomfortable discussion about kids, their time together had been just about perfect. The way Maggie had let the subject drop made him hopeful that maybe she might rethink the big family thing. It was a big maybe but a guy could hope.

This morning they'd gone kayaking, had another almost-uninterrupted lunch at a neat little diner, and then he'd left Maggie on her own while he did a phone interview and made a couple of phone calls. As soon as he was done, he went searching for her. He couldn't stay away from her.

She was outside, kicked back in an Adirondack chair, talking on her phone. The sight made him smile and he pulled his phone out of his pocket to snap a photo.

"Things are good," he heard her say. "No, there's nothing new to report. I've told you everything already." She heard the small click of his camera and started slightly. "Gotta go. We'll talk again later." She pressed the disconnect key and looked up at him. "Hey there," she said, languidly stretching.

He bent over and pressed a kiss on top of her head.

At his touch she smiled and hooked her finger into the collar of his shirt to pull him closer for a kiss.

Aaaaannd.... that was all it took for the blood to rush from his head to his groin. She was an addiction; the more he touched her, the more he needed to touch her. He tugged her up from her chair and pulled her close to kiss her properly. Her body, warm from the sun, fit against his as if she'd been made for him. Dimly aware of being out in the open, he walked her backwards to a nook between the stone of the fireplace and the exterior wall. Dipping his head to the curve of her neck, he nibbled his way to her ear, chuckling at her mm's of pleasure. He abandoned her ear to claim her mouth, that beguiling mouth and then slipped his hands beneath her shorts to knead her sweet, perfect ass. He heard her breath catch and felt his own pulse ratchet up. He nudged her legs apart with one knee and she hooked one leg up around his thigh, drawing him in closer, grinding against his dick.

From a chaste kiss on top of her head to hard and hungry in a matter of seconds, that's what she did to him. Now it was tongues and teeth, gasps and maneuvering. She slid her hands into his shorts and squeezed and stroked him, making his breath catch. She knew just how to handle him, but he knew what she liked, too, and caught a fistful of her hair with one hand and slid the other down to her soft, wet center. She made that little sound against his mouth, the one he loved, and in moments they were both panting.

Maggie broke the kiss. "Inside," she managed. "Got to go inside."

He couldn't wait. Right now, against the wall. He threw a glance over his shoulder and, fuck it all, there were a couple of boats idling by, too close for comfort. Maggie was right.

With his back to the lake, he shielded her and moved her inside the sliding doors. Sometimes they took their time, leisurely explorations in bed, sharing sweet strokes and whispers, and other times, like now, the spark combusted, needy and savage. It was a feverish race to strip, clothes falling helter skelter, and in seconds he had his hands on her, lifting and positioning her on the edge of the dining room table. "Eyes on me," he managed, his hand grasping his dick, lining it up with her notch.

"Condom." Her eyes were glazed with need. "Hurry."

"No. We're both clean and you're on the pill." He frowned because he couldn't believe his own words. He'd never, ever not worn a condom. Never ever considered being bare, taking that risk.

Maggie shook her head. "Are you sure? Really sure?"

He was sure, all right. This woman, what she did to him, his need for her right this second; he didn't fucking care. He gripped her hips and rocked into her, completely, and Maggie gasped. He had to stay completely still for a moment, give them both time to adjust, to feel. He tipped his head back, squeezed his eyes shut. The sensation of filling Maggie's silky tightness with no barrier was fucking staggering. He was afraid if he even breathed too hard, he'd be finished.

"Garrett," she breathed.

"Give me a second," he managed.

"What did you do?" Her eyes were huge. "Without a –"

He didn't have to protect himself from Maggie. He wanted to give her everything. "Hold on." He positioned her legs, those gorgeous legs, gripped her carefully and pulled out slowly. Groaning at the hot, wet friction, he slid back in again. Slowly, slowly, filling her up, inch by inch.

His legs were weak with pleasure.

"Ohhhh, Garrett," Maggie breathed, her back arched.

He opened his eyes and drank in the sight before him. Maggie, flushed, laid out like a feast, her gaze still locked on him. He looked down, at their bodies connected in the most primal fashion, and he shuddered fiercely. It broke him, the excruciating need to be connected on every imaginable level with this woman.

His woman.

"Garrett,"Maggie moaned, and he felt her clenching around him.

"Hold on, baby," he hissed. Maggie flung her arms out and grabbed the edges of the table, and he let go, pumping into her with fast, hard strokes. It was beyond anything, the way she fit around him, the scent of her skin, the sound of their flesh meeting, desperately giving and receiving. Over and over, in and out, with the little sounds Maggie made making him feel like a fucking god. He could feel his balls tightening at the same moment that her breath started hitching, and she shrieked his name and he felt her convulsing around him, and he came and came and came like a flood, all the while her eyes locked onto his. Her brown eyes, glazed with passion and something else, something he couldn't name, but something that spoke to him so far down in his soul that it almost hurt.

She uncurled her hands from the edges of the table and caressed his face. He turned his face into her palm and kissed it. "Baby," she whispered, still breathless, and some bottomless thing that felt like elation and longing and homecoming all confused and combined churned through him with such force that he had to shut his eyes so she wouldn't see the moisture that was stinging, threatening to spill. Too much, she gave him too much, but he wanted it all. He collapsed over her, pressing his face into her warmth. She wrapped her arms around his neck and her legs around his waist, and she was all around him and he was lost in her and she was everything.

Chapter 21

Maggie awoke slowly, deliciously comfortable in Garrett's bed. She reached a sleepy arm out in his direction. Feeling nothing but his cool pillow, she opened her eyes. Sunlight wafted into the room, little motes shimmering in the air. They'd driven back to Denver late the evening before, after their five perfect days at Grand Lake.

Well, almost perfect. She'd tucked the conversation about children far, far back in her mind so there would be no cloud hanging over their time together, and neither one of them had raised the topic again.

Sitting up, she stretched languorously. Where was he? Rising, she picked up the shirt he'd stripped off the night before and tugged it over her head. He liked it when she wore his shirts. She liked it, too, wrapping herself in his scent. She hurried to brush her hair and teeth, eager to find him. Maybe he was out by the pool. If so, she had a good use for one of those chaise lounge chairs.

Rounding the opening to the kitchen, she saw him standing at the window, his back to her. He was already dressed in jeans and a hoodie. Well, he'd have to take them off again. She'd help. She tiptoed in and slid her arms around him, laying her cheek against his back. "Good morning."

Stiffening, he stepped away and turned to face her. His

expression was emotionless, his stance rigid.

It took her a second to realize something was wrong. "Hey." She smiled up at him, expecting to get a smile in return.

There was no smile. Not even a hint.

She tried again, moving toward him. "What is it?"

He side-stepped, putting the island between them. Unblinking. Silent.

Something was really, really wrong. "What is it, Garrett?"

Without breaking eye contact, he picked up a printed page from the island top and held it out to her, his arm stiff.

Maggie stepped forward on unsteady legs to take the paper from his hand. She glanced down to see a print-out of an article. 'What's this?"

"Read it." His voice was low.

Maggie blinked and lifted the paper. "'What really happened between Garrett Long and his sister?'" She gasped and jerked her gaze back to Garrett. "Garrett, what is this?"

"Read it," he repeated, his tone harsh. "Tell me if it rings a bell."

Maggie held the paper up higher with hands that were beginning to shake slightly, and read the article.

What really happened between
Garrett Long and his sister?

By Brent Buchanan

Long may be at the top of his game professionally, but could he hit rock bottom with this shocking news?

It's no secret that remarkable talent and unchecked admiration can encourage narcissism,

> especially when the adulation begins at a young, immature age. When everything you want is yours for the taking, not even those closest to them are always safe from the sway of their whim.
>
> Well known for trying to keep his personal life private, Garrett Long, star quarterback for the Denver Renegades, may have a very good reason to shut down inquiries about his past. According to a source very close to him, there is a history of mental illness in his family that may tie in with an allegation by a family member that, at the age of fifteen, Long sexually assaulted his twin sister, Emily Long Nicholson.

The article went on but Maggie couldn't continue reading. Ice skating up her spine, she lifted horrified eyes to Garrett. "Oh my God, Garrett, this is terrible."

Eyes narrowed, he crossed his arms over his chest. "You think?"

She shook her head, scanning it again. "How does Buchanan know any of this?"

He made a rough, derisive noise. "You tell me."

Wait, what? 'You tell me'? "What do you mean?"

"I don't know, Maggie, let's think about it. You're the only person in the whole fucking world I've shared that with, right here in my own house. Does that narrow it down for you?"

She stared at him in disbelief, a horrible foreboding making her stomach drop "Garrett, it wasn't me." He couldn't possibly think it was her. Could he?

"No? Well, then, who the fuck was it? Who else could have talked with Buchanan?"

Unnerved, Maggie gaped at him. "Not me! Come on. How could you think I would do something like that?"

He shook his head in disgust. "I actually believed you when you said you didn't know him when you talked to him at the retirement home."

"I – I didn't! I don't! I don't know him!"

Garrett stared at her with such hostility that she found it hard to breathe. She shook her head. "I don't know him, Garrett. I don't know where he got this but it wasn't from me."

"I think you're lying. You sit down with him on Sunday. I tell you all of this –" he snatched the paper from her" - on Tuesday. It's printed less than a week later. Fucking coincidence?"

No. No, she had to make him understand he was wrong. "You're telling me that you think I – what – intentionally met up with him and made a plan to trick you into telling me about your parents; your father?" Surely he saw how ludicrous that was. "First of all, you're the one who asked me to go to the retirement home. I was supposed to fly home that day, remember?"

He just glowered at her.

"I didn't know anybody there except you and Eleanor and Tyler. I certainly didn't know Brent Buchanan. He never introduced himself, and I already told you what we talked about. It was nothing, only a couple of minutes, and then Tyler came over to get me. And I didn't ask you to tell me about your parents, Garrett. Don't you remember? You wanted to tell me. I even tried to stop you, when I saw how hard it was for you."

He scoffed. "Did you? You didn't manipulate me into telling you exactly what he's been trying to dig up for months?"

She reared back. "Manipulate you? How in the world did I manipulate you? You asked about my dad and I asked about yours and then I remembered you didn't like talking about your family so I told you never mind but you insisted. Don't you remember?" She heard herself babbling, pleading, as if from a distance.

"If I looked at your phone, would I see any messages to him? Calls? Emails? I saw you texting a lot and I heard you on the phone at Grand Lake. I heard you. You told him you didn't have anything new to report. That you'd told him everything already."

What was he talking about? Why wasn't he listening to what she was saying? Maggie stared at him. "I was talking to my mother, Garrett, not Brent Buchanan. "I was telling her I wasn't sure when I was going home."

"Yeah, right."

"I'll show you," she said desperately. "I'll get my phone and you can look at the texts, at the numbers –"

"Don't bother," he bit out, wadding the piece of paper and dropping it into the trash. "I'm sure you've deleted anything relevant but it doesn't change the fact that I haven't told anyone but you the things that are written in that article. You can't twist that fact. You did this."

"I did not!"

"What about your bank account? Any nice new fat deposits?'

Money? She couldn't even string words together to respond to such an accusation. She could feel the fury emanating from him, waves of it. She could see it in his flared nostrils, fisted hands. Her heart was beating as fast as an animal caught in a trap. This Garrett frightened her.

"Garrett, do you hear yourself? What you're accusing me of is horrible. Stop and think about it for a minute."

"You did this, Maggie. You." He spat the words at her.

She didn't understand. She just didn't understand. Why didn't he believe her? "You're wrong." She crossed her arms protectively, rubbed her shoulders. "You're wrong Garrett."

"Nobody but you, Maggie," he repeated, the muscles of his jaw working. "And now it's out there for the whole fucking world to see."

Her heart sank even lower. He was right. It was going to be all over the news. His worst nightmare and there would be no escape. The damage could never be repaired. She hated it for him, would do anything to be able to fix it for him, yet he actually believed she was responsible.

"Did you even think for a minute about how this would affect Emily?" Instead of raising his voice, his tone grew lower, deadly in its delivery.

Did he really believe that she would ever intentionally hurt his sister? The sister he'd tried so hard to protect? She tried again. "What possible reason would I have to betray your confidence, Garrett? There is nothing on this earth that could make me hurt you or Emily." Her voice broke.

He heard nothing. "How about my career? Did you think about how it would affect my career? The people I work with, my teammates, the whole fucking franchise? This shit is going to go viral. It's never going to go away. My team could have a perfect season and win the fucking Super Bowl again and all they're going to talk about is whether or not I fucked my sister." He flinched as he threw the words at her. "Thanks for that."

No. She rounded the island and grabbed his arm. "Listen to me, damn it. It wasn't me. I swear to you, it wasn't me."

He wasn't listening. He jerked his arm away and glowered down at her, his eyes narrowed to seething slits.

He really believed she would betray him like this. After the last few days, everything they'd shared, how close they'd grown, how much she loved him. The knowledge that he believed her capable of such duplicity was crushing. She tried one last time. "You know me, Garrett. You know I wouldn't – "

"I don't know you. I don't know who the fuck you are."

She reeled as though he'd struck her, and tears started sliding down her cheeks.

"Get your shit and get out of here."

She put a hand on the island top to steady herself. "Garrett."

"Don't be here when I get back."

Shocked speechless, her vision blurred, Maggie watched him stalk away without a backward glance.

Garrett drove to the Renegades facility and parked. There was a group inside waiting for him; his publicist, his agent, the media relations team, the head coach; hell, probably the general manager and owner, too. All waiting for him to arrive, to hear what he had to say and decide if they believed him and, if they did, to discuss how to manage the fallout of an article that accused him of molesting his sister.

Written by Buchanan, with help from his 'very close' source, Maggie.

It had to be Maggie, because the only other person who knew about his father's attempt to accuse him of his own filthy behavior was his high school coach and he'd died years ago. Even Emily didn't know what their father said at the football game so many years ago.

But he'd trusted Maggie. He'd shared it with her, all the ugliness, right there in his own home.

And she'd handed it to Buchanan.

It was the worst motherfucking day of his life.

Killing the engine, he propped his elbows on the steering wheel and dropped his head in his hands.

He'd awoken that morning with Maggie snuggled next to him in a tangle of sheets. He'd lain there a while, watching her sleep, trying to figure out how he'd gotten so lucky. What were the chances that they'd meet? Who even knew there was someone out there like her? He'd been thinking about how to go about coaxing her to move to Denver when his phone had chimed. Not once, not twice, but repeatedly, until he finally eased away and got up to see what the hell was so important.

Well, he'd found out, and the betrayal was so sharp his legs had almost gone out from under him.

Then reading, and re-reading the article. He could hardly take it in. The names, the details, the whole fucking story. Everything he had confided in her, in black and white for the world to read. Twisting his words and insinuating that he'd molested Emily.

He couldn't believe it.

He couldn't fucking believe it.

She was good, he gave her that. Staring at him with surprised, sleepy eyes, acting as innocent as a lamb. If there had been any possible chance it could have been anyone but her who fed the details to Buchanan, he'd have jumped to take it. But there wasn't anyone else. There was only Maggie.

He clenched his jaw to fight a wave of nausea and then dug his phone out of his front pocket. Before he went inside, he had to call Emily and tell her that, because of him opening his mouth, and because of Maggie, their lives were about to fall apart.

Again.

Maggie numbly settled herself into her seat in the airplane, a clump of sodden tissues gripped in one hand and the crumpled article in the other.

The last few hours were a blur. She didn't know where Garrett had gone or how long he would be, but she knew she had to leave before he returned. There was nothing more she could say to him.

In a stricken daze, she'd put on the same clothes she'd yanked off the night before, still tangled on the floor with Garrett's. She shoved her things into her bag. She'd requested an Uber with trembling hands and then slipped out the front door to wait. She'd cried all the way to the airport, grateful to the silent driver who had passed her a box of Kleenex. She'd cried at the ticket counter, handing over her credit card for the next available flight. She'd cried through security, on the train, on her long trek to the gate, and through five long hours until her flight was ready to board. Her phone had vibrated repeatedly with incoming texts and calls; some from friends but most from numbers she didn't recognize.

None of them were from Garrett. Her stupid heart still jumped each time she checked. Finally she sent a short text to her parents to let them know she was on her way home and then turned her phone off.

It was all a nightmare. She didn't know how Brent Buchanan got the information. She didn't know why Garrett didn't believe her. There had to be a way to prove she wasn't involved. She kept seeing his face, so cold, so angry; remembering how harshly he'd spoken to her. The way he'd said he didn't know who she was. She didn't know who he was either. She felt the first tiny fluttering of disappointment in him, of anger for his lack of trust. How could he possibly think she would do such a thing? Had she ever given him any reason to doubt her honesty? What would she have had to gain from such a betrayal?

He should have known better.

She was gone. His house felt like a tomb. Garrett walked into his bedroom, where the bedcovers were still rumpled and twisted. He glanced around the room and then in the bathroom. Some of Maggie's things were still there. Her perfume, her toothbrush, her lipstick. He swept them into the trash and then sat down heavily on the side of the bed, elbows propped on his knees and his face in his hands.

The meeting had gone about as well as could be expected under the circumstances. It had come as a profound relief to discover that nobody put any stock in the inference that he'd actually molested Emily. It was no secret to management that Buchanan had been harassing him for months. When culpability was raised, he'd had no choice but to name Maggie along with Brent Buchanan. It had been hard to do. Hard to admit he'd been deceived so effortlessly. From that point on, all energy had been focused on determining the best course of action. While discussion had swirled around him about lawsuits for defamation of character and the need for him to make a public statement, he'd found himself tuning out and thinking back to Maggie's reaction when he told her about that night. How she'd cried for him and Emily and then wrapped herself around him, consoled him with kisses, sanctioned his anger and grief and gave him solace with her compassion and with her body. How changed he'd felt afterwards.

Nobody was that good of an actor, were they?

His conversation with Emily had been a revelation, too. He felt like he'd failed her again but what he didn't expect was her reaction to the article. She was furious on his behalf but insisted she couldn't care less about the insinuation of abuse. Dan knew the true story about their parents, as did her closest friends, so what did she care what total strangers chose to believe based on a tawdry article? She would make her public statement and continue to live her life.

Then she'd asked about Maggie. When he told her Maggie was responsible, Em had laughed in his face. There was no convincing her that Maggie was to blame. She'd told him to get off his ass and figure out who was really behind it. She'd lost patience with him and suggested he needed counseling. She said he needed to let go of the past and realize that Maggie was the best thing that had ever happened to him.

He fell back on the bed, crossing his arms over his face, and smelled Maggie's scent on the sheets. He tried to block the image of her in the kitchen with the article in her hand, turning pale, eyes huge, backing away from him.

Part of him wanted to believe Maggie, to rebel against the idea that she'd betrayed his confidence. But it was less than ten days ago that he'd met her. In ten days she'd sneaked past his walls and made him trust her and managed to make him spill his rancid guts. How had that happened? He should have known better. Hell, he'd known Ty for years and even Ty didn't know the stuff he'd offered up to Maggie.

She had fooled him, plain and simple. He thought about his parents, how batshit crazy they were, but how they had excelled at hiding it from everyone. It was no stretch to think that Maggie could have hidden her true nature for the short amount of time they'd spent together.

It had to be Maggie. He'd trusted her and she'd betrayed him. It was more than he could stand. The constant nausea that was simmering just below the surface threatened to rise again.

His phone chimed, indicating someone was at the front gate. He wasn't expecting anybody and he sure as hell wasn't in the mood to entertain. Pressing the app to bring up the video, he frowned when he saw Tyler Hurst's face on his screen.

Ty could see him on the exterior screen, too, and didn't mince words. "Open up, Garrett."

Cursing under his breath, Garrett activated the gate without a word. He'd like to tell Ty to get lost but he knew the hardheaded bastard wouldn't hesitate to knock his gate down if he really wanted to get in.

Ty was pulling his vehicle to a stop when he got to the front door and jerked it open. Leaning against the door casing, arms crossed, he watched Ty open the passenger door for Eleanor.

Eleanor, too. Great.

Ty lifted an eyebrow when they reached the door and saw Garrett's expression and his rigid stance. "Relax, kid."

Like he could relax. Garrett stepped away from the door. "I guess you saw it."

"Yep." Ty held the door open so Eleanor could slip in beneath his arm. "How did it happen?"

"Maggie," Garrett replied shortly, leading the way through the foyer to the great room. He turned and realized they were still standing in the foyer, astonishment on their faces.

"That's ridiculous," Eleanor clamped her purse under her arm and marched into the room. "There's no way Maggie would do that. Where is she?"

"Gone."

Ty and Eleanor exchanged looks again. "Was that her idea?" Ty asked.

"Mine," he said shortly.

Ty nudged Eleanor onto one of the sofas and sat beside her, studying Garrett carefully. "Why do you think it was Maggie?" he asked calmly.

"It wasn't," Eleanor interjected quickly. "I'm telling you, there's no way."

Garrett sat down on the opposite sofa and clasped his hands behind his head. "She's the only person I've ever told that stuff to. Ever," he repeated. "Six days ago. Convenient timing, don't you think?"

"There has to be another explanation." Eleanor rose and moved to sit beside Garrett. "Maggie wouldn't do that, Garrett. I know she wouldn't."

Ty grunted in agreement.

Garrett ignored them. "Facts are facts. You saw her talking to Buchanan at the retirement home You don't think that was just a coincidence, do you?"

Eleanor put her hand on his arm. "Garrett, do you really believe Maggie would do such a thing?"

Why was everybody so fucking obstinate? First Emily, now them. "There's no other explanation."

"But why? What possible motive would she have?"

Did they think he hadn't tried to work that out? "No idea."

Ty looked skeptical. "Eleanor's right, buddy. It doesn't make sense."

Garrett tried to stifle his growing temper. "Nothing changes the fact that I've never shared those details with anyone else."

Eleanor chewed on her fingernail, in deep thought. "Something just doesn't add up. I'm going to figure it out."

Chapter 22

"Maggie? There's someone here to see you."

Maggie drew her knees up closer to her chest and squeezed her eyes shut. It was sometime in the afternoon, judging by the light edging through the sides of the window shades but she had no interest in getting up to see anyone. From beneath the covers, she heard the door open and sighed.

"Sweetie, your friend Eleanor is here."

Eleanor? Maggie blinked and pushed the covers down just enough to see her mother standing beside her childhood bed, elegant as always in linen pants and a sleeveless tunic. She sat on the edge of the bed and rubbed her back. "Would you like to come down and talk with her?"

"Eleanor Hurst?" Her voice sounded ragged.

Her mom nodded, worry apparent on her face.

How did she even know where to find her? Was she here to accuse her of conspiring with Buchanan, too? To call her ugly names and make frightening threats? If so, she needed to get in line behind a few hundred thousand other people.

Maggie shook her head.

Her mother sighed. "Maggie, I know you're hurting but

enough is enough. You have to get up eventually. Why don't you come downstairs and see your friend?"

"I don't know if she's my friend," she managed. She didn't know anything anymore.

"She seems very worried about you."

Maggie waited for her mother to add 'we all are.'

"If you don't come down, I'm going to let her come up."

Wow, her dainty little mother was going all tough love on her. Maggie would have been amused if she wasn't so tired.

"Fine." She heaved in a deep breath and sat up. "Tell her I'll be down in a minute."

Her mom squeezed her shoulder and rose. "That's my girl. Take your time."

That was mother-speak for 'tidy up' but Maggie couldn't find the energy to care what she looked like. She trudged in the bathroom, looked in the mirror and sighed. Her hair was matted and her eyes were puffy. She'd been wearing the same pajamas for a couple of days, pajamas she'd borrowed from her mom so they were a little on the snug side. Okay, a lot on the snug side. It wasn't a good look.

Who cared.

She tugged her dad's extra robe on, cuffed the sleeves up and tied the belt. She brushed her teeth. She made her way downstairs and found Eleanor and her mother sitting in the study off the living area. They both rose when she appeared.

"Hey, Eleanor." Maggie gave her a little hand wave.

She was startled when Eleanor stepped forward and gave her a big hug. It was a weird hug because Eleanor was so little and she was so pregnant, but it felt good and she didn't know why but it made tears well up in her eyes.

"Maggie, I'm so glad to see you."

Maggie didn't know what to say to that so she just tried to smile. It felt strange on her face.

Eleanor stepped back, looking hard at her and squeezing her

hands before sitting back down. If she thought anything of Maggie's bedraggled appearance, she was kind enough not to say anything.

Maggie's mother excused herself and Maggie sat down in the chair beside Eleanor and looked at her dully.

"So." Eleanor leaned forward, "How do you think Brent Buchanan got the information for the article? Because I know it wasn't you."

At Eleanor's abrupt show of support, the tears stinging behind Maggie's eyes began to leak and her throat clogged up. She held up a 'wait a minute' hand and looked away.

"I am so going to kill him," Eleanor hissed under her breath. "He is so dead."

Maggie pulled herself together. "I have no idea," she managed. When she first got home, she'd tried to contact Buchanan, to force him to tell her how he got the story, but the telephone number and email address she found online was either outdated or he wasn't interested in returning her messages.

"Well, you and I are going to figure it out."

It was nice to have someone like Eleanor rally around her but she didn't share her confidence. It all seemed hopeless.

"Have you talked with Garrett?"

"You mean since he threw me out?" Maggie asked tiredly. "No. I had to turn my phone off but it doesn't matter because he's not going to call. He's convinced I'm to blame."

She'd had no choice but to turn her phone off because the media was relentless. She'd shut down her Facebook and Instagram accounts and she couldn't even stay at her own home. The incessant phone calls were bad enough, but when strangers began knocking on her door wanting statements, interviews, and photographs, she knew she needed to leave. So she was back home with her very worried parents, emotionally spent, and hiding from the world.

She didn't recognize her own life anymore.

"Well, I know you're not to blame," Eleanor said staunchly. "We said as much."

"How was he?"

Eleanor hesitated.

Still convinced she'd played a role in the publication of that horrible article. "Never mind. It doesn't matter."

"Once we get to the bottom of this and find out who really is responsible, everything will be fine."

Maggie knew better. She didn't see any way for things to ever be fine again. She thought what she and Garrett had found together was special but she was mistaken. It was just attraction and sex. If it had really been special he'd have believed her.

"He said you were alone when he confided in you," Eleanor prompted her.

"Yes, in the den." Maggie remembered how all she'd wanted to do was comfort him, make him understand he wasn't to blame. "Just us. Nobody else."

Eleanor looked thoughtful. "Nobody in the flesh," she mused. "But what about some other way? Was the television on?"

"You think the television was spying on us?"

"The use of smart TVs and other electronics in surveillance is common nowadays, and don't even get me started on what I think about smart speakers," Eleanor stated briskly. "Whether Brent Buchanan went to those lengths is the question." She drummed her fingers on the arm of the chair. "Did anyone else come to Garrett's house while you were there?"

Maggie thought back. In some ways it felt like years ago. "He had poker night with some of his teammates."

Eleanor shook her head. "That wouldn't be it."

"He had food delivered a couple of times," Maggie mused. "And there was the contractor." She blinked at the memory. "One of the men with the contractor was in the den when I brought Lilah in from swimming." She scooted forward on her chair, trying to think through the fog. "He was over by the television. He said he was on his way to get something from their truck, and made some snarky remark about taking a look around."

Eleanor's eyebrows winged up. "So he wasn't where he was supposed to be?"

"Not at all. He was giving me the eye in my swimsuit and asking questions about Lilah, and I didn't like it. When I told him he ought to get back to work, he called me a bitch under his breath."

Eleanor snapped her fingers. "That's it. That's got to be it. Did you tell Garrett about him?"

Maggie nodded. "He wasn't too concerned and I never gave it another thought."

Eleanor reached over and patted Maggie's knee. "I've got a good feeling about this, Maggie."

Garrett's cell phone rang.

Eleanor.

He sighed. He had just managed to extricate himself from another frustrating conversation with Emily, who was still convinced Maggie was innocent, and he had a feeling Eleanor was going to jump on the same bandwagon. He couldn't deal with her, too.

He sat, knees on elbows, shoved his fingers through his hair and pressed his hands against his head until the phone stopped ringing.

Now that some time had passed, now that he wasn't so white-hot with fury, the question that kept him from sleeping at night, from functioning during the day, was why. Why did Maggie tell Buchanan the things he'd shared with her? It made no fucking sense. What was the connection? What had he missed?

He didn't understand how he could be so angry with her and

still miss her so much.

His phone started ringing again. Eleanor again, as stubborn as her husband. He might as well get it over with. He tapped the answer key, sat back and took a deep breath.

"Hey, Eleanor."

"I have a hunch," she said abruptly. "If it turns out to be correct, you're going to feel like crap and, even though I love you, that's going to make me very happy. Do you remember the day you had some men at your place to talk about remodeling something?"

He scrubbed a hand over his face. "Of course." That was the day when Maggie had worn a shirt over her bikini, when he'd crashed her nature walk with Lilah, the first night they'd watched a Harry Potter movie. He remembered every little detail.

"Well, that day when Maggie brought your niece inside for lunch, one of the workers was in the den next to your kitchen."

Garrett frowned. "Yeah, I remember her telling me about it. So?"

"Maybe he was up to something. Maybe he wasn't just working for your contractor."

He huffed impatiently. "Are you suggesting he was working with Buchanan? To bug my house or something?" He knew Eleanor believed Maggie wasn't to blame but this wasn't Mission Impossible.

"That's exactly what I think," Eleanor said firmly. "The timing fits."

Garrett was taken aback. "That's kind of far-fetched," he said, with a little less vehemence.

"More far-fetched than Maggie working with Buchanan? Breaking your trust?"

Garrett hesitated.

"Exactly. Why don't you go take a closer look around your television, the whole den in fact, lamps, underneath things, and maybe also call the contractor to get more information on the guy. His name was Chase. Find out if he was new to the job or quit shortly thereafter."

Garrett's mind was spinning at the crazy premise that their conversation might have been recorded. It was ridiculous.

Wasn't it?

"I will," he said slowly, rising from his chair.

If he found something, if there really was something, if it turned out to be true, then that meant…

"I saw Maggie," Eleanor said abruptly.

He winced but he didn't respond.

"I swear to God, Garrett, I wish I could send Ty to break your nose again."

He closed his eyes and squeezed the back of his neck.

"Now go look."

"Yeah," he said hoarsely. Setting his phone down, he blew out a breath and rose from his desk to go to the den. It was an outlandish idea but he'd do what Eleanor suggested and take a look around. He wasn't doing anything else, anyway.

His television was mounted on a bracket, with an inch or so clearance between the television and the wall. He ran his hand along the wall behind the television but felt nothing. He then ran a hand along the back edge of the television itself, and on the far side he felt an oblong object stuck to the metal bracket.

The fuck?

He couldn't get a good look into the narrow space so he strode to the pantry to get a flashlight. Fingers of alarm, of dread, curled in his stomach as he flattened against the wall by the television to shine the light into the crevice.

He saw it. Something that didn't belong there. Something with a tiny flashing light.

The feeling of dread coalesced into disbelief, then fury, then – horror.

He phoned the Denver police and then he sat, shoulders hunched, face in his hands, and thought about how deeply he'd fucked up.

Maggie was seated on a cushioned glider in the sunny Hurst back yard, watching the adorable Hurst children shrieking in the sparkly swimming pool with their stupidly handsome father. She didn't want to be there, held hostage to the happy scene, but she hadn't been able to come up with an excuse quickly enough when Eleanor called and invited her over. Now she was holding a glass of iced tea, a rusty smile pasted on her face, when all she wanted to do was get away from their painfully perfect family and go back home.

"I'm so glad you came over." Eleanor carefully settled on the bench beside her. "How are things now that you're back at your own house?"

Maggie's parents had wanted her to stay with them a while longer but she'd decided to stop hiding and take her life back. The first thing she'd done was delete all the calls from media on her phone, and then she'd gone home with her head held high and given firm "no comments" to the stubborn handful of reporters who had been camping out on her street.

"Better now that the reporters have finally gone away. I'm still getting a lot of phone calls, though."

Eleanor squeezed her hand. "I know things are really difficult right now but I'm sure they're going to get better."

Maggie's antennae went up at the note of satisfaction in Eleanor's tone. "Why? Has something happened?"

Stepping out of the pool, Ty dried off and joined them.

Eleanor nodded. 'You were right to be suspicious of the man you came upon in Garrett's den. I called Garrett to tell him about it and he found a recording device on the back of the television."

Maggie's eyes widened. "A bug, like in a spy movie?"

"Yes, exactly like that. They're easy to buy. He called the contractor and the police tracked the employee down. Apparently he's connected with Buchanan and they came up with the plan when the contractor was hired to do work for Garrett."

"They're both in a lot of legal trouble," Ty interjected. "It was all over the news last night. The site has issued a retraction and apology."

Maggie could scarcely take it in. She looked back and forth at Ty and Eleanor, and wondered why she didn't feel at least a little bit happy. "Well, that's that, then." She lifted the glass to her lips, took a sip, but tasted nothing. "Mystery solved, thanks to you, Eleanor." She wondered how Garrett had reacted to the truth. How he felt now about his lack of trust, the way he treated her. It didn't really matter, though. She was glad he'd found out who was really to blame but beyond that, it wasn't her business anymore. She wasn't investing any more of her energy into thinking about him.

Eleanor gazed at her. "Maggie, Garrett is going to want to talk to you, to apologize."

Maggie's stomach flipped. "I hope not."

"I'm sure of it."

Something in her tone made Maggie glance at her. Eleanor gave her an encouraging but weak smile. Oh, no. No, no, no. Maggie stood up abruptly. "He's here, isn't he?"

Eleanor reached for her hand. "Not yet, no."

Maggie felt like a giant fist was squeezing her lungs. "But he's on his way."

Eleanor hesitated.

Oh hell no. "I'm sorry, Eleanor, but I'm leaving." Maggie placed her glass on a side table and scooped up her bag. "I don't want to see him." She hoisted her bag over her shoulder. "You make sure he understands that I don't want to see him."

Eleanor rose, distressed. "Maggie, won't you consider listening to him?"

Listen to the man she'd fallen head over heels in love with, who hadn't hesitated to believe the worst of her and had sent her packing? "Like he listened to me?" Maggie replied shakily. "No, I'm sorry, Eleanor, I won't. I have nothing to say to him."

Ty held a hand up to Eleanor. "I'll walk Maggie out to her car."

She was desperate to leave but she waited while Ty pulled a shirt over his head, and then followed him through the house to the driveway.

"Before you go," he began, when they reached her car. "Can I tell you a couple of things?"

She really, really, really wanted to leave.

"I'll make it quick. Don't worry, Garrett's plane doesn't land for another couple of hours."

"Okay."

"I've known him a while now. You know he was really young when he was drafted, right?"

Maggie nodded.

"You also probably know he had a lot of baggage when he started out. Major trust issues. Still does, really."

That was the mother of all understatements. Maggie nodded again.

"His first years in the league were pretty turbulent, and when he came to Denver he was spiraling out of control, on his way out. He finally had a come-to-Jesus moment –"

"When you broke his nose," Maggie interjected.

"He told you about that?"

"Yes."

Ty gave her a half-smile. "Yeah, well, he started coming around, making better decisions, and he's made a success of himself. I'm proud of him, but he's still got those trust issues, even with me. Football comes easy to him but in his personal life, well, it's not easy for him to let people in."

"I don't understand why you're telling me this," Maggie said helplessly.

Eleanor's big, handsome husband squeezed her shoulder. "Because when we were in Denver, when you were with him, he was different. Not shut down like the last couple of years. I saw a new man. Centered, happy. And the fact that he shared such personal things with you says a lot about how he feels about you. You get that, right?"

Maggie felt tears well up in her eyes. She'd seen that new man, too, had fallen in love with him.

"I'm just saying, this whole mess with Buchanan, the way it looked, must have really wrecked him. You know, he finally has someone he trusts, he opens up and goes for it, and then this happens. Now I wasn't there, I don't know how it went down, and I'm guessing it was pretty bad, but I just want you to think about it for a second from his point of view."

She nodded. "I understand, Ty, but I've got to go now," she managed. "Please let me go."

"You go ahead." He opened her car door for her. "But just think about it. Think about how good you are for him."

Maggie slid into the driver seat and looked up at him. "The problem is, Ty, after all of this, I don't know if he's good for me."

Garrett sat in his rental, on the street outside Maggie's house in Baton Rouge, drumming his fingers on the steering wheel. He'd called Ty when his flight landed and learned that the second Maggie learned he was on his way, she'd gotten the hell out of there.

He didn't blame her. What could he possibly say to her that would make up for his behavior? It was the question he'd been asking himself since he'd found the device behind the television. Why would she want to hear his feeble apology after he'd kicked her out of his house in such a fury?

Remembering his behavior made him sick to his stomach. It was his worst fear realized. He was just as much a bastard as his father. He'd crushed Maggie with his accusations, with his lack of trust. Beautiful, open, honest Maggie. He could still see her face, pale and horrified at his cold indictment. How she literally staggered when he told her to go.

He was just as sick and twisted inside as he'd always feared.

Leaning forward, he rested his forehead on the steering wheel and swallowed against the nausea rising in his stomach.

Flying to Baton Rouge was probably a colossal mistake but he couldn't stay home and do nothing. Everywhere he looked, there were reminders of Maggie. He could see her, perched on the island, cross-legged on the chaise by the pool, in the den with her long legs draped over the side of his chair. In his office where the painted rock rested on his desk, in his bedroom where her scent still lingered. Even in the damned laundry room, where she'd forgotten her swimsuit hanging on the drying rack.

So instead of going to Ty and Eleanor's, he was able to talk them into giving him her address and he drove straight to her house. It was a small, old-fashioned place on an oak-lined street with a neat front yard. There were pots of flowers on the steps to the front porch and a swing on the far end with bright pillows in each corner. It looked like Maggie.

He inhaled and then blew out a long breath.

Her little red car was parked at the end of the driveway so he knew she was home, but he didn't have the courage yet to get out of his vehicle. He'd have to, soon, though, because even though the sun was setting, the air was smothering and he was sweating like a three-hundred-and-fifty-pound tackle.

A car rolled up behind him and turned into her driveway. He sank low into his seat and watched as a blonde stepped out of her car with a grocery bag and walked to Maggie's front door. She knocked and the door opened, but Garrett couldn't see Maggie. The blonde went inside and the door closed behind her.

He rubbed his chin, wondering if having someone else around would be an advantage or disadvantage. He doubted that any charm he could muster would work in his favor with any friend of

Maggie's. Maybe she would at least listen to him, though, with her friend there for back-up.

Before he could make up his mind, another vehicle turned into her driveway, and he sank back down again. This time, two women jumped out of an SUV, one balancing pizza boxes and the other carrying a cardboard box of wine tucked in the crook of her arm like a football. These women didn't even knock, they just pushed the door open and disappeared inside.

Maggie had her defensive line in position and from the look of things, she and her friends were setting up for a long girl's-night in. If he wanted to get to her on her own, he would have to wait until tomorrow.

But he didn't want to wait. He hadn't flown across the country to hide in his car. Losing here was not an option.

Drawing in another deep breath, he opened the door and stepped out of the rental car. Why was it so fucking hot here? It was like getting out of an oven, into a bigger oven. His shirt was soaked from sweat so he opened the back door to dig a dry shirt out of his bag. Hurrying, he stripped off the wet shirt, tugged on the clean one, tucked it in and wiped his hands on his jeans.

He walked up the driveway, to the walkway, to the front porch. It was ridiculous how fast his heart was beating. He hadn't felt this anxious, this sick to his stomach, in all his years playing ball. Not since he was a kid. Lifting his hand, he knocked on the door.

He heard voices inside, and then the door swung open. A tall brunette with a glass of wine in her hand gaped at him, her eyes growing huge.

"Hi." His voice was croaky. He cleared his throat. "I'm looking for Maggie."

She blinked a couple of times and then shut the door in his face.

He blew out his breath and waited.

And waited.

And waited.

The door opened again and now there were three women eyeing him, none of whom were Maggie. The tall brunette, the blonde, and a short brunette, all armed with large glasses of wine and identical suspicious expressions.

"Hi," he said again. "I'd like to talk to Maggie, please."

Eyes narrowed, the tall brunette put her finger to her mouth, silently admonishing him to be quiet. He nodded his understanding. She shoved the other two women through the door and onto the porch, and followed them, closing the door quietly.

"You have some nerve showing up here," she bit off. "You broke Maggie's heart."

"She doesn't want to see you," the short brunette added.

"God, you really are gorgeous," the blonde said.

The other two turned on her, practically hissing.

"I'm sorry, I'm sorry," the blonde said, not looking sorry at all. She sipped her wine and eyed Garrett up and down. "So what's your plan to fix this, superstar?"

The door opened again. "What are y'all doing –" Maggie appeared in the doorway, and broke off when she saw him. "– Out here," she finished weakly.

"Surprise, Maggie, Garrett Long is here to see you," the blonde announced.

"I see that," she said quietly, wrapping her arms tightly around her middle. She was wearing pink sweatpants and a t-shirt that said "there's no tired like teacher tired." She looked pale, and thinner than he remembered. He winced. He had done this to her.

"What do you want us to do?" the tall brunette asked Maggie, wrapping a protective arm around her waist and glaring at Garrett. "Shall I call the police?"

"Just say the word," said the blonde, pulling her phone out of her back pocket.

"Maggie doesn't need the police, she has us," said the small brunette belligerently.

Damn it if he didn't like these women, even if they were united against him. Maggie deserved friends who had her back.

He should have had her back.

He watched Maggie sigh and hand her glass of wine to the tall brunette. "It's okay. Y'all go back inside."

The short brunette and blonde erupted in protest. The tall brunette took another sip of her wine and shook her head. "Come on, Alicia, Toby. Maggie's a big girl." She nudged the other two back through the door. "We're right here if you need us." Then she pointed a finger at Garrett. "You," she said simply, narrowing her eyes to slits.

He got the message.

She followed the others inside and closed the door.

Maggie wrapped her arms around herself. "My girlfriends," she said unnecessarily.

"I figured." He hated like hell to see her so spiritless. He hated himself for causing it. He wanted to reach for her but he shoved his hands in his pockets instead. "Maggie –"

He broke off. Fucking hell, he didn't know what to say. He had nothing.

She looked up at him, her brown eyes dim. No hint of interest or affection. Not even anger.

He couldn't get enough air. He took one hand out of his pocket and rubbed his chest where it hurt and tried again, his eyes fixed on her. "Maggie, I'm sorry. So sorry."

She just looked at him. He knew it wasn't enough. Words didn't mean anything. There was no way to convey how much he regretted hurting her. Nothing he could say. Nothing he could do. He had no way to tell her.

"Maggie," he began again, because he couldn't just stand there. "I know you don't want to –"

"Stop," she said, interrupting him.

He closed his mouth.

"Can we just – can we just not do this?" she asked in a low voice. "Please."

He felt his stomach drop. "Not do this now, or –?" He didn't want to finish the sentence.

"You can't just show up like this. I'm not –" she trailed off and gazed off in the distance. "I have company."

"Tomorrow?" he asked quickly, hopefully. "Can I come back tomorrow?"

Everything hung on her answer. He held his breath. He rubbed his chest again but the ache didn't go away.

She gazed at him for a torturously long moment, then sighed. "Tomorrow."

Chapter 23

Maggie tugged at the hem of her top and glanced around her little living room, second-guessing her decision to have Garrett meet her back at her house. Sharon thought it was a good idea, home-field advantage as it were, but Alicia and Toby had voted for a public place like a coffee shop. The problem with a public place was, well, the public. It was going to be difficult enough to talk with him without anyone interrupting every five minutes to ask for an autograph or photo.

And she could do without having her face pop up on TMZ again. Ever.

She'd texted him to come at ten a.m. It was a quarter 'til and he'd been waiting in his rental car outside on the street for at least ten minutes already. She could see him in the driver's seat, his perfect profile staring straight ahead. Maggie sighed.

Taking a deep breath, she opened her front door, stepped out on the front porch and watched him turn his head swiftly toward her. He opened the door and stepped out. She watched as he ate up the distance between the car and her porch, never taking his eyes off of her.

"I'm early," he said unnecessarily, taking the steps up to the porch and stopping a foot away.

He was awfully dressed up, wearing gray slacks and a dark blue dress shirt with the sleeves pushed up. It struck her all over again how handsome he was, how lean and graceful.

"It's fine." She gestured to him to enter. "It's too hot to sit in your car."

He moved inside and glanced around before turning to her. He looked huge in the small room. "This is nice." He offered her a hopeful little smile. "Colorful."

She was too tired for small talk. "Want some coffee?"

"Only if you're having some."

She needed something to do with her hands, so she nodded. "I'll be right back."

"Can I help?"

She shook her head and escaped to her kitchen where she leaned against the counter for a moment. She definitely should have met him someplace else. Having him inside her home was unsettling. Too late, though. She busied herself with the coffee, and when she returned with a mug in each hand, she found him examining her framed festival posters. He took the mug she offered and sat carefully on one end of her sofa. She opted for the chair that was angled nearby and then lifted her gaze.

His blue eyes were trained on her, making her breath hitch. "I'm really sorry about just showing up here last night," he began, holding the mug between his big hands.

Maggie sipped her coffee, unsure of what to say.

"I thought I was going to see you at Ty's, but he said you didn't want to see me, and I – I didn't know what else to do." He paused. "And I didn't think you'd answer if I called or texted."

He was right. She took another sip.

He set the mug down on the side table and leaned forward, rubbing his hands back and forth on his thighs. "Maggie, I know I handled things really badly back in Denver that morning."

There was nothing to say to that.

"I wasn't thinking straight. I was in shock and nothing made any sense, you know." His gaze dropped and he shook his head. "It doesn't matter. None of that matters. I should have realized it couldn't be you, should have known. You tried to tell me, over and over again, but I wouldn't listen." He paused again, studying her face. "I'm just so sorry. You have no idea. Can you – do you think you can forgive me?"

Here went nothing. She sighed. "I want to." She rotated the mug in her hands. "I'm trying to, because I do understand why you thought I had something to do with it because of the circumstances and the timing, but –," she trailed off and glanced at him. He was leaning forward, his arms resting on his thighs, hands clasped. She shook her head slightly. "I didn't know who you were, Garrett. You went from being this man who – who cared for me to someone else, someone who frightened me, who was sure I was evil, and capable of intentionally hurting you." She shrugged. "I don't know what I'm supposed to do with that."

His head dipped down and his shoulders slumped. "You're right." His voice was low. "I was a fucking bastard. I know it. I totally lost my shit." Pulling in a deep breath, he lifted his gaze. "I never should have doubted you. I swear nothing like that will ever happen again. I'll do whatever it takes to make it up to you, Maggie. Just give me the chance."

She had rehearsed what she needed to tell him. She could do it. "I've done a lot of thinking since I got home."

"Okay." He leaned forward, his gaze fixed on her. "Tell me."

"I didn't have a clue about that side of you, Garrett, and it made me realize there's a lot I don't know. Everything between us happened too fast. I was all caught up in the moment, but that's so not who I am. I don't – I don't leap into bed with someone I've only known a week."

"I think we were both caught up," he said slowly. "But I don't have any regrets on that score. It wasn't just sex, Maggie. It was way bigger than that. It's something I've never felt before. You know that. You felt it, too, didn't you?"

She didn't know what she felt. She didn't trust herself anymore.

When she didn't reply, he winced. "Anyway, we can't change that now, so how can I convince you to give me another chance? How do we go forward from here?"

This was the hard part, the worst part, the part she wasn't sure she could get through. "I don't think we can."

He sat back like she'd struck him, his expression blank. "What – wait a minute. It's over? You're saying it's over?"

Maggie looked down, unable to continue.

"No. No, Maggie, I refuse to accept that," he said firmly. "I've just found you. I'm not going to lose you. We can figure this out. I can fix this. You just have to forgive me and let me make it up to you."

She clasped the sides of her face, struggling to find the right words. "Garrett, forget the whole horrible article part of it for a minute. Say we get past that, okay? I was engaged to someone else just a month ago, and you don't believe in marriage at all. How did we go from that, to this, in two weeks? What would even happen from here?"

He leaned forward, an earnest expression on his face. "It's simple. I want you to come back to Denver, Maggie. Move in with me. I was going to talk with you about it that morning, before - before I fucked up. What do you think?"

Maggie stared at him, aghast. Moving in with him in Denver was simple? Simple for whom? Did he really think she would quit her job and leave her family and friends to move across the country to live with him? Based on two weeks living inside a bubble? And after the last few days when he'd believed her capable of selling his secrets to his worst enemy? From the look on his face, he did. He looked like it was the perfect plan while all Maggie saw was a giant red flag flapping in hurricane force winds.

But why wouldn't he think it was the answer? She was the one who had been happy to put her whole life on the back burner. Why wouldn't he think that she'd just abandon it completely?

"Think how great it would be." He moved to sit on the edge of the sofa, closer to her. "We're good together. You know it."

"Move in with you after just two weeks?" she managed. "Mason and I dated over a year before we even talked about moving in together."

He frowned at her reference. "You and Mason lived in the same city," he countered.

"Why don't you move to Baton Rouge then?" She knew he couldn't, she didn't want him to, anyway, but she needed to make the point that her life was important, too.

He looked frustrated. "Maggie, I can't move to Baton Rouge. I have a contract. My team's in Denver."

"What about my job?"

"That's different. You could teach in Denver."

Maybe she could but that wasn't the point. "I love my job here. And what about my friends, my family?"

"People move all the time, Maggie. You could fly back and forth as much as you want."

"On a teacher's salary?"

"No, on mine."

"So now we've gone from meeting two weeks ago to me leaving my life behind, moving into your house and letting you support me?"

His frustration was building. "Not supporting you, Maggie. I know you love teaching but you can do that in Denver. And money's not an issue. I can easily afford to do whatever it takes to make you comfortable there. If that means flying you back and forth whenever you feel like it, why wouldn't I want to do that? Why wouldn't you let me? Hell, I'll buy a jet. Whatever it takes. I want us to be a real couple. I want to come home to my girlfriend every day. Doesn't it sound good to you at all?"

She set her mug on the table beside his and clasped her hands together. "Do you see how lopsided this is?"

Garrett drew in a deep breath. "I do. I'm asking a lot, I know that." He was silent for a moment. "But weren't you happy? I know I was."

Maggie swallowed. "Of course. It was amazing but we weren't living in the real world. We were playing pretend in a time warp. Time was going to run out eventually. Maybe not the awful way it did, but it was always going to end."

"You were always planning on ending it?" He looked stunned.

She was making a mess of this. "No, listen to me. I was hoping in some ridiculously optimistic, unrealistic way that things would miraculously work out, but I realized, once I got home, that it was never going to work out, not long-term."

"But why?" He stood up, agitated, rubbing the back of his neck. "Why can't it?" He moved closer, hunkered down in front of her and took her hands. "Maggie, the way I feel about you – I've never felt like this. You feel it, too, I know you do. We can figure it all out."

That was the closest he'd come to seriously saying he loved her, but even if he said the words, it didn't change things. "Garrett, my real world is here. Your world, well, I don't fit into it. It's not a normal life. It's all that media attention, photos on gossip sites, women chasing you, so many demands and obligations all the time, and when your season starts, you said yourself that it becomes all-consuming. Twelve hours a day, six days a week, right?"

He rubbed circles on her wrists with his thumbs. "I know how to handle all the crap, Maggie, and I'd be coming home to you after those long days. I want to come home to you."

"You know how to handle it, but I don't. Did you know that when I got home, I had to turn off my phone because it wouldn't stop ringing, and had to go stay with my folks because there were so many people lying in wait for me? Looking through these windows? And I didn't dare go online for fear of what I'd read about myself, or even go out in public. I hated it, Garrett. And that was here in Baton Rouge. What would it be like in Denver?"

"I can protect you from all of that."

"I don't want a life that has to be protected that way. My life is here, Garrett. It's simple and safe and I know who I am."

"Maggie, you can't –," he let go of her hands and stood, looking away for a minute, his jaw working. "Don't give up on us, please."

He was trying so hard but she couldn't cave. She had to remember what was at stake. Beyond the other problems, valid on their own, she'd be crazy to go forward with a man who didn't want what she wanted, not even someone who was perfect in every other way. So it had to be said. She stood and led him back to the sofa and sat beside him. "Garrett, say we can manage all of it. Figure it out, like you want. There's one problem we can't ignore."

He looked like he was bracing for a blow. "I know what you're going to say."

She nodded. "Marriage and children. Not today, not next month or even next year, but someday, I want a family."

There. She wouldn't manipulate him into feeling guilty about it or, worse, tempt him to make promises he didn't want to keep. But, if he was at least open to it, they had a chance.

He closed his eyes for a moment as if he was in pain. "I know how important it is to you, Maggie," he said slowly. "I really do."

She nodded, waiting.

"Let me say this," he began. "If someone had told me a month ago that I'd meet someone like you, I wouldn't have believed it, but here we are. So, marriage, yeah. I can see that. I can. But kids?" He shook his head. "I can't do it, Maggie."

It broke her heart. It was such a waste. She'd seen him with Lilah, she knew what kind of man he was. If only he could see himself through her eyes.

"I can't do it," he repeated. "I can't bring a child into this world knowing the kind of problems they could inherit. Even if I only had one parent with issues I'd be worried, and I have two. The odds are stacked against me, against any child of mine." A few long, long moments passed. He blew out a long breath. "Couldn't I be enough for you, Maggie?" His voice was low and rough.

Maggie squeezed her eyes shut against his raw plea. This man, laying himself low for her, was breaking her heart all over again.

"I would want your babies, too," she managed, placing her hand on top of both of his. "I would want them."

He lifted his face and she felt another twist of pain at the moisture in his eyes. "No," he finally said, shaking his head. "I'm sorry, Maggie. Not even for you."

She nodded, unable to speak. It was her line in the sand and he couldn't cross it.

"So. That's it, then," he said, his jaw twitching. "There's nothing more to say."

She could only look at him, unable to speak past the lump in her throat.

"Yeah," he said flatly. "Okay." He nodded. Wiping his hands on his thighs, he rose.

Maggie followed him toward the door.

He opened it and turned, his gaze heavy, and cleared his throat. "Friends can hug, right?"

Maggie slid her arms around his lean waist. It was the last time she'd rest her head against his warm chest. She closed her eyes to savor the feeling one more time. He bent down to hold her tightly for a long moment and then curved one of his big hands around her cheek. She lifted her face and he kissed her, just a light touch, then he let go and walked away.

Slouched down in the front center recliner in his media room, eyes trained on the wide screen, Garrett punched "x" repeatedly on the game controller in his hands. *Hike the football already, damn it. Stupid fucking game.*

The room was pitch black with the exception of the light from the screen so when the overhead lights blazed on, he was blinded for a minute. Then something hit him on the back of the head. "Fuck!" Still struggling with the intrusion of light, he pulled off his headset and rubbed the back of his head.

"Are you kidding me?"

He recognized the angry voice behind him and winced.

"Are you kidding me!" His sister's voice rose in volume. He sat up and twisted around to see Emily stalking across the room toward him. She looked thoroughly pissed.

Duke and Buddy, both snoring seconds ago, read the room accurately and eased around the recliners to head for the door. He wished he could sneak out with them.

He tried for a casual tone. "Hey, Em. What are you doing here?"

She stared at him incredulously. "What am I doing here? Well, you'd know that, wouldn't you, if you ever bothered to check your phone. Where is it?"

Leaning, he pulled it out of his pocket and showed it to her.

She snatched it out of his hand and pressed the home button. "Dead," she said accusatorily, holding it up to show him. "When you get around to charging it, you're going to find about a hundred or so messages. I'm so mad at you right now."

He retrieved his phone and stuck it back into his pocket. Yeah, he probably should have checked it but there wasn't going to be a text or message from Maggie and he really didn't care about talking to anyone else.

She looked around at the room again. "Exactly how long have you been down here?"

He had no idea. "An hour maybe?"

She looked at him suspiciously.

He shrugged. "I got home from the training center and came down here. It's relaxing." It was also about the only room in the house that didn't remind him of Maggie, and video games, usually pretty low on his list of priorities, had turned out to be the one thing that could vaguely distract him from his depressing thoughts.

Even if his shit virtual team was losing to the fucking Falcons.

"You look like hell." She plucked his shirt away from his chest, leaned closer, and sniffed. "Oh my God, you smell worse than Dude and Buddy."

He'd skipped his shower after his workout and practice. Lifting his arm, he sniffed. Yeah, it wasn't good.

Emily pressed her lips together. "Get upstairs. She spun on her heel and headed back toward the door. "Now."

When had his sister become such a hard ass? He rose and limped to catch up with her. From the stiffness in his knee, maybe he'd been there much longer than an hour. "Why are you here, Em?"

Ignoring him, she stomped up the stairs. "How about taking a shower so I can stand to be around you?"

"Nobody asked you to drive all the way from Santa Fe to show up uninvited and start insulting me, you know," he called after her. "Don't you have better things to do?"

She stopped, turned around and stomped back down, eyes flashing. "I have lots of better things to do, Garrett, but when my brother is having a crisis and won't answer my phone calls for days, what do you expect?"

He held his hands up. "Nobody's having a crisis."

She stomped on his bare foot.

Ow! Seriously? He hopped on the other foot and looked at the she-demon wearing his sister's body. It occurred to him that the apple of Lilah hadn't fallen far from the tree of Emily.

"I love you, you stupid dumbass, but I am so mad at you right now. Playing video games in the dark? What are you, ten years old? How is that going to help anything?"

"How is physically attacking me helping anything?"

She went from fury to broken in less than the blink of an eye. "I'm sorry," she wailed, hugging him. "I've been so worried! Claire said you told her to take the week off and you wouldn't open the gate for the maid and nobody could get in touch with you and that whole stupid article thing and I don't know what happened in Baton Rouge with Maggie but it couldn't have been good and you look like crap and– "

"What the hell has the maid got to do with anything?"

Still crying, she managed to push him and hug him at the same time.

"Okay, come on." He led her up the stairs and into the kitchen where he poured her a glass of water. "You sit down and catch your breath and I'll go take a shower and then you can explain to me why you drove six hours to ask why I didn't open the gate for the maid, okay?"

She glared at him through her tears. "Stop trying to be funny."

There was nothing remotely funny about anything these days, but he just chucked her gently on the chin and headed for his room. He hesitated at the door. He hated going into his room. The bed he'd slept comfortably in for years was too big now, too cold. For the first few nights after his return from Baton Rouge, he'd been up all hours, avoiding his bedroom, bumping around his silent, dark house. He wondered how Em would react if she knew that one night he'd actually fallen asleep wedged into the blanket fort under the table. He'd been pacing around the house, bleary eyed from lack of sleep, when he'd remembered the fort. He had repeatedly balked at letting the cleaning service dismantle it, using Lilah as a lame excuse, and even when he'd believed the worst of Maggie, like a fucking moron, he hadn't been able to take it down. So he'd crawled underneath the table where the pillows and things were still scattered on the floor, and damned if that wasn't the only time he'd actually slept for more than an hour or two since he'd returned home.

That was why he'd told the cleaning service to come back next week. He was tired of the strange looks they gave him when he reminded them to leave it alone.

He put his phone on the charger and continued on to his bathroom. Glancing in the mirror, he saw why Em had freaked out. His hair was dirty, his eyes were bloodshot, and he needed a shave. Maybe that's why he'd gotten a couple of odd looks at the training facility.

He stripped off the offending clothes and tossed them in the hamper. He picked up a shirt from the floor that hadn't quite made it into the hamper, and the milky stain on it made him wince. The night before, he'd parked in front of the television with a bucket of ice cream mixed with some kind of liqueur and tried to watch that movie Maggie loved so much, the one about the old man and the fat little boy, and damned if the opening sequence didn't get him all choked up just like she said it would. That old man sitting in his chair next to that empty chair – jeez. That was a hell of a way to start a kid's movie. He was never watching that shit again.

He wished he could tease Maggie about it.

He hit the controls in the shower and stepped in. There were memories here, too, memories that made his dick throb and his heart ache. Sighing, he dropped his head and let the jets of water beat him to death.

Man, he'd screwed things up. If he could reset the clock, he'd back it up and never take the trip to Florida. Never be on that deck, never see Maggie flying across the sand toward the little girl, never take her to dinner, and certainly never invite her to come to Denver.

He'd be fine. He'd be normal. He'd be meeting with his agent and business manager, composed and focused. He'd be transitioning from off-season to pre-season mode like he always did, watching film, studying the playbook, working out. He'd be at the facility doing drills and supersets and strategizing with the coaches.

Not twisted in knots, thinking about Maggie all the time, thinking about how screwed up he was, how he'd disappointed her. How she was the only thing he wanted, and how the one thing she wanted was the one thing he couldn't give her. How she'd changed everything and now his life sucked.

After his shower, he dressed and headed back through the house to find Emily on her cell phone in the den, looking out the back window.

"Yes, playing a stupid video game. His phone was dead."

"Who is that?"

Em held a 'quiet' finger up and he frowned at her. "Okay, I'll tell him. Talk later." She pressed the disconnect button and looked him up and down. "Well, you look a little better, at least."

"Who was that?" he repeated.

"Claire. I promised her I'd let her know when I got here. She's got a ton of messages for you."

"Look, Em, I'm sorry you were worried, honestly, but there was no reason to come all this way."

"Agree to disagree." She sat down on the sofa in the den. "Come sit down. I want to talk to you."

He sat down in the armchair and made a 'get on with it' motion. It was either going to be about Maggie or their mother, or worse, both.

"So what exactly is going on with you and Maggie?"

"None of your business?"

Emily ignored his remark. "Claire said you came back from Baton Rouge in a serious funk. What happened?"

"We were together before and now we're not. That's it. End of story."

She studied him for a long moment.

Sometime she made him wish he'd had a twin brother instead of a sister. A brother wouldn't get all up in his face and make him talk about stuff that was none of his business. "She wants kids, Em, okay? And I don't want to talk about it."

She huffed. "Well, put your big boy pants on. We're going to talk about it whether you want to or not."

He closed his eyes and pinched the bridge of his nose.

"I have one question. In a perfect world, would you like to be married and have kids?"

He knew damn well she was going to have more than one question. "There's no such thing as a perfect world, Em."

She didn't speak. He opened his eyes to see her glaring at him.

Whatever. "Okay, maybe, in a perfect world with the right woman."

She continued glaring at him.

"With Maggie," he finally said. "In a perfect world, yes, I'd want kids with Maggie. And another couple of Super Bowl rings, a couple of pet unicorns and world peace."

"God, you're such an ass." She stood up. "Wait here. I have something to show you."

Garrett watched her stride from the room and come back a few moments later with a handful of papers. "Remember when I called you and asked you to babysit Lilah?"

"Of course I remember. I don't have Alzheimer's."

"Sometimes I think you have some kind of brain damage," she muttered.

"Funny."

"And it went well, didn't it? Looking after her?"

Except for that first night, he recalled with a half-smile. He'd never fully recover from the horror of that blue popsicle-cheese pizza projectile vomiting. "Yeah, thanks in large part to Maggie."

"Well, with or without Maggie, I knew it would. I knew you'd take wonderful care of her. Here, take a look at these." She handed him the papers and perched on the arm of his chair.

He glanced at the top sheet and saw it was a crayon drawing of – what was that? A stick man and a small stick man and two blobs with – were those antenna? Or tails?

"That's you and Lilah and those round things are Dude and Buddy." Em gestured toward the blobs. "Look at the next one."

A small stick man standing on top of a big stick man, another stick man with long hair, two more blob-dogs and drunken zig zags.

"You're holding Lilah, that's Maggie, and you're all looking at clouds."

He held back a smile and flipped to the next sheet.

"Can you guess?" Em looked at it with him, over his shoulder.

This one defied description. Squinting, he turned it sideways but that didn't help so he turned it again and studied the frenzied tangle of stick people and lines and blobs. Wait. One of the stick people had a blue hat and the other had hair sticking out both sides of its head and their faces were smushed together. Him kissing Maggie? Garrett didn't know whether to laugh or cry at that one. "Tea party, maybe?"

"Tea party!" Em laughed. "I don't think she'll ever forget the tea party."

He wouldn't either. Maggie's hair in those funny pigtails, her mouth tasting like Oreos. Pushing that memory away, he flipped through the remaining pages, amused by Lilah's zealous art interpretations of swimming in the pool, painting rocks and a particularly bizarre floor plan that made it appear that his house was ninety percent bathrooms. "Can I keep these?"

Em squeezed his shoulder. "Of course." She moved back to the sofa and sat forward, her expression serious again. "Garrett, Lilah can't wait to see you again. All she talks about is Uncle Garrett this and Uncle Garrett that."

He knew where she was going with this, but spending little bits of time with random kids who belonged to other people was not a legitimate assessment of his psychological capacity to have kids of his own. No way was he willing to take even the smallest chance of subjecting an innocent kid to the abuse he and Em had endured. He was tired of repeating himself.

"You know, I was a little worried when I was pregnant." Emily twisted her hair around her finger. "I mean, not over the top freaked out like you, but I did wonder if I was going to be able to keep it together."

This was news to him. "You never said anything."

She shrugged. "You and I have the same genes, dummy. But I've got Dan, and he believed in me, and he was so ready to crush the whole daddy thing from day one that it was impossible for me not to be just as excited. We're a team. And if I needed help, I'd get it, but I don't. I'm fine. You're fine. We're not the same as them, Garrett."

She didn't get it. "Did you know," he said carefully, "that when I went to his funeral, mom kept going on and on, weeping about how I was just like him? She's been saying that my whole life. She could be right. I could be the kind of man who abuses his kids." He gave Em a hard look. "His daughter. He was diseased, Em, depraved. I'm his son. It's different for me."

She rose in agitation. "Oh, my God, Garrett, why are you so smart about most things and so stupid and stubborn about this?"

"Don't mince words, Em," he said dryly.

She rolled her eyes. "Do you think I would ever have brought Lilah to stay if I thought, for one tiny second, that she wouldn't be safe with you? That you wouldn't protect her with your life if necessary?"

"Do you think I want to have this fear, Emily?" he countered. "Do you think I enjoy it?"

She shook her head. "Let me ask this – did you have any impulse at all to act crazy around Lilah? What about when she made such a mess with the paint and the dogs? Did you feel like hitting her or calling her names or locking her in a closet?"

He shuddered. "Of course not."

"Of course not! Have you ever wanted to belittle anyone or punish them for – I don't know – breathing too loudly? Or gone through a case of vodka in a week?"

"No."

"No, of course not. Garrett, we're thirty years old. Don't you think that if you had some kind of hereditary mental problem it would have shown up by now? Beyond being impossibly hardheaded, that is?"

Garrett leaned forward and examined his clasped hands. Their parents had been young when he and Em were born. Did that mean that something sick would have shown up in him by now?

A tiny wedge of something silvery made him wonder if Em was on to something.

"Don't you?" she demanded.

"Maybe," he said thoughtfully.

Emily scooted to the edge of the sofa and patted his hands. "And think about this. You're all about goals, right? Remind me how old we were when you decided you wanted to become a professional football player? And not just any kind of player but a quarterback?"

Where was she going with this? "I don't know, twelve? Thirteen?"

"Okay, so it became your goal, right?"

Nodding, he waved a hand to hurry her up.

"Really big odds against your ever getting to the level you are now, right?"

"Okay, yeah."

She gave him the universal palms-up 'what the hell' gesture. "You had faith in yourself that you could make it to the pros and you made it happen. Now that you're the tiniest bit open to the notion that you don't have any crazy lurking beneath the surface, why don't you have a little bit of that faith in yourself that you could be a kick-ass dad? You've faced much bigger odds. You don't think that's a worthy goal?"

Faith. That's what Maggie said she had. It's what she wanted him to have.

He felt the tiny wedge expand a little.

"Maggie's like Dan, you know. Rock solid."

Maggie *was* rock solid. Ready to crush the mom thing.

"You know, I really would protect Lilah with my life," he mused out loud.

"I know you would."

Maybe, with Maggie, he could be a kick-ass dad.

"You might be on to something," he murmured. It was something to think about, anyway.

Emily lifted her arms in a 'hallelujah' wave and sank back onto the sofa. "Thank you, Jesus." Then she sat up again. "Now let's talk about going to see mom."

Chapter 24

"Is this some kind of an intervention?" Maggie eyed Sharon, Alicia and Toby mock-suspiciously over the rim of her jumbo frozen drink. Sharon had coaxed her out of her house and oh, what a surprise, Alicia and Toby were already seated at their favorite table when they arrived at Superior Grille.

"It's a margarita-vention," Toby corrected her. "An intervention featuring tequila."

Her friends been very patient with her since Garrett had shown up on her front porch, not pushing her to tell them what had transpired the next day, but it seemed her time was up.

Sharon caught Maggie's hand and squeezed it. "Here's the deal, Maggie. We can see you're really struggling but we're done tiptoeing around you. The time has come for you to tell us what exactly is going on so we can either support you fully or straighten you out."

Alicia nodded. "We hate seeing you so sad. It's not like before, with Mason."

"Alicia's right," Toby said. "You were just pissed about Mason. Now you're broken. Garrett broke you."

Mason. Maggie couldn't drum up an iota of feeling one way or the other about him anymore, but just thinking about Garrett made her chest tight, made it hard for her to breathe. She tasted her margarita, trying to think how to sum it all up. From the time she woke up until the time she finally managed to fall asleep, all she seemed to do was relive their entire last conversation. How anxious he'd been. How good he'd looked. That last hug before he walked away, his shoulders slumped. Sometimes she felt mad at him all over again for his reaction to the article and sometimes she understood his reaction completely. Sometimes she was offended that her life seemed disposable to him and other times she wanted to chuck everything and catch the first flight to Denver. A lot of the time she wanted to beat him over the head for his refusal to understand he wasn't like his father and then her heart would ache for him because he believed so firmly that he was broken.

She missed his grin. His humor. His eyebrow. She missed the best sex she'd ever had in her life and was ever likely to have again.

He'd ruined Harry Potter for her, and bacon, and pit bulls.

She didn't know how to move forward.

"Earth to Maggie," Sharon said, squeezing her hand.

She touched the salt around the rim of her glass. It reminded her of the way Garrett had hunkered down and brushed every bit of sand off of her legs at the beach.

Gah.

"There isn't really a lot to say. He apologized for the way he acted about the article and asked me to move in with him."

Yep, that pretty much summed it up.

Her friends leaned forward collectively, eyes wide.

"What did you tell him?" Alicia managed.

Maggie clasped the sides of her face together. "No, of course."

"You said no?" Toby clutched her head.

Maggie nodded.

"Why did you say no?" Alicia demanded.

Because she was an idiot?

No, she had good reasons.

"He thought I was capable of selling him out to that reporter, for starts."

"No," Alicia said. "Not good enough. You already told us it looked bad at the time and he was really sorry and that you've forgiven him for that."

Maggie sighed. "Yes, but what if something like that happens again? And there are lots of other reasons. His life is so big, you know? It's crazy."

"I think you mean his life is exciting, Maggie. That's better than boring, right?" Alicia asked.

"I don't know. Boring sounds kind of good right now."

"No, boring is bad," Toby said. "Very bad."

Garrett certainly wasn't boring. "You know what he said when he asked me to stay longer? That I have a brightness he can't resist." As soon as she said it, she knew it was a mistake.

Her friends gaped at her in varying expressions of awe. Sharon pressed her hands to her face. "Maggie, you're making it really hard for me to support you."

"I'm about to buy your damn ticket back to Denver myself," Toby added. "And come with you. Maybe he's got a friend."

"He can't resist your brightness." Alicia shook her head, her eyes wide. "For real?"

"Okay, hold on." Sharon reached for her bag and took out a pen and a notebook. "Let's do a pros and cons list. What you just said goes on the 'pro' side. What do you have for the 'con' side?"

"Oh, good idea," Alicia said, scooting forward. "What about his temper? When he was mad at you about the article, did he, like, yell or anything?"

Maggie shook her head. "No, he was very quiet, very controlled." It made her shudder to remember the way he'd looked at her and spoke to her that morning when he was sure she'd betrayed his trust.

"Does that go in 'pro' or 'con'?" Toby asked.

"I vote for 'pro' on that one," Sharon said, scribbling in the notebook. "Yelling would be 'con.'"

"Put 'sex' in the 'pro' column." Toby looked at the columns over Sharon's shoulder. "Right, Maggie?"

She leaned forward and rested her forehead on the table. "Yes." She bumped her forehead on the table a couple of times, as if that would dislodge the memories that still curled her toes.

"Put sex in bold capital letters," Alicia added, grinning.

Maggie couldn't believe they were actually making a list.

"Add 'lots of money'," Toby added. "Also add 'hot, hot, hot.' Make that bold, too."

"All we have are 'pros.' We need some 'cons,'" Sharon said, still scribbling.

All three of her friends looked at Maggie expectantly. "It's impossible to go anyplace without people making a fuss?" she offered weakly.

Toby made a 'so what' gesture. "So stay home!"

Alicia shrugged. "Seriously. Keep that booty locked down in the house."

Toby gave Alicia a high five.

Maggie made a face. "That's impossible with his job. And then, what about my life? This is my home. Mom and dad and you guys are here, and Denver is really far away."

"There are these handy little things called airplanes, remember?" Toby asked.

"We'll come visit every chance we get."

"Probably more often than you want us to."

Maggie rolled her eyes. "My job? I love my job."

Toby rolled her eyes in an exaggerated response. "What, there aren't any schools in Denver?"

They were not taking her seriously at all. "How about the fact that women chase him? Like there are Facebook groups devoted to stalking him?" She knew because she'd gotten hate messages from hundreds of them.

"You can't worry about crazy people, and if you're talking about that girl at the restaurant, you said he tore her number up," Sharon reminded her. "Plus he's not chasing them back, is he? He's chasing you."

"You also said before that he hasn't dated anyone in a while, so it's not like he's a player," Alicia added.

"And honestly, Maggie, you can't be mad if women think he's gorgeous. I think he's gorgeous," Toby said.

Alicia raised her hand, nodding. "Me, too."

Sharon raised her hand, too. "Me three. You can only be mad if he chases them back. So that's really not a pro or a con."

"I think it's a pro," Alicia offered. "Put 'trustworthy' on the pro side."

Was this really supposed to help her move forward? "I feel like I'm in elementary school again," Maggie said. "I also feel like anything I say, you're going to turn into a pro."

"Then what is it, really, Maggie?" Sharon asked her. "What are you not telling us? What's the real con?"

Maggie blew out a deep breath. "He doesn't want children. No ifs, ands, or buts. That's the major con."

Silence fell at the table. They all knew how much she wanted a big family of her own. It wasn't some passing fancy, it was a deep-seated longing for her own little piece of heaven.

Sharon put her pen down and squeezed her hand again. "No chance he'll change his mind?"

Maggie felt tears well in her eyes. "He's adamant about it."

Alicia bit her lip thoughtfully. "There's always adoption."

Maggie shook her head. "He's convinced he'll turn into his father no matter what. There's no convincing him otherwise. It doesn't make sense, especially when you see how amazing he is with his niece, but he just can't see it."

Toby propped her chin in her hand and studied Maggie. "Here's the bottom line, Maggie. Are you willing to wait for someone who might come along who makes you as happy as Garrett and wants children, or do you choose Garrett and no children?

"Garrett, who chased you through an airport and has ruined you for all other men forever," Alicia said dreamily.

"That airport photo." Toby shook her head and visibly shivered. "I kind of hated you when I saw it."

"You can't discount how important it is to Maggie to have her own family, though," Sharon insisted. "That's a biggie."

It was a biggie. Such a biggie. Maggie stared off across the restaurant, trying to visualize children with some really nice faceless, unnamed husband who wasn't Garrett.

It wasn't appealing at all. He could be the handsomest, smartest, funniest man in the world but he wouldn't be Garrett.

Garrett, who could cock that eyebrow and steal her French fries and make her snort and give her multiple orgasms for the rest of her life.

The poor imaginary guy didn't stand a chance.

She'd never want anyone more than she wanted Garrett.

But was it enough?

He'd asked her that. Her, Maggie Parrish. He'd humbled himself and asked if he could be enough.

"Maggie," Sharon said gently, squeezing her hand. "What are you thinking?"

She looked at the faces of her friends, and blinked.

He was enough. He really, really was.

"Guys," she said suddenly. "I have to get to Denver."

"Aaaaaand, our job here is done," said Sharon, bumping fists with Toby and Alicia.

If he could choose where he'd like to be at this moment, this place wouldn't even be in the top hundred. Or top thousand. Garrett looked around the private waiting room in the gold wing of Westgate Assisted Living and wondered again how in the hell he'd let Emily coerce him into this trip.

He'd been so deep in his own head after they talked that he hadn't noticed she'd disappeared from the room. His head was spinning, thinking about the startling points she'd made. He needed peace and quiet to do some serious thinking. About kids. And Maggie. And the possibility of a future that suddenly looked a whole hell of a lot brighter.

But Em had other ideas. She came back into the den with a packed bag. His packed bag, and she dropped the news that they were leaving for the airport. The real kicker was she'd conspired with Claire for a private flight, at his expense. It wasn't the money, it was the principle. And somehow she'd gotten him on the jet headed to Oklahoma City.

Good thing he loved his sister because right now he was thoroughly pissed at her.

As soon as he got this farce over with, he was high-tailing it to Baton Rouge as fast as he could to find Maggie. To tell her he was on board for the whole bunch-of-kids-white-picket-fence thing. That's where he wanted to be.

God, he hoped it wasn't too late.

"Sit down." Perched on a wingback chair, the object of his annoyance gestured toward the chair beside her. "You're making me nervous, pacing like that. And stop scowling."

"You said this wasn't going to take long." He stayed standing.

"We've only been here a few minutes. Cool your jets."

The door opened and he tensed.

Two women entered; one young woman wearing scrubs and a name badge, her hand at the elbow of the second, older woman.

Garrett took in his mother's appearance. The last time he'd seen her, at his father's funeral, she'd looked years older than her age. She'd been rail thin and hollow looking. Smelling of alcohol and cigarettes, she'd clutched at him with grasping, needlelike fingers, babbling almost nonsensically and then wailing when he shook her off.

She'd kept repeating, "You're just like your father." It had been her litany his whole life. He hated the words. He couldn't get out of there fast enough.

She looked a lot better now. She was still thin, but in the willowy way he recalled from his childhood. She wore a long skirt, a light sweater, and low heels. Her hair, once dark like Em's, was streaked with silver now, and pulled into a loose knot on top of her head. It struck him that she and Emily looked a lot alike.

He watched her gaze fall on Emily, who was almost bouncing with nerves. He didn't get why Em had this need to come here, to see her. He just hoped she got what she wanted from it and that he'd never have to come with her again.

Their mother smiled hesitantly. Em smiled back.

He didn't understand it. The woman had been no kind of mother at all. Em was setting herself up for major disappointment.

His mother's gaze traveled across the room and he stared at her coldly. He watched the tentative smile on her face falter, her eyes drop.

"How lovely that your children are here to visit you, Elizabeth." The aide smiled. "Let us know if you need anything. I'll be just down the hall." With that, she slipped out of the room, leaving the three of them alone.

The silence was palpable.

He watched her take a deep breath and cross the room to sit in the chair beside Em, her back straight and shoulders set. Clasping her hands in her lap, she let her gaze travel all over Em, and he could see her blue eyes collecting moisture. As if she couldn't help herself, she reached to quickly pat Em's knee, and then clasped her hands back together.

"Thank you both for coming." She glanced carefully at Garrett again. "I know it was a lot to ask."

Garrett made a scoffing noise. She paled and Em shot him a reproachful glance.

She straightened again and took a deep breath. "I want to thank you both for making it possible for me to get treatment here at Westgate."

He didn't want her thanks. It was all Em's doing. When she'd received a call from a hospital in Oklahoma City that their mother had been found unresponsive by a neighbor, Em had, for some unknown reason, decided to make it her mission in life to help her. She'd gone into overdrive to have their mother admitted to a good rehab facility. She'd spent a year there before moving to Westgate. Em constantly tried to update him on how she was doing. He didn't care. He insisted on paying for it because he didn't want Em and Dan to bear the burden.

"We're glad you're doing so well," Emily said. "I'm sorry it's taken us so long."

It was all he could do not to scoff again.

"Please don't apologize," their mother said quickly. "You never have to apologize to me."

That was certainly something they could agree on.

"Why did you want to see us?" he asked flatly, crossing his arms across his chest. "Why are we here?"

Em shot another look at him that was a clear warning and he answered with a slight shrug.

Their mother smoothed the fabric of her skirt for a long moment. Her gaze fluttered between the two of them. She took a deep breath. "There's something important that you both need to know. Something you should have known a long time ago. If I had been well, I would have –" she broke off, then glanced at Em, who gave her an encouraging nod.

She gripped her hands together tightly and took a deep breath. "When I was sixteen I started dating a boy who lived nearby. He was kind and handsome and I think I fell in love with him the first time I saw him and he felt the same." Her words fell out in a rush, but then she paused, her gaze focused somewhere beyond the room. "We started college together and had plans to get married, but when I was nineteen and he was twenty, when we were home from school for Christmas, his family's home caught fire."

She paused and took a deep breath that shook when she released it, and Garrett felt an uneasy prickle down his spine. A glance at Em's face told him she was bracing, too.

"He and his parents and sister – they didn't survive."

Em shot a glance at him but he didn't react. He was suspended in a weird limbo, just waiting.

Their mother took another breath before continuing. "Shortly afterwards, I discovered I was pregnant."

Huh.

This meant something, something monumental, but his thoughts were jumbled and he was damned if he was able to put it together.

"My parents were very upset and insisted that I immediately marry the son of my father's partner, a young man who admired me, but whom I had never liked very much." Their mother looked at Emily first, then Garrett. "Franklin Long was not your father."

He heard the words but didn't understand. His body felt unfamiliar, too heavy, his heart was beating too slowly. He had to lean against the wall. Still listening, waiting for her to finish.

"Your father was a beautiful, loving, intelligent man and I have never stopped loving him." She gazed at Garrett, her eyes filling with tears. "You look so much like him, Garrett."

What the fuck.

What the fuck.

What the fuck.

Garrett stared at his mother, his mind reeling. He knew Emily was as shocked as he was, he could tell she was struggling to remain composed but he couldn't look at her. His legs felt weak but he couldn't move.

"You're just like your father" was burned into his brain, words he'd hated his whole life, but she had not been referring to the piece of crap man who had made their lives a misery.

Franklin Long wasn't his father.

Franklin Long was nothing to him.

No relation.

His sickness had no relevance.

It was incomprehensible.

Garrett couldn't wrap his mind around it.

Slipping her hand into a pocket of her skirt, his mother withdrew a photograph and caressed it gently before passing it to Emily, who took it with a shaky hand. He watched Emily blink at the image and then jerk her eyes toward him, holding it out.

Wait, what again? He looked like his father, but Franklin Long wasn't his father.

He still couldn't move. If he pushed away from the wall, he might go down.

Em rose and crossed the room slowly, her face pale, and held it up to him. He dropped his eyes from her distraught face to the photo.

In the worn photograph, his mother, lithe and lovely and looking more like Emily's twin than he did, smiled up at a tall man with broad shoulders and wide grin. His arm was draped across her shoulder and she had a hand on his chest. A football helmet dangled from his fingertips.

His chest rising and falling with rapid breaths, Garrett took the photo with nerveless fingers and stared at it for a long moment, then looked across the room at his mother. There were tears falling down her cheeks. She met his eyes and nodded.

Emily returned to her chair and took her mother's hands in hers.

"I'm not asking your forgiveness because I don't deserve it. I should have left Franklin, should have gotten help. I was depressed, I drank too much, I took pills to forget, and I let you down, both of you, so badly. I let Michael down. I was weak. I have no excuses."

Michael. His father's name was Michael. He and Emily exchanged stunned glances. He was Garrett Michael, she was Emily Michaela. He felt a twisting in his gut and looked at the photo again.

"The night that Franklin – that night –" His mother covered her face with her hands and he tore his eyes from the photo to see her shuddering from across the room. "I was afraid you'd kill him and you'd be arrested. I wanted him dead but not like that. I was glad you left. It was better that way. Then it was only me he could hurt. I told him we'd be happier alone, that I would try harder to please him. I knew you'd be safe with the Staffords."

Garrett could remember every detail of that night. He remembered his mother screaming, trying to pull him off of his father. No. Off of Franklin. She wasn't trying to protect her husband? She was trying to protect him?

"I should have tried harder to tell you about Michael a long time ago, but I was - I was sick. But when that article came out, accusing you of mental illness, Garrett, of assaulting you, Emily," her expression crumpled. "I should have told you so long ago. I'm so sorry."

Emily rose from her chair and knelt at their mother's feet, speaking softly, reaching up to hug her. Garrett watched them cling together. Their mother looked at him, over Emily's head, emanating anguish, and he felt a sickening lurch in his stomach.

He had to get out of there.

Without a word, he straightened and headed for the door. Moving fast, almost running. Out of the room, down the main corridor, out the front door. Unseeing, mind blank, just putting distance between himself and the look on his mother's face.

At the far edge of the grounds there was a shady sitting area with a bench. He collapsed onto the bench and hunched over, hands clasped.

She was telling them the truth.

Franklin Long was nothing. Less than nothing.

He ought to be happy. He was happy. The weight he'd been carrying for so many years should be lifted. He should be ecstatic.

But he still felt numb.

He pressed his face in his hands. His eyes were burning. His throat was clogged. His thoughts were swirling, bits of his mother's halting speech vying for his focus.

His mother, grieving for his father, forced to marry that fucking bastard. She was just twenty when he and Em were born. A fucking kid herself. He could see it. He could see depression slipping into dullness and addiction. He could remember things now that supported her story. Franklin wouldn't have let her go. Feeding her alcohol, keeping her weak and compliant. Stealing her life from her.

He remembered other things. Vague little bits of memories, things he'd buried away, too angry to recall. Images of their mother, hugs, kind words, kisses. A birthday cake, half blue half pink. A playground, being pushed on a swing. Fingers smoothing his hair. Her running alongside him when he learned to ride a bike. Hazy memories from when he and Em were very small.

Before Franklin Long took her away, turned her into something less.

Leaving him and Emily alone.

A hand touched him on the shoulder. Jerking his head up, he found Em beside him. She looked pale, her eyes damp. "You okay?"

He blew out a deep breath. "Yeah. You?"

She sank onto the bench beside him, twining her fingers through his like they did when they were little. "I didn't expect that," she said quietly. "I'm kind of all over the place right now, trying to take it in."

Garrett huffed. "No kidding."

"You believe her?"

He turned to his sister, nodding. "Yeah. Yeah, I do."

"And that photo, Garrett. You do look just like him." She shook her head slowly.

Garrett nodded silently. The whole thing was a fucking tragedy. What would their lives have looked like if their real father hadn't died? If his mother's parents hadn't made her marry Franklin?

She touched his sleeve. "Will you come back inside with me? She's worried about you. She's waiting for us."

He and Em hadn't been the only victims. His mother had been through enough. She deserved forgiveness and he'd give it with an open heart.

But right now he had somewhere else to be. No time to waste. He had to get to Maggie because now he could offer her everything she wanted, with no hesitation.

He shook his head. "Can you get back to the airport on your own?"

Em looked worried. "Sure, why?"

"I've got to get to Baton Rouge. You take the jet home, I'll take the rental car. Tell mom about Maggie. Tell her she's going to like her when they meet."

Em's mouth dropped open. "*When* they meet?"

Garrett nodded firmly. "Yeah, when they meet. And, you know what; ask her if she's happy here or if she wants to move."

Em's eyes grew larger. "Move?"

"Yeah, Denver or Santa Fe; whatever. Just closer. But look, I've got to go." He rose, digging in his pocket for the keys to the car. "

Em stood and flung her arms around his neck. "Love you, Garrett. Be careful driving."

He hugged her back. "Love you, too, Em. And, uh," he hesitated. "I hate to say it, but thanks for being such a nag and making me come here with you." He kissed her on one cheek, then the other. "One for you, one for mom."

And now he needed to get to Maggie, because everything had changed.

Chapter 25

Maggie zipped her suitcase closed for the third time and hefted it off the bed, using both hands to lug it to the bathroom scales. Balancing it, she squinted at the number on the screen. Forty-nine pounds. Finally. Now she could drag it to the front door where it would wait until morning when the Uber picked her up to take her to the airport.

Now all she had to do was try to get a little sleep. She tugged on the pair of Garrett's boxers she'd found in the bottom of her duffle bag and his Renegades jersey and flopped into bed. It was going to be hard to fall asleep. Her body might be tired but her mind was still racing. It was scary, planning to fly to Denver without calling or texting Garrett beforehand. She knew she should give him a heads up; in fact she'd told her parents she already had. But she couldn't quite dredge up the courage. She was going to go with her instincts and just – show up. She hadn't quite worked out how she'd get through the gate, since she didn't know the code, but like Scarlett O'Hara, she'd think about that tomorrow.

Sharon, Toby and Alicia had followed her back to her house that evening, supposedly to help her pack but really because they were afraid she'd talk herself out of going. She might have. Not because she was waffling about the children issue, because for some weird reason she was totally at ease about that. Finally getting it through her own thick skull that Garrett was more important than anything else – the man Garrett, not the quarterback celebrity Garrett – was all it had taken.

No, what worried her was wondering if Garrett had already moved on. She hadn't heard a peep from him since he'd left her house two weeks ago. He might have decided it was all for the best. Her friends scoffed at her and kept reminding her of all the ways he'd shown her he cared, and Toby had even threatened to buy a second ticket and deliver her personally.

She hoped they were right. Tomorrow morning she was flying across the country with her forty-nine-pound suitcase to see if Garrett still wanted her. If he did, she'd unpack her bag and work out how to break the news to her principal that he'd need a new kindergarten teacher. If he didn't, she'd roll that suitcase right back out again and come home.

God, she hoped she wouldn't be coming right back home.

She went to bed and tried to turn her brain off but she was wide, wide awake. It was hot so she turned the ceiling fan on. She fluffed her pillow. Go up again to adjust the ceiling fan speed. Double and triple checked her alarm setting. Tossed her covers off. Got cold and pulled them back up. And finally, just when she was drifting off, the ceiling fan went off kilter and started thumping. Because, of course it did. She got up and turned it off, but the thumping continued, which made no sense.

Finally she realized someone was knocking on her front door.

In the middle of the night.

A chill ran down her spine.

This couldn't be good.

She slipped out of bed, her phone in her hand, pre-dialed to 911, and tiptoed nervously into the front room to peek out the window.

She blinked.

There was a big man on her porch.

A big man who looked like Garrett was on her front porch.

Sweet baby Jesus, Garrett was on her front porch. One hand propped up on the top of the door frame, the other rubbing the back of his neck.

Her heart thumped, stopped beating entirely, and then kicked back in high gear.

She stepped away, scrubbed her face, and then looked again.

It really was Garrett.

He knocked again.

Without taking her eyes off of him, she fumbled around on the wall for the porch light switch, wrestled with the deadbolt, and then twisted the door knob. It felt like it took ten minutes, but finally she flung the door open. Hand on her throat, she looked up at him. He looked exhausted. She couldn't get any words out. They were all scrambled and stuck together like a log jam.

His gaze roamed over her face and down to his jersey and boxers. And then he grinned, so wide and bright that it hurt her heart.

"What are you – how did you –"

"Shhh." He cut her off, sliding one hand behind her head and the other around her back to pull her close, and for a moment just held her, crushed against his chest, her head tucked under his chin. Maggie felt tears well in her eyes and she tipped her head up. His eyes were closed. "Just give me a second." His voice was low as he smoothed his big hand up and down her back. "One second."

"Come inside," she managed, backing through the door. Her suitcase was in the way so she pushed it aside. He glanced down at it and then lifted his eyes to her in question.

She slid her hands up to his cheeks and framed his face. "I was coming to Denver to tell you I'm okay with not having kids," she blurted.

His eyebrows shot up.

She nodded wildly. "Because you're enough, Garrett. I love you. I love you so much I'm sick with it. You're completely and totally more than enough. I've been so miserable without you. I've missed you so much. I hope you still want me because I want to come home to you and Buddy and Dude, and –"

"Shhh." Bending to her, he kissed her, sweetly, tenderly at first, and then hungrily, invading her mouth with warm strokes and swirls, claiming her, reminding her of her infinite desire for him until she was breathless, and clutching his shirt in fisted hands because her legs were jelly.

He pulled back a fraction, his hands moving to cup her face, and he nuzzled his nose against hers. "I love you, too, Maggie. You have no idea. I should've told you before but I was scared. And you'll get your babies."

Wait. What?

Taking advantage of her stupor, he slipped his hands beneath the rolled over waist of her stolen boxer shorts, squeezed her ass and lifted her up. Maggie automatically looped her arms around his neck and hooked her legs around his waist. "What did you just say?" she repeated.

"Where's your bedroom? This way?" He started through the living room and toward the hallway.

She used her hands on his face to try to make him look at her. "Garrett, what did you just say?"

He found her room, sat on the side of the bed, and collapsed backwards, bringing her with him "I love you, Maggie, and I want to have babies with you," he murmured into her hair. "Lots of them."

Straddling him, Maggie lifted up on her arms to study his face.

"As many as you want." He nodded, rubbing his hands up and down her back.

Oh, Lord, that felt good. She'd missed his big, warm hands.

"A dozen if you want."

A dozen? "Garrett," she managed. She had questions. So, so many questions.

He flipped her with ease, braced himself over her on one arm and pressed damp kisses down her neck, to her collarbone, pushing her jersey aside to kiss her shoulder. "You just tell me how many will make you happy and that's how many we'll have."

Who was this man? "Garrett," she tried again.

He put one finger over her mouth. "Hey, baby, I've driven all night." He kept nuzzling, her ear, her jaw, her throat.

"And I'm kind of tired." His hands reached for the hem of her jersey and tugged it over her head.

"And I have a lot to tell you." He kissed her, nibbled on her bottom lip, slid his tongue against hers again, made a satisfied noise that sent a surge of quicksilver through her body and stole her need to talk. Talking was overrated. She'd rather kiss him.

"But if you'd like to get started on the first one, I'm here and I'm all yours."

Epilogue

"Is he awake?"

"I wanna jump on the bed first!"

"No, me!"

Garrett grinned at the little voices on the other side of the door and glanced at the clock on the bedside table. It wasn't even six a.m. yet. Shaking his head, he hurriedly pulled the bed covers up and over his head. He heard Maggie's soft laugh on the other side of the door, too.

"Shh, boys. We have to sneak in, sneaky-like."

He heard his boys giggle. "Sneaky-like!" That was Michael, five already.

"Yeah, thneaky-like!" And that was Austin, almost three.

Stifling a chuckle, he started some over-the-top snoring. It was too much to hope that they'd be able to sleep late this morning, or any morning, really, because their boys consistently woke at the crack of dawn, running at full throttle the moment their feet hit the floor. He'd planned to get up first so Maggie could sleep in a little longer, get some much needed rest, but she'd kissed him and reminded him what day it was and he knew better than to argue.

"Daddy's thnoring tho loud!"

Giggles from Maggie, too. God, he loved that woman.

"Are we ready? Michael, can you open the door?"

"Uh huh." Little hands rattled the door. Garrett could picture Michael's narrow eyed concentration on the hapless knob, could see his feet planted in determination. Their eldest was intense in everything he did, while Austin bubbled his way through his busy little life. Their boys were as different from one another as a bird and a fish, but they were best of buds.

When he heard the door open, he threw in a couple of snorts and wheezes for special effect.

"Whoa, daddy is sleeping hard," Maggie whispered loudly. "It's going to take a lot of jumping to wake him up."

Okay, he'd better protect himself because knobby little knees and feet could do some serious damage to his junk, as he'd woefully discovered in the past. He flopped like a fish under the covers, safeguarding himself from imminent danger, and went for maximum volume on the snoring, which also amped up the giggles.

"Now?" he heard Austin ask, and Garrett could picture him hopping from one foot to the other, beside himself with merry anticipation.

"Now," Maggie said. The door flew open and he braced himself for the attack.

"Daddy! Daddy! Wake up!" Scrambling noises as small, wiry bodies towed themselves up and onto the bed and pounced on him. "Wake up, daddy!" Little hands pulled at the covers, jabbing and poking him.

So much giggling that it made his chest hurt but it was show time and he had a job to do. He flopped around underneath the covers some more, making the mattress shake, before sitting up abruptly and throwing the covers off of his head. "What? What's happening?" He grabbed one skinny torso and then the other, little arms and legs flailing, and tossed them gently, bouncing them on the bed. "What are you doing in my bed? Huh? Why are you waking me up?"

Full blown childish laughter now, little hands trying to fend him off and then coming in for another attack. Double-teaming him, the monsters.

"Waking me up so early in the morning! You're both in big trouble now."

"Mama said we could!"

He loved wrestling with his boys, reveled in the joy on their faces. He wished he could keep them this size, this happy, forever.

"Mama said you could?" He shot a grin at Maggie, who was perched on the far corner of the bed. Her hair was a messy halo around her face, her eyes shining, and she had one hand resting on the rounded swell of her stomach. "Mama wouldn't do that."

"She did! She did!"

"Well, she's in big trouble, too." He winked at her and her answering smile tugged at his heart. "You boys know what's going to happen now, don't you?"

"Tickle monster!" Michael shrieked.

"Tickle monther!" Austin squealed.

"That's right, tickle monster. You boys are going to get it now." He threw off all the covers and made the silly monster face that they loved. "Rawr!" Rising, he jerked his arms forward in monster fashion, fingers curling and flexing.

Faces alive with glee, they started scrambling away. "Nooooo!" Michael bounded off the bed first and headed for the door, then turned back around to grab his little brother, pushing him through the door first. "Run, Austin!"

"I'm coming! You'd better hide!"

Shrieks of laughter echoed as small feet flew down the hallway. He knew he had only a couple of minutes before he needed to thunder behind them so he dropped back onto the bed to quickly reach for Maggie. She giggled when he towed her into the middle and tugged her down. Throwing one leg over her thighs, he caged her in place beneath him and grinned. "Rawr."

"Rawr yourself," she laughed, skimming her soft hands up and down his shoulders and biceps.

He nuzzled the sensitive curve between her neck and shoulder, and then up to her ear, enjoying the soft hitch in her breath when he tugged gently on her earlobe with his teeth. This woman. She smelled so good and tasted even better. "Tickle monster is horny, mama."

She skimmed her fingers through his hair and then cupped his jaws with her hands, effectively interrupting his nuzzling. "That darned tickle monster is always horny." Her beautiful brown eyes glowed with humor and love.

"Yes, he is. Always, for you." He kissed her on the nose and then scrambled down a little to nuzzle the sweet valley between her breasts, and then further still to press a kiss on her stomach. Maggie was always beautiful but there was just something more when she was pregnant, some mysterious aura that made him ache with grateful contentment. "Hello little girl," he whispered to her belly before resting his cheek there for a moment. "Daddy can't wait to meet you."

Sighing, Maggie sifted her fingers through his hair again, the soft graze of her nails against his scalp making him shiver, his body tighten. "Happy Father's day," she murmured.

Father's Day. Unbelievable. Would he ever get used to the miracle that he was married to this woman, was daddy to their awesome boys and, soon, to a little girl he hoped would have Maggie's brown eyes and beautiful spirit? To think he could have lived a life without this gift. Without his partner, his love, warm and soft beneath him.

"Maggie." He lifted his head from her stomach, arching his eyebrow the way she liked as he slid a hand beneath the hem of her sleep shirt, creeping upwards.

Sneaky-like.

She shook her head, amused, and pushed his optimistic hand away. "No time, tickle monster."

He didn't like it, but she was right. Two little boys were waiting to be hunted and tickled within an inch of their lives and they wouldn't be patient for long and there was still stuff to do before their family and friends showed up for their annual barbecue.

"Hey, maybe mom could take the boys home with her tonight. What do you think?"

Maggie grinned. "Way ahead of you, babe. She already suggested it."

Garrett grinned.

Friends and family today.

Alone with Maggie tonight.

Best Father's Day ever.

ACKNOWLEDGMENTS

Thank you to all my wonderful, supportive friends and family who tolerate my reclusive nature.

Special thanks to:

Amanda Marchand Borowski, my mini-me, who doesn't complain (too much) when I send her bits and pieces and want immediate feedback even though she has a million things going on all the time. Love you, sweetie!

Alicia Boudreaux Marchand who takes the time to read and give me great input despite the fact she has four children under the age of twelve and barely a minute to call her own.

Debbie Wamsley for eagle-eye catches and for believing me when I say that a 'boop' really is a thing.

Kristi Marcum, for hooking me up with decent wifi so I could meet with my Beta girls and for the best hugs ever.

Sharon Chandler, for reading Little Bit Crazy early on and giving me a thumbs up.

Kelly Jackson, Wendy Raffaeli and Beth West, my Colorado Beta girls - You ladies have no idea how grateful I am for your laughter, support and great suggestions!

ABOUT THE AUTHOR

When I'm not writing, I love playing with stained glass, floating on the lake near my home and lazing around with a good book. Mother of two and Mamaw to four, I was raised in Louisiana and now live in the Ozark foothills with my husband of a-really-long-time, where I work in my pajamas, drink way too much coffee, wage a constant war with dog and cat hair, and love to watch deer and squirrels and one very cute chipmunk in our backyard.

Thank you so much for reading my book! I'm an independent author so every time a reader buys my book, I do a happy dance!

If you enjoy my book, I would appreciate it so much if you would leave a review on Amazon and/or Goodreads.

Many thanks,
Christy Marchand
cmarchandauthor@mail.com

MINE ALL MINE

By Christy Marchand

"Who says you can't find love in your own backyard?"

Excerpt

Eleanor landed among the scattered crates in the cool margin of space between the shrubs and the house with a painful, teeth-jarring thud. Carefully motionless for a moment, she drew in a deep breath and took stock of her situation.

She had banged her elbows, jabbed her ribs, and lost a shoe and several hairpins. Apparently she'd lost her mind, too, for even trying such a stunt. A normal person would call the real estate agent and make an appointment to see the house. A normal person wouldn't rummage around in a creepy old shed and then try to climb a stack of flimsy crates just to peek inside a house they had no intention of buying. Honestly, she didn't know what had gotten into her.

Small mercy it was an azalea she fell into and not something with stickers, Eleanor thought disjointedly as she struggled to push the crates out of the way and twist into a sitting position on the cool ground. She carefully dusted the dirt from her hands and smoothed back the hair that had begun to come loose from her chignon. Bigger mercy she hadn't broken a bone or given herself a concussion. God knows how long she'd have lain there, comatose or worse.

She shuddered. What a day. It was definitely time to go home and pull the covers over her head. Maybe she'd wake up and find that the whole morning was nothing but a terrible nightmare. That she still had a job, both her shoes, and her dignity.

She scrambled to her knees and began to feel beneath the low growing limbs for her lost shoe. She peered into the dense foliage. No shoe. It was probably lost forever inside the hungry, man-eating azalea. Suddenly she didn't even care; the shrub could keep the shoe. She just wanted to stumble back to her car and drive away as quickly as possible.

She debated whether to rise and fight her way out on foot, or crawl out beneath the lower branches. Since she was already on her hands and knees, she decided to opt for the latter.

"You okay in there?" A deep voice, humor undisguised, rumbled way above the screen of foliage.

Eleanor's hand went to her throat. Two enormous work boots, mud clumped around the soles, appeared on the other side of the shrub.

"Yes, I'm fine," she replied. "I'll be right out," she added, and then resisted the immediate temptation to thump herself on the side of the head. What an asinine thing to say.

"Take your time." Amusement seemed to ooze from the voice.

"If you don't mind, I'd just as soon climb out without an audience." Eleanor hated the note of desperation she heard in her voice.

"Too late. I saw the whole thing and must admit, I'm very impressed. I'm no expert, mind you, but I doubt many women can climb a stack of crates in high heels. Where'd you learn to do that?" The man spoke with a warm, lazy drawl.

Eleanor cringed with embarrassment and wondered what he saw when the limb snagged her skirt. "Listen, if you're a gentleman, you'll go away right now. I'm really fine. I don't need any help."

He laughed, a wonderful rumbly sound, and Eleanor's skin tingled in spite of herself. "Aw, come on out. Don't you want your shoe?"

So that's where it was. How had it managed to clear the azalea? "Just leave it on the ground," she replied.

The boots moved closer and the branches above her head began to rustle. "Don't be shy, now," he wheedled. "Stand up and let me help you get out."

"I can get out by myself. Really. Go away."

Paying no attention whatsoever, he simply laughed again. "Come on, honey, rise and shine."

Honey? Eleanor frowned, her brow wrinkling.

"Hellooo?" The shrubs rustled insistently.

She sighed. Okay, let's get this over with. Climb out, get your shoe from Mr. Helpful and get the heck away. Reversing her direction, she scooted backwards and clambered awkwardly to a standing position against the side of the house. Strangely hesitant to put a face to the voice, Eleanor smoothed her jacket sleeves and tugged at her skirt before raising her eyes to her insistent rescuer.

She looked where she expected to see his face, and saw his chest. A broad chest. She tilted her head, lifting her hand to shade her eyes against the glare of sunlight at his back.

He was big. No, not simply big. Huge. She was resigned to feeling small beside average people and tiny compared to tall people, but this man, even across the width of the azaleas, made her feel downright miniature. Eleanor pulled herself up as tall as she could on one shoe and stiffened her shoulders in unconscious reaction as her gaze traveled over the extraordinary length of his body. Her heart thumped slowly, painfully.

He was nothing like any man she'd ever seen before.

Made in the USA
Coppell, TX
12 October 2020

39658902R10193